CREATURE COLLECTION

Credits

Producers:

Clark Peterson and Bill Webb

Authors

Andrew Bates, Kraig Blackwelder, Carl Bowen, John Chambers, Trevor Chase, Ken Cliffe, Geoff Grabowski, Jess Heinig, Jeff Holt, Mike Lee, Ben Monk, James Stewart, Cynthia Summers, Richard Thomas, Mike Tinney, Jed Walls, Stephan Wieck and Stewart Wieck

Developers

Kraig Blackwelder, Trevor Chase, Ken Cliffe, Geoff Grabowski, Jess Heinig, Stephan Wieck and Stewart Wieck

Editors:

Carl Bowen, John Chambers, James Stewart and Cynthia Summers

Art Director

Richard Thomas

Layout and Typesetting

Matt Milberger

Interior Artists:

Jeff Holt, Brian Leblanc, Steve Ellis, Andrew Bates, Ron Spencer, Alex Sheikman, Andrew Trabbold, Guy Davis, Rich Thomas, Jeff Rebner, Mike Danza, Matt Mitchell, Steve Prescott, Drew Tucker, Langdon Foss, Melissa Uran, Talon Dunning, Mitch Byrd

Front & Back Cover Designer

Matt Milberger

Check out upcoming Sword and Sorcery Studio products online at:
http://www.swordsorcery.com

Distributed for Clark Peterson and Sword and Sorcery Studio by White Wolf Publishing, Inc.

This printing of the Creature Collection is done under the draft versions of the Open Game and D20 System Trademark licenses by permission from Wizards of the Coast. Subsequent printings of this book will incorporate final versions of those licenses.

S W O R D &
S O R C E R Y
S T U D I O S

PRINTED IN CANADA.

Table of Contents

Preface

Creature Collection is the first book in a series of products from Sword & Sorcery Studio. At its heart, this is a book of monsters and beings that could find a home in any fantasy setting. From the portentous Great Swan to the terrible Unhallowed to the magnificent Mithril Golem, gentle allies, monstrous enemies and unique nonpartisans are all presented here.

This book is made possible by the Open Game License (OGL), and requires use of the Dungeons & Dragons® Player's Handbook, Third Edition, published by Wizards of the Coast®. The OGL is a generous contribution to the roleplaying industry that will perpetuate this vital and engaging hobby. If the OGL can result in products like this one, fans of fantasy roleplaying games are well served indeed by the freedom creators and writers now possess to make their own contributions to the mythos.

Ostensibly a collection of over 200 creatures, this volume is also an introduction to a grand new world, the Scarred Lands, a place where as recently as 150 years ago, gods battled in a titanic struggle that raged across the face of the planet. Many of the creatures depicted herein have a place in the Scarred Lands, and some of the geography and personalities will become familiar to careful readers. But there's nothing stopping you from ushering a grotesque fatling, a nest of ratmen or any other denizen of our world into your own.

Future books from Sword & Sorcery Studio will contain more information on the Scarred Lands, while preserving your ability to use as much or as little of the setting as you like, and will still allow you to use of all the creatures, spells, magical relics and other wondrous things in your own unique fantasy campaign.

Enjoy!

The Producers, Writers and Editors @
Sword & Sorcery Studio

Introduction

The Scarred Lands were not always so. Less than two centuries ago, the world of Scarn was healthy — its forests were green, its seas pure, and its very heart pulsed with magic. The mortal races toiled the land and hunted the beasts, building entire civilizations, stone by stone. It was no paradise, but it was a prosperous world.

Of all Scarn's beings, both magical and mundane, the most awesome were the titans. The titans were entities of monstrous power, and their strength was derived from Scarn itself. The elements of the world and the skies above nourished them, granting them near-limitless abilities. Given sufficient time and patience, a titan could sculpt islands and mountain ranges, cut rivers, and breathe life into entirely new species of creatures. If they combined their powers, they could create entire continents. Even so, they were entities of raw fury, forces of nature that lacked the vital spark that would make them into something more.

Mighty though the titans were, they were not yet gods. But their *children*….

Although philosophers have difficulty explaining just why and how it could have happened, the children of the titans were not truly titans themselves. Like their progenitors, they drew some power from the world of Scarn, but the remainder of their potency derived from another source. They drew the greatest portion of their strength from the world's mortal races, feeding on the intensity of belief and on the vibrant mortal condition. The power these children called from the mortal races made them something new, something better. It made them gods.

The gods' enviable connection to the mortals of Scarn was destined to set them against their parents. For although the titans were at one with the essential elements of heaven and earth, they cared little for the world in their charge. If a titan was disappointed with how a coastline developed, he thought nothing of reducing it to sand with a series of tidal waves, cleaning the slate. If a titan grew bored with the thriving mortal races in her domain, she might give birth to horrific monsters to make things more "interesting."

The gods, who felt the suffering of the mortal races to their very souls, decided that the titans' reign had to end. Even the cruelest of the gods realized that if the titans were to cleanse the world of mortals on a whim — a very real possibility — loss of the mortals' faith and vitality would cripple the gods. So these celestial lords met in secret and plotted rebellion. When Denev, the titan of the earth itself, spoke out against her brethren, the gods took it as a sign — and the Titanswar erupted.

Eight gods and one titan went to war against a dozen other titans. The revolution shook the heavens'

pillars, shattered the blazing iron streets of hell, and raged across the face of the world. Under the force of combatants' blows, mountains split into rubble-strewn plains. Islands sank as warriors used them as stepping stones. Gods and titans alike spawned races of monsters and humanoids as foot soldiers in their feud. And divine blood spilled across Scarn, warping the very land.

Terrible though the war was, it finally came to an end. With the help of Denev, the gods were victorious. They could not kill the titans, once and for all, however — not even they possessed such power. Each titan had to be restrained or imprisoned, prevented from regaining his strength and seeking revenge. The gods pulled the teeth from Gaurak the Glutton before burying the Ravenous One beneath the earth, ensuring that he could not chew his way out. They cut Mormo the Serpent Mother into pieces, scattering the parts far and wide so the Queen of Witches could not reform. And so the gods dealt with each titan in turn, stripping them of their power and sealing them away.

Now, Scarn is no longer the world it once was. The land bears horrible scars where gods felled titans. The Kelder Mountains are split with chasms left by a heavenly axe. The Hornsaw Forest has grown gnarled and twisted after feeding on the spilled blood of Mormo. Great deserts and badlands linger where verdant fields once lay. An entire sea runs red with the blood of a titan who lies chained at its depths. The world has twisted and changed wherever the titans or their dismembered remains lie. Many of the monstrous races created by the titans and gods during the war still survive in the gouged reaches of the land. Those races favored by the gods prosper. The titans' chosen are less fortunate, watching and waiting from their wilderness exile, plotting to restore their fallen patrons.

Scarn is no longer. To many of its inhabitants, it is now simply the Scarred Lands — a wounded world that has yet to heal.

But there is hope. Cities begin to prosper once again under the watchful eye of their patron deities. Mortals sharpen their skills of war and magic, the better to hunt the monstrous beasts that prey upon the weak and injured. The followers of the gods are ever vigilant, careful that the titans' scattered minions do not succeed in restoring their heartless lords. The Scarred Lands are a place of fierce barbarism and intense struggle — and yet, the mortal races aspire to something much greater. With good fortune, bravery, sorcery and skill — and no small amount of providence — perhaps the Scarred Lands can be rebuilt. Perhaps Scarn can be restored.

But first, the heroes of the Scarred Lands must survive.

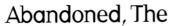

Abandoned, The

Large (Tall) Humanoid

Hit Dice:	2d8+4 (13 hp)
Initiative:	+0
Speed:	30 ft.
AC:	14 (-1 size, +5 natural)
Attacks:	Club +5 melee
Damage:	Club 1d6+4
Face/Reach:	5 ft. by 5 ft./10 ft.
Special Attacks:	Musk
Special Qualities:	None
Saves:	Fort +5, Ref +0, Will +0
Abilities:	Str 19, Dex 10, Con 15, Int 6, Wis 10, Cha 7
Skills:	Climb +6, Hide + 6, Listen +3, Jump +4, Spot +3, Wilderness Lore (Jungle) +4
Feats:	Power Attack, Run, Track
Climate/Terrain:	Jungle
Organization:	Solitary, pair, family (2-4) or tribe (5-20)
Challenge Rating:	1/2
Treasure:	None
Alignment:	Usually neutral
Advancement Range:	By character class

Description

When the Titans first fashioned the world and dabbled with the forms and shapes of Creation, the titan Gormoth was the first to create a servitor race of humanoids, a people who called themselves the Viren. However, Mormo, mother of serpents, grew jealous of the creation and poisoned her brother Gormoth. While Gormoth writhed in agony for a millennium, the Viren went ignored and forgotten.

Meanwhile, the titans created more beautiful and graceful races, and by the time Gormoth recovered, even he was no longer interested in the crude Viren. So, the Viren went deeper and deeper into hiding, for want of the other creatures' skills, and out of shame for their own forms and disfavor. In time, these people were forgotten by all except the ancient and the learned, and they became known as the Abandoned by those who knew them at all.

Today, only a small tribe of the Viren still exist, deep in the tropical jungles of the south, where other humanoid races cannot (or have yet to) intrude.

The Abandoned are shaggy wild men, with brown or black ragged fur all over their bodies. The have crude intelligence, but they remain painfully self-aware. They speak their own language composed of grunts, clicks and howls, and they know nothing of other races since they live in seclusion. Their first reaction to humanoid intrusion is to scatter, but fear quickly turns to anger as the injury and insult of ages comes to a boil. Knowledge of the Titans' overthrow might placate or even please the Viren, if it can be communicated somehow, but these wild people have little reason to believe that any gods or overlords would treat them any more fairly than they have been treated thus far. And yet, what secrets of the ancient world might these people simply take for granted?

Combat

The Abandoned typically scatter upon intrusion by any other kind of humanoid, seeking spots to watch strangers from afar and to hide their in-born shame. In time, however, observers yell and screech to each other, growing increasingly resentful of their "betters" until the tribesmen literally pour from the jungles, swinging whatever weapons come to hand.

Musk (Ex): The Abandoned exude a pungent musk that appeals to members of the race but that other races find nauseating. Anyone within 10 feet must succeed at a Fortitude save (DC 15) or be overcome by the stench. Those so affected suffer a -2 penalty on all saves, skill checks and attacks for 2d6 rounds.

Albadian Battle Dog

Small Animal (Dog)

Hit Dice:	2d8+4 (13 hp)
Initiative:	+4 (Dex)
Speed:	45 ft.
AC:	19 (+1 size, +4 natural, +4 Dex)
Attacks:	Bite +4 melee
Damage:	Bite 1d8+1
Face/Reach:	5 ft. by 5 ft./5 ft.
Special Attacks:	Lockjaw
Special Qualities:	Loose-skinned
Saves:	Fort +5, Ref +7, Will +0
Abilities:	Str 13, Dex 18, Con 15, Int 2, Wis 10, Cha 5
Skills:	Listen +6, Spot +6
Feats:	Dodge, Improved Bull Rush, Mobility
Climate/Terrain:	Any
Organization:	Solitary or pair
Challenge Rating:	1
Treasure:	None
Alignment:	Always neutral, or as owner
Advancement Range:	1-3 HD (Small)

Description

In the cold northlands of Albadia, the most popular pastime is dog-fighting. Men and women breed and raise dogs known as Albadian battle dogs. The dog is a marvelous and vicious fighter. Its loose folds of flesh help it avoid serious injury from most bites (the skin pulls away from the muscles before they can be pierced) and its strong frame provides balance and mobility.

Albadian Wolf

Some unknown number of years ago (but before the Divine War), an unsavory and unscrupulous breeder crossbred his battle dogs with wild dogs from the mountains just north of Albadia. It took several generations to get the mix he desired — one that combined the obedience of the battle dog with the stamina of the wolf — but he succeeded, at least well enough to begin to dominate the dog-fighting circuit. The Albadian's crossbreeding was eventually discovered, though, and he was hanged. (They take their dog fighting very seriously in Albadia.) Out of respect, the animals he'd created were set loose instead of slaughtered. The pack of two score dogs quickly carved out a territory among the wolves, and they

have managed to maintain it to this day. Now called Albadian wolves, these animals are larger (qualify as Medium-size), and they have 3d8+6 HD, but they do not have the special lockjaw attack as they are not disciplined enough to maintain their hold. They usually roam in packs of two to eight.

Combat

The Albadian battle dog relies mainly on its power and speed in combat. Injuries do not bother it overly much. They typically initiate combat with a bull rush and use their mobility to disengage and rush again if this proves effective against their opponent. Whenever it scores a solid blow with a bite, the battle dog locks its jaws and attempts to outlast its opponent.

Lockjaw (Ex): When a battle dog scores a hit with its teeth, it has the option of locking its extremely powerful jaws onto its victim. It loses its Dexterity bonus to AC, but each round thereafter it does bite damage automatically.

Loose-skinned (Ex): Because of its loose skin, the Albadian battle dog sustains only half damage from piercing weapons.

Alley Reaper

Medium-size Undead

Hit Dice:	3d12 (19 hp)
Initiative:	+2 (Dex)
Speed:	30 ft.
AC:	18 (+2 Dex, +6 natural)
Attacks:	Short sword +5 melee
Damage:	Short sword 1d6+2
Face/Reach:	5ft. by 5ft/5ft.
Special Attacks:	Fear
Special Qualities:	Incorporeal, undead
Saves:	Fort +1, Ref +3, Will +1
Abilities:	Str 15, Dex 15, Con —, Int 10, Wis 7, Chr 8
Skills:	Hide +6, Intimidate +4, Intuit Direction +6, Listen +4, Move Silently +6, Spot +4
Feats:	Dodge, Improved Critical, Quick Draw
Climate/Terrain:	Urban
Organization:	Solitary
Challenge Rating:	2
Treasure:	Standard
Alignment:	Always chaotic evil
Advancement Range:	4-7 HD (Medium-size)

Description

The alley reaper is the spirit of an assassin or cutthroat who died with blood on his hands. Belsameth considered that person particularly ruthless, cunning and deceitful and gave them an extended lease, not on life, but on the world. Little more than shadows, these spirits ostensibly appear to walk as men, concealing themselves under long, tattered, black cloaks. In truth, they have no substance. If a reaper's cloak is removed, all that's found underneath is a collection of prizes stolen from murder victims, and the weapon that the ghost used to kill in life. All of these items spill to the ground, although the reaper is still active and certain to attack those who dare provoke it.

An alley reaper stages a reign of terror over the ward or city in which it was killed, and probably on the group, watchmen or soldiers who killed it. Its appetite for revenge and death can never be sated, and when enemies from life are dispatched, anyone can become a target.

Reapers strike only at night. During the day, they fade from this world, leaving behind a fallen cloak and a collection of prizes. If these are all moved or taken, the ghosts arises the next night wherever its possessions are. If only some possessions are stolen, the reaper intuitively senses where they are and pursues them relentlessly. Perhaps the only way to put an alley reaper to rest is to locate its hidden possessions and await the rise of the spirit at sunset.

Combat

The alley reaper always seeks to ambush its victims, and then dismembers them horribly to inspire as much fear and uproar in the community as possible.

Fear (Su): A reaper may make a fear attack three times a night. Spectral winds fill its cape, making it resemble the wings of a vulture spread over a kill. From the shadows of the cape, the faces of the reaper's victims can be seen shrieking in horror. Those who see the reaper must succeed at a Will save (DC 15) or flee in fear for 2d4 rounds.

Incorporeal (Ex): An alley reaper is little more than a shadow, given form only by its cloak. When robed, it must pass through doors as a living person would. When disrobed, it can pass through objects and obstacles freely. Either way, only magical weapons and magical attacks can harm it.

Undead: The alley reaper is immune to mind-influencing effects, poison, sleep, paralysis, stunning and disease. It's not subject to critical hits, subdual damage, ability damage, energy drain or death from massive damage.

Amalthean Ram

Medium-size Magical Beast

Hit Dice:	8d10+48 (92 hp)
Initiative:	+3 (Dex)
Speed:	60 ft.
AC:	21 (+3 Dex, +8 natural)
Attacks:	Horns +13 melee
Damage:	Horns 2d10+5
Face/Reach:	5 ft. by 5 ft./5 ft.
Special Attacks:	Charge
Special Qualities:	Amalthean milk, damage reduction 10/+2, immunities, regenerate
Saves:	Fort +14, Ref +5, Will +9
Abilities:	Str 20, Dex 16, Con 23, Int 2, Wis 12, Cha 12
Skills:	Balance +8, Intimidate +4 (ram only), Jump +10, Listen +8, Spot +4
Feats:	Great Fortitude, Iron Will, Mobility, Run
Climate/Terrain:	Temperate to warm mountains
Organization:	Pair, family (3-4)
Challenge Rating:	6
Treasure:	None
Alignment:	Always neutral
Advancement Range:	6 HD (ewe, Medium-size)

Description

These unusual creatures are relatives of the big-horn sheep, but touched by the latent magic of the Scarred Lands. They are renowned for a single reason: The milk of an Amalthean ewe has incredible healing power that is said to be able to cure diseases, negate poison and even heal wounds. Many people covet this milk, particularly those without access to the divine powers of empowered priests — but the difficulty lies in obtaining the milk. The ewe is guarded by the Amalthean ram which — having been raised on a diet of Amalthean milk — is stronger and more resilient than any natural animal.

The Amaltheans are not herd animals; their remarkable resilience provides sufficient protection from predators, such that they don't need to rely on numbers to survive. They are commonly encountered in pairs, which mate for life. Amaltheans may live up to 75 years in the wild, thanks to their extraordinary health.

A few villages or nomadic tribes have managed to tame an Amalthean ewe, sometimes even the ram as well. These prize animals are usually well-kept secrets, for fear that outsiders may try to steal the village's sole source of healing. Regrettably, the Amaltheans are incapable of breeding in captivity. Even the most doting pair cannot seem to conceive offspring in human company. Their life span is also greatly reduced in captivity; without freedom, an Amalthean can live for only 40 years or so. When a village's ewe is nearing the end of her life, the elders often attempt to hire outsiders to fetch a wild Amalthean lamb — usually under the pretext that the animal is sacred to them, or that the gods demand Amalthean lambs as sacrifices from time to time.

Combat

The Amalthean ewe fights only to defend any lambs she might have. The ram, however, is rather belligerent, and he does his best to defend the ewe from anyone he deems a threat. He rarely fights to the death; if his opponents retreat, he is content not to pursue.

Amalthean Milk (Su): The milk of an Amalthean ewe has many beneficial effects. One draught cures 5 points of damage, 2 points of ability damage, neutralizes any non-magical poisons in the bloodstream and cures any non-magical diseases that the target may be suffering. A ewe can be milked for three draughts each day, but she can spare only one draught if she's currently nursing a lamb. Taking any more affects the lamb's growth adversely.

Charge (Ex): An Amalthean ram's charge inflicts double damage; triple if the ram is charging from an uphill position.

Immunities (Ex): Amaltheans are immune to poison and disease.

Regenerate (Ex): Amaltheans regenerate at the rate of 2 hit points per round.

Angler Ooze

	Large (Long) Ooze
Hit Dice:	4d10+12 (34 hp)
Initiative:	-1 (Dex)
Speed:	20 ft.
AC:	11 (-1 Dex, -1 size, + 3 natural)
Attacks:	Pseudopod +2 melee
Damage:	Pseudopod 1d6 and paralysis
Face/Reach:	5ft. by 10ft./10ft.
Special Attacks:	Acid, paralysis, dazzle
Special Qualities:	Blindsight, ooze
Saves:	Fort +7, Ref +0, Will -1
Abilities:	Str 8, Dex 9, Con 17, Int 1, Wis 6, Chr 1
Skills:	None
Feats:	None
Climate/Terrain:	Temperate marsh and underground
Organization:	Solitary
Challenge Rating:	3
Treasure:	None
Alignment:	Always neutral
Advancement Range:	3–4 HD (Large), 5-12 HD (Huge)

Description

The angler is a translucent, dull brown to brick-red ooze that slithers about in shaded or wet areas by day and waits for prey at night. Angler oozes at rest are typically about five feet across, snaking out to 15 feet when in motion (they cover the largest area when hunting). The slime's digestive acids, which cover its form, affect only animal matter, so it can conceal itself in brush and under ground-cover during the heat of the day without destroying its own surroundings.

Combat

The angler ooze's preparations for a night's hunt start at sunset. The angler finds a small tree or stump that's surrounded by low ground-cover such as ferns or tall grass, and slithers up it to a height of about four feet. At this point, it exudes a lemon-sized globule of slime that rapidly hardens and begins to glow. Small oozes proceed to use their sticky pseudopods to snag insects that are attracted. Larger specimens learn to wait for more satisfying prey.

Acid (Ex): Any successful melee attack made against the ooze inflicts 1d4 damage on the attacker from the acidic spray that erupts from the ooze's wound.

Paralysis (Ex): A paralyzing slime coats the whiplike pseudopods with which the angler attacks. A target must succeed at a Fortitude save (DC 13) or be paralyzed for 2d6 rounds.

Dazzle (Ex): If the ooze's attack is resisted aggressively, its form begins to roil and glow from within. Once the ooze loses half its hit points, any subsequent strike on it causes a bright flash. This reaction inflicts two more points of damage on the ooze but forces all within 15 feet to make a Reflex save (DC 17) or be blinded for 2d6 rounds.

Blindsight (Ex): The angler is blind, but its entire body is a primitive sensory organ that can detect heat, scent and motion within 35 feet.

Ooze: The angler ooze is immune to mind-influencing effects, poison, sleep, paralysis, stunning and polymorphing. It's not subject to critical hits.

Aquantis

	Large (Long) Beast
Hit Dice:	8d10+8 (52 hp)
Initiative:	+3 (Dex)
Speed:	30 ft., fly special (see below)
AC:	16 (-1 size, +3 Dex, +4 natural)
Attacks:	Bite +9 melee
Damage:	Bite 4d6+2
Face/Reach:	5 ft. by 10 ft./10 ft.
Special Attacks:	None
Special Qualities:	Water walking
Saves:	Fort +7, Ref +11, Will -2
Abilities:	Str 15, Dex 17, Con 13, Int 2, Wis 3, Cha 2
Skills:	Listen +4, Spot +10
Feats:	Flyby Attack, Lightning Reflexes
Climate/Terrain:	Any freshwater lake
Organization:	Pod (1-8) or cluster (9-20)
Challenge Rating:	5
Treasure:	Standard
Alignment:	Always neutral
Advancement Range:	8-11 HD (Large), 12-15 HD (Huge), 16-17 (Gargantuan)

Description

On the most remote shores of Lake Minagan, toward central Termana, is one of the most beautiful sights of nature in the Scarred Lands. Gazing upon a pod or cluster of aquantis as they swoop and turn in the wind and they ride the surface of the lake allows one to forget for a moment the world's devastation. These reptiles make use of vestigial wings and a flap of skin upon their back as sails of a sort. With these flaps unfurled, they seem to skate across the surface of the lake in search of fish or other prey upon which to feed. Humanoids in boats are certainly not exempt from the appetites of these colorful reptiles.

Aquantis can run across the water without the aid of the wind, but with it they can achieve remarkable speed in any direction (save directly into the wind). Their speed depends on the strength of the wind, but speeds over 100 feet per round are possible, especially if the beast is moving perpendicular to the wind.

A note of concern regarding the aquantis, there are rumors that a race of lizardmen living along the southern edge of Lake Minagan has been working for some time to domesticate these reptiles. Their labors have borne some fruit in recent years, and stories circulate about lizardmen pirates roaming about the gigantic lake in the interior of the continent, utilizing a dozen or so aquantis to harry and harm their targets. If such rumors are true, they bode ill for the merchants who have finally re-established trade across the breadth of the lake over the past generation.

Combat

The aquantis can be a deadly foe, especially when the wind is in its favor (and an aquantis waits to attack until it has a favorable path). It sweeps by boats and uses its long neck to reach onto the deck and pluck unfortunate sailors.

Water Walking (Ex): Although it would seem to be impossible for a creature so large, the aquantis is able to walk atop the water. This is a permanent effect.

Asaatth

Medium-size Humanoid

Hit Dice:	3d8+3 (16 hp)
Initiative:	+3 (+3 Dex)
Speed:	40 ft.
AC:	23 (+3 Dex, +5 natural, +5 serpent mail)
Attacks:	Scimitar +4 melee; short sword +4 melee; bite +4 melee; tail slap +4 melee; unarmed strike +4 melee; shortbow +6 ranged; javelin +6 ranged
Damage:	Scimitar 1d6+1; short sword 1d6+1; bite 1d3+1 and poison; tail slap 1d6+1; unarmed strike 1d3+1; shortbow 1d6; javelin 1d6+3
Face/Reach:	5 ft. by 5 ft./5 ft.
Special Attacks:	Poison
Special Qualities:	Keen senses
Saves:	Fort +2, Ref +4, Will +5
Abilities:	Str 12, Dex 17, Con 13, Int 15, Wis 14, Cha 13
Skills:	Alchemy +5, Escape Artist +3, Hide +3, Jump +6, Listen +5, Move Silently +10, Search +4, Spellcraft +9, Spot +3, Use Magical Device +3
Feats:	Blind-Fight, Combat Casting, Combat Reflexes, Expertise, Run
Climate/Terrain:	Swamp and deserts and surrounding temperate regions
Organization:	Pair, squad (3-7), war band (10-50 asaatthi, plus 1 4th to 6th level commander and 1 3rd level sergeant per 15 warriors), or clan (50-500 asaatthi, plus 1 7th to 9th level dire knight, 1-2 4th-6th level commanders, and 1 3rd level sergeant per 15 adults)
Challenge Rating:	2
Treasure:	Standard
Alignment:	Usually chaotic evil
Advancement Range:	By character class

Description

The asaatthi are an ancient race of reptilian warrior-wizards. It is said that their empire once extended from the Swamps of Kan Thet to the vast Ukrudan Desert. Scattered ruins hint at this ancient dominance but only isolated clans remain of the asaatthi themselves.

The snake-men were masters at crafting magical items that they used to further the greatness of their maker, Mormo, Serpentmother. The asaatthi focused on these talents so much that the rest of their culture crumbled away slowly. Many of their secrets remain lost to this day. Now, the once-great race knows only battle and magic.

The asaatthi have spent the many years since the Titanswar avenging fallen Mormo and searching for a means to free her from imprisonment. Although small in number, the snake-men are formidable foes. Everyone from barbarian champions to elvish arch mages respect the asaatthis' martial and magical prowess.

Asaatthi look continually for magic and lore that might free Mormo. Runners are reputed to venture into the Hornsaw Forest delivering new discoveries to a hidden clan of wizards hard at work trying to raise the Mother of Serpents.

An asaath is more slender than an elf though taller than a human. Its supple hide ranges in color from deep green to light tan with red, yellow or even blue markings. Despite its delicate appearance, the serpent-man is strong and fast and its skin is quite resistant to damage. It prefers loose robes and sashes in its clan design which provide its limbs — especially its long whiplike tail — a free range of movement. Jewelry adorns the asaath from head to toe, much of it ensorcelled to some degree. The asaath's golden eyes burn with savage intellect and intense hatred for the "gods' chosen."

Asaatthi speak Asatthi and Draconic, and almost all learn Common, the better to understand their enemies.

Asaatthi Characters

An asaatth may be of any class except barbarian; they are decadent, not savage. Most serpent-men encountered are fighters or clerics although monks, rogues and wizards are by no means uncommon.

Asaatthi Society

Asaatthi have a clan-based culture. Family and heritage are all important, with great ancestral warriors and wizards revered as saints. Their race's slow decline has resulted in two main groups: swamp- and desert-dwellers. The swamp-dwelling asaatthi live in their ancestors' decaying cities and venture forth to strike at humanoids. The desert-dwelling serpent-men are semi-nomadic, visiting hereditary ruins and other secret lairs while they hunt down their racial enemies.

Combat

The asaatthi are experts in warfare mundane and mystic. They prefer guerilla warfare due to their small numbers, but they are comfortable coordinating large-scale tactics (often directing other dark races against humanoids). Given a choice, the asaatthi will lay traps and ambush opponents, but they won't back down from a straight-up fight. Even so, the serpent-men are far from stupid. They'll retreat if the odds aren't in their favor and plan vengeance for another time.

Keen Senses (Ex): An asaatthi sees three times as well as a human in low-light conditions and has darkvision to 60 feet. A serpent-man can also scent creatures within 30 feet and discern their direction as a partial action.

Poison (Ex): Victims of an assatth's bite must succeed at a Fortitude save (DC 14) or fall into toxic shock for 2d4+2 minutes.

Skills: An asaatthi receives a +4 racial bonus to Move Silently and Spellcraft checks.

Barrow Worm

	Huge (Long) Vermin
Hit Dice:	15d8+30 (97 hp)
Initiative:	+0
Speed:	40 ft.
AC:	11 (-2 size, +3 natural)
Attacks:	Bite +19 melee
Damage:	Bite 2d8+6
Face/Reach:	5 ft. by 10 ft./5 ft.
Special Attacks:	Grasping mandibles
Special Qualities:	Vermin, sensitive to bright light
Saves:	Fort +11, Ref +5, Will +4
Abilities:	Str 23, Dex 10, Con 15, Int 1, Wis 8, Cha 4
Skills:	None
Feats:	None
Climate/Terrain:	Subterranean passages, aboveground crypts
Organization:	Solitary
Challenge Rating:	8
Treasure:	Standard
Alignment:	Always neutral
Advancement Range:	10-14 HD (Large), 16-18 HD (Huge)

Description

The barrow worm is a large creature, more than 15 feet long, with a powerful set of scythelike mandibles at its "head." The worm has no obvious eyes or other sensory organs — rows of fine bristles along its length detect minute changes in vibration, temperature and air pressure in its vicinity.

Barrow worms are a common hazard in crypts or subterranean passages, preying upon unwary animals or individuals that pass too near their lairs. A barrow worm locates a long, narrow fissure or tunnel into which it can squeeze, coiling itself back into the darkness like a great spring. When a victim passes close by, it strikes, grabs the target in its sharp, serrated mandibles and then recoils back into its hole, making it difficult for the victim to escape and nearly impossible for others to assist him.

Combat

The barrow worm stays back in its fissure, far from any sources of light, and detects likely victims by changes in air pressure and vibration. It is not a very intelligent predator, and once it locks its mandibles around a victim, it tries to drag the target inside its hole, whether the prey fits or not. The mandibles continuously saw at the victim, causing deep wounds until the worm can be persuaded to let go. Piles of refuse — bits of clothing, armor and equipment — found in mounds around a particular hole are often a dead giveaway that a barrow worm awaits inside.

Grasping Mandibles (Ex): When the barrow worm strikes an opponent with its mandibles, it bites down and traps the victim like the jaws of a trap, sawing away at its body until it breaks free or dies. On each subsequent round, a victim must succeed on a Strength check (DC 22) to break free, or he suffers and additional 2d8+6 bite damage, automatically.

Vulnerable to Bright Light (Ex): If a barrow worm is subjected to bright light (full sunlight or a magical flare), it must make a Will save (DC 18) or retreat back into its lair, releasing any victim it might have trapped in its mandibles.

Vermin: Immune to mind-altering effects.

Bat Devil

Medium-size Monstrous Humanoid

Hit Dice:	2d8+2 (11 hp)
Initiative:	+4 (Dex)
Speed:	30 ft., climb 10 ft., fly 80 ft.
AC:	17 (+4 Dex, +3 natural)
Attacks:	Bite +3 melee; 2 claws +1 melee; short sword +3 melee
Damage:	Bite 1d6+1; claw 1d3+1; short sword 1d6+1
Face/Reach:	5 ft. by 10 ft./5 ft.
Special Attacks:	None
Special Qualities:	Blindsight, pedal dexterity
Saves:	Fort +1, Ref +9, Will +2
Abilities:	Str 12, Dex 18, Con 12, Int 11, Wis 14, Cha 14
Skills:	Climb +5, Hide +5, Listen +20, Spot +8
Feats:	Blind-Fight, Flyby Attack, Lightning Reflexes
Climate/Terrain:	Temperate and warm land, caverns
Organization:	Solitary, family group (3-12), roost (4-48)
Challenge Rating:	1/2
Treasure:	Standard
Alignment:	Usually neutral
Advancement Range:	By character class

Description

The bat devils are rather inaccurately named; this sentient race of bat-people suffers from a bad reputation that it hasn't fairly earned. One of the few humanoid races naturally capable of flight, bat devils stand around six feet tall when fully upright. Their batlike features and huge, leathery wings tend to frighten other races, which have dubbed the bat-folk "devils" out of superstition. (Their name for themselves is the Piterin, or "the flying people.")

Bat devils typically eat monstrous insects and birds, which they catch on the wing, but they have been known to augment their diet by carrying off young herd animals. As they see little difference between a rancher's herd and wild prey, their occasional predations only add to their reputation among men. Worse, due to the actions of a few rogue (and likely insane) individuals, bat devils are rumored to snatch away and eat unattended children, even though the average bat person is no more likely to steal a child than is the average elf.

Bat devils have a relatively simple society, due to their lack of reliance on material goods. They tend to gather in roosts, led by the wisest female. Most roosts have at least one member who has eavesdropped enough to master at least conversational Common,

and under dire circumstances, a roost may send heavily robed emissaries into settled lands to conduct business of one sort or another.

Bat-Devil Characters

A few bat devils have scrounged enough knowledge from other races to become passable fighters or rogues. Druids exist among their numbers, but are very rare. Many of them are multiclassed rogues.

Combat

Unless given no means of escape, bat devils prefer to fly away from combat at the earliest opportunity. When forced to defend their roosts, they wield scavenged weapons with their feet, engaging opponents as they remain airborne. If cornered, a bat devil may fight with the long claws on its feet or even deliver a wicked bite.

Blindsight (Ex): Using echolocation, a bat devil can sense creatures within 120 feet. Magically imposed silence negates this ability.

Pedal Dexterity (Ex): A bat devil can use his feet with the same ease as a human uses his hands. Bat devils are fully capable of using their feet to wield weapons, hang upside down or use writing utensils.

Belsamaug

Medium-size Humanoid (Goblinoid)

Hit Dice:	4d8 (18 hp)
Initiative:	+6 (+2 Dex, +4 Improved Initiative)
Speed:	30 ft.
AC:	15 (+2 Dex, +3 studded leather armor)
Attacks:	Dagger +5 melee, throwing dagger +6 ranged
Damage:	Dagger 1d4; throwing dagger 1d4
Face/Reach:	5 ft. by 5 ft./5 ft.
Special Attacks:	None
Special Qualities:	Invisibility, keen senses, locate prey, melding, darkvision 80 ft.
Saves:	Fort +1, Ref +6, Will +1
Abilities:	Str 11, Dex 14, Con 11, Int 10, Wis 11, Cha 10
Skills:	Hide +2, Listen +3, Move Silently +2, Spot +3, Wilderness Lore +4
Feats:	Alertness, Improved Initiative, Track, Weapon Focus (Dagger)
Climate/Terrain:	Any
Organization:	Pack (4-8)
Challenge Rating:	2
Treasure:	Standard
Alignment:	Always neutral evil
Advancement Range:	3-9 HD (Medium-size)

Description

Most travelers feel safe under the light of the moon, but wise explorers know the danger of such assumptions. When the moon looks down upon the Scarred Lands, Belsameth's children are summoned to roam the night and hunt unwary prey.

The belsamaug are a vicious race of goblinoids that rage and hunger beneath the soil by day. By night, a belsamaug materializes from the ground and prepares to hunt. A belsamaug is a sinister creature, standing about four feet tall, with long and narrow implike features. Belsamaug emphasize their narrow frames and opal eyes with skintight leather costumes, and are often adorned with past victims' knives and daggers, which the creatures keep as trophies of their kills.

Belsamaug usually travel in groups. Often likened unto a pack of wolves, belsamaug are experts of luring and herding prey. They prefer easy prey, and their keen senses allow them to track a victim through the harshest of climates. It is said that belsamaug can sniff out the wounded, the ill, or even the old from miles away, and relentlessly pursue these weak opponents.

While the belsamaug can only rise at night, their most terrifying aspect is that they can be seen only in the moonlight. Where moonlight does not strike them, they are invisible. Reflected moonlight reveals a belsamaug, but acute visual senses do not. A belsamaug often taunts its opponents, darting from one shadow to the next.

While most of these vile creatures stick to rural roads, more than a few have found their way into tents and country estates. Woe betide the city with belsamaug in its streets.

When the moon finally passes from the sky, the belsamaug's reign of terror is briefly at an end. It seeks a safe place, and melds back into the earth from whence it came. Only one small trace is left behind — a smooth hunk of basalt to mark its resting place. The few sages who know this secret debate what significance this basalt stone carries, some theories being that it is the mark of Belsameth or a portion of the goblin's heart. Regardless, if this stone is shattered, the belsamaug is slain and never rises again.

All belsamaug speak their own dialect of Goblin.

Combat

Like wolves, these creatures attack in packs, herding their opponent until she lies exhausted and unable to put up a fight. From there, it's only a matter of time before she falls to the belsamaug's daggers.

Invisibility (Ex): When not standing underneath moonlight, a belsamaug is completely invisible. Attacks against the belsamaug are therefore at a 50% chance of missing, even if a normal attack roll is successful.

Keen Senses (Ex): Belsamaug have an exceptional sense of smell and receive a +2 bonus for any Track tests.

Locate Prey (Su): Three times a night, a belsamaug can locate the nearest wounded, sick or infirm creature within 500 feet.

Melding (Ex): When moonlight touches the resting place of a belsamaug, it rises out of the earth to hunt the weak. When the moon sinks out of the sky, a belsamaug melds back into the earth, leaving only a basalt stone to mark its passing. This power is automatic, and it takes two rounds before the melding is complete. During this time, the belsamaug is unable to take any action. Should the basalt stone be destroyed for any reason, the belsamaug is killed instantly.

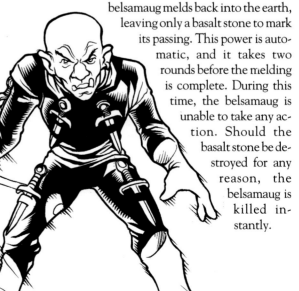

Berserker Wasp

Diminutive Vermin

Hit Dice:	10d8–20 (25 hp) (swarm)
Initiative:	+1 (Dex)
Speed:	Fly 60 ft.
AC:	15 (+4 size, +1 Dex)
Attacks:	Sting +9 melee
Damage:	Sting 1d10 and poison
Face/Reach:	5ft. by 5ft. (swarm)/o ft.
Special Attacks:	Poison sting
Special Qualities:	Vulnerable to cold, vermin
Saves:	Fort +0, Ref +2, Will -1
Abilities:	Str 1, Dex 13, Con 6, Int 1, Wis 8, Cha 2
Skills:	None
Feats:	Combat Reflexes, Track
Climate/Terrain:	Rain forests, temperate plains
Organization:	Solitary, Swarm Cloud (3-30)
Challenge Rating:	5
Treasure:	Standard
Alignment:	Always neutral
Advancement Range:	11-14 HD (swarm)

Description

Berserker wasps are four-inch-long insects with red bodies and double sets of shiny black wings. When enraged, their wings produce a deep, raspy buzzing, which in swarms of a hundred or more produces a bone-shaking drone that panics even well-trained beasts.

Berserker wasps are a hardy, adaptive breed of insect that does not build nests, but rather attacks and paralyzes large animals, using them as living hosts for their eggs and as nourishment for the hatchlings when they emerge. The wasps are dormant in the winter, emerging from burrows in the earth during the second week of spring. Queens then take to the air, attracting as many males as possible, and proceed to travel through the forests and grasslands, looking for a place to lay their eggs. Scouts range up to a mile ahead of the swarm, seeking out possible victims. Berserker wasps are drawn exclusively to the scent of blood, and their sensitive olfactory bulbs can sense a wounded person or animal up to a league away. When a victim is found, the swarm envelops it, stinging it hundreds of times until the insects' paralyzing poison takes effect. Then the queen and her males burrow into the still-living body and make their nest, laying eggs and feeding on the victim's tissues until the young hatch, up to a week later. After another week, the young have developed wings and the swarm moves on, leaving little more than a skeleton to mark their passing.

These insects have proven to acclimate quickly to changes in climate. Though the species originated in the equatorial rain forests of Termana, their swarms have made slow but steady progress northward (some say abetted by Virduk's trade ships to feast on the livestock of Vesh), encroaching into more densely populated fiefdoms. The insects' purposeful approach has rightly worried local nobles, many of whom dismiss rumors of Virduk's intent (as he has hardly been unaffected) and are instead convinced that some malevolent intelligence is directing the wasps' efforts.

Combat

Berserker wasps depend on speed and sheer numbers to bring down their prey, summoned by pheromones broadcast from their wide-ranging scouts and roaring down upon victims seemingly out of nowhere.

Poison Sting (Ex): Berserker wasps inject a powerful paralytic poison with each sting. Every time a victim is successfully stung, he must succeed at a Fortitude save (DC 17) or suffer 2 points of Dexterity ability damage per sting. This loss is temporary.

Vulnerable to Cold (Ex): Berserker wasps take double damage from cold-based attacks.

Vermin: Immune to mind-altering effects.

Blade Hood

Large (Long) Animal (Snake)

Hit Dice:	6d8+12 (39 hp)
Initiative:	+2 (Dex)
Speed:	40 ft.
AC:	15 (-1 size, +2 Dex, +4 natural)
Attacks:	Slash +9 melee
Damage:	Slash 1d10+4
Face/Reach:	10ft. by 5ft/5 ft.
Special Attacks:	Constriction
Special Qualities:	None
Saves:	Fort +4, Ref +7, Will +0
Abilities:	Str 18, Dex 15, Con 14, Int 8, Wis 7, Chr 14
Skills:	Escape Artist +4, Listen +6, Move Silently +5, Spot +6
Feats:	Alertness, Spring Attack
Climate/Terrain:	Arid regions and subterranean
Organization:	Solitary
Challenge Rating:	3
Treasure:	Standard
Alignment:	Always neutral
Advancement Range:	3-6 HD (Large), 7-9 HD (Huge)

Description

Blade hoods are large, clever serpents that inhabit remote wilderness areas and underground lairs. They are not venomous but they make up for this shortcoming with other adaptations. They're usually deep violet to black in color, although lighter variations such as rose and tan have been seen. Adults reach an average 30-foot length, and their bodies are stout and muscular, enabling them to crush even armored prey with relative ease.

The blade hood's most distinctive feature is its knifelike growths that emerge along its spine and from behind its jaws. When the serpent inflates its hood, its long jaw-scales spread out like the spokes on a chariot wheel. The serpent uses these appendages to tear through clustered prey or to strike solitary targets with a slashing motion. The shorter blades that run the length of the snake's spine are used to shred victims that are being constricted.

Blade hoods burrow deep lairs that usually have at least one large chamber. If a serpent makes a number of kills at once, it eats one on sight and drags the rest back to its tunnel to be swallowed later. Valuables are occasionally left in the dust of these chambers, or are scattered en route.

Combat

Blade hoods use surprise when possible, but can become impatient and charge forth, relying on their speed to run prey down. They are cautious about attacking any tool-wielding creatures they encounter. The serpents strike with slashing passes to test a potential victim. If a target fails to put up much of a fight, the snake seeks to constrict it to death.

Constriction (Ex): To use the constriction attack, the snake must make a successful melee attack with its jaw-blades. The blade hood then wraps its body around the victim (which must be Size Large or smaller) and inflicts another 2d6 points of crushing and cutting damage that round, and in each round thereafter until the victim is dead or the snake is dislodged. A successful Reflex save (DC 13) allows a target to escape a constriction attempt, and an Escape Artist or Strength check (DC 17) allows a held victim to escape.

Blight Wolf

Large (Long) Beast

Hit Dice:	8d10+40 (84 hp)
Initiative:	+8 (+4 Dex, +4 Improved Initiative)
Speed:	90 ft., fly 60 ft.
AC:	21 (-1 size, +4 Dex, +8 natural)
Attacks:	Bite +10 melee, 2 claws +5 melee; or tail +10 melee
Damage:	Bite 2d6+3; claw 1d6+1; tail 1d8+3
Face/Reach:	5 ft. by 10 ft./5 ft.
Special Attacks:	Chilling howl, poisonous bite
Special Qualities:	Frenzy, damage reduction 2/—
Saves:	Fort +11, Ref +6, Will +2
Abilities:	Str 16, Dex 18, Con 20, Int 5, Wis 10, Cha 3
Skills:	Hide +10, Listen +10, Move Silently +10, Spot +15
Feats:	Alertness, Combat Reflexes, Dodge, Spring Attack, Track
Climate/Terrain:	Wastelands
Organization:	Pack (2-8)
Challenge Rating:	5
Treasure:	Standard
Alignment:	Always chaotic evil
Advancement Range:	9-11 HD (Large)

Description

The blight wolf is another creature spawned in the terrible contest of magic between the gods and the titans, believed to have been born when a pack of wolves lapped at the blood of the fallen titan Mormo. Since then these fell wolves have prowled the forsaken wastes and desolate places of the world, preying upon all they encounter.

The blight wolf has the dark, furry head of a wolf, but the rest of its body is covered in lustrous black scales, and its paws are tipped with cruel talons. A pair of batlike wings sprout from its shoulders; though not strong enough to allow true flight, the wings permit a wolf to jump for long distances and pounce upon victims from improbable heights. The creature's tail is long and scaly, and ends in an iron-hard barbed point. Its eyes are black as pitch, and its howl sounds like a wind blowing out of the netherworld itself.

Blight wolves are drawn to those of good alignment, particularly lawful good, and they attack such individuals relentlessly, often to the exclusion of all else. Followers of Corean are particular targets.

Combat

The blight wolf chills its enemies' hearts with its baleful howl and then overwhelms them with sheer ferocity. The wolves are extremely crafty creatures and can show surprising patience, attacking savagely for a few heart-stopping moments, then fading into the darkness, only to strike again an hour later. They keep this up until the enemy is exhausted, and then move in for the kill.

Chilling Howl (Su): Blight wolves emit a baleful howl that strikes terror in any who hear it. Victims must succeed at a Will save (DC 19) or become panicked for 1d6 rounds, suffering a -2 on all saves and fleeing from the beast. Wolves may use this howl once per night.

Poisonous Bite (Ex): The blight wolf's bite is so poisonous it is said that if one so much as laps from a well, the water will be poisoned for weeks afterward. A victim bitten by a blight wolf must succeed at a Fortitude save (DC 21) or suffer 2d4 Constitution ability damage. This loss is temporary.

Frenzy (Ex): Blight wolves are immune to charm, mind control, fear and sleep effects. They are also immune to paralysis and subdual damage.

Bloodmare

Large (Long) Beast

Hit Dice:	10d10+50 (105 hp)
Initiative:	+2 (Dex)
Speed:	240 ft.
AC:	15 (-1 size, +2 Dex, +4 natural)
Attacks:	Bite +11 melee, 2 hooves +6 melee
Damage:	Bite 1d8+2; hooves 2d6+1
Face/Reach:	5 ft. by 10 ft./5 ft.
Special Attacks:	Equine lure
Special Qualities:	Tireless, damage reduction 5/+1
Saves:	Fort +12, Ref +9, Will +3
Abilities:	Str 15, Dex 15, Con 20, Int 12, Wis 10, Cha 15
Skills:	Listen +5, Move Silently +10, Spot +9, Track +7
Feats:	Alertness, Blind Fighting, Trample
Climate/Terrain:	Grasslands
Organization:	Solitary
Challenge Rating:	6
Treasure:	Standard
Alignment:	Always lawful evil
Advancement Range:	8-15 HD (Large)

Description

Bloodmares were once bred by the Warlock Kings (who some claim were the original inhabitants of Hollowfaust) as steeds for their champions and generals. After their empire was destroyed, many of these creatures escaped into the wild, where they continue to haunt lonely grasslands and forests far from civilization. A bloodmare is a tall, powerful warhorse, clean-limbed and strong,

with a black coat that reflects no light and eyes the color of clotted blood. Its teeth and hooves are sharply pointed, allowing it to tear flesh from its prey.

Bloodmares were bred with a taste for horseflesh, the better to fight and kill an opposing mount in the thick of battle. These days, this appetite for steeds draws bloodmares to caravans or other traveling parties, appearing just at full dark where the horses have been tethered. The creature magically calls to the horses, inciting them to stampede. Any horse that breaks free from its line or is released by its master bolts for the bloodmare, which runs into the distant hills. It leads until the other horse is exhausted, turns back and attacks its prey, killing and eating it. The bloodmare returns each night so long as the group still has horses to prey upon, disappearing only after the last has been killed.

In recent years, several evil lords (including the Jade Lord, new master of Canal Isle) have tried capturing wild bloodmares and turning them into warhorses once again, with mixed results.

Combat

If cornered by hunters, a bloodmare is a fearsome opponent, using its strength and speed to lash out with its pointed hooves and sharp teeth.

Equine Lure (Su): The bloodmare has the ability to call a horse that can hear its cry. Any horse hearing the call must make a Will save (DC 17) or do everything in its power to follow the creature. If someone is riding the horse at the time, the rider may make a Ride check (DC 19) to keep the mount under control.

Tireless (Ex): Bloodmares can run from sundown to sunrise without tiring.

Bone Lord

	Large (Tall) Aberration
Hit Dice:	12d8+36 (90 hp)
Initiative:	+0
Speed:	60 ft.
AC:	18 (-1 size, +9 natural)
Attacks:	(See below) bites/claws +15 melee
Damage:	Bite/claw 1d8+4
Face/Reach:	5 ft. by 5 ft./10 ft.
Special Attacks:	Multiple natural weapons
Special Qualities:	Alter shape, cold resistance, immunity
Saves:	Fort +9, Ref +4, Will +9
Abilities:	Str 18, Dex 10, Con 16, Int 9, Wis 20, Cha 5
Skills:	None
Feats:	Ambidexterity, Blind Fighting
Climate/Terrain:	Any
Organization:	Solitary
Challenge Rating:	6
Treasure:	Double Standard
Alignment:	Always neutral evil
Advancement Range:	8-12 HD (Large), 13-18 HD (Huge)

Description

The bone lord is a colony of small organisms that knit piles of bones together. A kind of communal intelligence stimulates the colony to move the construct at will, creating a kind of vehicle with which the colony can travel, hunt and defend itself. The colony appears in the form of a pink-gray fungus that grows on the surface of the bones, swelling at the joints and thickening in places that are analogous to muscles. The shape and weapons — claws, teeth or clublike bones — that a bone lord can form vary widely, depending only on the kind of bones available to the colony.

No one knows what hideous magic created bone lords. Perhaps a wizard's experiment went catastrophically wrong, or perhaps, as some sages whisper, the creatures were once mortals cursed by a vengeful god for the wrongs they committed against the gods. Regardless, these monsters have only been encountered in recent times, arising from the grisly remains of scattered battlefields and lurching about in search of living prey.

The bone lord needs fresh blood to nourish its colony and finds a cool, shadowy place to lie in wait for a passing victim. Prey are torn apart and a victim's blood is absorbed through the bones and distributed to all parts of the colony. After feeding, the bone lord lies dormant for weeks, storing metabolic energy, while the bones of its prey bleach in the sun. Once the bones are properly bleached, the colony absorbs them into the construct and moves on to another hunting spot.

Combat

A bone lord is a seemingly random collection of skulls, limbs and daggerlike ribs. It can alter its shape to adapt to changing situations. The creatures can bear amulets, jewelry, or bits of clothing or armor left over from past victims and even use them to entice curious adventurers.

Multiple Natural Weapons (Ex): The bone lord is capable of manifesting numerous natural weapons to fight its enemies. In the first round of combat, the bone lord will manifest 1d4 fanged jaws, claws, or bladed ribs to attack its enemies in that round. Each subsequent round, the bone lord will manifest one additional natural weapon up to a maximum number of attacks equal to its hit dice.

Alter Shape (Ex): As a free action, the bone lord may alter its shape each round with a successful Dexterity check (DC 18) in order to take the best advantage of the surrounding terrain, perhaps allowing it to pass through small tunnels or expand outward to fill a cave mouth.

Cold Resistance (Ex): The bone lord takes half damage from cold attacks, but double damage from fire.

Immunity: Bone lords are immune to polymorphing effects.

Bottle-Imp

Tiny Undead

Hit Dice:	4d12 (26 hp)
Initiative:	+7 (Dex)
Speed:	Fly 30 ft.
AC:	22 (+2 size, +7 Dex, +3 natural)
Attacks:	Knife +10 melee; or bite +10 melee
Damage:	Knife 1d4+4; bite 1d6+4 and sleep
Face/Reach:	2.5 ft. by 2.5 ft./5 ft.
Special Attacks:	Sleep bite
Special Qualities:	Retreat, smoke form, teleporting bottle, damage reduction 15/+2, undead
Saves:	Fort +1, Ref +11, Will +1
Abilities:	Str 18, Dex 25, Con —, Int 13, Wis 10, Cha 10
Skills:	Hide +7, Listen +6, Move Silently +7, Search +5, Spot +4
Feats:	Dodge
Climate/Terrain:	Any, usually urban
Organization:	Solitary
Challenge Rating:	4
Treasure:	None
Alignment:	Usually neutral evil
Advancement Range:	2-3 HD (Tiny), 5-6 HD (Small)

Description

Rumor has it that these horrible shadowy creatures are crafted from the ghosts of children by using dark rituals. They often serve as deadly assistants and helpers to malevolent wizards or necromancers, so that their murderous impulses can be better indulged.

Bottle-imps seem to be made of shadow and smoke, which grants them surprising reach for their size. They live inside small enchanted bottles, which are sometimes "given" to people that the giver wants dead. However, their bottles might turn up in surprising places, even washing ashore on beaches.

A bottle-imp can range up to 100 yards from its bottle, always connected by a small tether of smoke (which can be disrupted without injuring the imp, although the imp senses the disturbance). It emerges only at night. It refuses to come out into daylight even if threatened with death. It carries a small knife that does serious damage for its size.

Combat

Although bottle-imps are not the most imposing creatures, they can make terrifying combatants. They dart around with surprising speed, biting at faces and throats in order to incapacitate their opponents before slashing with their knives. Some necromancers who command bottle-imps wear their bottles at their waists, releasing the imps to aid them in combat.

Sleep Bite (Su): Anyone bitten by a bottle-imp must make a successful Fortitude save (DC 16) or fall into a deep slumber for 10-60 minutes.

Smoke Form (Ex): Bottle-imps are partially substantial and can squeeze through any opening that a Fine creature could.

Retreat (Su): When a bottle-imp is reduced to 0 hit points, it automatically retreats into its bottle and pulls in the stopper. This is a free action.

Teleporting Bottle (Su): The only way to permanently destroy a bottle-imp is to break its vessel. The vessel is treated as hardness 10 with 10 hit points. Of course, if the imp senses an attack on its bottle, it usually activates the bottle's teleportation power to escape. The bottle grants the ability to teleport up to 100 yards away, three times per day. The imp has usually scouted out the surrounding area to find the most innocuous location to hide its bottle in the event of an emergency (wine cellars and gutters are favorites).

Undead: Bottle-imps are immune to poison, sleep, paralysis, stunning and disease. They're not subject to critical hits, subdual damage, ability damage, energy drain or death from massive damage.

Brewer Gnome

Small Fey

Hit Dice:	2d6 (7 hp)
Initiative:	+2 (Dex)
Speed:	20 ft.
AC:	13 (+1 size, +2 Dex)
Attacks:	Club +3
Damage:	Club 1d6
Face/Reach:	5 ft. by 5 ft./5 ft.
Special Attacks:	Belch, flame breath, spells, spell-like abilities
Special Qualities:	Magical brewing
Saves:	Fort +0, Ref +5, Will +1
Abilities:	Str 10, Dex 14, Con , Int 13, Wis 12, Cha 14
Skills:	Alchemy +18, Appraise +4, Bluff +4, Craft (Brewing) +21, Escape Artist +1, Hide +2, Knowledge (Nature) +6, Sense Motive +3
Feats:	Brew Potion, Craft Wondrous Item
Climate/Terrain:	Any temperate except near large cities
Organization:	Clan (5-14)
Challenge Rating:	1
Treasure:	Standard
Alignment:	Usually chaotic neutral
Advancement Range:	2-5 HD (Small)

Description

Mislabeled as gnomes, brewer gnomes are actually one of the fey races that still walk the Scarred Lands. These gnomes travel the countryside collecting strange ingredients to make the brews for which they are famous or infamous, depending on whom one asks.

When they are not collecting ingredients, brewer gnomes find a secluded glade or mountaintop to set up camp and do their brewing. The brewer gnomes then proceed to have a large party until they are all quite worse off for it.

The gnomes are happy to barter with anyone who happens upon their encampments, or who encounters them during their searches for strange ingredients. Anyone who manages to survive a few of the brewer gnomes' drinks during formal introductions is accepted as a trading partner. Brewer gnomes are happy to collect gems and potions of all kinds, and they also barter their goods for ingredients-collection services from travelers. They do not let their casks of brew go cheaply.

Brewer gnomes stand three feet tall and dress in bright colors. They travel in extended families. Some clans have taken in ogres or hill giants who get their fill of drink in exchange for carting around heavy casks and for eating anyone who acts rude to the brewer gnomes.

Combat

Brewer gnomes prefer the bottle to the bastard sword, and never enter combat voluntarily. If they are attacked or their possessions are being stolen, the gnomes either attempt to escape with what goods they can or drive off the attacker depending on the situation.

Belch (Su): A brewer gnome may spend its move action imbibing some of its Silver Moon Ale and then belch the powerful fumes from the brew at any opponent within five feet in the subsequent round. The victim must succeed at a Fortitude save (DC 11) or pass out. The victim is not merely asleep. Rousing him requires several rounds of slapping and yelling in his ear or any blow that causes damage. Left alone, the victim wakes up in (at most) four days. The belch attacks counts as a poison attack.

Flame Breath (Su): As a full round action, the gnome may quaff some of its highest proof brew and then breathe it out on opponents while magically lighting it into a 10-foot flaming cone. Anyone within the cone takes 2d4 damage. Characters who succeed at a Reflex saving throw (DC 11) take only half damage.

Magical Brewing: Brewer gnomes create many wonderful concoctions. The following are but a few of the possible brews. In general, all brews cause the drinker a -1 Dexterity, Wisdom and Intelligence penalty per mug, and a +1 Strength, Constitution and Charisma bonus for every three mugs. These bonuses and penalties all fade at a rate of one point per hour once the drinking stops. The brews are stored in casks, each holding a dozen mugs of drink.

Passionberry Cider — This lovely cider is fermented from rare passionberries, and it seems to augment the berry's amorous side effects. Anyone drinking the cider gains +1 Charisma every two mugs instead of every three. They also suffer a -2 penalty per mug on any saving throws for charming or suggestion magic, to disbelieve illusions, or on any Sense Motive skill rolls. If a drinker sees or speaks with any reasonably suitable mate (preferred sex and same race), he must pass a Will saving throw (DC 11, before the -2 penalty above) to avoid becoming infatuated with his newfound love.

Pond Scum Stout — Although no one cares to know what the brewer gnomes put in this stout, no one complains of its excellent hearty flavor. The stout gives +1 Strength per two mugs not three, and anyone drinking it is immune to fear effects for one hour per mug.

Silver Moon Ale — A smooth draught that can go right to one's head. Anyone except dwarves, gnomes and fey races who drinks the ale must succeed at a Fortitude saving throw (DC 11) or pass out. The difficulty of the saving throw goes up by one with each successive cup imbibed. Anyone who passes out remains asleep for one year per mug unless they are woken up (as per "Belch").

Those who do not succumb to the ale's slumber find themselves in an abundantly cheerful mood, and if the moon is visible, they also gain the ability to fly (as a spell-like ability, caster level 12, activated once per mug drunk).

Waterfall Wine — This bubbly white wine grants the ability to breathe underwater for one hour per drink.

Spells: Brewer gnomes cast spells as fourth level sorcerers.

Spell-like Abilities: Turn invisible twice per day.

Butcher Spirit

Small Undead

Hit Dice:	6d12 (39 hp)
Initiative:	+8 (+4 Dex, +4 Improved Initiative)
Speed:	40 ft.
AC:	20 (+4 Dex, +1 size, +5 natural)
Attacks:	None
Damage:	None
Face/Reach:	5 ft. by 5 ft./5 ft.
Special Attacks:	Gaze, shudder, possession
Special Qualities:	Darkvision 120 ft., incorporeal, undead
Saves:	Fort +2, Ref +6, Will +4
Abilities:	Str 10, Dex 18, Con —, Int 10, Wis 9, Cha 6
Skills:	Animal Empathy +9, Hide +6, Listen +6, Spot +5
Feats:	Improved Initiative
Climate/Terrain:	Any
Organization:	Solitary, convocation (3-18)
Challenge Rating:	4
Treasure:	None
Alignment:	Usually neutral evil
Advancement Range:	5-8 HD (Small); 9-12 HD (Medium-size)

Description

Butcher spirits are what remains of animals once sacrificed in religious rites to feed the relentless hunger of the titan Gaurak. The animals' wholesale slaughter was avenged by an angry Denev, who sought to destroy the ravenous lord's cults by allowing animal spirits to remain in the world to lash out at their murderers. Butcher spirits linger at the places of their death, haunting long-abandoned temples or interrupting ceremonies at secret altars still dedicated to the Voracious One. Robbed of life, these spirits hate all people and humanoids in turn, whether they venerate Gaurak or not. Sometimes butcher spirits even assume the bodies of people to experience the world again, and to commit offenses against humanoids that cannot be performed from beyond. Butcher spirits are often solitary, seeking revenge for all their fellow creatures slaughtered at a site. However, some druids know the tale of a convocation of dead animals that haunts a ruined temple in the swamplands of southern Darakeene just inland from Liar's Sound.

Combat

Butcher spirits are usually tied to the location of their sacrifice. They possess intruders to wreak havoc abroad until the first rays of the sun return them to their haunts.

Gaze (Su): Those who make eye contact with a butcher spirit must succeed at a Will save (DC 20) or be unable to take actions unless attacked or the spirit releases its gaze.

Shudder (Su): The butcher spirit passes through the body of a target, overwhelming him with the fear that the animal felt at the time of its sacrifice. The victim must succeed at a Will save (DC 20) or suffer a -4 morale penalty to all attacks, saves and skill rolls for 1d12 rounds.

Possession (Su): After trapping a person in its gaze, a butcher spirit can enter his body and assume complete control. The target must succeed at a Will save (DC 16) to resist possession. A possessed being is used to cause as much havoc to surrounding humanoids as possible. Sunrise dispels the possession; the butcher spirit returns to its haunt, while the host regains control, and is probably held responsible for his seeming actions.

Incorporeal (Ex): This creature has no material form. It is seen only as an apparition. It is immune to nonmagical weapons, although magical weapons and spells affect it normally.

Undead: A butcher spirit is immune to poison, sleep, paralysis, stunning and disease. It's not subject to critical hits, subdual damage, ability damage, energy drain or death from massive damage.

Carnival of Shadows, The

Far to the southeast of Ghelspad, and well south of Asherak where the Blood Sea comes to an end, is a place beyond human curiosity called the Bay of Tears. This bay is the terminus of the currents that flow past the body of Kadum, the Mountainshaker, who lies forever bound to a great rock at the bottom of the sea. There beneath the waves, he writhes, gouting blood from where his heart has been torn out, as salt waters burn his eternal wound.

The Bay of Tears is so named because of the terrible curse that hangs over it. The fish and sea creatures that by necessity taste the blood of Kadum breed strangely, turning crafty, hostile and vile. And those who eat the catch from the bay are often sickened… or changed.

At the mouth of the Bay of Tears lies Blood Bayou, a vast salt marsh that's flooded at high tide and sequestered from the sea when the tide is low. Inland, the marsh's backwaters are shallow, stagnant lakes flooded only by storm surges.

In this place of darkness and disease, the blood of Kadum, rich with curses and magic, coalesces and seeps into the very land. It is a place of sickness, a blight that will not heal until the seas are cleansed, the land is purged, and Kadum's ever-flowing blood is stanched.

There are some evils in the world that are not a result of the Titanswar. Like flaws in glass, they have always been there. But when the gods and titans turned their attention toward each other in a struggle for the heavens, these evils prospered and grew fat on the scraps of war. It is in Blood Bayou that one such evil has come to dwell.

Some call him The Laughing Man, or the Momus, or the Jack of Tears. Whatever he's called, the King of the Carnival of Shadows has held court at the dark heart of Blood Bayou for at least two centuries, as there is evidence he occupied this land before the Titanswar, though perhaps in a different form. He has since grown mighty on the power of the blood of Kadum.

Yet the Laughing Man is not a mere menace to be feared and destroyed. Mad, capricious and deadly being that he is, he also possesses a certain gallows humor, a fondness for bravery and honesty, and a seemingly insuperable compulsion to keep his word. Though feared by those those who know of him, the Jack of Tears has never sent his krewes marching abroad as an army — although he swears that they will if any attempt is made to unseat him.

Indeed, Momus has actually offered his services as advisor and even court magician to other kingdoms that can bear him. Although his magic is dark and unappealing, it is rumored capable of raising plains into mountains, curing plagues and destroying armies. The prince's price is so high and his magic so fearsome, however, that he has never been called upon (at least to anyone's knowledge). Such offered aid, and fear of the combined power of the krewes roused for war, makes the Jack of Tears an uneasy fixture in the Scarred Lands' political arena despite his geographical separation — a distance he seems to prefer.

Krewe of Bones

Blood Bayou is a place of death and decay, and the Carnival of Shadows rejoices in it. Those things that are dead-yet-walk serve in the Krewe of Bones. This society is the most military of the krewes. There is little alternative — with so many members of the group nearly mindless, shambling creatures, the only alternative to discipline and strict regimentation is a chaos that the other krewes could not permit.

Even the most independent or even rebellious of the krewe's members are at lest of a strategic or military bent. Those members willing to accept commissions and intelligent enough to command are assigned positions leading units of less intelligent undead. Those who are disinterested in such matters are placed on "detached duty in the Krewe of Mangroves" or on "indefinite furlough" and allowed to go about their business until they are "called up" to serve the krewe. The whole matter is treated with grave formality, and krewe members are essentially subject to conscription in time of need.

The Krewe of Bones has the honor of providing the Jack of Tears' personal guard, and will lead the carnival in war should that ever prove necessary.

Each unit in the Krewe of Bones is uniformed by its officers. While there are no standards, uniforms tend to be both flamboyant and sensible. Most members wear intimidating gear on parade or when attending court functions — often the half-rotted heads of enemies or necklaces made of enemy fingers — if only to remind other carnival members who it is that will save their asses in times of war.

Lord Quick, the leader of Plagues, envies the permanence of Baron Mirth's servants and believes that the baron steals his followers.

Baron Mirth

The leader of the Krewe of Bones, Baron Mirth is like the force he commands — the personification of discipline and order. Mirth knows well that he is subordinate to his commander in chief, the Jack of Tears. Rumor has it that the baron was created by the Momus himself, and that he was once one of Demoiselle Antunes' more fortunate lovers. Whatever the truth, the skeletal baron swaggers through the carnival, secure in his position and publicly jovial about all matters. In private, however, he argues that the carnival must expand to protect itself, and sees every intruder or counterattack against a raiding party as an excuse to lobby the dispassionate Jack for a campaign of conquest.

Mirth is a huge creature, almost seven feet tall, dressed in brilliantly polished armor and a flowing scarlet cape. He carries a bastard sword and a shield emblazoned with an unmarked scarlet field. He goes about at all times escorted by at least a dozen of his crack shock troops. A lady's man, the baron keeps a small harem of undead concubines.

Krewe of Mangroves

Blood Bayou itself is home to many singular creatures, hateful beings who have chosen to lurk in the mud and mire, away from a world that shuns them. It's a place of misfits and madmen, and also of terrible beasts — lifewrack and seawrack dragons, spiders grown huge and cunning amid the glades, deadly alligator men and other beasts without names. These misfits together form one of the most powerful krewes in the carnival.

The Krewe of Mangroves is, perversely, the least active of the Prince's societies. It exists to protect and aid the interests of the exiles and misanthropes who choose to make the bayou their home. Most such beings have little or no interest in the outside world. It's also the poorest of krewes. While the leaders of other groups go to the court of the Laughing Man dressed in finery, the leaders of the Mangroves rely on barbarian splendor.

And splendid it is. With their fur caps and bone jewelry, their carved-wood fetishes and canes, spider-silk robes and swamp-tanned leather, the members of this krewe are terrible to behold. Though there may be no precious metals or jewels among their garb, how can a mere display of wealth match the majesty of renegade wizards in cloth-of-man colors, with their leashed alligators? Can mere money compare to the meticulous perfection of the alligator-man warriors with their countless bone ornaments?

Internally, the Krewe of Mangroves is the least formal and probably the most welcoming of the Laughing Man's societies. The bayou is a dangerous place for isolated spiders and alligator warriors, who must respect each other if they are to take shelter with one another from time to time. The krewe exists to protect its members and give them a social outlet. It's not that members exist in harmony — many are at constant war with each other — but those who are not engaged in hostilities can be counted on for a friendly word or help in desperate times.

The Krewe of Mangroves has strained relations with the Krewe of Plagues; Lord Quick forever looks for ways to expand his domain and claim more members for his group from among these outcasts.

Demoiselle Antunes

The leader of the Krewe of Mangroves is the Demoiselle Antunes, whom some say has inhabited the bayou since before the Titanswar. None know how old the Demoiselle really is. She seems to have been the same late middle age for as long as anyone willing to talk about the matter can remember. Surely the Jack of Tears knows her age, but he isn't telling.

Jovial in her evil, the Demoiselle is known for her string of lovers as well as for her penchant for transforming unfaithful paramours into a wide variety of fitting shapes. Transformation is not her only strength, though. The Demoiselle far outstrips any of the others in the carnival for her knowledge of formal magic. Her name is often associated with The White Lady, a powerful magician from a time *before*, who disappeared under questionable circumstances. The Demoiselle leads her krewe almost by default, being its most powerful member willing to accept the position.

Krewe of Plagues

The most festive of the Jack of Tears' krewes, the Krewe of Plagues is the very image of the danse macabre. Brilliant in their gold-and-scarlet regalia, with the music of their lepers' castanets and bells, Plaguers are the ill and misshapen of Blood Bayou. This krewe offers the world's deformed outcasts shelter, safety and relief from the agonies of their ailments.

Of course, relief is not without price. Most who join were in some way sick or twisted before. When they enter into the service of Lord Quick, they become bearers of various horrific diseases but are kept alive by Quick's good graces and potent magic. They live painlessly but transmit ailments among each other just as other people shake hands.

Although they revel in their illness, all krewe members know that they survive at the sufferance of their leader. Those who displease him die quickly and horribly. Others who commit grave offenses are forced to perish slowly as Lord Quick revokes his protection bit by bit.

Unlike the other Bayou societies, the Krewe of Plagues has very few interests of its own. Unlike Waves, it isn't constantly on the alert for intruders, nor is it self-involved as are the Krewes of Bones and Mangroves. Instead, most Plaguers live at the Jack of Tears' great rickety seaside festival as a staff of permanent revelers. They serve as courtiers and messengers for the Laughing Man, and give the ever-ambitious Lord Quick eyes and hands all over the carnival.

The krewe's idle state and loose organization make it dangerous. Members can be anywhere at any time, accomplishing any overt or covert deed. And though the Laughing Man decrees that members of other krewes and guests of the carnival never be infected with a Plaguer's disease, anyone else can be killed with but a touch from a member. Of all the bayou's groups, outsiders would fear this krewe most, if only they knew about it.

Given the gruesome existence that Plaguers live, their suicide rate is high despite their painless afflictions; those who remain for long are either mad or given wholly to wickedness for its own sake.

Lord Quick

The master of the stricken, Lord Quick dresses as the quintessential troubadour and masquerader: in harlequin's garb and constantly disguised. Unlike the Jack of Tears, however, he wears a domino over his face rather than holding up a mask. For all his smiles, Quick's breath reeks of carrion, his teeth are blackened and chipped, and his tongue is a rainbow of diseased colors.

A brutal political player, Lord Quick is different from his fellow krewe leaders. He seems much more on par with the Laughing Man, and there is much speculation about his origins. Some believe that he was a force of evil, like the Laughing Man himself, who came to be allied with the Jack of Tears. Others believe him to be a lieutenant of the titans, hiding from the wrath of the gods. Whatever the case, he is the only krewe leader to ever cause the Jack of Tears to lose his temper, and he seems to be the only one who entertains designs on the Momus' throne. That he still lives and retains his position despite these facts would seem to mean something — but perhaps nothing more than that the King of the Carnival is amused by the antics of his minions.

Krewe of Waves

The Krewe of Waves consists of the Jack of Tears' aquatic followers. This does not include pirates. Although buccaneers of Bloodport are wary of Queen Ran, leader of the Krewe of Waves (and sometimes pay her tribute) they are independent of the Krewe of Waves and the Jack of Tears in general. The members of the Krewe of Waves make their home *in* the ocean and are a dark and mysterious breed.

Cold and aloof as their deep, black homes, the members of the Krewe of Waves largely eschew the pageantry and comic air affected by members of other krewes. These creatures live by war and raiding, swimming up from below to attack ships at sea or coming ashore in the dead of night to seize captives and take booty back to their lairs.

The main duty of the Krewe of Waves appears to be border security for the Bay of Tears, the waters around which form a bottleneck to unknown lands beyond. The Krewe does not allow boats from the continents of Termana, Ghelspad or Asherak pass into the water beyond the Bay of Tears. Therefore, the lands beyond remain a mystery. Evidently, there is some sort of civilization beyond, for captured Bloodport pirates report sighting strange galleons in the distance that seemed disinterested in crossing the waters that are home to the Krewe of Waves.

Most of the members of this krewe are shark-folk, creatures twisted from the carnivorous fish that first fed upon Kadum's bleeding body. These vicious creatures can survive in the open air for several hours and are a terrible menace to seaside communities. Other members of the krewe include sea hags and their close allies the krakens. Vast and terrible creatures, skilled in black magic and weather-witching, the krakens are the leaders of the krewe. They call up fogs and storms to cover and protect the shark-folk during raids, and in return reap the tribute and respect of their lessers.

The Krewe of Waves is coldly formal. When it takes part in the carnival at all, which is only to demonstrate propriety to the Jack of Tears, leaders are resplendent in robes made of pearls and gold coins. Even warriors glitter and shimmer in coral and mother-of-pearl beads.

Though they dress far less spectacularly in their dim ocean homes, krewe members are almost painfully formal in their interactions. Complex webs of respect and loyalty bind these creatures, with every kraken owing fealty to their queen. In turn, each kraken has a court of hags and communities of shark-folk that look to it as their protector and leader. Even the shark-folk are strictly regimented, formed into military units with complex hierarchies.

The Krewe of Waves has close ties with the Krewe of Bones. Baron Mirth lays claim to all aquatic undead, and many shark-folk attacks are aided by his walking and swimming corpses. In return, the Krewe of Waves treats its drowned victims with special care to ensure that as many as possible rise from the dead.

Queen Ran

A vast black kraken, Queen Ran is the ice-hearted ruler of the Krewe of Waves. She is a vicious, wicked creature who delights in the riches that descend upon her black and frigid domain. As brutal and uncompassionate as the sea she rules, Queen Ran dresses in cloth of diamonds and carries the scepters of drowned kings in her many arms. A black magician of the darkest sort, even worse than the Jack of Tears himself, Ran is said to strike pacts with infernal princes, dealing with them as one ruler to another.

Carnival King, Jack of Tears

Medium-size Outsider (Chaos, Evil)

Hit Dice:	18d8+90 (171 hp)
Initiative:	+3 (Dex)
Speed:	30 ft.
AC:	24 (+3 Dex, +11 Natural)
Attacks:	Wand +20 melee
Damage:	Wand 6d6+2
Face/Reach:	5 ft. by 5 ft./5 ft.
Special Attacks:	Spells
Special Qualities:	Damage Reduction 10/+1, SR 24
Saves:	Fort +11, Ref +9, Will +15
Abilities:	Str 15, Dex 17, Con 20, Int 20, Wis 18, Cha 24
Skills:	Bluff +14, Climb +10, Concentration +10, Diplomacy +14, Escape Artist +12, Forgery +18, Gather Information +13, Hide +15, Intimidate +16, Knowledge (arcana) +14, Listen +20, Move Silently +18, Perform +18, Pick Pocket +18, Read Lips +20, Scry +20, Search +18, Spellcraft +12, Spot +18, Use Magic Device +16, Use Rope +20
Feats:	Combat Casting, Spell Penetration, all Item Creation and Metamagic Feats
Climate/Terrain:	Blood Bayou
Organization:	Unique
Challenge Rating:	10
Treasure:	Triple Standard
Alignment:	Always chaotic evil
Advancement Range:	None

Description

Perhaps the Jack of Tears was once nothing more than an evil spirit. It could be that he once roamed the night roads in a corpse-cart or a circus wagon, the wheels of which left tracks of blood, and he inflicted ill luck, miscarriage and sudden death wherever he went. Certainly, this is the origin many wizards attribute to him, but the jealous have always taken delight in casting aspersions.

Whatever the Jack of Tears once was, he became something more when he came to Blood Bayou and fed upon the blood of Kadum. The Laughing Man is not a child of the titans any more than are most inhabitants of the Bay of Tears. He has simply grown mighty on the intensity of Kadum's suffering.

Whatever his origin, the Jack of Tears is now the undisputed ruler of Blood Bayou and the krewes based there. These krewes are groups he has bound together for the common good and goals of all the unsavory characters who call the Bay of Tears their home.

Though he is a jesting figure, the Laughing Man is undoubtedly a force of evil, one who is wise enough to

make himself useful to his neighbors so that they tolerate his existence. But to the individuals who deal with him, the Laughing Man is a merciless trickster who twists words and grants requests with a ruthlessly literal ear.

The Jack of Tears rules his swamp-kingdom from a great, rickety carnival that lies in the center of the bayou, connected to the ocean by a channel so that members of the Krewe of Waves can come and go freely. Here, on a brightly painted throne of children's toys, he presides over the endless festival of his minions and holds audiences with those daring or foolish enough to approach him.

The Jack of Tears has never been brought to battle. His scepter Foolscap is a thick wand, white on one end and black on the other. The black end causes 6-36 points of damage with but a touch. The white end cures all illnesses and wounds and restores all lost abilities, levels and amputated limbs. The white end works on the Jack of Tears as well as on anyone he agrees to bless... for a price.

Combat

The Jack of Tears uses his magical wand and spells in combat.

Spells: Spellcasting abilities of an 18th-level sorcerer.

Outsider: Not affected by critical hits, death from massive injury, poison, paralysis, sleep, disease or any attack that must target a living subject.

Carnival Krewe, Alligator Warrior

Large (Tall) Humanoid

Hit Dice:	6d8+18 (45 hp)
Initiative:	+6 (+2 Dex, +4 Improved Initiative)
Speed:	40 ft., swim 30 ft.
AC:	24 (-1 size, +2 Dex, +3 studded leather armor, +10 natural)
Attacks:	Weapon +9; bite +9 melee, tail slap +7 melee; javelin +7 ranged
Damage:	By weapon +4; bite 1d6+4; tail slap 1d6+2; javelin 1d6+4
Face/Reach:	5 ft. by 5 ft./10 ft.
Special Attacks:	None
Special Qualities:	None
Saves:	Fort +8, Ref +4, Will +1
Abilities:	Str 18, Dex 15, Con 16, Int 12, Wis 8, Cha 6
Skills:	Climb +4, Disable Device +5, Escape Artist +2, Hide +4, Jump +3, Listen +4, Move Silently +6, Search +3, Spot +6, Swim +12, Wilderness lore +4
Feats:	Alertness, Dodge, Improved Initiative, Multiattack, Spring Attack
Climate/Terrain:	Swamps
Organization:	Solitary
Challenge Rating:	3
Treasure:	Standard
Alignment:	Usually lawful evil
Advancement Range:	7-10 HD (Large)

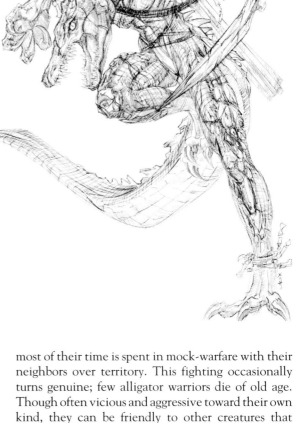

Description

Solitary swamp-dwelling predators, alligator warriors are some of the most dangerous inhabitants of Blood Bayou. It's unclear if they existed before the area came to be saturated with the blood of Kadum. If they did, it's impossible to say what they were like originally.

Alligator warriors are extremely territorial and independent. They typically gather for only three purposes. The first is for mating, and in the early spring the booming sounds of alligator-warrior males calling out territorial challenges creates an incessant evening din. The second is for organized activities such as meetings of their krewe or festivals and dances. Despite their predatory bent and solitary nature, these creatures can become gregarious by intention. The third occasion is to hunt intruders. When the territory populated by alligator warriors is invaded, they put aside their own disputes to stalk an invader, picking off stragglers or overwhelming an individual if it is weaker than the whole of the attackers.

Alligator warriors are unsophisticated creatures that focus on solitary hunting, preferably by ambush. They are masters of the pitfall, trap and snare, and most of their time is spent in mock-warfare with their neighbors over territory. This fighting occasionally turns genuine; few alligator warriors die of old age. Though often vicious and aggressive toward their own kind, they can be friendly to other creatures that inhabit their domains. Alligator warriors often serve as the genteel companions of other bayou denizens. They favor magicians and giant swamp spiders as companions, both of whom can provide the warriors aid and assistance in their constant territorial sparring.

Combat

Alligator warriors favor javelins, which they hurl with the use of a throwing stick, and knives or short swords. Most alligator warriors wear bone-studded leather armor.

Carnival Krewe, Blood Kraken

Large (Long) Magical Beast

Hit Dice:	7d10+21 (59 hp)
Initiative:	+1 (Dex)
Speed:	swim 60 ft.
AC:	24 (-1 size, +1 Dex, +14 natural)
Attacks:	8 tentacles +9 melee; squeeze +9
Damage:	tentacle 1d6+3; squeeze 1d6+3
Face/Reach:	5 ft. by 10 ft./5 ft.
Special Attacks:	Ink, sticky grasp, spells
Special Qualities:	None
Saves:	Fort +5, Ref +3, Will +8
Abilities:	Str 17, Dex 12, Con 16, Int 14, Wis 17, Cha 13
Skills:	Diplomacy +8, Hide +3, Innuendo +5, Intimidate +3, Knowledge (arcana) +10, Listen +7, Scrying +6, Spellcraft +5, Spot +2, Use Magic Device +3
Feats:	Blind-Fight, Forge Ring, Craft Rod, Enlarge Spell, Leadership, Maximize Spell
Climate/Terrain:	Undersea, seashore
Organization:	Solitary
Challenge Rating:	5
Treasure:	Triple Standard
Alignment:	Always lawful evil
Advancement Range:	8-10 HD (Large), 11-14 HD (Huge)

Description

These inky black creatures are the leaders of the Krewe of Waves and are the terrors of shipping and coastal villages throughout the Bay of Tears. Though blood krakens are relatively small (usually 8 to 12 feet from tentacle tip to tentacle tip) and shy from physical conflict, their leadership abilities and mastery of the magic of weather and destruction make them extremely dangerous, especially when supported by their coteries of followers.

Most krakens have personal entourages of several sea hags and a number of shark-folk. Such raiding parties might be as small as a school of 8 to 12 or as large as a village of 50 or more.

Blood krakens as a group owe allegiance to Queen Ran, the leader of the Krewe of Waves. Through her, they are members of the Carnival of Shadows, though by and large they find the chaos of the carnival distasteful. Most blood krakens are vain creatures, proud of themselves and their power. They bedeck themselves in the riches of the surface world, covering their arms with rings and bracelets, gilding and piercing their beaks, and crowning themselves with a wide variety of circlets, tiaras and diadems.

Most wield scepters or other wands of office salvaged from wreckage, and these can include swords and elaborately carved wooden legs — anything striking.

Combat

Blood krakens are typically reticent to enter combat, preferring for their followers to take care of such matters while they stay back and offer magical support. When forced into combat, krakens favor combat magic or attempt to strangle victims with their powerful arms.

Ink (Ex): Blood krakens can spew a thick ink cloud, which obscures vision in a 60-foot radius. Not even darkvision can penetrate it. They may do this once every three hours.

Sticky Grasp (Ex): When struck by one of the Kraken's tentacles, a target is seized and crushed, taking damage automatically every round unless the kraken is killed or releases the victim voluntarily. Size Small or larger individuals can be held by up to two tentacles at the same time.

Spells: Blood krakens have access to spells of the War, Destruction, Law, Evil and Water spheres as an 8th-level cleric.

Carnival Krewe, Necromantic Golem

Huge (Long) Undead Construct

Hit Dice:	9d12 (58 hp)
Initiative:	+0
Speed:	90 ft.
AC:	14 (-2 size, +6 bone armor)
Attacks:	2 large arms +16 melee, 4 small arms +11 melee
Damage:	Large arms 2d8+9; small arms by weapon type +4
Face/Reach:	10 ft. by 10 ft./10 ft.
Special Attacks:	None
Special Qualities:	SR 8, damage reduction 4/+1, undead construct
Saves:	Fort +6, Ref +3, Will +0
Abilities:	Str 28, Dex 10, Con —, Int —, Wis 4, Cha —
Skills:	None
Feats:	None
Climate/Terrain:	Swamp
Organization:	Solitary or company (2-3)
Challenge Rating:	7
Treasure:	None
Alignment:	Always neutral
Advancement Range:	6-8 HD (Large), 10-16 HD (Huge), 17-25 HD (Gargantuan)

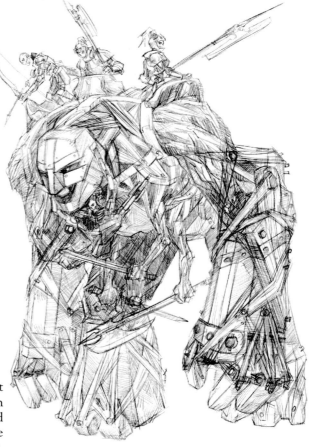

Description

Not every corpse is reanimated sufficiently intact to serve as an individual warrior, and many who begin undeath in good repair become so severely damaged that they can no longer perform field service. From these remnants are made the so-called necromantic golems. They are golems only in that they are constructed, usually by sewing or lashing remains together, perhaps around carefully constructed hardwood frames. The rest of the process is *almost* natural, as the powers of the blood and curses that saturate Blood Bayou give life to the dead tissue. Within a few hours or at most a few days, the pieces of the golem gain a dark communal life and begin acting as parts of a single, terrible undead behemoth.

The art of constructing these abominations is well studied among war-machine makers of the Krewe of Bones. Not just slapped-together hunks of meat and bone, necromantic golems are the product of long hours of careful craftsmanship. Built not only for the battlefield, but as works of art to be used in the carnival, these monstrosities are the pride of the Bones.

A necromantic golem has no set form — the statistics presented here are for an average construct used to support infantry in battle. Larger golems are created for siege work, and even sea-going golems exist for naval operations. The version described below can carry four skeletons in the howdah built onto its hunched back. These skeletons are typically armed with crossbows or long lances, with which to fire or jab down into a press of men. The golem itself has two large arms ending in bone-armored clubs. These are typically used

against cavalry or fortifications but work well enough against smaller targets. The golem also has four small arms facing its front. These typically carry human-sized weapons and are used to attack opponents too close to the front of the golem for troops in the howdah to hit.

Combat

An automaton, a necromantic golem does its masters' bidding fearlessly and without hesitation. If riders in the howdah are destroyed durign battle , the golem will still attack anything in sight except members of the Krewe of Bones who are its masters.

Undead Construct: A golem is impervious to critical hits, subdual damage and death from massive damage trauma. It's immune to poisons, diseases, blinding, deafness, drowning, electricity, sleep and spells and attacks that affect respiration and living physiology. It cannot be stunned or affected by attacks or spells of mind-altering nature (enamoring or charming spells, for example), or by spells based on healing/harming. It is also immune to ability damage, energy drain, or death from massive damage. It cannot be turned as it has no mind capable of fearing holy power, but it may be destroyed if a cleric generates a destruction result with a turning attempt.

Carnival Krewe, Plague Wretch

Medium-size Humanoid

Hit Dice:	3d8+12 (25 hp)
Initiative:	+0
Speed:	30 ft.
AC:	15 (+5 natural)
Attacks:	Punch +5 melee
Damage:	Punch 1d4+2
Face/Reach:	5 ft. by 5 ft./5 ft.
Special Attacks:	Touch of Death
Special Qualities:	Damage reduction 4/—
Saves:	Fort +7, Ref +1, Will +1
Abilities:	Str 15, Dex 10, Con 19, Int 10, Wis 10, Cha 7
Skills:	Balance +1, Bluff +3, Climb +2, Diplomacy +1, Intimidate +4, Jump +2, Listen +3, Perform +4, Spot +2, Tumble +2
Feats:	Endurance
Climate/Terrain:	Swamp
Organization:	Throng (1-8), revel (6-36)
Challenge Rating:	2
Treasure:	Standard
Alignment:	Usually neutral evil
Advancement Range:	By character class

Description

Plague wretches are servants and victims of the dreadful Lord Quick, the leader of the Krewe of Plagues. These beleaguered people are the primary inhabitants of the ongoing festival that is the Laughing Man's capital.

Burdened with dozens of diseases and beholden to the twisted madness of their leader, most wretches who survive even a short time in the carnival are quite mad. Though they may have pursued adventuring professions prior to their existence here, most have forgotten their skills after endless rounds of drinking and celebrating.

Plague wretches are possessed of a tremendous, unnatural stamina and energy, part of the same gift that allows them to survive — even prosper — under the burden of their maladies. Wretches are generally willing to do anything to avoid the displeasure of their lord. They live by his leave alone.

Combat

Plague wretches typically use no tactics in a fight — and few need to. They can shrug off sword blows, and their victims are typically too terrified to resist them. While their touch is not immediately fatal, those who do escape them are usually dead long before they reach the bayou's borders.

Touch of Death (Ex): Plague wretches have a deadly touch, so they rarely use weapons. Not only do their blows do a startling amount of damage, those hit must succeed at a Fortitude save (DC 18) or contract any kind of virulent disease. Once a victim fails such a save, she takes one point of Constitution ability damage every twelve hours until the illness is somehow cured or the victim dies. Disease effects are not cumulative with multiple hits.

Cathedral Beetle

Large (Long) Vermin

Hit Dice:	6d8+18 (45 hp)
Initiative:	+1 (Dex)
Speed:	40 ft., fly 30 ft.
AC:	17 (-1 size, +1 Dex, +7 natural)
Attacks:	Bite +9 melee
Damage:	Bite 3d6+4
Face/Reach:	5 ft. by 10 ft./5 ft.
Special Attacks:	Acid spray
Special Qualities:	Vermin
Saves:	Fort +8, Ref +3, Will +2
Abilities:	Str 18, Dex 12, Con 16, Int 1, Wis 10, Cha 13
Skills:	Climb + 6, Listen +8, Spot +4
Feats:	Improved Bull Rush, Power Attack
Climate/Terrain:	Temperate and warm hills, forests, mountains and prairie
Organization:	Solitary, pack (1-6), or mating cluster (4-16)
Challenge Rating:	4
Treasure:	None
Alignment:	Always neutral
Advancement Range:	7-8 HD (Large), 9-12 HD (Huge)

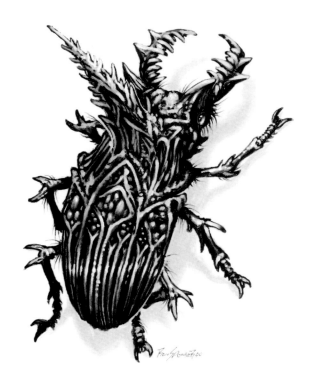

Description

The cathedral beetle is neither the most dangerous threat roaming the Scarred Lands, nor the most fantastic, but it is certainly one of the most striking. This immense insect, fully nine feet long and four feet at the "shoulder," is notable for its ornate bronze-colored carapace. The ridged "horns" adorning its head look something like fluted spires, while its wing cases seem to be engraved with an arch pattern like the vaulted molding on the interior of a cathedral — hence the name.

Cathedral beetles were previously found only in deep forests, but the disasters of the Titanswar drove many of them from their homes, scattering them to a variety of new territories. Unfortunately, they proved very adaptable and are now a moderate menace to anyone unlucky enough to cross their paths. The beetles are always ready to add meat to their diet.

Like other beetles, cathedral beetles have a notoriously unselective palate. If it's organic, a cathedral beetle can probably eat it, be it flesh, wood or bone. They are content to remain in an area as long as there's food, but their lack of intelligence makes them prone to overeat a region's organic life. When out of food, they take to the air clumsily, migrating to more promising regions — including pasturelands and fields.

Combat

The cathedral beetle, like other beetles, has mandibles with tremendous crushing power. If it perceives a foe as edible — that is, smelling more of flesh or vegetable matter than of metal or stone (which may rule out heavily armored foes) — it usually tries to bowl them over with a bull rush, pin them with its weight and begin eating them. If the foe resists, it tries to bite sufficiently large chunks until its prey stops resisting. If the beetle perceives a threat as inedible, or too dangerous to be worth its while, it sprays a cloud of acid from its mouth and retreats in the confusion. This can get horribly messy when multiple cathedral beetles are involved. The beetle does not spray acid unless pressed severely, as acid-dissolved opponents are difficult to eat.

Acid Spray (Ex): The cathedral beetle can spray a cloud of acid directly in front of it, which covers a cone 20 feet long. Creatures caught within the cloud take 4d6 points of acid damage, half that with a successful Reflex save (DC 17). The beetle must wait one hour before it can build up enough acid to spray again.

Vermin: Immune to mind-influencing powers.

Cave Moth

	Tiny Ooze
Hit Dice:	1d10 (5 hp)
Initiative:	+0
Speed:	5 ft., fly 20 ft.
AC:	12 (Size)
Attacks:	Wrap +1 melee
Damage:	Wrap 1
Face/Reach:	2.5 ft. by 2.5 ft./0 ft.
Special Attacks:	Smother
Special Qualities:	Blindsight, transparent, ooze
Saves:	Fort +2, Ref +0, Will -5
Abilities:	Str 6, Dex 10, Con 10, Int —, Wis 1, Cha 1
Skills:	None
Feats:	None
Climate/Terrain:	Underground
Organization:	Flurry (5-10)
Challenge Rating:	1
Treasure:	None
Alignment:	Always neutral
Advancement Rate:	2-3 HD (Small); 4-10 HD (Medium-size)

Description

The cave moth is a nearly transparent form of ooze that makes its home in dungeon passages and cave networks. Flurries of cave moths flap through corridors in search of prey. While digesting its kills, the creature builds up gases within its body that are lighter than air, allowing it to float. By undulating, the cave moth can propel itself through the air.

On dungeon walls, the cave moth looks like nothing more than glistening wet stone. While airborne, it is almost impossible to spot, as its translucent form and silent motions combine with the caverns' darkness to confound the senses.

Combat

Usually found either clinging to walls or flying through dungeon corridors, the creature is attracted by the subtle moisture created through other creatures' respiration. The moth attempts to wrap itself around a target's head in an effort to suffocate its prey. Cave moths are also attracted by the gases given off by burning torches and smother them with their bodies, thinking the brands are prey. These unlucky creatures are killed. However, they are rarely solitary, and other moths flock to attack intruders who now flounder in the dark.

Blindsight (Ex): The cave moth is blind, but its whole body acts as a primitive sensory organ that can locate prey by its exhalation.

Smother (Ex): With a successful attack, the cave moth wraps itself around the head of a victim, cutting off his air supply. A successful Strength or Escape Artist check (DC 15) dislodges the creature. Otherwise, the only option is to attack it with weapons, in which case the moth and its victim suffer the same damage. A victim is considered to be drowning until the moth is killed or dislodged.

Transparent: Cave moths are difficult to see, requiring a Spot check (DC 15) to notice one.

Ooze (Ex): Cave moths are immune to mind-influencing effects, poison, paralysis, sleep, stunning and polymorph. They are not vulnerable to critical hits.

Cave Shrike

Huge (Long) Ooze

Hit Dice:	12d10+48 (114 hp)
Initiative:	-2 (Dex)
Speed:	15 ft., climb 15 ft.
AC:	9 (-2 size, -2 Dex, +3 natural)
Attacks:	4 Tentacles +15 melee
Damage:	Tentacles 1d6+5
Face/Reach:	5 ft. by 10 ft./100 ft.
Special Attacks:	Sticky tentacles
Special Qualities:	Vulnerable to electricity, ooze
Saves:	Fort +12, Ref +2, Will -1
Abilities:	Str 21, Dex 6, Con 18, Int —, Wis 1, Cha 2
Skills:	Hide +5, Spot +12
Feats:	Blind Fighting
Climate/Terrain:	Subterranean caverns
Organization:	Solitary
Challenge Rating:	6
Treasure:	Standard
Alignment:	Always neutral
Advancement Range:	10-11 HD (Large), 12-15 HD (Huge)

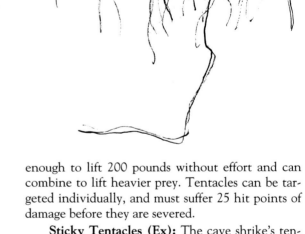

Description

The cave shrike is a horrific denizen of the lowest subterranean pits. It has a quivering, protoplasmic central body ringed with a number of slimy, elastic tentacles that can reach victims up to 100 feet away. Three large eyes spaced equidistantly around the central body stare fixedly into the darkness, constantly searching for prey.

Cave shrikes are rare and hideous creatures that ooze their way onto the high ceilings of ancient caverns, hiding in the abyssal darkness where no torchlight can reach and waiting patiently for animals and other cave dwellers to pass below. The creature then grabs its intended prey swiftly in one or more ropy tentacles and draws it high into the air before dropping it on the many stalagmites that rise sharply from the cavern floor. Once the impaled victim expires, the cave shrike picks the rotting corpse apart, absorbing bits of the victim through the jelly-like membrane of its central body.

Dark stories persist of tribes of goblins or kobolds that worship cave shrikes as gods, creating their homes under a monster's shadow and providing it with sacrifices from the outside world. The creature's name comes from cavern explorers who were attacked by one of these things and who misinterpreted its strikes as the attacks of cave-dwelling birds.

Combat

The cave shrike's method of attack is simple — pick up a victim and drop it from a great height, usually 80 to 120 feet. Each tentacle is easily strong enough to lift 200 pounds without effort and can combine to lift heavier prey. Tentacles can be targeted individually, and must suffer 25 hit points of damage before they are severed.

Sticky Tentacles (Ex): The cave shrike's tentacles are covered with a sticky ooze that helps them grip — and makes it difficult for prey to escape. A victim hit by a tentacle must succeed at a Reflex save (DC 16) or become entangled. Anyone struggling to break free from a tentacle's clutches must make a successful Strength or Escape Artist check (DC 16). Beginning the round after its latches onto its prey, the cave shrike will lift them 30ft. into the air each round (until it decides to drop them or they free themselves).

Vulnerable to Electricity (Ex): Cave shrikes suffer double damage from electricity-based attacks.

Ooze: Immune to mind-influencing effects, poison, sleep, paralysis, stunning and polymorphing. Not subject to critical hits.

Celestian

	Huge (Tall) Giant
Hit Dice:	6d8 (27 hp)
Initiative:	+0
Speed:	Fly 50 ft.
AC:	8 (-2 size)
Attacks:	None
Damage:	None
Face/Reach:	15 ft. by 15 ft./15 ft.
Special Attacks:	Weather control, spells
Special Qualities:	Immunities, vulnerabilities, SR 13
Saves:	Fort +5, Ref +2, Will +3
Abilities:	Str —, Dex —, Con —, Int 16, Wis 12, Cha 14
Skills:	Concentration +6, Intimidate +7, Knowledge (arcana) +6, Spellcraft +6, Spot +4
Feats:	Quicken Spell
Climate/Terrain:	Any
Organization:	Solitary or Gusts (3–12)
Challenge Rating:	4
Treasure:	Standard
Alignment:	Usually chaotic evil
Advancement Range:	5-12 HD (Huge)

Description

In the eyes of the divine races, the giantkin were blasphemers who fought against the gods, and they were justly punished. The Hundred-Handed Ones, a cadre of the strongest and most arrogant giantkin, were given a most ironic punishment by the storm god Enkilli for the role the giants played in the Divine War. Enkilli tore the giants' physical forms asunder and made them as hollow as the wind. These giants who had crushed dwarves with one hammering blow of their mighty fists, became no more powerful than a spring breeze—doomed to an eternity as creatures of the clouds and mists.

But the celestians, as they are now known, are not as dim-witted as most of their giantkin brethren. Since the Divine War, they have taken new strength from the realms of magic. Their accursed transformation only increased their fury, so the celestians spread destruction wherever they go.

A celestian's form is that of a cloud, thin and translucent. Its eyes are crystal-blue and nearly opaque; the rest of its body wavers and shifts as it moves. Though its size never changes, a celestian can take almost any form imaginable, including the

guise of an ordinary cloud. A celestian can make itself heard in just as many ways, but it almost invariably retains the booming voice of its "old" days.

The celestians' status among other giants lies in tatters. Regarded as little more than diminutive cousins, their fall from grace has created a great deal of tension between them and other giantkin. Clashes between giants and celestians are common—and marvelous—to behold. The true focus of celestians' ire, however, is the war against the gods and their servants. They are as bitter as the titans themselves and immediately abhor any priests they encounter, targeting such clerical opponents before all others.

Combat

Celestians move freely like the air, and they often strike with little warning, descending directly over their foes. Consisting of a vaporous substance, these creatures are unable to harm an opponent physically. However, they are formidable magic-users, and combined with their limited weather control, they are still capable of inflicting the damage for which giants are infamous.

Weather Control (Su): A celestian is capable of causing strong winds as a free action. Anyone within 50 feet of a celestian using this power moves at half his normal speed. Those using thrown or missile weapons that travel within this stormy area of effect suffer a –6 on their attack rolls. Tiny (or smaller) flying creatures within the area of effect are blown out of the air and injured by falling.

Spells: Celestians are potent sorcerers, and are treated as sorcerers of the celestian's HD in level.

Immunities (Ex): Celestians can only be injured by magical weapons. They are immune to polymorph, poison, paralysis and electrical spells and attacks.

Vulnerabilities (Ex): As they are cursed by the gods, celestians do not receive their spell resistance against clerical magic (but they do against druidic or arcane magic). Furthermore, for all their fury, they fear being cursed by the gods again and do not seek to draw their attention. Therefore, celestians may be turned or destroyed by clerics of any alignment (they may not be rebuked or commanded however, so even evil or neutral clerics still turn or destroy celestians). Note that this does not mean the celestians are undead, they are simply vulnerable to turning as though they were undead.

Cerulean Roc

Large (Tall) Magical Beast

Hit Dice:	16d10 (88 hp)
Initiative:	+4 (Dex)
Speed:	20 ft., fly 170 ft.
AC:	14 (-1 size, +4 Dex, +1 natural)
Attacks:	Beak +16 melee, 2 talons +11 melee
Damage:	Beak 2d10+1; talons 2d8
Face/Reach:	10 ft. by 10 ft./10 ft.
Special Attacks:	Chaos effects
Special Qualities:	None
Saves:	Fort +10, Ref +9, Will +8
Abilities:	Str 12, Dex 18, Con 10, Int 13, Wis 17, Cha 19
Skills:	Escape Artist +16
Feats:	None
Climate/Terrain:	Sky
Organization:	Solitary
Challenge Rating:	9
Treasure:	Standard
Alignment:	Usually chaotic neutral
Advancement Range:	16-20 HD (Large)

Description

The majestic cerulean roc is also known more pejoratively as "the chaos bird," for it throws the natural laws of nature into disarray wherever it goes. Meeting cerulean rocs has proven to be an especially harrowing experience for travelers caught out in the open — be it on land or sea — where they are unable to escape the effects of the bird's flight.

No one knows for certain where the cerulean roc nests. Some hold that the roc springs from the cerulean ether itself, for the bird is sometimes sighted during those hours when the sky is most radiant. Whenever a cerulean roc approaches or departs, it always does so from the distant horizon, and those with the power of flight who have pursued it only find to their dismay that it simply disappears into the vault of sky. There appears to be no rhyme or reason to a cerulean roc's coming or going.

Cerulean rocs seldom approach civilized lands. They prefer to travel the skies above the wilder realms of the Scarred Lands. Other flying beasts rarely prey upon cerulean rocs, perhaps because most beasts are wary of the rocs' unpredictable powers.

Combat

Cerulean rocs rarely need to enter combat, but they use their sharp beaks and terrible talons when they must.

Chaos Effects (Su): Whenever a cerulean roc flies overhead, one of the following eight effects occurs (roll 1d8).

1d8 Roll	Effect
1	Bend Starlight/Sunlight: At night, the stars in the heavens appear to bend, twist, spin and change position, such that travelers cannot use them to determine direction. In daylight, the sun itself appears to change position in the sky, moving higher or lower, or moving to an illogical point in the heavens (due north, for example). This warp remains in effect until the next dawn or dusk.
2	Windstorm: The winds begin to move, whip and howl; slowly at first, then gaining intensity. Halfway through the duration of the 3d4-round windstorm, those present must make a Reflex save (DC 17) or be cast to the ground for 2d4 points of damage per round. The players must make this save every round for the remainder of the storm. After 3d4 rounds, the winds die away suddenly.
3	Spectral Flash: Multi-colored lightning fills the skies overhead, blinding all who fail a Fortitude save (DC 14) for 3d4 rounds.
4	Desert Wind: A dry thirst grips the throats of those beneath the cerulean roc and causes them to make attack rolls, skill rolls, or save rolls at a penalty of -3 until they have satiated their thirst by drinking three days' rations of liquids. A Fortitude save (DC 16) resists the effect.
5	Relocate: All creatures and small landmark items (boulders, trees, etc.) in the vicinity safely teleport 100-600 feet in a random direction (roll 1d8: 1= north, 2= northeast, 3 = east, etc.).
6	Luck: The cerulean roc flies upon the winds of fortune, and fortune brings success. Rolls to attack, saves and skill rolls are made at a +3 bonus for the next day.
7	Contentedness: A feeling of wellbeing permeates anyone who is affected. Natural healing rates double, only half rations need be consumed to fill one's belly, and sleeping times are halved for the next week.
8	Wealth: Gold dust falls from the Roc's wing tips but disappears as it strikes the ground. Anyone in the area with a suitable container can roll 1d20+Dexterity modifier and multiply the result by three. The result is the number of gold pieces worth of gold dust the character can collect.

Charduni

Medium-size Humanoid (Dwarf)

Hit Dice:	1d8+2 (6 hp)
Initiative:	+0
Speed:	20 ft.
AC:	19 (+6 splint mail, + 2 large shield, +1 natural)
Attacks:	Charduni warscepter +3 melee; net +3 melee; shortbow +1 ranged
Damage:	Charduni warscepter 1d10+2; shortbow 1d6
Face/Reach:	5 ft. by 5 ft./5ft.
Special Attacks:	None
Special Qualities:	Darkvision 90 ft., dwarven traits
Saves:	Fort +4, Ref +0, Will +1
Abilities:	Str 15, Dex 10, Con 14, Int 10, Wis 12, Cha 8
Skills:	Appraise +1, Climb +1, Craft (Mining) +2, Intimidation +2, Intuit Direction +4, Listen +2, Spot +1
Feats:	Exotic Weapon Proficiency (Charduni Warscepter)
Climate/Terrain:	Temperate and warm land and underground
Organization:	Squad (4-9), slaver patrol (10-30 charduni, plus 1 slavemaster of 5-7th level), war troop (20-120 charduni, plus one 3rd-level assault-master per 10 charduni, two 6th-level war-masters, one 8-10th level war-general, two 4-6th level necromancers, and possibly undead troops as well)
Challenge Rating:	1/4
Treasure:	Standard
Alignment:	Always lawful evil
Advancement Range:	By character class

Description

Like the namesake bloody god these dark-skinned dwarves worship, charduni embrace conquest, domination and war. Disciplined, regal and decadent, these dwarves rule their kingdom from the city of Chorach with a terrible, iron grip.

Charduni are infamous as slavers and necromancers — anyone unfortunate enough to be captured by a charduni slaver patrol is cast into their Thorn Mines, where victims are worked to death and reanimated to continue their labors. While most of the iron ore from the mines goes to charduni smiths for use in armor and weapons, the precious metal ores are smelted and forged into the many baroque adornments on the charduni nobility.

Charduni soldiers are depicted as fearsome warriors. Bards tell bloody stories of the charduni riding into battle, swathed in the decadence of their conquests and brandishing their warscepters, a terrifying weapon made in the likeness of the one wielding it. Charduni soldiers fight to the death, eagerly

awaiting their return as undead. Fallen soldiers relish the opportunity to rise and strike another blow for their dark god. War-generals, the nobility of the charduni, often ride into battle with a retinue of undead to strike fear into their enemies.

The charduni emperor and prophet, named The One in White, is said to possess skin of wrought iron and a voice of velvet. From his palace in Chorach he reputedly keeps constant council with Chardun himself. The emperor's prophecies of conquest are followed with an unholy fervor.

Before the Divine War, the charduni empire was vast, encompassing a significant portion of the continent of Ghelspad. However, during the war, these dwarves fought fiercely alongside their god, facing some of the largest losses of any of the Scarn races. As a result, after the Divine War, the remnants of the charduni withdrew to Chorach. Already, however, the charduni have begun to expand their borders, and neighboring kingdoms live in fear of their wrath, knowing that it is only a matter of time before the charduni seek to lay claim on their territory again.

Charduni are slightly taller than other dwarves, but less broad. Their skin darkens with age, going from light gray to deepest black. As the charduni age, their skin also becomes more and more dense until the oldest charduni truly have skin like steel (charduni's natural armor class bonus ranges from +0 to +6 with age). They weigh twice as much as a normal dwarf due to the density of the elder charduni's flesh and bone. Lower caste charduni decorate themselves with iron and bone while the nobility are resplendent in baroque jewelry and accoutrements of silver, platinum and gemstones. All charduni warriors and priests use warscepters, with high priests and war-generals commonly wielding enchanted varieties.

Combat

The extremely militant charduni fight with a disciplined, cunning style. As units, they are adept at carrying out orders and implementing complex tactics. Charduni are especially adept at using their size to their advantage, and their infantry are trained to take down larger and more numerous foes. Their leaders are tacticians of the highest order, and their troops will die to fulfill the smallest command. Charduni are known to employ shock troops of undead in their ranks.

Dwarven Traits: Charduni share all of the common racial bonuses inherent to dwarves.

Chardun-Slain

Medium-size Undead

Hit Dice:	5d12 (32 hp)
Initiative:	+0
Speed:	20 ft.
AC:	19 (+4 scale mail, +5 natural)
Attacks:	Punch +8 melee; warhammer +8 melee; javelin +5 ranged
Damage:	Punch 1d6+3; warhammer 1d8+3; javelin 1d6+3
Face/Reach:	5 ft. by 5 ft./5 ft.
Special Attacks:	Finishing blow
Special Qualities:	Undead
Saves:	Fort +4, Ref +1, Will +1
Abilities:	Str 16, Dex 10, Con —, Int 10, Wis 10, Cha 11
Skills:	Climb +7, Intimidate +10, Intuit Direction +3, Jump +5, Listen +5, Ride +9, Search +5, Spot +11
Feats:	Armor Proficiency (Medium)
Climate/Terrain:	Any land
Organization:	Solitary, fist (4-6), company (20-50)
Challenge Rating:	2
Treasure:	Standard
Alignment:	Usually chaotic evil
Advancement Range:	4-10 HD (Medium-size)

Description

A good soldier never stops fighting, even after he's dead. The god Chardun, the Great General, awarded distinguished soldiers and units the gift to carry on their wars after death. Chardun-slain rise one full solar cycle after their deaths, apparently at the behest of the

Great General, and resume whatever assignment cost them their lives, be it laying siege to a town, guarding a bridge or winning a battle. A year is a long time, so most Chardun-slain undertake bizarre imitations of their duties: If they died in battle, they might rise and attack the fort built atop the battleground. If they died protecting a merchant caravan, they might find another band to "escort" to the same destination. After completing their tasks, symbolic or otherwise, the Chardun-slain bury themselves and become normal corpses.

Combat

Although they lack conventional intelligence, they rely on whatever martial prowess they had in life. They fight like trained soldiers, be it in man-to-man combat or during a coordinated siege. A few Chardun-slain use whatever armor and weapons they carried to war in life.

Finishing Blow (Su): Whatever force reanimates the Chardun-slain aids them in "recruiting" others. Those struck by a Chardun-slain who have fewer than 10 hit points remaining must succeed at a Fortitude save (DC 17) or suffer double damage. This supernatural attack does only normal damage to characters under spells of holy protection.

Undead: Chardun-slain are immune to poison, sleep, paralysis, stunning and disease. They're not subject to critical hits, subdual damage, ability damage, energy drain or death from massive damage.

Charfiend

Medium-size Monstrous Humanoid

Hit Dice:	2d8+2 (11 hp)
Initiative:	+5 (+1 Dex, +4 Improved Initiative)
Speed:	40 ft.
AC:	12 (+1 Dex, +1 natural)
Attacks:	Bite +2 melee; 2 claws +2 melee
Damage:	Bite 2d4; claw 1d6
Face/Reach:	5 ft. by 5 ft./5 ft.
Special Attacks:	Foul odor
Special Qualities:	Desecrate, immunities
Saves:	Fort +4, Ref +1, Will -1
Abilities:	Str 11, Dex 13, Con 13, Int 10, Wis 8, Cha 8
Skills:	Balance +3, Climb +4, Hide +8, Jump +10, Listen +3, Search +1, Spot +4
Feats:	Improved Initiative
Climate/Terrain:	Any land or underground near cities
Organization:	Solitary, pack (2-8)
Challenge Rating:	1
Treasure:	None
Alignment:	Always chaotic evil
Advancement Range:	3-5 HD (Medium-size)

Description

A race of scavengers that feeds upon dead flesh, charfiends earned their name through their preference for well-done meat. These creatures often lair in the ruins of burned buildings, emerging only to feed. The stench of burning hair, scorched skin and sizzling fat stimulate a charfiend's appetite, and the creatures are drawn irresistibly to burning homes, funeral pyres and even sacrificial rites. Despite their own foul odor, charfiends can smell burning flesh for miles.

The charfiend's stench and hideous presence defiles holy places until they are rededicated with the proper purification spells. In the Titanswar, Mormo created the charfiends to spread such sacrilege, thereby leaving worshipers unable to communicate with their gods.

The Titanswar was a banquet for these creatures; in these less incendiary times, many charfiends go hungry. The smartest of the breed resort to starting their own fires....

Combat

When discovered feasting, charfiends usually flee unless they have a clear advantage. When facing an obviously inferior foe, charfiends circle around their prey, first slashing at him with their claws, then closing in until they overwhelm the victim and tear him apart with their teeth. If cornered, charfiends fight like wild animals, endangering themselves just long enough to escape.

Foul Odor (Ex): The stench of scorched flesh and acrid smoke clings to charfiends' fur. Upon first encountering a charfiend, all those within 10 feet must succeed at a Fortitude save (DC 12) or become nauseated, suffering a -2 penalty to all attacks, saves and skill checks for 1d8 rounds.

Immunities (Ex): Charfiends are immune to fire.

Desecrate (Ex): Through the sheer foulness of their presence, charfiends counter and dispel sanctifying and consecratory spells wherever they go as if they were dispelling the magic as a 3rd-level wizard.

Child Trap

Medium-size Plant

Hit Dice:	2d8 (9 hp)
Initiative:	-3 (Dex)
Speed:	Immobile
AC:	12 (-3 Dex, +5 natural)
Attacks:	None
Damage:	None
Face/Reach:	5 ft. by 5 ft./5 ft.
Special Attacks:	None
Special Qualities:	Intoxicating lure, plant, soporific gas, digestion
Saves:	Fort +4, Ref +-3, Will +0
Abilities:	Str 10, Dex 4, Con 13, Int —, Wis —, Cha —
Skills:	None
Feats:	None
Climate/Terrain:	Tropical
Organization:	None
Challenge Rating:	1/4
Treasure:	Standard
Alignment:	None
Advancement Range:	1 HD (Small), 2-5 HD (Medium-size)

Description

This unassuming tropical plant is one of the more lethal beauties ever to be transported to the verdant shores of the Lush Isle in the Blood Sea. While philosopher-kings and world-wise mendicants alike find peaceful rest in contemplating its delightful exterior where it grows wild in various locales all over the Scarred Lands, the scurrilous denizens of the Lush Isle have chosen well their island's first line of defense against the casual interloper. For, while the organism is calming and delightful to contemplate from afar, its appetite for prey has earned the sedentary predator its name countless times over.

The child trap attracts curious animals (or unmonitored children) with its bright, shining colors and by emitting a delightful display of iridescent gas from an orifice directly in its center. The gas dances and weaves on air currents churned by a cluster of vibration-sensitive fronds. The gas is intoxicating and sleep-inducing, and the same substance coats the inside of the trap's leaves and fronds as a sticky resin. When a hapless victim is lured in and lulled, the plant's fronds reach out to claim a meal.

Once prey has been drawn into the center of the plant, its leaves close up and lock together in a prickly egg-shaped bulb. Inside, resin dissolves the skin, flesh and bone of the animal, which are all absorbed. Waste material fills an underground bladder in the trap's root system, and that bladder creates more gas to attract future meals. A trap is sated for a month on a meal the size of a large dog, but it can devour a human adult given enough time.

The child trap's outer surface is coarse and tough due to the bone, hair and clothing it absorbs, but it is quite vulnerable to fire. In fact, the intoxicating, sleep-inducing gas it emits is explosive when exposed to open flame. Child traps are resistant to most herbicidal poisons, but they cannot digest metal. A resourceful scavenger — such as those who guard the Lush Isle's coast for their pirate masters — might find all sorts of trinkets in the gullet of a gorged child trap. A large enough quantity of metal, such as a full suit of plate armor, virtually chokes a child trap to death.

Combat

Digestion (Ex): A creature trapped within the plant's bulb suffers 1d10 damage per hour until killed and processed. Half of the damage inflicted on the plant is inflicted on a victim inside. A would-be meal is expelled once the plant loses half its hit points. Possessions made of anything but metal are totally ruined after one hour of digestion.

Intoxicating Lure (Ex): From a distance, the addictive gas the child trap emits induces euphoria. Any potential prey that could be enticed must succeed at a Will save (DC 16) to resist the effect.

Plant: Child traps are impervious to critical hits, subdual damage and death from massive damage trauma. They're not affected by spells of mind-altering nature (enamoring or charming spells not specifically designed for plants, for example), paralysis, poison, sleep, polymorph or stunning.

Soporific Gas (Ex): As potential prey draws closer, the same gas puts him to sleep, hopefully within reach of the plant's fronds. The creature must succeed at a Fortitude save (DC 18) to avoid falling asleep.

Coal Goblin

Small Humanoid

Hit Dice:	2d8+2 (11 hp)
Initiative:	+2 (+2 Dex)
Speed:	30 ft.
AC:	16 (+1 size, +2 Dex, +2 leather armor, +1 Dodge)
Attacks:	Short sword +3 melee; or net +5 ranged; or shortbow +5 ranged
Damage:	Short sword 1d6; arrow 1d6
Face/Reach:	5 ft. by 5 ft./5 ft.
Special Attacks:	None
Special Qualities:	Darkvision 120ft.
Saves:	Fort +1, Ref +5, Will +1
Abilities:	Str 11, Dex 15, Con 13, Int 12, Wis 13, Cha 11
Skills:	Hide +8, Listen +3, Move Silently +8, Open Lock +3, Spot +3
Feats:	Dodge
Climate/Terrain:	Any, particularly underground
Organization:	Murder party (3-5), band (11-20, led by a 3rd-level rogue), nest (25-100, led by a 7th-level rogue, and three 3rd-level scouts), temple (50-300, led by a 9th-level priest, a 7th-level rogue, five 3rd-level guards and five 3rd-level scouts)
Challenge Rating:	1/4
Treasure:	Standard
Alignment:	Usually neutral evil
Advancement Range:	By character class

Description

Before the Titanswar, many sub-breeds of goblinkin lived all across Scarn. The goblins were humanoid vermin, creatures born from the polluted portions of the world and dedicated to malice. However, the Titanswar destroyed many goblin warrens, and entire clans were wiped out for merely getting in an army or dragon's way.

Those who fought died, but those who hid survived.

The largest and most dangerous clan of survivors was the coal goblins, creatures with jet-black skin and an inherent gift for stealth. Their leaders took them deep underground, emerging from time to time only to watch the progress of the war. During this troubled time, the coal goblins learned to pray, and Belsameth, goddess of assassins, answered.

Coal goblins now ply the trade of murder to get by. Although they grow mushrooms and hunt for subsistence, they also waylay sleeping travelers for their goods. A good portion of their income comes from the faithful of Belsameth, though; many a Belsamite priest knows how to contact a nest of coal goblins should they be needed. Some nests have even moved quietly into the cities, where they lair in sewers and tunnels. They emerge in secret to victimize the urban population and fulfill their needs. And always, they keep their patroness in their prayers....

Coal Goblin Characters

Coal goblins favor rogue when multiclassing; many of their heroes are rogue/clerics who follow Belsameth. Their clerics usually take the specialty domains of Evil and Trickery. Fighters and sorcerers are more rare than are rogues and clerics.

Combat

Coal goblins never get involved in mass brawls if they can help it. If they cannot overcome their opponents with traps, sneak attacks and missile fire, they retreat as best they can in order to fight another time. If cornered, they fight like rabid animals (and they're tougher than they look). If a way out exists, they don't stand and fight unless the advantage is clearly theirs.

Darkvision (Ex): Coal goblins can see up to 120 feet in pitch darkness as if it were bright light.

Skills: Coal goblins are born to stealth. They receive a +6 racial bonus to both Hide and Move Silently checks.

Cold Slime

Large Ooze

Hit Dice:	7d10+21 (59 hp)
Initiative:	-2 (Dex)
Speed:	10 ft., climb 10 ft.
AC:	15 (-1 size, -2 Dex, +8 natural)
Attacks:	None
Damage:	None
Face/Reach:	5 ft. by 10 ft./5 ft.
Special Attacks:	Envelop
Special Qualities:	Ooze, freezing air
Saves:	Fort +8, Ref +0, Will +0
Abilities:	Str 17, Dex 7, Con 17, Int 2, Wis 6, Cha 1
Skills:	Climb +15, Hide +15, Move Silently +15
Feats:	None
Climate/Terrain:	Any cold
Organization:	Solitary
Challenge Rating:	3
Treasure:	Standard
Alignment:	Always neutral
Advancement Range:	8-10 HD (Large), 11-16 HD (Huge)

Description

Cold slimes are transparent oozes that inhabit frozen regions both above and below ground. They are naturally slow under most circumstances, but after feeding on the warmth of a victim, cold slimes are much more agile and only slightly more viscous than water.

Some scholars have proposed that cold slimes may be a bizarre hybrid of water elemental and slime or perhaps water elementals that, for whatever reason, simply prefer a semi-solid state to a fluid one.

Cold slimes make stealthy guards in frozen climates, often being mistaken for a layer of ice on the ground, on trees or on walls.

Combat

Cold slimes respond to most stimuli by attacking. They envelop victims in their near-solid mass and drain the target's heat, seeking to gain a warmer, more liquid state once more.

Envelop (Ex): If the cold slime succeeds at a grapple check against a single target, the victim must succeed at a Reflex save (DC 22) or become enveloped within the slime. The victim loses 1d10 hit points per round until he breaks the grapple hold, as the creature leeches away his body's heat.

Once a cold slime envelops its victim, it takes only half the damage caused by piercing weapons from exterior foes — its enveloped victim takes the other half.

Freezing Air (Su): The air around a cold slime is extremely frigid as the ooze constantly soaks up any ambient heat. Those within 10 feet of a cold slime must succeed at a Fortitude save (DC 17) or suffer a -2 penalty to all attacks, saves and skill checks until they leave the creature's vicinity.

Ooze: A cold slime is not affected by attacks or spells that involve poison, sleep, paralysis, polymorph or stunning, or that influence the mind. It has no physiological weak points and is therefore immune to critical hits.

Coreanic Steed

Large (Long) Magical Beast

Hit Dice:	5d10+20 (47 hp)
Initiative:	+2 (Dex)
Speed:	55 ft.
AC:	16 (-1 size, +2 Dex, +5 natural)
Attacks:	Bite +9 melee, 2 hooves +4 melee
Damage:	Bite 1d3+4; hooves 1d8+2
Face/Reach:	5 ft. by 10 ft./5 ft.
Special Attacks:	None
Special Qualities:	Detect evil, detect lie, immunities, speak with master
Saves:	Fort +5, Ref +3, Will +3
Abilities:	Str 18, Dex 15, Con 19, Int 10, Wis 14, Cha 14
Skills:	Search
Feats:	None
Climate/Terrain:	Savannah
Organization:	Solitary (with master if already called), herd (4-24)
Challenge Rating:	2
Treasure:	None
Alignment:	Always lawful good
Advancement Range:	3-7 HD (Large)

Description

Legends tell of a young paladin named Permenthes who traveled the fertile plains of the Scarred Lands during the Age of Sun. He was known far and wide for his many good deeds, but he was susceptible to the deadly sin of pride. It was pride that drove young Permenthes to erect a temple to his deity, Corean, upon a hill in the midst of what was once the vast and fertile plain of Merses. At first he exhorted, then commanded, then coerced the people of the plain to help him, telling them to forget their planting and harvesting since mighty Corean would provide for them.

It is said that one day he grew especially angry with an old man who appeared too lazy or weak to help haul stone for the temple foundations. In his wrath, Permenthes rose to strike him, only to find that Corean had assumed the visage of an old man. Once the god had dropped his disguise, he looked down upon Permenthes and said, "Let the strong serve the weak, let the proud be humbled, let the blind see the light of truth. For you have demanded service, Permenthes, where you have failed to serve. You raise a temple upon a mount of pride, not humility. Without the light of wisdom, blindness has overtaken you."

Permenthes suddenly realized he had been stripped of his holy powers, and he begged his lord to forgive him and allow him to atone for his sins. Corean said, "I will make you an example to all. You will serve me forever, and you will be a light unto my Holy Champions, a reminder to them that service to others is blessed in my name." And before the eyes of the common plainsmen, Corean transformed Permenthes into a great white stallion to serve forever as the mount for heroes of Corean. Where the temple foundations had been laid, Corean summoned a fountain to irrigate the land.

It is believed that the descendants of Permenthes now occupy the legendary plain and still drink from the holy Fountain of Corean. It is the privilege of a holy warrior, himself long in Corean's service, to summon a Coreanic steed when the time has come. Although only paladins know for certain, legends say that when a holy knight calls for his steed, he must first pray before a fountain or well that lies within a sacred vale or field, and the quest to find his sacred mount becomes known to him.

Once a Coreanic steed answers the call of a paladin, the steed serves its master until one of them dies or until the paladin falls from the grace of Corean. The Coreanic steed can understand and obey any commands given by its master, although it asserts its own judgment when necessary in the course of fulfilling its instructions.

Coreanic steeds that still await their call to serve a paladin of Corean travel in small herds across the Bleak Savannah. They are known to help lost or weary travelers by escorting them back to their homes, or even by defending travelers from attacks by the various titan-spawned races that still inhabit the plains.

Combat

Coreanic steeds use a powerful two-hooves-one-bite combination in combat.

Detect Evil (Sp): This ability can be performed once per day, in a 20-foot radius for 10 minutes. The Coreanic steed stamps the ground and neighs furiously when it senses evil.

Detect Lie (Sp): The steed can also detect lies once per day, in a 20-foot radius for a duration of 10 minutes. The Coreanic steed stamps the ground and neighs furiously when it senses a lie.

Immunities (Ex): Coreanic steeds are immune to charm spells, due to their fierce loyalty to their riders. They are also immune to fear-based attacks.

Speak with Master (Ex): Although the Coreanic steed seldom does so, it can speak with its master in a secret language known only to the faithful.

Crescent Elk

Large (Long) Animal

Hit Dice:	3d8+9 (22 hp)
Initiative:	+2 (Dex)
Speed:	70 ft.
AC:	14 (-1 size, +2 Dex, +3 natural)
Attacks:	Antler rake +6 melee, 2 hooves +1 melee
Damage:	Antler rake 2d8+4; hoof 1d4+4
Face/Reach:	5 ft. by 10 ft./5 ft.
Special Attacks:	None
Special Qualities:	None
Saves:	Fort +6, Ref +3, Will +1
Abilities:	Str 18, Dex 15, Con 16, Int 2, Wis 10, Cha 12
Skills:	Listen +12, Spot +12
Feats:	Balance
Climate/Terrain:	Temperate to cold hills and mountains
Organization:	Herd (5-30)
Challenge Rating:	1
Treasure:	None
Alignment:	Always neutral
Advancement Range:	1-2 HD (Large), 4-5 HD (Large)

Description

The crescent elk is one of the hardier animals to populate the Scarred Lands. A crescent elk stands roughly five feet at the shoulder and is built gracefully but solidly. The creature gets its name from its antlers, which curve up and forward like a pair of crescent moons. Both males and females sport these antlers, which they do not shed seasonally as other animals might.

Crescent elk are simple herbivores. Although they are generally dangerous when cornered, they are still preyed upon by hunters such as hill howlers. Even humans eat crescent elk if they can catch them; the meat is nutritious and filling, if somewhat bitter. The animals have an impressive sense of balance and can navigate steep slopes as can mountain goats.

A few nomadic tribes of elves in the southern reaches of the grasslands becoming better known as Virduk's Promise have actually managed to domesticate crescent elks, using them as pack animals and mounts. Crescent elk bulls can support up to 180 pounds without losing much of their agility. Properly trained war elk can effectively fight at their rider's command, attacking the target of their rider's choice or, if no specific orders are given, selecting a target of their own.

War elk are notorious for accepting only one rider in their entire lifetime, which makes their market value relatively poor. Recently weaned crescent elk can sometimes be found for sale at trade centers where nomads come to barter. The price usually runs about 300 gold coins, which doesn't include the cost of training.

Combat

In the wild, crescent elk are inclined to run rather than fight. They stand and do battle only when cornered or defending their calves. A crescent elk usually lowers its head and rakes with its sicklelike antlers against opponents that run low to the ground and might strike for the underbelly, such as wolves. If facing predators that are more likely to strike for the head, neck or heart (which many humanoids might do), an elk is more likely to rear up, striking downward with sharp hooves and sharper antlers.

Desert Falcon

Large Animal (Bird)

Hit Dice:	4d8+12 (30hp)
Initiative:	+6 (+2 Dex, +4 Improved Initiative)
Speed:	50 ft., fly 100 ft.
AC:	11 (-1 size, +2 Dex)
Attacks:	Bite +7 melee, 2 claws +2 melee
Damage:	Bite 1d6+4; claw 1d4+2
Face/Reach:	5 ft. by 10 ft./5 ft.
Special Attacks:	None
Special Qualities:	Shadowless
Saves:	Fort +7, Ref +3, Will +2
Abilities:	Str 18, Dex 15, Con 16, Int 4, Wis 13, Cha 8
Skills:	Hide +8, Intimidate +7, Intuit Direction +7, Move Silently +15, Spot +18
Feats:	Endurance, Improved Initiative
Climate/Terrain:	Desert
Organization:	Solitary
Challenge Rating:	2
Treasure:	Standard
Alignment:	Always chaotic neutral
Advancement Range:	3-6 HD (Large)

Description

The wide-spanned desert falcon is an animal of prodigious stamina. It makes its home in the mountains that ring the Desert of Onn, and it is capable of flying all the way across the wasteland without stopping (at least north to south, as no one seems to know the extent of the desert westward, though perhaps the great falcons can manage that as well), should circumstances dictate. It lives on ratroos, Ubantu tribesmen and any other creatures it can catch alone in the great golden expanse.

Falcons are solitary and territorial monsters in their aeries or in the air, and they consider their territory to be all they survey. Although they could carry a man, they do not allow themselves to be ridden or even approached. Even falcon chicks learn to fend for themselves immediately after being hatched. Wounded, grounded falcons lash out at anything that moves within a wing's reach.

Variants

Another species of the falcon lives on the icy tundra surrounding the Knife Mines of southern Fenrilik. An even larger variety is reputed to live on the virtually impassable cliffs of the Lush Isle and subsists on whales that surface for air, but such rumors remain substantiated only by a handful of captured pirates.

Combat

Falcons swoop straight down on prey rather than circle or wait. If the intended victim is part of a group — and if the falcon is hungry enough — it swoops down and tries to pluck its meal right from the midst of the pack. Alternatively, the falcon swoops low to the ground, trying to scatter a pack and isolate its prey. The falcon scoops up its prey and returns to the nest to devour it.

Shadowless (Ex): A desert falcon casts no shadow on the ground as it flies. Prey animals must either hear the raptor approaching or happen to glance up at the right time to avoid being snatched up.

Dire Monitor

Large (Long) Animal

Hit Dice:	6d8+6 (33 hp)
Initiative:	+5 (+1 Dex, +4 Improved Initiative)
Speed:	20 ft., swim 60 ft.
AC:	13 (-1 size, +1 Dex, +3 natural)
Attacks:	Bite +8 melee and 2 claws +3 melee; or tail swipe +8 melee
Damage:	Bite 2d8+3; claw 1d10+1; tail swipe 3d6+3
Face/Reach:	5 ft. by 10 ft./5 ft.
Special Attacks:	Tail swipe
Special Qualities:	None
Saves:	Fort +6, Ref +3, Will +1
Abilities:	Str 16, Dex 13, Con 13, Int 8, Wis 9, Cha 5
Skills:	None
Feats:	Combat Reflexes, Improved Initiative
Climate/Terrain:	Subterranean pools and rivers
Organization:	Solitary
Challenge Rating:	4
Treasure:	Standard
Alignment:	Always neutral
Advancement Range:	4-9 HD (Large)

Description

The dire monitor is a powerfully built reptile that can reach lengths of up to twelve feet or more, half of which is made up of a very strong, whiplike tail. A dire monitor's skin is reddish-black or brown and has a rough, pebbly texture. Its blunt snout is lined with rows of razor-sharp teeth that curve backward and help the monitor trap its prey within its jaws.

The dire monitor is an aggressive predator that prefers subterranean pools or small, stygian lakes, where it can lurk nearly unseen in the shadows until suitable prey passes by. With only the very top of its head and eyes above the surface of the water, the monitor digs its claws into the rock or mud bottom and then lunges at its prey, locking its jaws around a victim. The lizard then uses its powerful body to pull the victim under the water, clawing and biting all the while. Few creatures have strength enough to wrestle with the big reptile and hold their breath at the same time. Many drown long before the monitor's claws and teeth finish them.

After several kills, the skeletons and equipment of the monitors' victims often serve to lure even more victims into reach. In a chilling display of intelligence, some of these creatures have even learned to carry small pieces of gold or jewelry and deposit them at the edge of their pools, just close enough to tempt a curious — or greedy — creature.

Combat

The dire monitor remains deathly still until the moment of attack, nearly always catching its prey by surprise. It attempts to lock its jaws around the creature's throat, but a limb or a shoulder is equally effective. It then flexes its powerful body and yanks the creature off balance, causing it to fall into the pool. Once underwater, the reptile holds its victim until it drowns. A monitor dragged out onto dry land is still a formidable opponent, using its whiplike tail to knock its victims off their feet.

Tail Swipe (Ex): Dire monitors forced to fight on land can use their tails to terrible effect. If a creature is struck by a tail swipe, it must succeed at a Reflex save (DC 18) or be knocked prone.

Dragon, Mock

Huge (Long) Animal

Hit Dice:	6d8+18 (45 hp)
Initiative:	+1 (Dex)
Speed:	40 ft., swim 20 ft.
AC:	17 (-2 size, +1 Dex, +8 natural)
Attacks:	Bite +11 melee, 2 claws +6 melee; or tail slap +11 melee; or crush +11 melee
Damage:	Bite 2d8+5; claw 2d6+2; tail slap 2d6+5; crush 2d8+5
Face/Reach:	10 ft. by 30 ft./10 ft.
Special Attacks:	Spit Venom
Special Qualities:	None
Saves:	Fort +8, Ref +3, Will +3
Abilities:	Str 20, Dex 12, Con 16, Int 3, Wis 12, Cha 10
Skills:	Listen +6, Spot +2
Feats:	Power Attack
Climate/Terrain:	Temperate and warm hills
Organization:	Solitary or pair
Challenge Rating:	4
Treasure:	Standard
Alignment:	Always neutral
Advancement Range:	9-12 HD (Huge)

Description

After the Titanswar ended, the surviving dragons — the living weapons of the Titans — quickly decided that it was better if they went to ground to avoid the victorious gods and their servants. It was difficult to hide, however, as any report of something even vaguely dragonlike would bring down inconvenient mobs of pious would-be dragon-slayers. It was then that one of the most cunning of their number devised a clever plan — to spread decoys throughout the land, in order to hide in plain sight.

Through unknown means, this dragon was able to reconfigure some of the giant lizards of the Scarred Lands into mock dragons — cunning facsimiles that look sufficiently convincing to fool most observers. The scales have taken on the same brilliant hue, the eyes are the same menacing yellow, but the creature is a sham.

For all its menacing demeanor, the mock dragon is relatively harmless — at least when compared to its true draconian architect. Its "wings" are nothing more than modified fins poking out from its back, useful only for collecting the sun's heat on cool days. They cannot breathe fire, although they were given a convincing enough capacity for spitting poison.

And the dragon's plan has been working beautifully. Each year, a few more encounters with "dragons" are recorded, a few more "dragon-slayers" triumph, and a few more people forget that the mock dragon is a pale, pale shadow of the true dragons of Scarn. As far as buying time goes, the mock dragon is a rousing success.

Combat

The mock dragon starts combat with a tail slap, preferring to expend as little energy as possible. If irritated further, the dragon will spit its venomous cloud and then attack with its claws and teeth, focusing on one opponent at a time. Only as a last resort will the dragon use its second venom attack, preferring to save it as a prelude to fleeing the combat.

Spit Venom (Ex): The mock dragon can exhale a blast of venom in a cloud of mist 20 feet in diameter centered up to 20 ft from the dragon. The venom does 3d4 points of damage, and it blinds victims for 2d20 minutes. A successful Reflex save (DC 14) halves the damage and negates the blindness effect. The dragon can attack in such a fashion only twice before its venom reserves are depleted; it must rest for 24 hours before they refill.

Dragon, Tar

Hit Dice:	Gargantuan Dragon (Tar)
	30d12+180 (375 hp)
Initiative:	+3 (-1 Dex, +4 Improved Initiative)
Speed:	40 ft., fly 120 ft. (poor), swim 30 ft.
AC:	35 (-4 size, +30 natural, -1 Dex)
Attacks:	Bite +38 melee, 2 claws +33 melee;
	tail +33 melee; crush +38 melee
Damage:	Bite 2d12+12; claw 2d8+6;
	tail 2d10+20, crush 3d8+18
Face/Reach:	20 ft. by 50 ft./15 ft.
Special Attacks:	Breath weapon, frightful presence, great bite
Special Qualities:	Blindsight, darkvision 1,000 ft., damage reduction 20/+1, immunities, SR 28, tarred skin
Saves:	Fort +22, Ref +15, Will +19
Abilities:	Str 35, Dex 9, Con 22, Int 15, Wis 16, Cha 12
Skills:	Alchemy +24, Intimidate +32, Knowledge (Religion) +18, Knowledge (Local) +35, Listen +27, Search +37, Sense Motive +27, Spot +38, Swim +23
Feats:	Alertness, Cleave, Endurance, Improved Critical (bite only), Improved Initiative, Multiattack, Power Attack
Climate/Terrain:	Warm or tropical hills and mountains, and underground
Organization:	Solitary (unique)
Challenge Rating:	15
Treasure:	Quadruple Standard
Alignment:	Usually lawful evil
Advancement Range:	25-28 HD (Huge), 29-35 HD (Gargantuan)

Description

Like most other dragons, tar dragons come in many sizes and ages, but only two have been seen in the Scarred Lands since the great war. One of these was a fledgling dragon that was slain in its infancy. The only known surviving tar dragon dwells in the southern portion of Termana. It is known to the wild natives of the area as Orraganjus, or "Vomit Eater."

The tar dragon is an immense creature of vast knowledge. He appears to be more stout than most dragons. His agility seems likewise less than that of other dragon breeds, but he is by no means clumsy. The strength he possesses more than compensates for any deficiencies of speed.

Combat

When the tar dragon hunts, he typically works up a full load of his breath weapon — and since the location of his lair is unknown, he's likely to be hunting whenever he's encountered. Therefore, he has enough to capture four medium-sized creatures. Although he is a poor flyer, the tar dragon's under-sized wings can keep him aloft and out of melee range of his victims until he has immobilized as many of them as possible with his breath weapon. Once his foes are captured in his tarry vomit, or once his initial supply is exhausted he lands to either devour his captured prey or to melee with any remaining foes. (He exhausts his weapon supply after six rounds, since two new loads of vomit build up while he uses the first four.) He targets those foes who manage to maintain use of their weapons (i.e., those whose weapons do not get stuck on his body).

Since the tar dragon has a mammoth appetite, he uses his frightful presence only if his foes are initially too numerous or if the battle has turned against him and he needs an opportunity to retreat.

Breath Weapon (Su): The tar dragon 's breath weapon is literally its vomit, which is can disgorge up to 120 feet (horizontally) from itself. This foul-smelling load of bile is inky black and mucilaginous. Any victim that fails a Reflex save (DC 33) is stuck completely within the adhesive puke, and is subject to drowning rules. A victim so caught may attempt a Strength roll (DC 22) to first pull himself part way out, and then another Strength roll (DC 18) to extricate himself completely. Those who make the Reflex save begin partially caught and need only the second Strength save to escape.

These saving throws assume that the tar dragon puts the minimum-required size of discharge on an opponent. The dragon may store four "loads" at any one time. One load is required to capture a Medium-size opponent or smaller, while a Large opponent requires two loads. A Huge victim requires three loads, and a Gargantuan one must be the victim of the full four loads. Anything less than the required number of loads partially captures an opponent that fails its save, and a successful Reflex save allows the victim to escape the breath weapon entirely. A tar dragon works up one new "load" every second round.

Frightful Presence (Ex): Merely by raising himself to his full height or by flying overhead, the tar dragon can terrify any creature or being (except other dragons) with less than 31 HD. Victims of this attack must make a Will save (DC 30). Creatures with 6 HD or less who fail must flee at top speed for 4d8 rounds, while those with 7 or more HD are paralyzed with fear for 4d8 rounds.

Great Bite (Ex): Whenever the tar dragon scores a critical hit with its bite attack (critical threat range is 18-20) or merely succeeds with a bite attack against an immobilized foe, the dragon swallows the prey whole. (In the latter case, the tar dragon must eat its own vomit as well, hence the translation of its name by the Termana natives). Anyone who is swallowed must make a Fortitude saving throw (DC 26) each round against the noxious contents of the beast's stomach, lest he black out. The victim is dead and digested in 1d4 hours. The existence of even the slightest undigested bit allows the victim to be raised from the dead, but once he is digested completely, the victim cannot be recovered.

Tarred Skin (Ex): Bludgeoning and slashing weapons that touch the tar dragon (i.e., succeed at hitting at least AC 6 as if it had been a touch attack) become stuck in the same sort of tarry substance that the dragon uses as it's breath weapon. The tar dragon keeps itself covered with its own tar. Weapons can be pulled free only with a Strength roll (DC 16). Piercing weapons are not affected.

Dragon (Wrack)

Weapons of the titans, the wrack dragons were created to serve their masters as officers and warriors in the war against the gods. Few wrack dragons survived the war or the concerted cleansing operations the gods staged immediately afterward. However, those that did are the craftiest of their breed, and many still lead the remnants of the forces they once commanded (or the descendents of those remnants, in the case of more short-lived and prolific troops).

Wrack dragons are fierce and terrible beasts. All have a natural aptitude for magic, and all are clever and malicious. They are formed from elemental wrack — natural elements exposed to destructive energies and imbued with a negative spiritual resonance. The titans amplified and shaped this energy into great, lithe, beasts of war.

There is more than one sort of wrack dragon. Some were formed from water-wrack, the debris of the ever-churning ocean filtered and strained and imbued with a primal hate. Poisonous beasts, these creatures served as the lieutenants and scouts of the titans. Others were formed from fire-wrack; embers, ash, burnt bones and tongues of flame. These served as the officers and the shock troops of the titans. Finally, some were made from life-wrack, the leavings of the constant struggle for survival. These are creatures of bleached bones and storm-twisted tree-limbs, of young animals flash-roasted in grass fires and of the withered hate of scrub trees struck by desert lightning. These creatures were the magicians, assassins and advisors of the armies of the titans.

Today, those wrack dragons that survive mostly live a quiet or isolated existence. Though they are not elementals in a technical sense, they are as much forces of natural might as they are living creatures. They need eat only a little to sustain themselves, and they neither mate nor age. Wrack dragons are thus an ever-diminishing breed, for they were never born, and with the death or imprisonment of their creators, there will be no more of them. In a sense, wrack dragons are already dead.

Those that remain are of many minds. While the sea drakes are not stupid, most are too narrow of focus to adapt to new existences. They ravage the lands around them because that is their nature. The more powerful drakes are typically more circumspect in their approach, and many even live undetected. Some, particularly those created at the end of the war, are embittered with their creators, who brought them into existence to fight a war that was already lost and left them to survive at the mercy of hostile gods. They live a furtive existence in the dark places of the world. Others remain loyal, even now, and work diligently to rescue their masters. Many of both types retain command of much-reduced units of troops. Some still possess the weapons and armor the titans equipped them with during the war, though by the end of the struggle, most such gear was of the shoddiest sort; the magic in the equipment has long perished, leaving the dragons with only their formidable natural weaponry.

Dragon, Firewrack

Huge (Long) Dragon (Wrack)

Hit Dice:	16d12+96 (200 hp)
Initiative:	+4 (Dex)
Speed:	60 ft., burrow 10 ft.
AC:	32 (+4 Dex, -2 size, +20 natural)
Attacks:	Crush +27 melee; bite +27 melee
Damage:	crush 2d10+13; bite 2d6+13
Face/Reach:	15 ft. by 15 ft./15 ft.
Special Attacks:	Breath weapon, frightful presence
Special Qualities:	Immunities, damage reduction 10/+3, SR 15
Saves:	Fort +16, Ref +14, Will +11
Abilities:	Str 36, Dex 18, Con 22, Int 12, Wis 13, Cha 10
Skills:	Listen +10, Spot +14
Feats:	Cleave, Great Cleave, Power Attack,
Climate/Terrain:	Caves and volcanic wastelands
Organization:	Solitary, Section (2-4)
Challenge Rating:	10
Treasure:	Standard
Alignment:	Always lawful evil
Advancement Range:	14-24 HD (Huge)

Description

Firewrack dragons were the generals and elite warriors of the armies of the titans. While they ae not as magically adept or clever as their woodwrack cousins, they are larger and more capable in combat. Firewrack dragons are great assemblages of coals and charred wood, burnt bones and scorched animals killed in forest blazes. They are constantly wreathed in foul smoke, and they glow with dark orange radiance.

Fighters to the last, firewrack dragons combine the aggressive instincts of the lesser seawrack with a keen intellect focussed on finding the most direct way to the soft underbelly of a problem. Most firewracks died in the Divine War, and those that did not were hunted down shortly thereafter — how many places can a 30-foot-long mass of smoldering timbers and burnt flesh hide? Most of those that do survive exist underground or in blasted volcanic wastelands where their smoldering hides do not betray them.

Firewrack dragons are hot to the touch, but not su-

pernaturally so. Anything pulled into contact with their charcoal forms is likely to be burnt, but they are not surrounded by a corona of flames nor do their very footsteps melt metal and stone.

Combat

Firewrack dragons are the thickest and most heavily built of their kind. They have doglike legs, and they use their bulk and burning mass to good advantage in combat. They most commonly smash against or roll over opponents, searing them. Firewracks typically single out and attempt to neutralize the most dangerous opponent as quickly as possible, and tend to concentrate on enemy magicians, even to the exclusion of equally dangerous warriors. Firewracks almost always use their breath weapon in the first round of combat if opponents are within range.

Breath Weapon (Su): Once every three rounds, a firewrack may breathe a hideous combination of smoke and fire. Composed more of agony and cruelty than actual heat, this pale but brilliant flame sears all it touches. Against living creatures, it causes flash burns, peeling skin and illness. Against other objects, it causes scorching and smoldering flames. Against plants it causes disease, rot and wilting. Targets take 9d10 initial damage, plus 1d10 more each hour for 2d6 hours unless they are magically cured of disease. Those who succeed at a Reflex save (DC 21) take half the initial damage, and those that succeed at a Fortitude save (DC19) resist the diseased after-effects completely. This gout is a 75-foot-long cone.

Frightful Presence (Ex): The ghastly presence of the wrack dragon strikes fear and confusion into those who face it. Foes or bystanders within 180 feet of the wrack dragon must succeed at a Will save (DC 20) to resist the fear effect generated by the dragon's unnatural aura. Those who fail the saving throw become panicked for 3d6 rounds if less than 3 HD or levels (they flee the scene), while those of 4 or higher HD or levels become shaken for 1d6 rounds (-2 to all actions).

Immunities (Ex): Firewrack dragons are immune to fire and disease.

Dragon, Seawrack

Huge (Long) Dragon (Wrack)

Hit Dice:	10d12+40 (105 hp)
Initiative:	+8 (+4 Dex, +4 Improved Initiative)
Speed:	60 ft., swim 60 ft.
AC:	28 (+4 Dex, -2 size, +16 Hide)
Attacks:	Bite +17 melee, 2 claws +12 melee
Damage:	Bite 1d10+9; claw 2d6+3
Face/Reach:	10 ft. by 10 ft./15 ft.
Special Attacks:	Breath weapon, frightful presence
Special Qualities:	Immunities, damage reduction 8/+2, SR 12
Saves:	Fort +11, Ref +11, Will +8
Abilities:	Str 28, Dex 18, Con 18, Int 12, Wis 12, Cha 6
Skills:	Listen +10, Spot +14
Feats:	Cleave, Improved Initiative, Leadership, Power Attack
Climate/Terrain:	Any water, coastal land or swampland
Organization:	Solitary, Pair, Group (2-4)
Challenge Rating:	6
Treasure:	Standard
Alignment:	Always neutral evil
Advancement Range:	8-14 HD (Huge)

Description

The most common of the wrack-dragon breeds, the seawrack is a dangerous opponent, resistant to lesser magic and more than capable of vanquishing a large number of foes. These creatures were the officers of large units of regular troops, and most have an instinctual predilection to taking a severe, direct approach to matters. In percentages, few of these dragons survived — most died fighting the armies of the gods. However, they vastly outnumbered their cousins and remain the most common sort of wrack dragon, even today.

Seawrack dragons are not sea creatures per se. Most prefer dank lakes, bayous and other inland waters rich with life.

Seawrack dragons are simple creatures, most of which expended the troops under their command in short-term campaigning long ago. Those that survive do so because they are in isolated or unsettled areas. Seawrack dragons are the only social wrack dragons, and many still retain their small-unit command structures from the Titanswar and are thus found in small groups.

Combat

Seawrack dragons keep their tactics simple — attack from ambush, weaken as many foes as possible with a breath attack, and then pick the remaining ones off, starting with the most dangerous.

This doesn't make them stupid, it just means that they're not subtle. A seawrack dragon can easily pick out a man using magic, can spot officers and can devise plans that exploit enemies' weaknesses. After all, they are small-unit commanders. Most just don't apply themselves to long-term planning for conquest or growth — they are content to survive and destroy what they can. Many seawrack lairs are surrounded by large barren areas, dead zones where the plants are stunted and the water is made undrinkable by the dragon's venom.

Breath Weapon (Su): As often as once every five rounds, the seawrack dragon can breathe a choking cloud of noxious fumes. This cloud is 20 feet in radius and is centered up to 40 feet in front of the dragon. Those caught within it must succeed at a Fortitude save (DC 16). Those who fail are incapacitated with nausea for 1d4+1 rounds. Those who succeed still suffer -3 to attack rolls and must pass a Concentration check (DC18) to cast spells for the next 1d4+1 rounds.

Frightful Presence (Ex): The ghastly presence of the wrack dragon strikes fear and confusion into those who face it. Foes or bystanders within 180 feet of the wrack dragon must succeed at a Will save (DC 20) to resist the fear effect generated by the dragon's unnatural aura. Those who fail the saving throw become panicked for 3d6 rounds if less than 3 HD or levels (they flee the scene), while those of 4 or higher HD or levels become shaken for 1d6 rounds (-2 to all actions).

Immunities (Ex): Seawrack dragons are immune to poison and paralysis attacks.

Dragon, Woodwrack

Huge (Long) Dragon (Wrack)

Hit Dice:	18d12+108 (225 hp)
Initiative:	+7 (+3 Dex, +4 Improved Initiative)
Speed:	60 ft., climb 40 ft., fly 90 ft., swim 50 ft.
AC:	29 (+3 Dex, -2 size, +18 natural)
Attacks:	Bite +26 melee, 4 claws +21 melee
Damage:	Bite 2d10+10; claw 2d6+4
Face/Reach:	10 ft. by 10 ft./15 ft.
Special Attacks:	Breath weapon, frightful presence, spells, whirlwind attack
Special Qualities:	Immunities, damage reduction 8/+3, SR 18
Saves:	Fort +17, Ref +14, Will +14
Abilities:	Str 30, Dex 16, Con 22, Int 14, Wis 16, Cha 10
Skills:	Animal Empathy +14, Concentration +18, Hide +16, Knowledge (arcana) +10, Knowledge (history) +5, Listen +14, Move Silently +18, Scry +16, Spellcraft +12, Spot +10
Feats:	Cleave, Dodge, Expertise, Flyby Attack, Improved Initiative, Mobility, Power Attack, Spring Attack, Whirlwind Attack
Climate/Terrain:	Woods and Marsh
Organization:	Solitary
Challenge Rating:	12
Treasure:	Standard
Alignment:	Always neutral evil
Advancement Range:	16-17 HD (Huge), 19-24 HD (Huge)

Description

Lightning fast and deadly, and impossibly stealthy for a creature so huge, the woodwrack dragons were the assassins and magicians of the titan army. They acted as commanders of detached or guerrilla troops, and also served as advisors and roaming sorcerers in the service of their more combative firewrack cousins.

Woodwrack dragons prefer to live in forests and marshes, particularly dark or tropical ones where they are closest to the forces from which they were birthed. While woodwrack drakes were never terribly common, a greater percentage have survived the years since the war than have other forms of wracks. More flexible in their thinking and more circumspect in their behavior, as well as naturally stealthy, many woodwrack dragons lurk quietly in forgotten places, pursuing whatever long-term plans they have developed in the years since the titans' final defeat.

Woodwrack dragons have a natural affinity for animals of all sorts and often use this to their advantage. When strangers walk within the bounds of their woods, they know it, and those hunting for the dragon's lair are likely to be ambushed long before they near their goal.

Combat

Woodwrack dragons aren't straight-up fighters, preferring to attack from ambush. Most seek to get into the midst of their prey before attacking, either by launching themselves downward from the treetops (usually carrying those treetops down with them to clutter the battlefield). If they cannot fly, they wait in the contours of the forest floor until their targets stand almost on top of them.

Once in combat, woodwrack dragons use their speed combined with their spring attack or flyby attack feats to assault their foes and move away. They also use magic to assist them in combat. Many use stealth, combat and manipulation spells as a matter of course, attempting to avoid direct confrontation. Woodwracks also tend to use their breath weapons for indirect attacks rather than for simple damage, sawing down trees with a slash of lighting or igniting blazes with the super-hot air surrounding the bolt.

Breath Weapon (Su): The woodwrack dragon can breathe a crack of lightning as often as once every five rounds. This is a cylinder 30 feet long by 5 feet wide. The breath weapon does 10d10 damage, halved if the target succeeds at a Reflex save (DC 22).

Spells: As a 12th-level sorcerer.

Whirlwind Attack (Ex): The woodwrack dragon's whirlwind attack feat consists of two separate claw attacks made against every target within the creature's 15-foot reach.

Frightful Presence (Ex): The ghastly presence of the wrack dragon strikes fear and confusion into those who face it. Foes or bystanders within 180 feet of the wrack dragon must succeed at a Will save (DC 20) to resist the fear effect generated by the dragon's unnatural aura. Those who fail the saving throw become panicked for 3d6 rounds if less than 3 HD or levels (they flee the scene), while those of 4 or higher HD or levels become shaken for 1d6 rounds (-2 to all actions).

Immunities (Ex): Woodwrack dragons are immune to electrical attacks.

Dragonman

Medium-size Humanoid

Hit Dice:	8d8+27 (63 hp)
Initiative:	+5 (+1 Dex, +4 Improved Initiative)
Speed:	40 ft.
AC:	21 (+1 Dex, +10 natural)
Attacks:	Fists +12 melee, or by weapon type
Damage:	Fists 1d4+4
Face/Reach:	5 ft. by 5 ft./5 ft.
Special Attacks:	Imposing presence
Special Qualities:	Immunities, damage reduction 5/—, SR 16
Saves:	Fort +5, Ref +3, Will +10
Abilities:	Str 19, Dex 12, Con 17, Int 16, Wis 15, Cha 16
Skills:	Listen +10, Spot +15
Feats:	Alertness, Improved Initiative, Iron Will, Toughness
Climate/Terrain:	Any
Organization:	Solitary
Challenge Rating:	10
Treasure:	Double Standard
Alignment:	Any (but usually determined by dragon type)
Advancement Range:	By class or 8-12 HD (Medium-size)

Description

There are rumors that occasionally, rarely in truth, a dragon adopts the guise of a mortal human and lives out a lifetime among men. This possibility, and the reasons behind it, is debated constantly. However, if it is true, then it would explain the existence of dragonmen. A dragonman is the offspring of a dragon and a human, presumably conceived while the dragon was guised in human form.

Dragonmen can live harmoniously within human society and pursue any number of careers. They are highly prized by wizards for research purposes, and many powerful wizards would pay handsomely to have a living, breathing dragonman at their disposal.

Dragonmen can live several human lifespans and never quite feel comfortable in human society. Likewise, dragon soci-

ety is more or less closed to them. As a result, dragonmen almost always keep their true nature a secret. They keep very few friends, and avoid society's mainstream (under most circumstances).

Combat

Dragonmen fight depending upon what martial prowess they've learned in their lifetimes. They can study any trade, so some are warriors, some are clerics, others sorcerers and still others are bakers.

Imposing Presence (Ex): A dragonman can draw himself up and unsettle his foe. Any the creature of 8 or fewer HD and within 30 feet of the dragonman is susceptible to this effect. Any creature must succeed at a Will save (DC 18) to avoid the fear effect. Upon failure, a creature is shaken for 2d6 rounds, performing all actions with a −2 modifier on the roll.

Immunities (Ex): Dragonmen gain +10 on their saves against sleep and paralysis effects. They take half damage from attacks to which their parent dragon is immune.

Heightened Senses (Ex): A dragonman sees twice as well as a human in all conditions (regular and low light).

Dread Raven

Small Beast

Hit Dice:	2d10+2 (13 hp)
Initiative:	+3 (Dex)
Speed:	10 ft., fly 80 ft.
AC:	16 (+1 size, +3 Dex, +2 natural)
Attacks:	Peck +1 melee and 2 talons +0 melee
Damage:	Peck 1d4; talons 1d3
Face/Reach:	5 ft. x 5 ft./5 ft.
Special Attacks:	Spells
Special Qualities:	Keen senses
Saves:	Fort +1, Ref +6, Will +2
Abilities:	Str 7, Dex 17, Con 12, Int 10, Wis 14, Cha 7
Skills:	Hide +7, Listen +3, Read Lips +6, Spot +6
Feats:	None
Climate/Terrain:	Temperate and cold woods, hills or barrens
Organization:	Flock (1d6)
Challenge Rating:	1
Treasure:	None
Alignment:	Usually neutral evil
Advancement Range:	None

Description

Particularly intelligent and nasty, dread ravens gather like plagues in places of blight, warfare and devastation. Larger and more intelligent than their more common kin, dread ravens pose a threat to travelers because of their appetite for flesh and because they are often trained to serve as spies for evil humanoids, sorcerers and overlords.

Dread ravens are similar to sentry crows; both are inclined to deal with the people of the world. However, somewhere along the line, dread ravens took a dark turn, perhaps as a result of training by malicious or abusive masters. Perhaps King Virduk of Calastia contributed to this unfortunate development; he is said to have become obsessed with bird-sentries after his defeat of the dwarves at Iron Tooth Pass.

Dread ravens look much like dire ravens — huge black birds, three feet in length, with a correspondingly large wingspan. They have orange-yellow beaks and a definite cast of intelligence to their eyes.

Combat

Dread ravens are scavengers more so than hunters. They seek to prey upon those who have already fallen, the more tender the flesh the better (thus their preference for the remains of children, women and sheltered lords). If starving, they will seek to snatch small children from their parents and peck their victims apart in sheltered roosts.

Spells: A dread raven can cast spells as a third-level sorcerer. Each dread raven has its own selection of individual spells; "pecking order" in a dread-raven flock often depends upon which bird has the most deadly and useful spells.

Keen Senses (Ex): A dread raven gains a +6 bonus to Spot checks in daylight.

Dream Snake

Tiny Magical Beast

Hit Dice:	2d10-2 (9 hp)
Initiative:	+3 (Dex)
Speed:	20 ft.
AC:	16 (+2 size, +3 Dex, +1 natural)
Attacks:	Bite +0 melee
Damage:	Bite 1d4
Face/Reach:	2.5 ft. by 2.5 ft./0 ft.
Special Attacks:	Coma, energy drain
Special Qualities:	Etherealness
Saves:	Fort +2, Ref +3, Will +1
Abilities:	Str 3, Dex 16, Con 9, Int 2, Wis 12, Cha 4
Skills:	Hide +12, Listen +5, Move Silently +16, Spot +9
Feats:	Dodge
Climate/Terrain:	Any
Organization:	Solitary or pair
Challenge Rating:	3
Treasure:	Standard
Alignment:	Always neutral
Advancement Range:	2-3 HD (Tiny); 4-6 HD (Small)

Description

These monsters hide in the Ethereal Plane and consume sleeping creatures' energy. They care not for a victim's physical remains, leaving them for scavengers.

Dream snakes are typically found near large concentrations of living beings. Dream snakes find creatures with strong life forces most appealing. A rat is but a snack, while a horse offers a feast. The serpents find human-like intellect and willpower to be great delicacies, making wizards and clerics their primary targets.

A dream snake looks little different from a mundane asp, if one can see it at all. An adult is roughly three feet long and two inches in diameter. It has black and bright-blue banding, and a flat head. The serpent cannot normally be seen on the Material Plane. Spells or abilities that pierce the Ethereal Plane or use of magic detection spells reveal the dream snake as a smoky, translucent shape. In dreams or on the Ethereal Plane, the monster looks completely solid and can be interacted with normally.

Combat

A dream snake only attacks a victim in whom it has induced a coma. Whether this state makes the victim's energy more appealing or simply makes for an easier target is unknown. From the Ethereal Plane, the dream snake follows its Material Plane target until it lies down to sleep. Then, the snake coils ethereally around the target's neck, uses its coma inducing power and attaches its open mouth to the victim's own. It then feeds on the target's life energy until the victim dies, the snake is forced to flee or the snake is killed.

Etherealness (Ex): A dream snake lives its life in the Ethereal Plane. While there, anyone in the Material Plane cannot harm the dream snake (except with force magic, gaze attacks, and a few other exceptions. The dream snake cannot affect creatures on the Material Plane except through dream magic such as its coma power below.

Coma (Su): The dream snake may only use coma on a single living, sleeping target. If the victim fails a Will save (DC 18), then the dream snake has successfully brought the victim's sleeping spirit across to the Ethereal Plane, however the victim remains in a coma-like, deep sleep while the dream snake proceeds to feast on the victim's life force. In this state, the victim appears to others on the Material Plane as if he is suffering a horrid nightmare as he clutches his throat as if choking while still sleeping. The victim cannot be awoken from the coma except by dispelling the magic of the coma effect, which returns the victim's spirit to his body on the Material Plane; the victim can then be woken normally.

On a successful saving throw, the target still enters the Ethereal Plane, but is lucidly dreaming and has control of his dream self. He may combat the dream snake (which is probably wrapped around his throat) as one ethereal creature fighting another. The victim's dream self is treated as having all of his normal statistics but no gear or equipment. The victim may try to awaken himself (Will save at DC 13) and thereby leave the Ethereal Plane altogether, or his sleeping body may be wakened normally by others in the Material Plane.

Energy Drain (Ex): The bite of the dream snake inflicts one negative level per bite. A victim of energy drain dies once she has as many negative levels as HD. Each negative level suffered by a victim imposes penalties: -1 penalty on attack rolls, ability rolls, saving throws, skill rolls and on effective level. A spell-caster also loses a single spell as if she had cast her highest level currently memorized spell. The serpent gains 5 temporary hit points from each negative level it inflicts. See other rulebooks for details on regaining negative levels.

Drendari, Demigoddess of Shadow

Medium-size Outsider (Avatar)

Hit Dice:	35d8+140 (297 hp)
Initiative:	+17 (+13 Dex, +4 Improved Initiative)
Speed:	40 ft.
AC:	38 (+13 Dex, +15 natural)
Attacks:	Sword of Shadow +32/+27/+22/+17/+12 melee
Damage:	Sword of Shadow 1d6+7
Face/Reach:	5 ft. by 5 ft./5 ft.
Special Attacks:	Charming song, rogue abilities, spells, spell-like abilities
Special Qualities:	Avatar, damage reduction 20/+3, keen senses, shadowcloak, SR 28
Saves:	Fort +22, Ref +31, Will +25
Abilities:	Str 16, Dex 36, Con 18, Int 22, Wis 24, Cha 35
Skills:	Appraise +25, Balance +36, Bluff +37, Climb +33, Concentration +37, Decipher Script +34, Disable Device +35, Disguise +31, Escape Artist +37, Forgery +30, Hide +47, Innuendo +22, Intimidate +28, Knowledge (arcana) +23, Knowledge (geography) +24, Knowledge (history) +27, Knowledge (planes) +27, Knowledge (religion) +34, Listen +33, Move Silently +37, Open Lock +27, Perform +26, Pick Pocket +32, Read Lips +25, Scry +20, Search +28, Sense Motive +14, Spellcraft +17, Spot +34, Swim +19, Tumble +30, Use Magic Device +23
Feats:	Ambidexterity, Blindsight, Combat Casting, Dodge, Improved Critical, Improved Initiative, Silent Spell, Spring Attack, Still Spell
Climate/Terrain:	Any
Organization:	Solitary (unique)
Challenge Rating:	16
Treasure:	Standard
Alignment:	Always chaotic neutral
Advancement Range:	None

Description

Daughter of Enkili and a siren, Drendari is a minor demigoddess in the pantheon of the Scarred Lands. She holds dominion over shadow, and rogues of all races revere her. Since her patronage is small and secretive, few Scarred Lands myths even mention her. Those legends that do contain some exploit of Drendari are usually one of two types. First, being the daughter of the trickster god, Drendari myths often feature her pitting Madriel (goddess of light) and Belsameth (goddess of darkness) against one another with the goddess of shadow coming out the better for her trickery.

The second style of story, told among thieves, shows Drendari intervening to aid those robbers who were wise enough to pray and make sacrifice to her before

they embarked upon a job. Sample stories tell of the hero trapped in a necromancer's crypt as he trips the alarm by taking the necromancer's black opal from its protective housing. Just as deathly terrors close in on the hero, he hears Drenari's silver bell laughter and is whisked away by walking the shadows with his goddess.

Some tales of intervention also say that Drendari takes too much liking to some few thieves and steals them away with her into the realm of shadow. Most of the subjects of these stories are never seen again, but some do return to the physical world. If they do return, though, they pine endlessly for their goddess' touch, trying in vain to recreate the sound of her laughter or picture her face again.

Thieves who pray to Drendari regularly receive a +2 bonus to Hide as shadows seem to stretch from the walls to embrace the thief. Thieves who worship Drendari and are particularly adept at hiding amid shadows (rolling Hide skill check totals of 35 or higher) can hear her acknowledge their presence while in her realm. Her carefree laughter and her beautiful voice soothe the properly pious thief, although such sounds are apparent to no one else. Male thieves (with high Charisma scores) who get such acknowledgements may experience her presence even more intimately. Some claim to feel her fleeting touch or a quick caress. Others hear their name called out amid the laughter or even feel her hands about them, gently pulling them deeper into the shadows.

When Drendari cares to take an active role in the physical plane, she either aids her worshippers directly — the rare time it meets her whim to do so — or plays out some deceitful game by meddling in the affairs of some other deity's mortal province.

Combat

When Drendari does manifest her avatar in the physical plane, she uses her Shadowcloak ability to remain unseen. She usually refuses confrontation and simply uses her spell-like abilities to walk through shadows to escape. If she does engage in combat, it is through the use of her spells and sneak attacks with her Sword of Shadow.

Avatar: The statistics provided are merely for the avatar image Drendari may project into the physical plane. The demigoddess' actual statistics are dramatically higher on her own plane. If her avatar is destroyed on the physical plane, she cannot form another one for 1d4 months. If her avatar is somehow imprisoned, then she is trapped from appearing elsewhere on any plane, and her father Enkili will be pissed off at anyone responsible.

Avatars are not affected by critical hits, death from massive injury, poison, paralysis, sleep, disease or any attack that must target a living subject.

Blindsight (Ex): Unless an area is in absolute light or darkness, Drendari can sense her surroundings through communion with the shadows.

Charming Song (Su): True to her mother's lineage, Drendari's voice can charm any male humanoid that hears it. All victims who hear her song may attempt a Will saving throw (DC 18) to resist the charm.

Keen Senses (Ex): Drendari has darkvision up to 200 feet. She may also see invisible and ethereal creatures.

Rogue Abilities: Drendari possess all the rogue class special abilities. She can be treated as a 35th-level rogue.

Shadowcloak (Ex): As a free action, Drendari may wrap herself in supernatural shadow, hiding her from all forms of sight. She is effectively treated as being invisible whenever she likes. Divine spells that create light or darkness may counter the Shadowcloak effect for 1d4 rounds.

Spells: Drendari uses magic as a 12th-level cleric and a 16th-level sorcerer.

Spell-like Abilities: Drendari may use any spell whose name contains the word "shadow" or "shade," or other spells whose main function deals with shadow, an unlimited number of times per day, no more than once per round.

Sword of Shadow: The wielder of this +4 short sword may strike at any single opponent within 60 feet if the opponent is casting a discernable shadow or if there is some other shadow within five feet of the opponent. The wielder must also be in shadow or casting a discernable shadow to use this ability. As the strike is essentially made through a mystical bridge between the wielder's and the opponent's shadows, the opponent is considered flanked by the shadow strike unless he actively defends against attacks coming from nearby shadows.

Drowned Lady

Tiny Animal

Hit Dice:	1d8-1 (3 hp)
Initiative:	+0
Speed:	Swim 90 ft.
AC:	12 (+2 size)
Attacks:	Envelop +3 melee
Damage:	Special
Face/Reach:	2.5 ft. by 2.5 ft./0 ft.
Special Attacks:	Envelop
Special Qualities:	None
Saves:	Fort +1, Ref +0, Will -1
Abilities:	Str 10, Dex 10, Con 9, Int —, Wis 9, Cha 4
Skills:	Listen +3, Spot +1
Feats:	None
Climate/Terrain:	Freshwater lakes or rivers
Organization:	School (1-6)
Challenge Rating:	1/4
Treasure:	Standard
Alignment:	Always neutral
Advancement Range:	1-2 HD (Tiny)

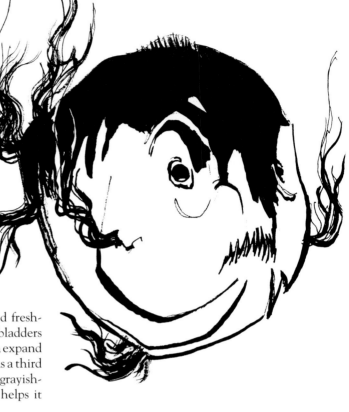

Description

The drowned lady is a moderately sized freshwater fish that appears tall and thin when its bladders are empty. The fish has a large mouth that can expand horizontally to fit around an object as much as a third larger than the fish itself. The fish is a dark, grayish-brown in color, a natural camouflage that helps it blend in with the muddy river floor.

The drowned lady is an unusual creature that lingers in the water's depths, constantly eyeing the brighter depths above for movement and likely prey. When a fish — or even a swimmer — passes overhead, the drowned lady rises from the depths and locks its jaws around the victim. Once it has enveloped part of its prey, the fish sucks water into five bladders located around its body, swelling it into a large, ovoid shape and consequently increasing its weight. Then the drowned lady sinks back to the river floor, pulling its victim along with it. It sits there for days, slowly digesting its meal.

Drowned ladies are favorites of nobles whose strongholds incorporate moats or lakes as part of their defenses. The fish eagerly attacks swimmers as well as other fish, making the waters hazardous for attackers or potential escapees.

Combat

The drowned lady's method of attack is almost entirely passive, with it acting as a millstone and dragging a victim to a watery grave. Its jaws are mostly cartilage, making them elastic, very strong and very difficult to remove once they have closed around a hand or foot. To make matters worse, a thrashing victim often attracts other drowned ladies in the area, hoping for a meal of their own.

Envelop (Ex): If a drowned lady successfully hits its target, it automatically swallows or envelops a larger creature's hand or foot. The victim must then make a Swim check (DC 16) each turn to stay above water. A drowned lady's grip is very elastic and strong, requiring a Strength roll with a DC of 20 to dislodge the fish while it lives.

Dune Delver

Large (Long) Beast

Hit Dice:	10d10+20 (75 hp)
Initiative:	+0
Speed:	Burrows 40 ft.
AC:	15 (-1 size, +6 natural)
Attacks:	Bite +11 melee
Damage:	Bite 1d10+2
Face/Reach:	5 ft. by 10 ft./5 ft.
Special Attacks:	Feeding tubes
Special Qualities:	None
Saves:	Fort +5, Ref +0, Will -1
Abilities:	Str 15, Dex 11, Con 15, Int —, Wis 5, Cha 5
Skills:	Listen +15
Feats:	Alertness, Blind Fighting
Climate/Terrain:	Desert
Organization:	Solitary
Challenge Rating:	5
Treasure:	Standard
Alignment:	Always neutral
Advancement Range:	8-12 HD (Large)

Description

Desert nomads share horrific tales around the campfire of the strange and terrifying dune delver, a rarely seen creature that escapes the blistering desert heat by burrowing deep under the sand and sending thick, tentacle-like feeding tubes to the surface to lie in wait for passing prey.

The dune delver's actual body is a spherical mass of muscle and cartilage almost 10 feet across, with broad, blade-like "flippers" set equidistantly around its body to both help it move through the sand and to anchor it when hunting for food. When disturbed, the delver extends four tentacle-like feeding tubes, each tipped with a large, bulb-like mouth filled with curved teeth that help it grab and swallow prey.

Dune delvers are voracious and not very intelligent, and they attack anything that creates enough vibrations in the sand above their bodies. Anything larger than a small lizard causes one or more of the mouths to explode upward from just beneath the surface, in an attempt to grab the victim and swallow it. Anything pulled into the delver's mouth is swallowed automatically, whether it's sand, people or burning torches.

Combat

The dune delver's senses for detecting prey are acute, but its ability to bite and swallow victims is somewhat less accurate. Generally, the delver does not use more than two of its feeding tubes to try and grab victims; if sorely pressed, the creature tries to maneuver its prey so as to place them directly over one of the two "reserve" mouths and take them by surprise. As long as the delver senses vibrations in the sand, it keeps trying to swallow whatever is up there. The only way to kill a delver is to dig up its body — some 20 feet beneath the sand — or feed it something lethal such as iron spikes or burning oil (and even that may take some time).

Feeding Tubes (Ex): The dune delver's mouth-tipped feeding tubes are capable of grabbing and swallowing a man-sized target in a single action. If the delver scores a hit in combat, one of its mouths has successfully grabbed a victim. If the roll causes a critical hit, the target is swallowed automatically. If not, the victim is allowed to roll a Reflex save (DC 16) to avoid being sucked into the tube. Victims can attempt to cut their way out of a feeding tube, but cannot use anything larger than a dagger and must inflict more than 15 points of damage within three rounds or it's too late. Each feeding tube can withstand 40 hit points of damage from external attacks before it's severed.

Dwarf, Forsaken

Medium-sized Humanoid

Hit Dice:	1d8+1 (5 hp)
Initiative:	+0
Speed:	15
AC:	14 (+4 scale mail)
Attacks:	Warhammer +0 melee; repeating crossbow +0 ranged
Damage:	Warhammer 1d8+1; repeating crossbow 1d8
Face/Reach:	5 ft. by 5 ft./5 ft.
Special Attacks:	Dwarven traits
Special Qualities:	Dwarven traits
Saves:	Fort +3, Ref +0, Will +0
Abilities:	Str 11, Dex 10, Con 13, Int 10, Wis 10, Cha 8
Skills:	Craft: Trapmaking +4, Listen +1, Spot +1
Feats:	Exotic Weapon Proficiency (Repeating Crossbow)
Climate/Terrain:	Mountains and underground
Organization:	Solitary, pair, group (5-8) or band (10-100 forsaken dwarves, plus 1 leader of 4th to 6th level and 1 cleric of 3rd to 5th level)
Challenge Rating:	1/2
Treasure:	Double Standard
Alignment:	Usually lawful evil
Advancement Rate:	By character class

Description

Forsaken dwarves are an evil race of dwarves living within Krakadöm, the largest of the Kelder Mountains. Territorial in the extreme, the dwarves often kill trespassers on their divine mountain and mutilate their bodies, then leave the corpses to rot on long pikes overlooking the Kelder Mountains' many passes as a warning to others. Though relatively recent immigrants to the region, having moved there since their own realm in the World's End Mountains was destroyed during the Divine War, the dwarves have spent the last century and a half carving an enormous kingdom from the living rock of Krakadöm.

It is said that the forsaken dwarves were not always so malicious. Before moving to the Kelder Mountains, the forsaken dwarves were a good and just people. Many believe that the hardships experienced in the Divine War — the hundreds dead, the loss of their ancient kingdom and the long trek to their new home — scarred the dwarves' souls as much as it did the lands to which they are tied. Others, primarily forsaken elves, whisper that the dwarves' change in demeanor has a much darker origin, one inexorably tied to the dark influence of something that dwells within Krakadöm itself.

Forsaken dwarves appear much like their more kindly brethren. Standing between four and four and one half feet in height, they are extremely stocky, making their weight comparable to that of an average human. Hair color ranges from blond to black, though forsaken dwarves invariably go gray early in life. The main differences between forsaken and regular dwarves are the forsaken's wan and gaunt faces, their nasty dispositions and their shortened lifespans; few live more than 200 years.

Forsaken dwarves speak the Dwarven tongue and many also speak Elven and the language of the riders of the Kelder Steppes, their closest human neighbors.

Forsaken Dwarf Characters

The majority of forsaken dwarves are fighters (their preferred class), though clerics and multiclass fighter/clerics are not uncommon. Forsaken dwarf clerics may choose two of the following domains: Chaos, Destruction and Earth. Very few forsaken dwarf rogues exist, and those that do are typically scouts and spies. Forsaken dwarf spellcasters are practically unheard of.

Combat

The forsaken dwarves seldom venture forth from their underground homes, thus, they've become quite adept tunnel fighters. Forsaken dwarves are expert trapmakers, often setting deadfalls or collapsing tunnels on intruders. Invariably, their tunnel fighters strike in ambush from secure position, first riddling their victims with crossbow bolts and then closing to finish the survivors with their mighty warhammers.

Dwarf Hound

Medium-size Animal

Hit Dice:	5d8+25 (47 hp)
Initiative:	+4 (Improved Initiative)
Speed:	80 ft.
AC:	12 (+2 natural)
Attacks:	Bite +8 melee
Damage:	Bite 1d10+3
Face/Reach:	5 ft. by 5 ft./5 ft.
Special Attacks:	Deafening bark
Special Qualities:	Darkvision 60ft., Immunities
Saves:	Fort +6, Ref +0, Will +0
Abilities:	Str 16, Dex 11, Con 20, Int 4, Wis 8, Cha 8
Skills:	Intimidate +5, Intuit Direction +5, Listen +5, Spot +5
Feats:	Improved Bull Rush, Improved Critical, Improved Initiative
Climate/Terrain:	Subterranean caverns, castles
Organization:	Solitary or trained packs (2-4)
Challenge Rating:	3
Treasure:	None
Alignment:	Always neutral
Advancement Range:	3-6 HD (Medium-size)

Description

Legends say that the first dwarven hounds were a dozen prize mastiffs presented to the dwarf King Thorvann by the human King of Darakeene as a gesture of gratitude for dwarven aid against the goblin invasions. It's not likely that the human king expected the dour dwarves to do much with the gift, but the dwarven king surprisingly fell in love with the dogs and began breeding them in his underground halls. The breed that resulted was nothing less than extraordinary, a magical mixture of canine loyalty and strength combined with the dwarven passion for deep, dark places and veins of glittering ore.

Dwarf hounds are short and broad, possessed of enormous strength and stamina. They are not swift runners, but they can fit through even the narrowest passages and lope along with their masters at a tireless trot. The dogs have short coats ranging in color from

coal black to a reddish-gold and have large, golden eyes. They have been bred for great intelligence, and miners often use the dogs to sniff out veins of ore deep within the mountains. When it scents a vein, it lets loose with a thunderclap bark that echoes for miles through underground tunnels (an attribute that makes them amazing watchdogs as well) How the animals actually smell gold and the like is a mystery to human trainers and is a secret the dwarves prefer to keep to themselves.

Dwarves are happy to sell puppies to human trainers, but they are always very expensive, and the dogs are never happy outside close passages and dim lighting. For this reason, they are rarely seen in human lands except as watchdogs in some wealthy lord's castle.

Combat

A dwarf hound's loud bark is indeed worse than its bite. The hounds are utterly fearless in defense of their masters and don't back down from any attacker, no matter how large or dangerous. Once they attack a target, nothing can deter them except death.

Immunities (Ex): Dwarf hounds are immune to fear, sleep and paralysis attacks, as well as subdual damage.

Deafening Bark (Ex): When in battle, a dwarf hound barks constantly. The pure volume of the bark can confuse or even stun foes. Opponents within 60 feet in an enclosed area or 20 feet in an open area must make a Will save (DC 16) or be disoriented. In an enclosed area, a failed save means the foe is unable to move or attack that round while success means movement at 1/2 speed and attacks at -4 are possible. In an open area, a failed save means -4 to hit while a successful save reduces this modifier to -2. Dwarves used to fighting near these hounds make their Will save at DC 12 with failure being the equivalent of a success for others and success meaning no effect.

Dweller at the Crossroads

Medium-size Outsider (Evil)

Hit Dice:	8d8+40 (76 hp)
Initiative:	+5 (Dex)
Speed:	60 ft.
AC:	22 (+5 Dex, +7 natural)
Attacks:	None
Damage:	None
Face/Reach:	5 ft. by 5 ft./5 ft.
Special Attacks:	None
Special Qualities:	Wish, vanish, SR 20, damage reduction 15/+2, outsider
Saves:	Fort +11, Ref +11, Will +10
Abilities:	Str 19, Dex 20, Con 20, Int 20, Wis 19, Cha 18
Skills:	Bluff +11, Diplomacy +11, Innuendo +11, Intimidate + 11, Listen +11, Sense Motive +11, Spot +11
Feats:	None
Climate/Terrain:	Any crossroads
Organization:	Unique
Challenge Rating:	6
Treasure:	None
Alignment:	Always neutral evil
Advancement Range:	None

Description

Many legends portray crossroads as places of fateful meetings and supernatural encounters. It's said that if a man wants something more than his very soul, he can find it at the crossroads at midnight.

No one knows who or what the dweller at the crossroads may be; most believe it to be a kind of demon, while others think it is merely one more incarnation of Enkili, the trickster god. Regardless, a traveler on a quest who pauses at a crossroads at midnight is likely to meet a stranger in a flowing black cloak, his face concealed in the depths of a dark hood. He offers the traveler his heart's desire, but there's always a price to be paid, sooner or later. Many travelers make the deal, believing that they can cheat the hooded stranger, but their efforts always end in tragedy, the stuff of bardic legend.

Combat

The dweller at the crossroads reaps a harvest of human souls by fulfilling any mortal's fondest wish. This wish must relate to a mortal's immediate need or must be crucial to allowing her to complete a quest that she currently undertakes. The dweller appears only to people when they are in great need, so the temptation is usually fierce. But, as always, there is a price, seemingly in proportion to the wish that's granted. For example, a questing knight might seek a weapon to slay a mighty creature; the dweller presents the knight with a sword, but it turns out to be subtly cursed, so that once the knight's foe has died he must then go on to kill someone every night. Or a peasant suffering under the reign of a terrible lord might wish for the tyrant's death — only to find himself put in the tyrant's place, completely incapable of the task set before him and hated just as badly by the rest of the populace. Whatever its motives, the goal of the dweller is corruption and misery to any who accept its offer. Anyone foolish enough to try and attack the dweller is left holding empty air, as the mysterious entity vanishes into the darkness.

Wish (Su): The dweller at the crossroads can fulfill a single wish for a single mortal once per night. This wish is dependent on conditions set by the dweller in the manner of a bargain with the mortal in question.

Vanish (Su): If attacked, the dweller can disappear into the darkness but cannot return to the mortal plane until the following night.

Outsider: The dweller is immune to poison, disease, paralysis, mind-influencing effects, and any form of attack which requires a living target.

Ebon Eel

	Medium-size Animal
Hit Dice:	3d8 (13 hp)
Initiative:	+3 (Dex)
Speed:	Swim 60 ft.
AC:	13 (+3 Dex)
Attacks:	Bite +5 melee
Damage:	Bite 1d8+2
Face/Reach:	5 ft. by 5 ft./5 ft.
Special Attacks:	Blinding spray
Special Qualities:	None
Saves:	Fort +0, Ref +3, Will +0
Abilities:	Str 15, Dex 17, Con 10, Int 1, Wis 6, Cha 4
Skills:	None
Feats:	Cleave, Power Attack
Climate/Terrain:	Shallow saltwater coastlines
Organization:	Solitary
Challenge Rating:	1
Treasure:	Standard
Alignment:	Always neutral
Advancement Range:	2-6 HD (Medium-size)

Description

The ebon eel is a voracious and territorial predator that favors shallow-water caves and the wrecks of sailing ships, lying in wait to dart out and trap unwary passersby in its powerful jaws. The eel can reach up to nine feet in length and is colored a deep cobalt blue. Its long snout is filled with a double row of razor-sharp triangular teeth.

This species of salt-water eel is famous for its attacks on swimmers and treasure divers in the wreck-strewn waters of the Liars' Sound in southern Ghelspad, sometimes lurking within split-open treasure chests or within the hollows of a suit of ceremonial armor. The eel attacks its victims by exuding an amber-tinted cloud of liquid from pores around its head that spreads quickly through the water and attacks the prey's eyes, causing them to swell shut. Thus blinded, the victim is an easy meal for the predator's lightning speed and powerful jaws.

Ebon eels are absolutely fearless and extremely territorial; any creature that enters its territory is attacked without hesitation.

Combat

Unless an unlucky creature sticks its face or hand into the eel's hiding place, its normal method of attack is to spend up to a minute lying in wait and pumping its blindness-producing toxin into the surrounding water. When the victim begins to thrash and churn the water, the creature strikes, darting in to bite deeply and then swimming away again.

Blinding Spray (Ex): The ebon eel initiates its attack by exuding a chemical irritant into the water that causes pain and swelling in a victim's eyes. Individuals within 10 feet of the eel must make a Fortitude save (DC 17) or be blinded for 1d6 minutes. This roll must be made each turn for unaffected creatures within 10 feet of the eel as long as it is still alive.

Elf, Forsaken

Medium-Size Humanoid

Hit Dice:	1d8-1 (3 hp)
Initiative:	+1 (Dex)
Speed:	30 ft.
AC:	16 (+1 Dex, +5 chain mail)
Attacks:	Rapier +0 melee; longbow +2 ranged
Damage:	Rapier 1d6-1; arrow 1d8
Face/Reach:	5 ft. by 5 ft./5 ft.
Special Qualities:	Elven traits
Saves:	Fort +1, Ref +1, Will +0
Abilities:	Str 9, Dex 13, Con 8, Int 11, Wis 10, Cha 13
Skills:	Hide +3, Listen +4, Move Silently +3, Search +4, Spot +4
Feats:	Dodge, Point Blank Shot
Climate/Terrain:	Any land
Organization:	Solitary, squad (6-10), war band (21-40), village (10-100), city (30-300)
Challenge Rating:	1/2
Treasure:	Standard
Alignment:	Usually chaotic neutral
Advancement Rate:	By character class

Description

Another casualty of the Divine War, the forsaken elves are a mere shell of their former selves. When the gods rose against the Titans, these elves of the western plains of Termana battled alongside a demi-god particularly beloved by them, only to watch horrified as their patron was betrayed by one of his own divine servants and slain by the Titan Chern. Maddened by the loss, the furious elves fell upon Chern and helped bring the haughty Titan down. It was a pyrrhic victory, however, as well over half their number was slain during the conflict. As if that were not enough, it became evident after the war that their race, previously blessed with the near immortality of other elves, had been infected with the curse of death that other races lived under, and most of their already rare children were born malformed or dead. Thus, while still longer-lived than a man, the forsaken elves are a race in steady decline. Those

that remain today are those that can remember the Divine War — there hasn't been a forsaken elf born healthy in the last 150 years.

Forsaken elves are humanoids with pale skin, long pointed ears, large eyes and long spindly limbs. Their eyes are black with brightly colored irises. They wear ornate clothing of surpassing beauty, full of intricacies that the elves themselves find beautiful but most other races find overly busy. Elven weapons are delicate but strong, forged by the finest craftsman to be as beautiful as they are deadly.

Forsaken elves speak Elven. Many also speak the languages of other races.

Forsaken elf settlements are clustered on the edge of the plains humans have re-named Virduk's Promise, Before the Divine War, the elves had a more organized structure under a single king, but with the decimation of the race, the kingdom has degenerated into its current state of disarray. Those visiting one of these surviving settlements will find some of the finest, most ornate architecture in the Scarred Lands. However, those with the ability to see through illu-

sions will find that many of these great structures are little more than crumbling ruins, their appearance shored up by magic. Also, many buildings stand abandoned, their inhabitants either having died in the war of the gods or since. Amphitheaters that once echoed with the joyful songs of elven bards are now silent. Temples to dead gods lie as forsaken as the elves themselves, their only inhabitants doleful priests who outlived the beings they worshipped.

Changelings

As a result of their steady decline and few viable births, forsaken elves have taken to stealing the young of their more vital human neighbors. These babes (usually female) are taken to be used as slaves and, when they reach maturity, mothers, through whom the elves hope to reinvigorate their race. (Often, these humans are returned to human lands decades later, as elderly, burned-out husks incapable of relating to their own kind.) In their place, the elves sometimes leave their own twisted offspring, whom forsaken elves now find distasteful. Usually, these changelings are veiled by illusion to fool the human parents into believing the elven babies are their own. When the illusion wears off, the humans often believe it is their own child who has become ill. Even if they realize what has happened, the elves themselves are long gone.

Half-Elves

The vast majority (95%) of all the half elves of the Scarred Lands are the result of the union of a forsaken elf and a human. The scions of unions between forsaken elves and humans, these unfortu-nates are viewed as halfbreeds by both of their parent races. To the humans, they are the end product of an ongoing campaign of kidnapping and rape perpe-trated on their kind. To the elves, half-elven vitality merely points out the elves' own weakness and the depths to which they have been driven. Viewed objectively, however, half-elves combine some of the best of the two races characteristics.

Typical half-elf stats are: Str 10, Dex 11, Con 10, Int 11, Wis 10, Cha 11. Half-elves of the Scarred Lands possess the usual half-elven special qualities.

Forsaken Elf Characters

Forsaken elves favor multiclass fighters; leaders tend to be fighter/wizards. Illusionists and enchanters are more popular than actual wizards among those spellcasters who aren't also fighters. Forsaken clerics still venerate their fallen god, but with only their own faith to empower them, they may only cast 1st and 2nd level spells from the following domains: Chaos, Knowledge, Magic and Trickery. To date, not a single forsaken elf has managed to muster enough faith in one of the "foreign" gods to become a fully powered cleric.

Combat

After having the majority of their warriors slain, with few being born to replace them, forsaken elves came to favor surprise and guerilla tactics. They attack from positions of cover with frightening speed and ferocity, raining down arrows and spells on the opposition, then having their land and aerial cavalry, mounted on warhorses and giant eagles (or hariers) respectively, swoop down to deal the final blow.

Emperor Stag

Large (Long) Beast

Hit Dice:	8d10+56 (100 hp)
Initiative:	+5 (Dex)
Speed:	180 ft.
AC:	21 (-1 size, +5 Dex, + 7 natural)
Attacks:	Antlers +14 melee and 2 hooves +7 melee
Damage:	Antlers 2d6+7; hooves 1d8+2
Face/Reach:	5 ft. by 10 ft./5 ft.
Special Attacks:	Piercing antlers
Special Qualities:	Run like the wind, damage reduction 8/+1, speak with animals
Saves:	Fort +12, Ref +7, Will +7
Abilities:	Str 21, Dex 21, Con 25, Int 20, Wis 20, Cha 19
Skills:	Hide +11, Intuit Direction +11, Listen +13, Move Silently +11, Spot +13
Feats:	Alertness, Blind Fighting, Combat Reflexes, Dodge, Improved Critical (antlers)
Climate/Terrain:	Primeval forest
Organization:	Solitary
Challenge Rating:	6
Treasure:	None
Alignment:	Always lawful neutral
Advancement Range:	6-12 HD (Large)

Description

Rangers speak in reverent tones of a legendary creature called the emperor stag, a powerful spirit that rules over the deep forests and maintains the laws of wood and glen at the command of Denev, the Earth Mother. The stag is described as huge and majestic, with large, intelligent eyes and a rich brown pelt that glows in the twilight beneath the ancient trees. His rack of antlers spreads like the branches of a venerable oak and gleams like polished iron.

Within the bounds of its forest, the emperor stag is the chosen agent of the earth goddess and is able to cross its environs with the speed of the wind and bear witness to the acts of any who pass through its territory. The stag is able to speak the languages of all the animals that live in the forest, and many act as his eyes and ears, passing word back to him of what occurs in his

"realm." The emperor stag watches travelers and repays them in kind for every deed they do while in his forest: Acts of mercy are rewarded, and acts of violence are paid in full. The stag does not speak to travelers but can understand all of the major languages and can sometimes be seen just beyond the light of a camp, listening to the talk around the fire.

Another legend says that, in times past, a hero could vault upon the back of the stag and whisper a place he needed to go. No matter how far away, the stag would carry the hero there in the space of a single night, but the chosen servant of the goddess would not suffer being a beast of burden gladly. It would carry the hero where he wanted to go, but would be under no compunction to ensure that he survived the trip.

Combat

The emperor stag is a fearsome creature in combat, lashing out with its hooves and ravaging victims with its mighty array of antlers. The creature attacks only if provoked or to repay an act of wanton violence committed within its realm. If offenders are part of a large force, the stag can summon other denizens of the forest to assist its efforts.

Piercing Antlers (Ex): The antlers of the emperor stag are harder than iron and capable of penetrating the toughest armor. They have a +2 to attack and damage.

Run like the Wind (Su): The emperor stag is one of the earth goddess' swiftest servants. Once per night, it can run from one point to another with the speed of the wind, covering up to 100 leagues an hour.

Speak with Animals (Su): The emperor stag is able to speak with and be understood by any animal native to the forests.

Exemplar

Medium-size Humanoid (Human)

Hit Dice:	4d8+8 (26 hp)
Initiative:	+5 (+1 Dex, +4 Improved Initiative)
Speed:	40 ft.
AC:	13 (+1 Dex, +2 natural)/15 vs. subdual damage attacks (+2 Ironbone feat)
Attacks:	Hand +5 melee
Damage:	Hand 1d8+2
Face/Reach:	5 ft. by 5 ft./5 ft.
Special Attacks:	Monk abilities, special feats
Special Qualities:	None
Saves:	Fort +6, Ref +5, Will +7
Abilities:	Str 13, Dex 13, Con 15, Int 14, Wis 16, Cha 10
Skills:	Balance +7, Climb + 7, Escape Artist +2, Jump +7, Listen +4, Move Silently +5, Spot +2, Tumble +6
Feats:	Deflect Arrows, Dodge, Improved Initiative, Improved Unarmed Strike
Climate/Terrain:	Solitary or groups anywhere, temples
Organization:	Solitary, Group (2-5), Temple (10-30 plus 2 to 8 8-HD exemplars, 1 to 3 12-HD exemplars and 1 20-HD exemplar)
Challenge Rating:	2
Treasure:	None
Alignment:	Always lawful neutral
Advancement Range:	1-20 HD

Description

Like monks, exemplars are humans who have taken up a monastic lifestyle to perfect themselves through training in combat arts and meditation techniques. Exemplars revere the god Hedrada, who watches over them as they seek perfection. Rather than keep the souls of dead exemplars with him, Hedrada allows the souls to reincarnate on the physical plane in a human form to continue their pursuit of the ideal state they possessed prior to the attack of the wizard Tarkun centuries ago. Only those exemplars who attain their perfect self (20 HD exemplars), remain with Hedrada in the afterworld when they die.

Exemplars maintain a few monasteries in the Desert of Onn, where they live and train. They venture forth from their temples to find the new incarnations of their deceased comrades wherever those souls appear in the world. The reborn exemplars are brought back to the monasteries and are awakened to their true natures through meditation so that they may return to training and perhaps one day find and defeat their ancient enemy.

Exemplars also serve rotating four-year duties as bodyguards to the high priests in mighty Hedrad, across the Blood Sea, and they may be found guarding the temples in the city, traveling with the priests or journeying back and forth from Onn when their rotations begin or end.

The exemplars' recurring lifetimes have allowed them to master many special abilities largely unknown to even other monks. The exemplars share some of these secrets with other lawful neutral monks who come and train with the order for a sufficient amount of time, or who serve Hedrada or the exemplars in some exceptional way.

Exemplars live an ascetic lifestyle. They sleep on stone floors, eat the simplest raw foods, wear plain clothing and forgo all sexual activity. They even eschew the use of all weapons save their own body. They are reserved in manner but not taciturn if the situation calls for speech. Likewise, they are peaceful unless threatened or they learn the location of a sandmasker.

Combat

In combat, exemplars fight to the death, since they have no reason to fear it. Death is only a brief interruption in their training.

The statistics provided above are for a 4 HD exemplar with the Ironbone feat, but exemplars of all advancement ranges (1 HD to 20 HD) can be encountered. They may have none or all of the exemplar special feats described below, depending on their HD and the GM's discretion.

Monk Abilities: Exemplars possess all of the special abilities of a monk of level equal to the exemplar's HD.

Special Feats: Exemplars have trained through multiple lifetimes to perfect their bodies and achieve seemingly supernatural powers. These special abilities are treated as feats, mostly for system purposes. In order to learn one of these special feats from an exemplar, a PC or NPC monk must first gain the exemplar's trust through study or service. He may then gain one of the following special feats in lieu of a feat the character would normally gain through level advancement — all subject to the GM's adjudication, of course.

Ironbone — The exemplar hardens the bones in his hands, feet, shins, forearms, elbows and forehead through years of smashing these body parts into wooden beams. Exemplars use secret herbal compounds to heal their bruised flesh during training. They also infuse their skin and bones with elixirs to strengthen them.

The exemplar receives a +1 open hand damage modifier and +2 AC modifier against attacks that cause subdual damage. A Constitution of 13+ is a prerequisite for this feat.

Ironskin — The exemplar furthers his invulnerability training by having his entire body routinely pummeled and then soaked in a secret herbal preparation. At the end of years of such training, the exemplar's flesh is toughened, and his vital points are desensitized to injury and pain. The exemplar gains +1 to Fortitude saving throws and +2 AC against attacks that cause subdual damage (cumulative with Ironbone). When an opponent scores a critical threat against an exemplar with Ironskin, the attack roll to determine if the hit is critical is made as if the exemplar had +4 AC. The Ironbone feat is a prerequisite to Ironskin.

Energy of Life — Exemplars who master this feat need only five percent as much food and water as a normal human. A Constitution and Wisdom of 13+ are prerequisites for this feat.

Moving Meditation — Mastering this feat requires the exemplar to master his thoughts. By quieting his stream of consciousness and maintaining a calm and meditative mind throughout his activities, an exemplar removes his need for sleep entirely. He also gains a +1 to his Listen and Spot skill checks from his increased awareness. A Wisdom of 13+ is a prerequisite for this feat.

Ten Animal Style — By modeling their fighting style after the natural techniques employed by 10 different animals, the exemplars have mastered an arsenal of frightful hand and foot strikes. Any exemplar with this feat has +2 to his critical threat range for open-hand attacks. (If the exemplar normally threatens a critical hit on a roll of 20, he would threaten a critical on 18-20 with this feat.) This feat stacks with other effects or feats that expand the critical threat range, but it is applied after any effect that doubles the critical threat range (like the Improved Critical feat). A base attack bonus of +8 is a prerequisite for this feat.

Nerve Strikes — Through careful study of the anatomy and endless practice delivering the correct Ki strike to pressure points on an opponent's body, the exemplar masters the ability to incapacitate his opponents quickly with one well-placed blow. Exemplars who possess this feat and attack an opponent to cause subdual damage score x4 damage on critical hits. Prerequisites for this feat include being a monk of 10th level or an exemplar of 10 HD, and possessing a Wisdom of 13+.

Ki Projection — Master exemplars are able to project their Ki force over a distance to effectively make open-hand attacks against a remote foe as if the foe were within melee range. This effect has a range of the exemplar's HD (or monk's level) x3 in feet. The exemplar may not make more than one of his hand strikes into a Ki Projection attack each round, but he could still take a move action or use other attacks on foes within normal melee range if he is using a full action attack. Using Ki Projection does invite attacks of opportunity, however, just as any other ranged attack made from melee. Ki Projection can also be used as a very limited form of linear telekinesis to push small objects in a straight line away from the exemplar or to draw a small object toward the exemplar. This feat can only be mastered by a 12-HD or higher exemplar (12th-level or higher monk) with a Wisdom of 15+.

Cloud Running — Exemplars practice running over fragile surfaces while using their Ki to lighten their body. Through progressive practice on rice-paper floors, then sand, then water, and then the thinnest of ribbons stretched between poles, the exemplars master the ability to run so lightly they seem to levitate over the ground. Bards speak of exemplars running off cliffs to race across the clouds themselves.

As long as the exemplar has some surface other than empty air to run upon, he may pass over it without falling. He can run over thick clouds, thin ribbons or water, but he must be running at full speed to use the feat. While using this ability, the exemplar is +2 on Move Silently skill checks and anyone attempting to track his passage has a +15 DC modifier to such attempts.

This feat can be learned by only 6+ HD exemplars (6th-level monks), with a Dexterity of 13+.

Fatling

Huge (Tall) Aberration

Hit Dice:	6d8+27 (54 hp)
Initiative:	-4 (Dex)
Speed:	5 ft.
AC:	14 (-4 Dex, -2 size, +10 natural)
Attacks:	Crush +8 melee
Damage:	Crush 2d4+4
Face/Reach:	10 ft. by 10 ft./5 ft.
Special Attacks:	Spells, envelop
Special Qualities:	Damage reduction 4/—, immunities, oil secretion, SR 15
Saves:	Fort +11, Ref -2, Will +7
Abilities:	Str 19, Dex 3, Con 19, Int 11, Wis 14, Cha 3
Skills:	Animal Empathy +10 (lard worms only), Concentration +5, Intimidate +6, Listen +3, Scry +4, Sense Motive +3
Feats:	Enlarge Spell, Great Fortitude, Quicken Spell, Toughness
Climate/Terrain:	Any
Organization:	Solitary
Challenge Rating:	5
Treasure:	Double Standard
Alignment:	Always neutral evil
Advancement Range:	6-8 HD (Huge)

Description

After the Divine War, the gods may have buried Gaurak the Gorger beneath the earth, never to escape, but that doesn't mean his vile influence can't still be felt on the Scarred Lands. The highest priests and most favored of Gaurak's servants (all of whom worship the Titan in secret, often at hidden shrines or in refuse pits) are blessed by their buried lord. Gaurak's favor is clear to those who know what to look for: A patch of jaundiced, greasy melons grows up somewhere near the followers' shrines. Eating these repulsive fruits transforms an intended individual into a reflection of the Ravenous One himself. The servant becomes a fatling, a grotesquely obese monstrosity around whom other adherents to the Titan gather to perform their disgusting rituals, in hopes of currying the buried Titan's favor. Repugnant as a fatling might be, followers of Gaurak who honor the creature would give their very lives to protect the Titan's chosen.

Fatlings are inhumanly repulsive masses, literally rolls upon rolls of greasy sallow skin. They constantly sweat a foul-smelling slippery oil that allows them to lumber their bulk around when they choose to move at all. Almost unable to raise their own limbs, fatlings receive the further gift of lard worms (qv.), creatures that inhabit the priests' folds and eat whatever might be trapped therein.

As repulsive as fatlings are, there is one piece of knowledge that makes them all the more disturbing: They were once human.

Combat

Although fatlings would seem defenseless, they're actually quite potent. Blunt weapons are harmless to them, thanks to the creatures' excessive tissue. Sharp weapons may cut through fat, but damage is merely cosmetic. The abominations are also highly magic resistant. Fatlings have a variety of spells at their disposal, and anyone who gets too close can be pinned and suffocated under layers of blubber.

Envelop (Ex): Fatlings can make grappling rolls to envelop enemies in their layers of skin. Once a fatling captures an opponent, he simply waits for the victim to suffocate, at which point the priest's lard worms begin the process of consuming the victim. A Strength or Escape Artist roll (DC 15) is required to pry one's self free of a fatling's folds. Up to two allies can help liberate a victim if he manages to get a hand or foot free before being trapped (Escape Artist roll — DC 13 — to do so). Each assistant reduces the DC of escape attempts by 2. An enveloped victim is considered to be drowning.

Immunities (Ex): Blunt weapons deal no damage to fatlings. Slashing weapons do half damage, before damage reduction is applied. Only piercing weapons are truly useful against fatlings.

Oil Secretion (Ex): Fatlings exude a noxious, slippery oil from their skin that helps them move (and when they don't move for long periods, this oil pools around them). Individuals following a fatling or who get within 10 feet of him have to make a Reflex save each round (DC 16) or slip and fall to prone.

Spells: Fatlings cast cleric spells from the Death, Destruction, Evil and Trickery domains at 9th level.

73

Feral

Hit Dice:	2-16d8+4-32 (13-104 see below)
Initiative:	+0
Speed:	30 ft.
AC:	12-26 (+2-16 natural)
Attacks:	Shortspear +4-24 melee
	or 2 claws +4-24, thrown spear +2-16
Damage:	Shortspear 1d8+2-8, claw 1d6+2-8
Face/Reach:	5 ft. by 5 ft./5ft.
Special Attacks:	Howl
Special Qualities:	Damage reduction 5/+1 or cold iron, darkvision 60 ft., outsider, packsoul
Saves:	Fort +1-8, Ref +1-8, Will +1-8
Abilities:	Str 12-26, Dex 10, Con 14, Int 9, Wis 8, Cha 5
Skills:	Climb +6, Listen +11, Move Silently +5, Spot +9, Swim +9, Wilderness Lore +10
Feats:	Power Attack, Run, Track
Climate/Terrain:	Any
Organization:	Pack (1-15)
Challenge Rating:	See below
Treasure:	Standard
Alignment:	Always chaotic evil
Advancement Range:	None

Description

When seen in the Scarred Lands, ferals seldom have a purpose other than the utter destruction of anything in their wake. They are dispatched to the world at the whim of the demon god Vangal to please him with the path of rape and murder and other atrocities they leave in their wake. With a limitless appetite for bloodshed and the destruction of anything civilized, a pack of ferals falls upon a village and leaves naught but a crudely designed temple of gore and rubble to their god.

Fabricated from the most brutish souls that make their way into the Abyssal Volcano that is Vangal's home-realm, a single soul is splintered into as many as 15 parts to create a pack of Ferals. Forged thus from a single wicked soul, a pack of Ferals can operate with one mind. Their most fearsome aspect, however, is the fact that if any of the members are destroyed, their vital energy simply flows back into the remaining pack members to make them stronger. Thus destroying an entire pack of ferals becomes a progressively harder task.

Ferals also possess a keen tracking ability and instinctive sense of the wilds. They are occasionally used to hunt down those who have caught Vangal's attention or who possess some item or guard some person coveted by Vangal or one of his mortal priests.

Combat

Ferals always seek open ground to fight, preferring to spread out and attack foes from all sides. They use

crude spears to injure before closing it to finish a victim with their clawed hands.

Outsider: Ferals manifested in the Scarred Lands are less potent than they in their otherworldly form, and do not receive all of the normal immunities of being an outsider. Still, they do not sustain damage from any non-magical flame or cold attacks, and they are immune to poison.

Packsoul (Ex): Any single pack of ferals shares one soul. When any feral of that pack dies, the remaining pack members gain +1 Strength, +1 HD (and thereby +6 hit points), and +1 AC immediately.

Any pack of 15 ferals is composed of 2 HD creatures. As pack members are killed, the HD of each member escalates to 3 HD, 4 HD, etc. on up to a single remaining feral possessing 16 HD. Each feral's Strength escalates similarly from 12-26 (10 + their HD). A feral's saving throw modifiers are equal to half its HD, and the challenge rating of defeating a feral is one-third of its HD.

Note that if multiple feral pack members are killed at once (caught in an area-of-effect spell, for example) all surviving pack members still escalate based on the number of pack members killed.

Firedrake

Large (Long) Beast

Hit Dice:	8d10+48 (81 hp)
Initiative:	+3 (Dex)
Speed:	110 ft.
AC:	16 (-1 size, +3 Dex, +4 natural)
Attacks:	Bite +10 melee, 2 claws +5 melee
Damage:	Bite 1d10+3; claw 1d6+3
Face/Reach:	5 ft. by 10 ft./5 ft.
Special Attacks:	Living furnace, fiery death
Special Qualities:	Fire resistance
Saves:	Fort +12, Ref +5, Will +0
Abilities:	Str 16, Dex 17, Con 22, Int 2, Wis 7, Cha 6
Skills:	Balance +6, Climb +4, Hide +6, Jump +5, Listen +7, Move Silently +5, Spot +6
Feats:	Cleave, Combat Reflexes
Climate/Terrain:	Volcanoes and subterranean geysers
Organization:	Solitary, Pack (1-6 Adults)
Challenge Rating:	5
Treasure:	Standard
Alignment:	Always neutral
Advancement Range:	6-10 HD (Large)

Description

The firedrake is a large, wingless lizard that's found primarily near sources of geothermal heat such as geysers, dormant volcanoes and subterranean lava flows. The skin of the firedrake is knobby and black, like newly-forged iron, with numerous small, oval nodules running along its back that glow like rubies when exposed to firelight.

Firedrakes are fierce and aggressive, staking out a territory that supplies them with a ready source of heat and attacking any who violate their domain.

Occasionally, when a volcano becomes active and begins spewing lava, there are reports of firedrakes following flows and attacking anything in their path, apparently driven into a murderous frenzy by the volcano's activity.

The crystalline nodules on a firedrake's back are very rare and highly prized as forms of jewelry, with one egg-sized nodule going for as much as 2,000 gold pieces in some markets.

Combat

The firedrake attacks its victims with tooth and claw and inflicts horrible damage simply from the heat radiating from its body. When cornered in its own territory, the reptile tries to force opponents to fight dangerously close to scalding steam and lava flows, where it clearly has the advantage.

Living Furnace (Ex): Heat radiates from a firedrake like a blazing forge, and its touch ignites combustible material such as parchment, wood and clothes. Also, its claws and bite inflict an additional 2d8 points of heat-related damage with each successful hit.

Fiery Death (Ex): When it dies, a fire drake releases its heat energy in a final explosion that causes 3d8 damage to all victims within 30 feet (Reflex save at DC 16 for half damage). Unfortunately, this explosion often destroys or renders worthless most of the ruby-like nodules on its body. Roll 1d8-6 to determine how many remain intact.

Fire Resistance (Ex): The firedrake is immune to fire-based attacks.

Fleshcrawler

Medium-size Undead

Hit Dice:	5d12+15 (48 hp)
Initiative:	+4 (Dex)
Speed:	40 ft., climb (with tethers of sinew) 50 ft.
AC:	16 (+4 Dex, +2 armor)
Attacks:	Bite +7 melee, 2 claws +4 melee
Damage:	Bite 1d8+2; claw 1d4+2
Face/Reach:	5 ft. by 5 ft./5 ft.
Special Attacks:	Tethers of sinew, paralysis
Special Qualities:	Undead
Saves:	Fort +7, Ref +5, Will +3
Abilities:	Str 15, Dex 18, Con 16, Int 14, Wis 15, Cha 12
Skills:	Balance +5, Climb +15, Hide +10, Listen +3, Spot +5, Tumble +5, Use Rope (tethers of sinew) +20
Feats:	Armor Proficiency (Light), Blind-Fight, Multiattack
Climate/Terrain:	Underground and any land
Organization:	Solitary, cell (3–8) or host (7–12)
Challenge Rating:	4
Treasure:	Standard
Alignment:	Always chaotic evil
Advancement Range:	5–12 HD

Description

Fleshcrawler are wicked humans who have bargained with the dark lord and ultimately been taken to the Abyss where demon lords have made them undead and given them dark gifts. Fleshcrawlers are then sent back to the Scarred Lands to act as snatchers, bounty hunters or retrievers for a variety of demons.

At first glance, fleshcrawlers resemble pale humans in black leather armor sporting an array of ritualistic scars, brands and piercings. In the palms of their hands (and on the soles of their feet) are chitinous sheaths the size of a gold piece. From these small holes — as well as from their mouths — shoot lengths of grizzled flesh variously tipped with sharp hooks, claws or barbed spikes. The hand sheaths wield so-called tethers of sinews ending in barbed and bony spikes; the tether of sinew spat from the mouth (unrolling like a frog's tongue) ends in a hook, and is used for pulling back prey to be devoured. Fleshcrawlers use the tethers of sinews from the underside of their feet to anchor themselves to ceilings or walls, allowing them to hang like strange spiders in pursuit of their prey.

Fleshcrawlers use their tethers of sinews much as spiders use strands of silk, and they strategize well in three dimensions. They may hang from their foot tethers above doorways and attack their prey from above, or they may use them to climb walls, pull down a wall on opponents, or disarm an opponent.

The tethers of sinews retract almost instantaneously, and they do so with the fleshcrawler's full strength. A tether that gets trapped or severed is jettisoned, which appears to be no sacrifice to the fleshcrawler as the supply of tethers appears to be limitless.

Combat

Fleshcrawlers like to prepare ambushes for their chosen prey. When hunting in a cell, fleshcrawlers use pack tactics and work together like a well-oiled machine.

Tethers of Sinew (Ex): A fleshcrawler can shoot forth spiked or hooked tethers of sinews from its palms or mouth as a ranged attack (60 feet maximum) with an attack modifier of +5. Barbed spikes from the hands do 1d6 damage and snare the prey. If the fleshcrawler causes no damage because of its target's armor, the spike may catch on the prey's armor and allow the fleshcrawler to reel in its prey anyway. A roll that is one or two short of successfully striking an armored opponent still allows this effect. The sharpened hook at the end of the mouth tethers of sinew inflicts 2d6 damage and is covered with the fleshcrawler's paralytic saliva. A fleshcrawler may make three such tether strikes in a turn in lieu of its normal attacks. Furthermore, the fleshcrawler may attempt to sunder or disarm with these, even though they are ranged attacks. Fleshcrawlers additionally gain the use of the Point Blank Shot and Precise Shot feats for use only with the tether of sinew attacks.

Paralysis (Ex): The saliva of a fleshcrawler causes paralysis. A victim bitten by a fleshcrawler or hit by the hooked tethers of sinew from its mouth must succeed at a Fortitude save (DC 15) or be paralyzed for 3d6 minutes.

Undead: As undead, these creatures are immune to mind-influencing effects, poison, sleep, paralysis, stunning and disease. They are not subject to critical hits, subdual damage, ability damage, energy drain or death from massive damage.

Forge Wight

Tiny Elemental

Hit Dice:	6d8+24 (51 hp)
Initiative:	+3 (Dex)
Speed:	0 ft.
AC:	15 (+2 size, +3 Dex)
Attacks:	Special
Damage:	Special
Face/Reach:	2.5 ft. by 2.5 ft./0 ft.
Special Attacks:	Heat metal
Special Qualities:	Vulnerability, SR 13, immunities
Saves:	Fort +9, Ref +7, Will +4
Abilities:	Str —, Dex 16, Con 18, Int 4, Wis 4, Cha 4
Skills:	None
Feats:	None
Climate/Terrain:	Ancient forges
Organization:	Solitary
Challenge Rating:	4
Treasure:	None
Alignment:	Always neutral
Advancement Range:	None

Description

In ancient times, master smiths across the land would keep their forges hot through prayer and sacrifice to Thulkas, titan of iron and fire. In return, Thulkas would send a fire spirit to inhabit the smith's forge and keep it lit always. Unfortunately, the world changes; titans fall and the old smiths die.

Sometimes, if a castle was ruined in war or a smith died suddenly without an apprentice or heir, there would be no one to perform the rites to free the forge wight from its labor. A few of these forges remain in the depths of shattered fortresses or in towns long deserted, and the spirits trapped within their cold shells are twisted and bitter from their long, cold imprisonment.

Forge wights are fire spirits trapped in cold forges abandoned by the ages, and lash out at any unwary soul that passes too close. The spirit appears as a flickering tongue of pale flame, and it uses its power to affect metals carried by its victims. The spirit vents its anger on any mortal that stays within range but can be momentarily placated if hot coals are tossed into the forge. As soon as the coals die out, however, the spirit resumes its attacks, angrier than before.

An individual versed in the rites of Thulkas can perform the ceremony to free a forge wight from its prison, but there are very few clerics still alive who know such arcane lore.

Combat

The forge wight strikes out at its victims by heating and warping the metal weapons and armor they carry.

Heat Metal (Su): A forge wight can impart blistering heat to any metal object within 30 feet. The wight need only make a successful Intelligence roll (DC 12) to cause the metal on one person to become nearly red-hot. Weapons become too hot to hold and inflict 1d4 points of damage until dropped. Metal armor causes damage points to the wearer equal to its AC rating unless removed. The spirit can use this effect against only one target per round but may use the power an unlimited number of times. The effect lasts 2-8 minutes per use.

Immunities (Ex): Fire- and heat-based attacks cause the spirit no harm. Nor is it susceptible to critical hits, subdual damage or death from massive-damage trauma. A wight is immune to poisons, diseases, blinding, deafness, electricity and spells or attacks that affect living physiology. It cannot be stunned. Nor is it affected by attacks or spells of a mind-altering nature or spells based on healing/harming.

Vulnerability (Ex): A forge wight takes double damage from cold and water-based attacks.

Frost Ape

Medium-size Animal

Hit Dice:	2d8+9 (18 hp)
Initiative:	+0
Speed:	30 ft.
AC:	16 (+2 Dex, +4 natural)
Attacks:	Bite +4 melee; or club +4 melee; or rock +2 ranged; or ice spear +2 ranged
Damage:	Bite 1d4+2; club 1d6+2; rock 1d4+2; spear 1d6+2
Face/Reach:	5 ft. by 5 ft./5 ft.
Special Attacks:	None
Special Qualities:	None
Saves:	Fort +8, Ref +0, Will +0
Abilities:	Str 15, Dex 10, Con 16, Int 8, Wis 10, Cha 7
Skills:	Climb +8, Jump +5, Listen +2, Spot +3
Feats:	Alertness, Endurance, Great Fortitude, Toughness
Climate/Terrain:	Northern wastes
Organization:	Solitary or packs (2-6)
Challenge Rating:	1
Treasure:	Standard
Alignment:	Usually chaotic good
Advancement Range:	1-3 HD (Medium-size)

Description

The great apes now known as frost apes are not indigenous to the vast glacier continent of Fenrilik that they rule. They once inhabited the verdant jungle cliffs of the Lush Isle, guarding it with rough force against would-be intruders. When war errupted between the gods and Titans, the young god Chardun singled the great apes out for their strength and intelligence. He drafted them into service as soldiers against the armies of the Titans, stealing the entire race from their home and sending them to war. The impressment subsequently left the Lush Isle open for domination by the pirates of newly founded Bloodport.

What Chardun failed to account for was that the great apes would not kill intelligent creatures. While they would fight with savage ferocity, they only crippled their foes or pummeled them to unconsciousness. As long as it was within their power to allow a foe the chance to escape, they would do so, regardless of what tactical advantage it cost them. Although this leniency had served them well enough at home — where visitors knew to leave well enough alone — it proved disastrous on the battlefield. Despite superior prowess in small engagements and unlimited enthusiasm in large, open-field conflicts, the great apes' small modicum of mercy proved a greater liability than their prowess was worth. Furious that he had wasted his effort, Chardun banished the great apes to frozen, far-away Fenrilik.

Many of the great apes died in the first several years of their exile, but those that survived grew into a more hale and hardy breed known now as the frost apes. They are more bitter, harsh and brutal than their Lush Isle ancestors, but they still refuse to kill outright. They are not averse to letting an opponent die, but they do not force the issue.

Combat

Frost apes attack *en masse* with a basic grasp of infantry tactics. They surround their opponents, try to knock them down, then pound them with clubs, rocks and chunks of ice. They primarily attack an opponent's limbs, but a careful blow to the head suffices as long as it doesn't kill an opponent.

Garabrud, the Obsidian Hound

Huge (Long) Animal

Hit Dice:	23d8+115 (218 hp)
Initiative:	+2 (Dex)
Speed:	45 ft.
AC:	28 (-2 size, +2 Dex, +18 natural)
Attacks:	Bite +33 melee, 2 claws +28 melee
Damage:	Bite 3d12+12; claw 2d6+5
Face/Reach:	10 ft. by 20 ft./10 ft.
Special Attacks:	None
Special Qualities:	Damage reduction 25/+5, SR 38
Saves:	Fort +17, Ref +8, Will +7
Abilities:	Str 35, Dex 14, Con 18, Int 7, Wis 12, Cha 10
Skills:	Listen +14, Spot +10, Wilderness Lore +8
Feats:	Track
Climate/Terrain:	Any
Organization:	Solitary (unique)
Challenge Rating:	14
Treasure:	None
Alignment:	Always lawful evil
Advancement Range:	None

Description

Garabrud, the Obsidian Hound, is a thing of dread legend across the face of the Scarred Lands. Purported to be one of three great guardian mastiffs that served the titan Gaurak, the Glutton, the Obsidian Hound is the only such mastiff still seen roaming the land.

The Obsidian Hound's behavior is well chronicled by the bard Adrometus, who was the first to follow the hound and observe its tracking and killing behavior. Adrometus' ballads tell that the hound normally behaves as any other wild creature — sleeping and hunting. However, at seemingly random times, the hound is roused from its placid state and becomes the dread beast all of the Scarred Lands have come to fear. At these times, the hound begins to flawlessly track some newly designated prey — no matter how far away or hidden the hound's chosen prey may be. No normal or magical means has yet been found to hide the hound's prey from the beast.

The hound continues to close in on its prey, never resting and scarcely deviating from the most direct path. The beast tramples through villages and tends to ignore those seeking to hurt or deter it. Only a foe who can actually hurt the nigh-invulnerable hound might warrant its attention when it is tracking a victim.

Once the hound has caught and killed its prey (devouring them as well), it either immediately begins the chase for its next victim or resumes its natural state by taking up residence wherever it can find a food supply near where it brought down its latest prey.

For those victims fortunate enough to be far away from the hound when it begins its pursuit, the hound's coming is presaged in the victim's dreams. The victim's sleep is haunted by nightmares of the hound's baleful howl and of being run down and torn apart by the beast. The intensity of the nightmares increases the closer the hound draws to its prey. When the wizard Dolomar took refuge in the dwarven citadel at Burok Torn to escape the hound, it is said that the intensity of the wizard's nightmares drove him to suicide over the year the hound spent burrowing at the bedrock of the citadel to reach him.

No one knows how the beast selects its victims. Adrometus speculates that the god Chardun might have somehow gotten command over the hound since Gaurak's downfall, as most of the hound's victims seem to be those who have angered or disappointed the Conqueror.

Combat

Garabrud attacks with its powerful bite, and if its opponent is Size Large or bigger, the hound also rakes with its front paws.

Goblin Bear

Large (Long) Animal

Hit Dice:	10d8+50 (95 hp)
Initiative:	+4 (Improved Initiative)
Speed:	60 ft.
AC:	22 (-1 size, +13 natural)
Attacks:	Bite +14 melee and 2 claws +9 melee
Damage:	Bite 1d10+5; claw 2d6+2
Face/Reach:	5 ft. by 10 ft./5 ft.
Special Attacks:	Shoulder spines, neck-breaking shake
Special Qualities:	Thick-headed
Saves:	Fort +12, Ref +3, Will +3
Abilities:	Str 21, Dex 10, Con 20, Int 2, Wis 10, Cha 5
Skills:	Listen +2, Spot +2
Feats:	Alertness, Improved Critical, Improved Initiative, Sunder
Climate/Terrain:	Temperate forests
Organization:	Solitary
Challenge Rating:	6
Treasure:	None
Alignment:	Always neutral
Advancement Range:	8-14 HD (Large)

Description

The goblin bear is in fact neither a goblin nor a bear, more closely resembling a giant wolverine, with a blunt, muscular body, a short, toothy snout and long, sharp, curved claws on all four feet. The beast is the size of a small pony and has a glossy, reddish-brown pelt.

Goblin bears are voracious omnivores that have earned their name through aggressive assaults on travelers' campsites. Constantly searching for food to ease their all-consuming appetite, goblin bears have been known to brazenly walk into a camp and begin rooting through packs in search of provisions, insolently daring someone to do anything about it. Most travelers familiar with the breed wisely choose to stand aside and let

a beast eat what it finds, because the goblin bear is easily enraged and stubborn to a fault, fighting drawn-out, bloody battles over little more than a moldy biscuit and a strip of beef jerky.

If left alone, goblin bears are generally lazy creatures that eat what they can reach easily, ignoring the outraged cries of the camp and then finally moving on. On a more sinister note, however, there have been reports of some goblin bears that have developed an exclusive taste for fresh meat and thus provide far greater dangers to unsuspecting travelers.

Combat

An enraged goblin bear is aggressive and headstrong, attacking without regard for safety or survival and giving ground to no one, no matter how big or fearsome. Goblin bears prefer to leap onto their prey, bearing them to the ground and savaging them with tooth and claw, trusting to their spiny flanks to keep other attackers at bay.

Shoulder Spines (Ex): Goblin bears have twin ruffs of barbed shoulder spines that run from the point of the beast's shoulder all the way to the point of its hips. These barbs stand erect when the creature is enraged. Whenever an enemy makes a successful hit in melee combat against the goblin bear, the bear may make a free roll to hit with its spines, causing 1d6+5 damage if it succeeds.

Neck-breaking Shake (Ex): If a goblin bear gets a good enough hold on an enemy with its teeth, it shakes its victim savagely from side to side, intending to break the target's neck or spine. If the goblin bear causes a critical hit with its bite, it may automatically roll for damage from a neck-shake (2d10+5 damage in addition to the critical damage).

Thick-headed (Ex): The thick-headed goblin bear is immune to fear and mind-influencing attacks, as well as subdual damage.

Golem, Bone

Medium-size Construct

Hit Dice:	1d12+3 (9 hp)
Initiative:	+1 (Dex)
Speed:	30 ft.
AC:	13 (+1 Dex, +2 natural armor)
Attacks:	Claw +1 melee
Damage:	Claw 1d6
Face/Reach:	5 ft. by 5 ft./5 ft.
Special Attacks:	None
Special Qualities:	Immunities, variable construction, construct, damage reduction 5/+1
Saves:	Fort +4, Ref +1, Will +0
Abilities:	Str 10, Dex 12, Con 11, Int 1, Wis 10, Cha 11
Skills:	Open Lock +8
Feats:	Endurance, Great Fortitude, Toughness
Climate/Terrain:	Any
Organization:	Solitary
Challenge Rating:	1/2
Treasure:	Standard
Alignment:	Always neutral
Advancement Range:	None

Description

Bone golems are a favored tool of Scarred Lands necromancers, if a particularly dangerous one. They make excellent traveling bodyguards, grave robbers and collection agents for the more organized guilds of necromancers in the Scarred Lands' large cities.

Bone golems seem to house residual intelligence from the spirits of the dead from which the golems are constructed. This glimmer of intelligence makes the golems relatively easy to control, and they carry out complex lists of commands with plodding, methodical surety. They cannot speak, nor — it is assumed — can they hear any voice other than that of the one who created them. Their hands bend into various utilitarian shapes, making the golems — if not exactly master thieves — at least able to open locked doors and carry out their grim business.

The main flaw in the bone golem's design is that its body wears out very quickly. Shingles and flakes of bone rub off constantly, leaving dusty tracks and prints wherever the construct goes. A bone golem disintegrates completely over the course of a month. To stave off its inevitable decay, a bone golem must constantly incorporate new bones into its body. Many necromancers keep golems supplied by keeping them busy at collections work. However, one who cannot supply a golem sufficiently — it requires at least five complete human skeletons each month — may wind up the golem's next victim.

Considering the way they are created and the means by which they sustain themselves, bone golems are often surrounded by angry ghosts, which the golems' necromancer master must somehow keep in check.

Combat

Bone golems do not rely on trickery or subtlety in their attacks. When given a command, they pursue it straightaway, surmounting obstacles with only the requisite amount of force. When they are in need of sustenance, they batter their foes to the ground, strip the flesh from them, break off as much bone as they need and absorb it directly into their bodies.

Immunities (Ex): Bone golems are immune to cold. Piercing weapons do not harm them, and slashing weapons do half damage.

Variable Construction (Su): A bone golem's hands can assume the shapes of various simple tools such as knife-sized blades, hammerheads, cups, clamps wedges, crude saws and lock-picking prongs. This provides the golem with some ability to open locks, as reflected by the skill above.

Construct: Impervious to critical hits, subdual damage and or death from massive damage trauma. Immune to poisons, diseases, blinding, deafness, drowning, electricity and spells and attacks that affect respiration or living physiology. Cannot be stunned. Not affected by attacks or spells of mind-altering nature (for example enamoring or charming spells) or spells based on healing/harming. Fire and acid spells or attacks deal half normal damage.

Golem, Copper

Large (Tall) Construct

Hit Dice:	12d12+60 (138 hp)
Initiative:	-1 (-1 Dex)
Speed:	20 ft.
AC:	20 (-1 size, -1 Dex, +12 natural)
Attacks:	Fist +17 melee
Damage:	Fist 2d10+6
Face/Reach:	5 ft. by 5 ft./10 ft.
Special Attacks:	Electrical conduction
Special Qualities:	Construct, damage reduction 20/+1, SR 24
Saves:	Fort +13, Ref +3, Will +4
Abilities:	Str 23, Dex 8, Con 20, Int —, Wis 10, Cha 1
Skills:	None
Feats:	None
Climate/Terrain:	Any
Organization:	Solitary
Challenge Rating:	6
Treasure:	None
Alignment:	Always neutral
Advancement Range:	9-15HD (Large)

Description

Copper golems are constructed through the use of magical tomes or by wizards of 15th-level or higher. Construction requires 54,000 gp and two months. Construction also requires the services of a highly trained blacksmith (Craft skill of at least +10) and access to a prodigious amount of copper ore. The end result is an inspiring animated statue with a gleaming surface of beaten copper.

Copper golems obey the simplest of verbal commands given by their creators. Alternately, command can be bestowed upon another if the wizard fashions a magical copper ring (10,00 gp cost and three weeks work) at the time of the golem's creation. Whoever wears the ring may control the golem through verbal commands, but the golem runs amok, destroying the nearest object or creature it can see if the ring is destroyed. The golem's rampage continues until the construct is destroyed.

Combat

The golem attacks with one blow each round.

Construct: The copper golem is impervious to critical hits, subdual damage and death from massive damage trauma. It's immune to poisons, diseases, blinding, deafness, drowning and to spells or attacks that affect respiration or living physiology. It cannot be stunned. It's not affected by attacks or spells of mind-altering nature (enamoring or charming spells, for example), or by spells based on healing/harming. Fire and acid spells or attacks deal half normal damage.

Electrical Conduction (Ex): The copper golem does not receive its standard Spell Resistance to electrical attacks. Instead, these attacks deal no damage, but actually heal the golem. For every four points of damage the golem would have taken from the attack had it failed any applicable saving throw, the golem heals one point of damage. This conduction is the only means of healing a copper golem.

Once the golem has recovered to its maximum hit points, it stores the remaining electrical energy and discharges it on opponents when it strikes. It can discharge up to 10 points of stored electrical damage with each of its blows (in addition to its normal crushing damage).

The golem can store no more than half its maximum hit points in electrical damage, and any energy not discharged within 10 minutes of being absorbed dissipates out of the golem without effect.

Golem, Lead

Hit Dice:	20d12+120 (250 hp)
Initiative:	-3 (Dex)
Speed:	20 ft.
AC:	30 (-2 size, -3 Dex, +25 natural)
Attacks:	Pulverizing fist +36 melee
Damage:	Pulverizing fist 4d12+14
Face/Reach:	10 ft. by 10 ft./15 ft.
Special Attacks:	Poisonous gas
Special Qualities:	Damage reduction 40/+3, SR 31, construct
Saves:	Fort +18, Ref +3, Will +12
Abilities:	Str 38, Dex 4, Con 22, Int —, Wis 10, Cha 1
Skills:	None
Feats:	None
Climate/Terrain:	Any
Organization:	Solitary
Challenge Rating:	11
Treasure:	None
Alignment:	Always neutral
Advancement Range:	13-25 HD (Huge)

Description

Lead golems are constructed by wizards using an appropriate magical tome or by an 20th-or-higher level wizard using appropriate spells. Either way, it takes three months and 89,000 gold pieces to construct a lead golem. Due to the lead gases involved, the construction is hazardous work; at the end of the construction time, the wizard must make a saving throw as if he were struck by the golem's poisonous gas attack.

Lead golems are massive constructs. Their weight alone overwhelms the floors of most normal buildings, and their fists can batter structures to rubble in minutes. Their sculpture includes some aperture from which it releases its poisonous gas, commonly its mouth or a hole in its chest.

The dark elves of Dier Drendal are especially fond of creating lead golems, often crafting them with massive clawed hands with which to dig tunnels. Such golems have also been used in the dark elves' attacks on the dwarves of Burok Torn.

Lead Golems follow commands only from their creators. They normally understand and obey basic verbal commands, but can be "programmed" with fairly complex instructions if the creator invests about an hour drilling them into the golem.

Combat

Lead golem smash!

Spell Resistance: The lead golem receives its normal Spell Resistance against all spells except those that would transmute its metal into other substances. The spell must specifically target metal to bypass the resistance. If the golem fails any applicable saving throw, it is most commonly slowed to half movement and attack speed for the duration of the spell rather than actually being transmuted. The GM can decide the exact effects based upon the spell description.

Poisonous Gas (Su): Once every five rounds, a lead golem may billow out a 30-foot-long cone of poisonous gas. Anyone caught in the cone must succeed at a Fortitude save (DC 20) or pass out in a number of rounds equal to their Constitution and die in an equal number of rounds after they pass out.

Construct: A lead golem is impervious to critical hits, subdual damage and death from massive damage trauma. It's immune to poisons, diseases, blinding, deafness, drowning, electricity and spells or attacks that affect respiration or living physiology. It cannot be stunned. It's not affected by attacks or spells of mind-altering nature (enamoring or charming spells, for example), or by spells based on healing/harming. Fire and acid spells or attacks deal half normal damage.

Golem, Mithril

Gargantuan (Tall) Construct (Golem)

Hit Dice:	30d12+450 (645 hp)
Initiative:	-3 (Dex)
Speed:	50 ft.
AC:	45 (-4 size, -3 Dex, +42 natural)
Attacks:	Fist +46 melee, stomp +41 melee
Damage:	Fist 6d10+20; stomp 4d20+20
Face/Reach:	30 ft. by 30 ft./15 ft.
Special Attacks:	None
Special Qualities:	Damage reduction 60/+4, SR 35, construct
Saves:	Fort +32, Ref +7, Will +16
Abilities:	Str 50, Dex 4, Con 40, Int —, Wis 10, Cha 1
Skills:	None
Feats:	None
Climate/Terrain:	Any
Organization:	Solitary (unique)
Challenge Rating:	18
Treasure:	None
Alignment:	Always neutral
Advancement Range:	None

Description

The priests of Corean tell the tale that the Mithril Golem was forged by their god to use against the titan Kadum in the Divine War. The myth holds that the Mithril Golem succeeded in holding Kadum by its tail for but an instant, but that was long enough for the bestial titan to be gutted and chained by the gods. However, Kadum's tremendous strength warped and damaged the otherwise indestructible Mithril Golem. After the Divine War, the golem's purpose fulfilled, Corean left the Mithril Golem behind on the land rather than taking it to the god's home.

While some heretics doubt such an origin, it is certain that following the Divine War, a colossal statue of nigh-indestructible metal was discovered on the coast of the Blood Sea. Acting on visions from their god, the priests of Corean constructed a temple around the statue, and from that temple has sprung the rapidly growing city of Mithril.

For the past 150 years, the Mithril Golem has stood motionless while the Mithril Temple of Corean and a growing city have been constructed around it. The faithful have no doubt that their god would rouse his construct to action should he ever desire its service — such as to answer the prayers of one of his high priests or to defend the city over which the Mithril Golem holds its silent vigil. Indeed, if the unfaithful seek proof of such, they need only look to the time when the priests and paladins of Mithril prayed to Corean to deliver unto them weapons of righteousness so as to cleanse the Blood Sea coast of the titan races.

A week later, one small finger from the Mithril Golem miraculously broke off and crashed to the ground. The mithril metal of the finger was melted in magical fire and forged into the holy swords of the paladins of Mithril.

Combat

The Mithril Golem uses its monolithic fists to pulverize nearly anything it hits. In addition to its fist attack, it can stomp any target of Size Large or smaller. It can stomp with one foot per round and can target all opponents in a 10-foot-by-10-foot area provided none of the targets in that area are Size Huge or larger

Construct: The Mithril Golem is impervious to critical hits, subdual damage and death from massive damage trauma. It's immune to poisons, diseases, blinding, deafness, drowning, electricity and spells or attacks that affect respiration or living physiology. It cannot be stunned. It's not affected by attacks or spells of mind-altering nature (enamoring or charming spells, for example), or by spells based on healing/ harming. Fire and acid spells or attacks deal half normal damage.

Golem, Silver

Medium-sized Construct (Golem)

Hit Dice:	6d12+24 (63 hp)
Initiative:	+4 (Dex)
Speed:	30 ft., fly 90ft.
AC:	23 (+4 Dex, +9 natural)
Attacks:	2 Claws +9 melee
Damage:	Claw 1d6+3
Face/Reach:	5 ft. by 5 ft./5ft.
Special Attacks:	Flame gout
Special Qualities:	SR 18, damage reduction 20/+1, construct
Saves:	Fort +9, Ref +6, Will +2
Abilities:	Str 16, Dex 18, Con 18, Int —/10, Wis 10, Cha 1
Skills:	None
Feats:	None
Climate/Terrain:	Any
Organization:	Solitary, patrol (2)
Challenge Rating:	5
Treasure:	None
Alignment:	Usually neutral
Advancement Range:	5-15 HD

Description

Silver golems are splendid-looking constructs. Usually humanoid in shape, with wings sprouting from its back, a golem is crafted in silver right down to each "feather" on its wings. Silver golems also sport a large red ruby somewhere on their bodies, commonly their foreheads.

Like other similar constructs, silver golems may be created by a wizard using a magical tome or by a 16th-level or higher wizard employing the proper spells. Construction also requires a skilled silversmith with a Craft (silversmith) skill of at least +12. The smith must be employed for four months. Once the smithwork is completed, the wizard must invest another month in creation of the golem. The materials cost is 54,000 gold pieces, at least 5,000 of which must come from a single ruby.

Silver golems understand and obey fairly long and complex instructions from their creators, including orders up to several sentences in length. For this reason, wizards often use silver golems as messengers, bodyguards and even as personal attendants.

A few rare manuals for silver-golem creation have been uncovered that are thought to have been penned by the god Corean himself. Such manuals create silver golems with a true rudimentary intellect of their own. Despite their apparent intelligence and consequent freewill, such golems have unerringly served their creators thus far.

Once a silver golem is destroyed, the ruby can possibly be pried from its housing and recovered. A successful Craft (jewelry) skill roll (DC 28) recovers the gem, failure means the ruby is shattered into pieces worth a total of 500 gold pieces. Assuming the heavy body of a silver golem can be taken to a smithy, it can be melted down into the equivalent of 30,000 silver pieces.

Combat

Depending on the situation and their instructions, silver golems usually attack from the air with their flame gout and then land to attack with their clawed hands. Unlike their larger plodding cousins, silver golems are quite fast and agile in combat.

Flame Gout (Su): Silver golems can issue forth a cone of fire 20 feet long from their ruby adornment. Anyone caught in the flames takes 3d6 points of damage or half that if they pass a Reflex saving throw (DC 15). The golem can use this attack every four rounds.

Construct: A silver golem is impervious to critical hits, subdual damage and death from massive damage trauma. It's immune to poisons, diseases, blinding, deafness, drowning, electricity and spells or attacks that affect respiration or living physiology. It cannot be stunned. It's not affected by attacks or spells of mind-altering nature (enamoring or charming spells, for example), or by spells based on healing/harming. Fire and acid spells or attacks deal half normal damage.

Golem, Wood

Medium-size Construct (Golem)

Hit Dice:	7d12+35 (80 hp)
Initiative:	-2 (Dex)
Speed:	15 ft.
AC:	18 (-2 Dex, +10 natural)
Attacks:	Fists +11 melee
Damage:	Fists 2d8+4
Face/Reach:	5 ft. by 5 ft./5 ft.
Special Attacks:	Thorns
Special Qualities:	Damage reduction 12/+1, weapon immunity (wood), SR 22, regeneration, wood construct
Saves:	Fort +12, Ref +0, Will +8
Abilities:	Str 18, Dex 6, Con 21, Int —, Wis 10, Cha 2
Skills:	None
Feats:	None
Climate/Terrain:	Any
Organization:	Solitary, grove patrol (1d4+1)
Challenge Rating:	5
Treasure:	None
Alignment:	Always neutral
Advancement Range:	5-10 HD

Description

Wood golems are human-sized constructs made from any hard wood that has died but not yet begun to rot. Wood golems are constructed by druids through the use of an appropriate magical tome or by a druid of 14th level or higher using appropriate spells. The cost is 20,000 gold pieces, and construction requires two months. If the druid spends an additional three months gathering components herself, she may eliminate the gold cost.

Once animated, the golem obeys simple commands given by its creator. However, for each week of the golem's animated life, the creator must roll a d100 and if the result is 01-03, the golem immediately loses its magical properties and becomes a lifeless husk.

Druid followers of the Earth Mother Denev are divided on the issue of constructing wood golems. Some see it as a heretical practice more akin to arcane magic than magic that involves the living embodiments of nature. Others feel that if the Earth Mother sees fit to grant them their incantations with which to construct a golem, then Denev clearly does not view these beings as heresy.

Combat

The wood golem attacks using its fists in a single pounding attack.

Thorns (Ex): As a free action, the wood golem may sprout thorns from its body. These deal an extra two points of damage when it hits with its fist attack. Anyone grappling the golem takes an automatic 1d6 damage each round.

Regeneration (Ex): The wood golem may regenerate one hit point per minute that it is in direct contact with a living tree. The golem cannot be healed any other way.

Damage Reduction 12/+1 (Ex): Wood golems ignore the first 12 points of damage from any strike from a non-magical weapon.

Weapon Immunity (wood) (Ex): Wood golems are immune to any strikes from wooden objects, including all weapons with a wood striking surface, whether such a weapon is magical or not. This also means two wood golems are immune to each other's attacks.

Spell Resistance: The wood golem receives this spell resistance as normal except against any spells specifically targeted to plants or wood. It receives its normal saving throw against such spells, but not its spell resistance.

Construct: As a creature of wood, a wood golem is impervious to critical hits, subdual damage and death from massive damage trauma. A wood golem is immune to poisons, diseases, blinding, deafness, drowning and spells or attacks that affect respiration or living physiology, and cannot be stunned. It is not affected by attacks or spells of mind-altering nature (enamoring or charming spells, for example), or by spells based on healing/harming.

Gore Beetle

Tiny Vermin

Hit Dice:	2d8+8 (17 hp)
Initiative:	+1 (Dex)
Speed:	90 ft., climb 90 ft.
AC:	18 (+2 size, +1 Dex, +5 natural)
Attacks:	Bite +3 melee
Damage:	Bite 1d6
Face/Reach:	2.5 ft. by 2.5/0 ft.
Special Attacks:	Gas sacs
Special Qualities:	Vermin
Saves:	Fort +7, Ref +1, Will –2
Abilities:	Str 8, Dex 13, Con 18, Int 1, Wis 6, Cha 5
Skills:	None
Feats:	None
Climate/Terrain:	Temperate to tropical urban or subterranean areas
Organization:	Solitary, nest (10-20 adults)
Challenge Rating:	1/2
Treasure:	Standard
Alignment:	Always neutral
Advancement Range:	1-3 HD (Tiny)

Description

The gore beetle is an armored insect the size of a small dog, with a head dominated by four compound eyes and a pair of large, saw-like mandibles. Gore beetles range in color from a dull brown to a grayish-black, and their carapaces are often crusted with clots of dried blood and flesh from eating carrion — hence their gruesome name.

Gore beetles are common sights in large cities or ruined castles, where there's plenty of refuse available for constructing nests and rotting meat available to feed themselves and their young. The primitive human natives within or at the edges of southern jungles actually venerate these insects, considering them gifts from the earth goddess that keep their villages clean. Most places, however, find the bugs a nuisance and put prisoners to work eliminating their nests.

Gore beetles collect bits of trash and waste and build low, irregularly shaped nests to guard their young and store food. They prefer to locate nests in dark, out-of-the-way places such as narrow, blind alleys and abandoned privies. Most times, the smell alone is enough to warn curious passersby away. Certain brave — or foolhardy — individuals nevertheless risk the mandibles of the beetles to carve open their noisome lairs and look for coins, jewels or other items dragged along with pieces of their former owners.

Combat

When defending their nests, gore beetles attack intruders aggressively, venting their gas sacs to irritate their foes and rushing forward to bite deeply with their mandibles. As long as a nest is threatened, the beetles fight to the death.

Gas Sacs (Ex): Gore beetles shunt waste gases from their digestive processes into a series of sacs located underneath their armor. When threatened, they vent this gas, inflicting nausea and eye irritation on their victims. Targets within 10 feet of a beetle must make a Fortitude save (DC 15) or suffer a -2 modifier to all rolls for 1d4 rounds. A beetle can use this attack once per day.

Vermin: Immune to mind-altering effects.

Gorgon, High

Medium-size Monstrous Humanoid

Hit Dice:	9d8+27 (67 hp)
Initiative:	+2 (Dex)
Speed:	30 ft., swim 30 ft.
AC:	19 (+2 Dex, +7 natural)
Attacks:	Scimitar +13 melee; or 8 bites +12 melee
Damage:	Scimitar 1d6+3; bite 1d4+2
Face/Reach:	5 ft. by 5 ft./5 ft. (snakes 20 ft.)
Special Attacks:	Poison, spells
Special Qualities:	Damage reduction 10/+1, immunities, SR 15
Saves:	Fort +9, Ref +5, Will +8
Abilities:	Str 17, Dex 15, Con 17, Int 15, Wis 15, Cha 11
Skills:	Alchemy +6, Bluff +3, Concentration +8, Decipher Script +4, Disguise +6, Hide +3, Intimidate +7, Knowledge (arcana) +6, Listen +3, Scry +2, Search +7, Spellcraft +3, Spot +5
Feats:	Ambidexterity, Alertness, Extend Spell, Quicken Spell, Weapon Focus (Scimitar)
Climate/Terrain:	Any land, often urban or subterranean
Organization:	Solitary, cabal (2-5)
Challenge Rating:	5
Treasure:	Standard
Alignment:	Usually lawful evil
Advancement Range:	8-12 HD (medium)

Description

One of the most twisted legacies that the Titans left behind is Mormo's parting gift to the world — the gorgons. These wretched creatures were birthed by the Serpentmother some 50 years before the Titanswar, and they served their mother obediently. They were certainly her most faithful creation. Now that Mormo has been hacked apart and buried, the gorgons work secretly to restore her.

There are two varieties of gorgon — the bestial low gorgon, and the humanoid high gorgon. Although nearly as different as humans and lions, both varieties of gorgon are repulsively interfertile; the females of both species can be fertilized by males of either kind. They lay clutches of 1d6 eggs, one in five of which typically hatches into a high gorgon — the rest become low gorgons.

A high gorgon resembles a solidly built human man or woman with slightly grayish, almost glistening skin. They have no body hair whatsoever — a fact that they often conceal with cosmetics, hoods or wigs. A small seam runs from the bottom of the breastbone down to just above the genitals. When the high gorgon wishes to reveal its true nature, the seam splits wide open, revealing a mass of intertwined serpents that strike out at the gorgon's enemies. High gorgons usually have yellow, amber or brown eyes, and their teeth are unusually perfect.

High gorgons speak Common flawlessly, and most know a few other languages. They can also communicate in the Gorgon tongue, which they keep secret from others. High gorgons often pose as members of obscure (and fictional) human cults, which generally convince adherents to grant a little more indulgence to the sects'… unusual customs.

High gorgons don't have an actual culture of their own; they imitate human society as best they can, all the better to fit in. They gather in small cabals to exchange information and magic, and they particularly prize any rumors that might lead to another piece of Mormo's severed remains. They have no real allies among the other races (save low gorgons), but they have been known to hire coal goblins, werewolves and even manticora as needed. The Hornsaw Forest is a place of high pilgrimage to high gorgons, who visit an underground temple there dedicated to the Titan's spilled blood.

Combat

High gorgons usually try to conceal their true nature if at all possible. They typically fight with weapons and spellcasting as if they were human, even to the point of adopting popular skirmish tactics. If there is no way to prevent their nature from being revealed, however, they pull their bellies open to bite at opponents with their serpentine heads. Their lairs are often defended with traps, magical and otherwise, as well as a kennel of low gorgons.

Poisoned Blade: High gorgons are in the habit of anointing their weapons with an acidic poison partially derived from their own. Anyone wounded by a high gorgon's weapon must make a successful Fortitude saving throw (DC 18) or suffer 1d4+3 additional points of damage.

Poison (Ex): The snakes growing from a high gorgon's belly are venomous. Anyone bitten by a snake must make a successful Fortitude saving throw (DC 19) or take 1d8 points of temporary Constitution damage. After one minute, the victim must make a second saving throw (same as the first) or suffer another 1d8 temporary Constitution damage. If a victim is bitten by multiple snakes during a gorgon's attack, the DC for the saving throw is raised by 1 for each bite after the first. For example, a character bitten by four snakes would have to make a Fortitude saving throw at DC 22 for the fourth bite. However, a victim may only suffer from one dose of venom at a time, ignoring subsequent bites until the initial venom does has run its course. Once the minute has elapsed and the venom has had its full effect, the character can be poisoned again.

Immunities (Ex): High gorgons are immune to poisons and sleep-based attacks, and they suffer half damage from cold-based attacks.

Snakes (Ex): A high gorgon can strike with up to eight snakes at once; these serpents can be severed if specifically targeted with an edged weapon (AC 20, 15 hp damage to sever). An average high gorgon has 10-15 snakes attached to its spine inside its abdomen.

Spells: Each high gorgon can still draw on a portion of its Titan-mother's power, granting the ability to cast spells as a sorcerer of a level equal to the creature's hit dice (usually 9th). They favor spells that diminish or warp their opponents, such as necromantic or polymorph spells.

Gorgon, Low

Large (Long) Beast

Hit Dice:	9d10+54 (103 hp)
Initiative:	+2 (Dex)
Speed:	50 ft.
AC:	20 (-1 size, +2 Dex, +9 natural)
Attacks:	Bite +14 melee, 2 claws +9 melee; or tail lash +14 melee
Damage:	Bite 4d4+6; claw 2d6+4; tail lash 1d8+6
Face/Reach:	5 ft. by 10 ft./5 ft.
Special Attacks:	Acidic spittle, pounce
Special Qualities:	Immunities, SR 18
Saves:	Fort +12, Ref +5, Will +3
Abilities:	Str 22, Dex 15, Con 23, Int 7, Wis 11, Cha 13
Skills:	Climb +8, Hide +4, Jump +8, Listen +8, Move Silently +7, Spot +5
Feats:	Run, Track
Climate/Terrain:	Temperate and warm, thick forests; broken lands and underground
Organization:	Pack (2-5), breeding herd (11-30)
Challenge Rating:	5
Treasure:	Standard
Alignment:	Usually neutral evil
Advancement Range:	8-12 HD (large), 13-15 (huge)

Description

It seems impossible to believe that the bestial low gorgons are related to their humanoid cousins, but that's exactly the case. Where the high gorgons are intelligent and subtle, the low gorgons are ravening and animalistic. Still, the blood of Mormo ties them to their bipedal cousins, and the two races are often found in one another's company.

A low gorgon looks something like a reptilian lion, with a ruff of writhing snaky tendrils where a mane would be. Its dark-green scales are thick, almost metallic, and its long, flexible tail ends in a bony knob like a mace.

Low gorgons are rather more common than their "high" brethren, but they still tend to avoid civilization unless they are imported by their kin. A few people have managed to train low gorgons as watchbeasts by raising them from the egg, but the gorgons have to be monitored carefully at all times lest they turn on their masters at the first sign of weakness.

Combat

Low gorgons are malicious brutes that seem to take exceptional pleasure in ripping living creatures apart with their teeth and claws. They stalk their prey for as long as they can, seeking to leap on the victim from above. A low gorgon typically focuses its claws and bite on one opponent, not relenting until it has felt its victim die in its jaws; it reserves its tail lash attack for those trying to flank it. When they hunt in packs, low gorgons demonstrate even further cunning, seeking out spellcasters, archers and other ranged combatants actively. (They even leap over the heads of defenders if necessary.) If directed by a high gorgon, low gorgons are capable of following complicated plans, although their natural impatience can sometimes hinder their efficiency.

Acidic Spittle (Ex): A low gorgon's saliva is remarkably acidic; the beast is capable of chewing through iron bars. Its bite attack inflicts an additional 1d6 points of acid damage to its prey. If the gorgon achieves a critical hit on its bite attack, the bite damage is doubled and the acid damage is tripled.

Immunities (Ex): Low gorgons cannot be poisoned.

Pounce (Ex): A low gorgon can leap as far as 30 feet (15 feet vertically) in order to attack with its claws; this attack is treated as a charge (+2 bonus to attack roll, -2 penalty to AC). It can attack in such a fashion from above. Thanks to its strength and agility, a low gorgon takes no damage from falls of 60 feet or less as long as it is conscious and mobile.

Great Harrier

Huge (Long) Beast

Hit Dice:	20d10+ 40 (150 hp)
Initiative:	+8 (+4 Dex, +4 Improved Initiative)
Speed:	40 ft., fly 150 ft.
AC:	12 (-2 size, +4 natural)
Attacks:	Bite +23 melee, 4 claws +18 melee; 2 wings +18
Damage:	Bite 2d6+5, claw 2d6+2, wing 1d6
Face/Reach:	10 ft. by 30 ft. / 10 ft.
Special Attacks:	Awesome presence, ward
Special Qualities:	Immunity, keen senses
Saves:	Fort +8, Ref +16, Will +5
Abilities:	Str 20, Dex 18, Con 15, Int 7, Wis 9, Cha 23
Skills:	Listen +20, Search +30, Spot +28
Feats:	Alertness, Flyby Attack, Improved Initiative, Power Attack
Climate/Terrain:	Forests and mountains
Organization:	Solitary, pair or cavalry patrol (5 - 8)
Challenge Rating:	8
Treasure:	Standard
Alignment:	Usually neutral good
Advancement Range:	21-23

Description

The greatest of beasts employed by the elves of Uria, a great harrier is a magnificent sight to behold in the skies of the Scarred Lands. During the Titans War, they were at the forefront of the Corean cavalries, talons unflinchingly rending the armies of their foes. In the present, though known mostly for their use in scouring the Scarred Lands for dragons and other great Titanspawn, harriers are mainly used to scout, patrol and defend Uria, one of the many islands west of Ghelspad. Difficult to train but amazingly loyal, these beasts are revered by Urians as an almost holy animal.

Non-combatant Urians on important missions often use them for travel as they can protect their riders from harm as well as take a battle to an enemy.

Rumors abound of wild harriers living in forest or mountainous regions, but as of yet, no true sightings have been confirmed. Should a harrier be captured, many nobles would pay a wealthy ransom for it.

Combat

In combat, a harrier is unrelenting. A victim usually can do nothing but look in awe as the screeching beast descends in a whirlwind of claws and fury.

Awesome Presence (Ex): A harrier is capable of entrancing foes with the terrifying nature of its magnificent beauty whenever it attacks, charges or flies overhead. Creatures with 20 or fewer Hit Dice (except for the Urians) within 210 feet of the harrier must succeed at a Will save (DC 21) to avoid this fear effect. On a failure, creatures with four or fewer HD become panicked for 4D6 rounds and those with five or more HD become shaken for 4d6 rounds.

Ward (Sp): A harrier, once per day, is capable of crafting a seal of protection around itself and its rider, which appears as a radiant sphere that encircles it. When used, the harrier and its rider gain a +10 deflection bonus to AC. This seal lasts for five rounds.

Immunity (Ex): Known as a symbol of valor, harriers are immune to any fear inducing effects.

Keen Senses (Ex): A harrier sees three times as well as a human in low-light conditions and four times as well in normal light. The harrier also gains a +8 bonus to Spot checks in daylight.

Flyby Attack: The harrier can attack at any point during, before, or after its move if it is flying.

Great Swan, The

Medium-size Animal

Hit Dice:	6d8+6 (33 hp)
Initiative:	+0
Speed:	10 ft, fly 100 ft., swim 15 ft.
AC:	20 (natural)
Attacks:	Peck +4 melee; wing slap +4 melee
Damage:	Peck 1d4-2; wing slap 1d6-2
Face/Reach:	5ft. by 5ft./5ft.
Special Attacks:	None
Special Qualities:	Blessing, damage reduction 20/—, SR 30
Saves:	Fort +3, Ref +2, Will +9
Abilities:	Str 7, Dex 10, Con 13, Int 18, Wis 18, Cha 18
Skills:	Animal Empathy +6, Escape Artist +8, Intimidate +6, Listen +4, Sense Motive +12, Spot +3, Swim +5, Wilderness Lore +4
Feats:	Alertness
Climate/Terrain:	Any
Organization:	Solitary
Challenge Rating:	3
Treasure:	None
Alignment:	Always lawful good
Advancement Range:	None

Description

When warrior-hero Adurn of Vesh fell at the Battle of Twisted Timbers, his crestfallen knights and men-at-arms set his remains adrift on a funeral pyre across Mountain's Tear Loch (now called Adurn's Tear). Although the army (interceding on behalf of the defeated dwarves of Burok Torn) had won its battle against Calastia and Boy-King Virduk, the spirit of Adurn's army was broken by the loss of its leader. It was only a matter of time before Virduk would rally his forces and strike back against the army that dared defy him. The priests tried in vain to appeal to Corean for aid, but the god would make no move since the battle was of their own choosing. In desperation, the priests accompanying Adurn's army prayed to Madriel the Redeemer for mercy, to help find a new champion who might rise to inspire the demoralized troops.

Almost immediately, the priests received a sign. Rather than burn out in the space of a night, Adurn's pyre burned for seven nights and cast a dancing light, in the shape of a swan in flight, across the looming Kelder Mountains. On the seventh night, Prince Thain, son of recently deceased King Gontric of the dwarves, descended from the mountains to thank his unsolicited allies, explaining that a great lowlands swan had called to him in his dreams and promised to save his people. It was then, upon Thain's arrival that a majestic swan took wing from the last ember of Adurn's pyre and disappeared beyond the horizon. Adurn's priests were no fools, and they beseeched

Thain to become the adopted lord of their army, creating a new alliance of man and dwarf against Virduk.

Whether this story is true or not, witnesses report sightings of a great, solitary swan all over the Scarred Lands, often in kingdoms where the people need an enlightened, just hero to lead them against oppression. It is said that anyone whom the swan — presumably the very embodiment of Adurn's soul — allows to touch it is blessed as a leader among men. Those who have been so favored make it a custom to bear a swan insignia as their heraldic symbol, although some imitators seek to gain the recognition that only these chosen deserve.

It is known widely that swan-images of any kind are outlawed in Calastia (where King Virduk's hatred of birds is ever-growing), and the animals are even hunted and killed in the kingdom.

Combat

The Great Swan never fights, not even in self-defense. If anyone should seek to attack it, it simply flies off beyond harm. It does the same to almost all who would try to touch it, except for those destined to lead kingdoms with an even and fair hand.

Blessing (Su): A person who touches the Great Swan is explicitly allowed to by the creature and is blessed as a result. He gains a point of Wisdom automatically, and he is capable of the Leadership feat thereafter, despite his level.

Grippett

	Large (Long) Beast
Hit Dice:	3d8+3 (17 hp)
Initiative:	+5 (+1 Dex, +4 Improved Initiative)
Speed:	30 ft., climb 20ft.
AC:	13 (-1 size, +1 Dex, +3 natural)
Attacks:	Bite +2 melee; 2 claws +0 melee; or tongue +5 melee
Damage:	Bite 1d6+1; claws 1d6; tongue 1d8
Face/Reach:	5 ft. by 15 ft./5ft. (15 ft. with tongue)
Special Attacks:	Swallow
Special Qualities:	Chameleon skin, mimic, darkvision 60 ft.
Saves:	Fort +4, Ref +2, Will +1
Abilities:	Str 10, Dex 13, Con 12, Int 6, Wis 10, Cha 11
Skills:	Hide +11, Listen +6, Move Silently +10, Spot +10
Feats:	Improved Initiative, Multiattack
Climate/Terrain:	Forests
Organization:	Solitary or pair
Challenge Rating:	3
Treasure:	None
Alignment:	Usually neutral
Advancement Range:	4-6 HD (Large)

Description

The grippett is a nocturnal, reptilian creature with striped skin and a large, prehensile tongue. Known for its abilities to blend into forests and mimic any noise it has heard, this creature lures unsuspecting adventurers into traps by imitating prey or fellow party members.

The grippett is capable of extending its tongue up to fifteen feet and can pull most smaller creatures right into its mouth to eat them whole. Larger prey is avoided or killed with the grippett's powerful jaws and claws, while the grippett uses its mimicry to join the chorus of its victim's own death scream.

A grippett resembles a large gecko lizard with a jaw that is hinged like a snake for swallowing prey. A typical grippett stands 6 feet high at the shoulder, extends some 20 feet from nose to tail. It weighs approximately 1,000 pounds. When not using its chameleon ability, its skin is a light brown or green laced with purple stripes. It has sharp teeth and claws, which it uses to climb effectively and hunt prey.

Combat

The preferred tactic of a grippett is to track a potential meal for long periods of time listening to noises that the grippett can then imitate. Then it finds a suitable hiding spot and waits while imitating these noises in hopes of luring prey. If the grippett succeeds in capturing prey, it climbs or runs to a safe spot to finish chewing its meal. If it fails to get a victim into its mouth, the grippett resorts to raking attacks with its claws and teeth.

Chameleon Skin (Ex): Grippetts receive a +10 bonus to Hide checks due to their ability to blend into their surroundings.

Mimic (Ex): The grippett can imitate any noise that it can remember. A successful Listen check (DC 19) is required to detect the ruse.

Swallow (Ex): Grippetts prefer to attack Size Small or smaller prey since it can use its tongue to reel such prey in and swallow them whole. The grippet's critical threat range with its tongue is 16-20, and if it succeeds with a critical hit with its tongue, the victim is pulled into the grippett's maw (instead of doing an additional die of damage). Once in the grippett's mouth, the victim can only attack with hand damage or with small melee weapons if they were already holding such when pulled into the maw. The victim takes 2d6 damage per round until dead (and then swallowed) or until the grippett dies. The grippett may not attack with its tongue while it has prey in its mouth.

Hag

More than simply witches or sorceresses, hags are a different breed of creature entirely — demented female monsters, corrupted by the influence of the titan of witchcraft. Women who have been cruelly ostracized from their homes, abducted by hags themselves or who delve too deeply into the mysteries of Mormo have all become hags. The dark blessings of Mormo infused these women with strange elemental power, allowing them to align themselves with the forces of the night and the darker aspects of nature. The arcane pact they swore with Mother Mormo keeps them from aging once they've achieved cronehood, at which point the passage of time does nothing but make her more powerful and more deeply attuned to her elemental power.

Hags typically embody all the less attractive features of old women: gaunt bodies, pendulous dugs, sharp noses, pointy chins, warts and hairy moles. This does not bother a hag at all. It is not for beauty that hags live, but for power. They receive it — at the cost of their humanity. Hags are huge, often standing 10 feet or more in height, a side-effect of the strange process that makes them what they are. As a woman becomes a hag, her teeth become longer and sharper, her skin hardens, she becomes wiry and tough, and she develops an understanding of the forces of nature, so that she is able to manipulate it in accordance with her will. On the whole, hags are deeply hateful individuals, despising the humanoid races with a passion and preying on them whenever opportunity permits. Hags frequently adorn themselves with the remains of their victims, wearing the bones, scalps or skins of those who have crossed their paths as horrific trophies.

Traditionally, any woman who was driven from her home, especially for unjust reasons, could become a hag by offering herself to Mormo for deliverance and retribution. Although Mormo, like all titans, cared little for actual prayers, her hag-children once used their divination powers to determine where next they might find a future sister. They spirited away likely candidates to their secluded wilderness lairs, there teaching the mortal women the dark ways of witchcraft bequeathed them by their colossal mother.

Even today, the hags still gather recruits, although their ability to create more of their ilk has been severely impaired by the severing of Mormo. They still select women who have suffered exile, although some will also choose young women from contented homes, plotting to ruin their young charges' lives out of spite. Female spellcasters who demonstrate strong magical talent and intense ambition are particularly prized targets.

The Metamorphosis

The hag feeds the woman a diet of strange fruits and herbs, raw fish, poisonous berries, gulls' heads, fungal tea or whatever bilious concoction is appropriate to begin the evolution. Step by step, the woman casts aside her humanity (or has it stripped from her by her "grandmother"); by the time she reaches late middle age, she has mastered the elemental ways of the hag women.

Untrained Hags

Not all hags are brought into being by other hags. There are some women who feel such deep hatred, anguish or rage that it sustains them through circumstances that would normally kill them. Sages are not quite sure how such creatures "spontaneously" erupt, although Yugaman has a theory, of course: hidden pools of Mormo's blood, bile or breast-milk shed during the Divine War.

Common Hag Powers

All hags have a strange affinity for the beasts of their terrain and are able to communicate with any animal or beast (magical or otherwise) native to their territory. All hags have some spellcasting ability and are treated as sorceresses. Several use charm effects to gather a bodyguard of creatures around them. Hags are also able to brew potions, and some may be talented at creating magical items of other sorts.

Hag, Brine

Large (Tall) Humanoid (Hag)

Hit Dice:	10d8+50 (95 hp)
Initiative:	+2 (Dex)
Speed:	40 ft., swim 80 ft., climb 10 ft.
AC:	20 (-1 size, +2 Dex, +9 natural)
Attacks:	Bite +13 melee, 2 claws +8 melee
Damage:	Bite 1d10+4; claw 2d8+2
Face/Reach:	5 ft. by 5 ft./10 ft.
Special Attacks:	Spells
Special Qualities:	Breathe water, darkvision 120 ft., scry
Saves:	Fort +14, Ref +6, Will +4
Abilities:	Str 19, Dex 14, Con 21, Int 15, Wis 13, Cha 14
Skills:	Alchemy +4, Animal Empathy +5, Handle Animal +10, Intimidate +10, Knowledge (ocean) +15, Scry +13, Swim +20
Feats:	Brew Potion, Great Fortitude, Lightning Reflexes
Climate/Terrain:	Deep ocean
Organization:	Solitary, pair
Challenge Rating:	6
Treasure:	Standard
Alignment:	Usually neutral evil
Advancement Range:	10-13 HD (Large)

Description

Brine hags are creatures of the deepest oceans, where they squat in lairs made of sharp stones, whale bones and sea shells. These gaunt monsters stand nearly twice the size of a man, with dark greenish-gray skin. Their noses and chins are cruelly pointed, their arms are disproportionately long, and their webbed, clawed hands and feet are unnaturally large. A brine hag often decorates the sea floor near her lair with rocks, bones, the wreckage of ships and anything else she can find to mark her territory. Brine hags with "apprentices" in training tend to pick caverns with air pockets or isolated islands so that their "granddaughters" can survive until the time of metamorphosis.

Reclusive in the extreme, brine hags rarely come to the surface, preferring to remain in the depths, away from the hated mortal races. From time to time, a brine hag may swim up to the surface, climb the side of a passing ship and drag a victim down to her lair as a means of putting variety in her diet. Other times, a hag might rise to the surface to frolic and ride the violence of a particularly fierce storm or to enter into battle with a storm hag. Innocent bystanders can and do get caught in the middle of the vicious battles between brine and storm hags. Some believe the hags deliberately fight when there are mortals at hand as a way of introducing an interesting random element into the conflict.

Brine hags frequently keep sharks as pets and guards for their demesnes. They may boast other marine creatures as allies and pets as well.

Combat

Brine hags fight intelligently, using their element to best advantage. They often open a combat by trying to hurl armored opponents into the water to drown, then attacking less heavily-armored foes with their terrible teeth and claws. Brine hags tend to use their spells to whittle down their foes' strength before combat or to execute last-minute escapes; brine hags prefer to taste blood on their tongues in combat and do not like fighting from a distance.

Spells: Brine hags are accomplished spellcasters, functionally the equivalent of 10th-level sorcerers (individuals may range higher or lower by up to five levels). They favor spells that control water and weather, as well as summoning spells.

Breathe Water (Ex): Brine hags can breathe in water or air, though they're more comfortable breathing the cold dense water of the deep ocean.

Scry (Su): When brine hags do take an interest in the surface, they are able to watch from a distance in their scrying shells, the iridescent shells of giant oysters that the brine hag has prepared for her own use. This scrying is sight-only and can be maintained for up to an hour a day; the hag may divide this time into multiple scrying sessions if she chooses.

Hag, Cavern

Large (Tall) Humanoid (Hag)

Hit Dice:	9d8+45 (95 hp)
Initiative:	+2 (Dex)
Speed:	50 ft., climb 60 ft.
AC:	23 (-1 size, +2 Dex, +12 natural)
Attacks:	Bite +13 melee, 2 claws +8 melee
Damage:	Bite 2d8+5; claw 2d6+2
Face/Reach:	5 ft. by 5 ft./10 ft.
Special Attacks:	Spells
Special Qualities:	Blindsight, immunities, damage reduction 5/+1
Saves:	Fort +13, Ref +5, Will +4
Abilities:	Str 21, Dex 15, Con 21, Int 17, Wis 13, Cha 15
Skills:	Alchemy +5, Animal Empathy +5, Climb +15, Heal + 2, Intimidate +8, Intuit Direction +5, Jump +7, Knowledge (nature) +10, Listen +5, Move Silently +10, Spot +8, Swim +5, Wilderness Lore +10
Feats:	Blind-Fight, Brew Potion, Endurance, Great Fortitude, Power Attack, Sunder
Climate/Terrain:	Underground (caverns only)
Organization:	Solitary, pair
Challenge Rating:	5
Treasure:	Standard
Alignment:	Usually lawful evil
Advancement Range:	7-10 HD (Large)

Description

Cavern hags are those hags who went underground and learned the secrets of earth and stone. By the time she attains full hag status, a cavern hag's eyelids have permanently grown together, making her stone blind — but no less dangerous for that. A cavern hag can smell an enemy's whereabouts to within inches.

The cavern hag devotes much of her time to her alchemy; her acute sense of smell allows her to easily distinguish one material from another, thus negating any handicap her blindness might otherwise give her. A cavern hag is torn between hate and resentment for all mortals and a buried longing for human companionship; most cavern hags compromise by making their lairs in deep caves near human settlements, where they can capture humans to torture and devour when the loneliness grows too acute. Subterranean beasts are the closest thing to a cavern hag's friends, particularly monstrous vermin; some cavern hags have even managed to tame barrow worms as pets.

Combat

A cavern hag generally prefers to ambush her victims. She almost always has means to extinguish intruders' light sources (particularly spells). Once her prey has been blinded, she sends in any pets she might possess to attack, hurling more spells as she advances. If a group seems particularly strong, she shadows them as they pass through her territory, picking off any stragglers one by one.

Spells: A cavern hag has the spellcasting ability of a sorcerer of a level equivalent to her hit dice. She favors spells that create darkness, manipulate stone and earth and summon monsters to fight for her.

Blindsight (Ex): The cavern hag can sense her surroundings and nearby creatures in total darkness by scent, hearing and the vibration of the air (which she detects through the fine hairs growing from her moles). She suffers no penalties in melee combat and can detect all foes within 120 feet as a sighted creature would (beyond that range, targets count as totally concealed). Negating the cavern hag's sense of hearing or smell reduces her blindsight, although she still fights as if using the Blind-Fight feat.

Immunities (Ex): Immune to illusions, visual effects, gaze attacks and other attack forms that rely on sight.

Hag, Ice

Large (Tall) Humanoid (Hag)

Hit Dice:	7d8+31 (62 hp)
Initiative:	+3 (Dex)
Speed:	50 ft., climb 10 ft
AC:	20 (-1 size, +3 Dex, +8 natural)
Attacks:	Bite +4 melee, 2 claws +9 melee
Damage:	Bite 2d8+1; claw 1d8+3
Face/Reach:	5 ft. by 5 ft./10 ft.
Special Attacks:	Breath weapon, heat drain, spells
Special Qualities:	Immunities, scent
Saves:	Fort +9, Ref +5, Will +6
Abilities:	Str 17, Dex 16, Con 19, Int 17, Wis 15, Cha 14
Skills:	Animal Empathy +10, Balance +5, Hide +5, Intimidate +10, Knowledge (nature) +10, Listen +5, Scry +8, Spot +5, Wilderness Lore (arctic) +10
Feats:	Iron Will, Toughness
Climate/Terrain:	Frozen or arctic land
Organization:	Solitary, pair
Challenge Rating:	6
Treasure:	Standard
Alignment:	Usually lawful evil
Advancement Range:	8-10 HD (Large)

Description

Wrapped in a tattered, dirty collection of the hides of their prey, ice hags haunt the northern lands, feeling it their sacred duty to protect the White Wastes of Fenrilik (where even the faceless giants do not tread) from incursions by humanoids. They haunt the wilderness outside settlements, avenging themselves on the mortals who once sent them outside to die of exposure.

Ice hags may dig dens in the ice for themselves and any attendant animals to sleep in. An ice hag may have various animal followers, from dire wolves to polar bears; they have also been known to strike pacts with sleet devils to share prey. At least one ice hag of notable age and cunning has positioned herself as the chieftainess of a tribe of ice ghouls, who bring her meat in exchange for her guidance and strength.

Combat

Unless her victim is a lone wanderer or obviously easy prey, an ice hag tends to order her menagerie of arctic allies to attack a party to soften the interlopers up. Once the party has been weakened — and she has evaluated their tactical preferences — the hag either attacks directly, using her breath weapon against the most dangerous spellcasters, or stalks the party, picking them off one at a time as they sleep. Her vicious claws and terrible strength serve an ice hag well in hand-to-hand combat.

Breath Weapon (Ex): An ice hag can breathe a cone of freezing air and sharp snow crystals at her enemy, causing 2d4 points of damage and blinding the victim for 1d4 minutes. A successful Reflex save (difficulty 15) halves the damage and prevents blindness.

Heat Drain (Su): The touch of an ice hag sucks heat and life from victims who fail a Fortitude save (DC 14). Each round the hag makes contact, if her victim fails the Fortitude save, she deals an additional 1d12 points of cold damage to her victim. Hit points drained in this way are added to the hag's hit point total, up to her normal hit points +10. Hit points above her normal max fade at the rate of one every 10 minutes. Any damage a hag inflicts in this way is in addition to her normal physical attacks; however, an ice hag may drain any given opponent's heat only once per round.

Spells: An ice hag is a potent spellcaster, with the full abilities of a sorcerer of a level equal to her hit dice.

Scent (Ex): The ice hag can sense creatures by smell with a range of 80 feet (if she's downwind), 20 feet (if she's upwind) or 40 feet (if the air is still).

Immunities (Ex): Ice hags are immune to cold and take double damage from fire on a failed saving throw. They are also immune to paralysis and sleep effects.

Hag, Moon

	Large (Tall) Humanoid (Hag)
Hit Dice:	12d8+96 (150 hp)
Initiative:	+4 (Dex)
Speed:	60 ft., climb 20 ft., fly 60 ft., swim 30 ft.
AC:	24 (-2 size, +4 Dex, +12 natural)
Attacks:	Bite +11 melee, 2 claws +16 melee
Damage:	Bite 2d8+2; claw 2d8+5
Face/Reach:	5 ft. by 5 ft./10 ft.
Special Attacks:	Stunning touch, spells
Special Qualities:	Flight, invisibility, damage reduction 10/+2, SR 16, magic items
Saves:	Fort +12, Ref +8, Will +12
Abilities:	Str 20, Dex 18, Con 27, Int 17, Wis 18, Cha 18
Skills:	Animal Empathy +10, Climb +5, Heal + 10, Intimidate +12, Intuit Direction +5, Jump +7, Knowledge (arcana) +5, Knowledge (nature) +10, Listen +5, Move Silently +3, Scry + 15, Spellcraft +10 Spot +5, Swim +5, Wilderness Lore +10
Feats:	Blind-Fight, Brew Potion, Craft Wand, Empower Spell, Sunder
Climate/Terrain:	High mountains and underground
Organization:	Solitary, pair
Challenge Rating:	9
Treasure:	Standard
Alignment:	Usually lawful evil
Advancement Range:	13-18 HD (Large)

Description

The most powerful of all the Scarred Lands' hags, moon hags hold dominion over nature, madness and night. These monstrous crones stand twice the height of a man when they draw themselves fully upright; their dark skin gleams with strange oils and their wide eyes shine with madness. They typically prefer to live in high, craggy mountains or deep woods. They choose only the bitterest and most magically apt women as candidates for the metamorphosis.

A moon hag's boundaries are often marked with piles of blood-stained stones and odd bundles of bones and sticks. Anyone who wanders past these signs, whether from ignorance or recklessness, takes his life into his own hands. Moon hags have a powerful affinity for the beasts of the night; their allies have been known to include bat devils, murdersprites and even high or low gorgons. Coal goblins, werewolves, harpies and other night-beasts faithful to Belsameth avoid moon hags, who in return hate the newcomers and their goddess.

Combat

A moon hag likes to enthrall her victims with spells before she closes in for the kill. She takes a deep

delight in sowing terror and confusion in her enemies. She frequently enters the presence of her enemies unseen, then begins using her spells and magic items to best effect. After her allies have scattered her foes, the moon hag attacks physically, slashing with her huge claws and biting with her enormous teeth.

Invisibility (Su): A moon hag may turn invisible at will but only during the night hours. Her invisibility is dispelled if she attacks, but she may reactivate it the next round.

Stunning Touch (Ex): Anyone hit by a moon hag must succeed on a Will save (DC 16) or become stunned for 1d6 rounds. Multiple hits require multiple saves.

Flight (Su): A moon hag can fly as quickly as she can run.

Spells: Moon hags, as the most powerful spellcasters among hagkind, have access to the spellcasting power of a sorcerer two levels higher than the hag's hit dice. They tend to use a mix of beguiling, stealth and necromantic spells. They may also cast divine spells from the Air, Animal, Healing, Luck and Water domains as a cleric of level equal to the hag's hit dice.

Magic Items: A moon hag will usually carry at least one wand and two potions that she crafted herself. Such items are usable by mortals, but often have unpleasant side effects — a wand might curse its wielder with ugliness, a potion might cause rapid hair growth while in effect, and so on.

Hag, Storm

	Large (Tall) Humanoid (Hag)
Hit Dice:	9d8+45 (85 hp)
Initiative:	+5 (Dex)
Speed:	40 ft., fly 80 ft. (good)
AC:	19 (-1 size, +5 Dex, +5 natural)
Attacks:	Bite +7 melee, 2 claws +7 melee, and 2 hair grapples +12 melee
Damage:	Bite 2d6+2; claw 1d8+2; hair grapple special
Face/Reach:	5 ft. by 5 ft./10 ft. (20 ft. for hair)
Special Attacks:	Hair grapple, spells
Special Qualities:	Damage reduction 5/+1, flight
Saves:	Fort +8, Ref +11, Will +6
Abilities:	Str 19, Dex 20, Con 20, Int 12, Wis 16, Cha 14
Skills:	Intuit Direction +10, Knowledge (nature) +5, Listen +8, Spot +5
Feats:	Brew Potion, Flyby Attack
Climate/Terrain:	Aerial
Organization:	Solitary, pair
Challenge Rating:	7
Treasure:	None
Alignment:	Usually chaotic evil
Advancement Range:	10-12 HD (Large)

Description

Storm hags are horrible crones that have shrugged off the tyrannical grip of gravity and mastered the secrets of the air. Once a storm hag reaches the point in her maturation process where she takes to the air, she dislikes touching the ground again; she will only do so in order to instruct a "granddaughter" or to brew a potion. Storm hags sleep in dark clouds during the day and come out to hunt at dusk. Their skin is a silvery, dusky gray like that of a storm cloud, their yellow eyes flash like lightning, and their long white hair balloons out around them as if constantly stirred by wind.

A storm hag hunts her prey from above, swooping down to carry off children or other small creatures to devour. Storm hags are leaner and more nimble than their sister hags, granting them the ability to soar and swoop as nimbly as bats. Of all the hags, the storm hag is least likely to have animal or beast allies at her beck and call; few creatures can keep up to her liking.

Combat

Storm hags are prone to flying down, catching their prey in their hair and then swooping back up into the sky, where they maul their opponents one-on-one with their cruel claws and terrible teeth. If a storm hag is not happy with the way a struggle is going, she lets her prey drop to the ground and tries again after the fall has softened it up a bit.

Hair Grapple (Ex): The long hair of a storm hag often appears to be blowing in the wind, but it's actually under her full control. Storm hags get an additional two grappling attacks per round; these provoke no attacks of opportunity. The hag can strangle or constrict grappled victims on successive rounds (1d6+4 damage per round) while making further grapple attacks. At most, a storm hag can entangle 4 medium-size, 6 small, 12 tiny or 24 fine creatures at once. The hair of a storm hag has a Strength rating of 15; it takes 10 points of damage from an edged weapon to sever a given lock.

Spells: Storm hags have the spellcasting ability of 9th-level druids. They favor weather-controlling magic above all other spells.

Flight (Su): A storm hag is capable of wingless flight.

Hag, Swamp

Large (Tall) Humanoid (Hag)

Hit Dice:	7d8+28 (59 hp)
Initiative:	+3 (Dex)
Speed:	40 ft., swim 40 ft.
AC:	17 (-1 size, +3 Dex, +5 natural)
Attacks:	Bite +4 melee, 2 claws +9 melee
Damage:	Bite 1d8+1; claw 1d6+3
Face/Reach:	5 ft. by 5 ft./10 ft.
Special Attacks:	Spells
Special Qualities:	Camouflage, immunities
Saves:	Fort +6, Ref +5, Will +7
Abilities:	Str 17, Dex 16, Con 19, Int 17, Wis 15, Cha 11
Skills:	Animal Empathy +5, Climb +10, Handle Animal +5, Heal + 5, Hide +4, Intimidate +4, Intuit Direction +3, Knowledge (nature) +10, Listen +5, Move Silently +10, Spot +10, Swim +7, Wilderness Lore +10
Feats:	Brew Potion, Track
Climate/Terrain:	Warm swamps or bayous
Organization:	Solitary, pair
Challenge Rating:	5
Treasure:	Standard
Alignment:	Usually lawful evil
Advancement Range:	8-10 HD (Large)

Description

Swamp hags lair in the deep bogs, swamps, bayous and marshlands that civilized creatures avoid. They are the smallest of their kind, rarely reaching nine feet in height. Their skin is typically a greenish brown, and their eyes are a bright, sickly yellow. A hag typically likes to "enhance" her appearance with whatever materials are at hand —moss, crocodile skulls, iridescent beetle shells and myriad twigs, teeth, bones, skins and baubles are all likely adornments. The more bones a swamp hag wears, the more power over life and death she displays.

Swamp hags are remarkably religious and share a common devotion for "Mama Mormo." Although they dislike leaving their fens, swamp hags are more willing than most to aid attempts to restore Mormo to health and power. They often cooperate with high gorgons toward this very end.

Like their cousins, swamp hags enjoy the company of beasts. These hags tend to have the largest menageries of any of their ilk. A swamp hag is rarely found without a contingent of monstrous vermin, reptiles or other swamp beasts as pets and bodyguards. Swamp hags are strangely domestic and build huts that they guard ferociously.

Combat

Swamp hags are wily opponents. Their deadliest advantage is their knowledge of the swamps they inhabit. By using their camouflage abilities, swamp hags can track a party for hours or days, harrying and weakening them if necessary. When the hag decides to enter combat, she always does so on her terms. A swamp hag will typically have her beasts enter the battle first to scatter or weaken the party, then the hag herself will enter the fray. Swamp hags despise clerics. While stalking a group, a swamp hag will identify the priests and healers in the party and make sure that they are poisoned by spiders, crushed by snakes or eaten by crocodiles before she turns her attention to any other opponents.

Spells: Like their sisters, swamp hags are quite talented at the magic arts. A swamp hag has the spellcasting power and spells of a 7th-level druid. They prefer spells that convince animals and plants to attack, ensnare or otherwise overbear their foes.

Camouflage(Ex): Swamp hags have greenish-brown skin that makes them hard to spot in a swamp, but they can also change color to blend even more perfectly with their surroundings. When in swampy terrain, they gain a natural +15 bonus to Hide checks as long as they remain perfectly still.

Immunities (Ex): Swamp hags are immune to all poisons and disease.

Halfling

Small Humanoid

Hit Dice:	1d8-1 (3 hp)
Initiative:	+2 (Dex)
Speed:	20 ft., climb 10 ft.
AC:	14 (+1 size, +2 Dex, +1 padded armor)
Attacks:	Club +1 melee; stone +6 ranged
Damage:	Club 1d6-1; stone 1d4-1
Face/Reach:	5 ft. by 5 ft./5 ft.
Special Attacks:	Throwing
Special Qualities:	Fearless
Saves:	Fort +0, Ref +3, Will +1
Abilities:	Str 8, Dex 14, Con 10, Int 12, Wis 12, Cha 13
Skills:	Balance +2, Climb +2, Hide +4, Jump +2, Listen +2, Move Silently +2, Spot +2, Tumble +2
Feats:	Alertness
Climate/Terrain:	Temperate lands, often on the outskirts of other civilized races' communities
Organization:	Outing (3-6), gathering (7-20, plus 1 leader of 3rd to 4th level), community (21-100, plus 1 leader of 5th to 7th level, 2-3 advisors of 3rd or 4th level, and 1 2nd-level constable per 15 people)
Challenge Rating:	1/4
Treasure:	Standard
Alignment:	Usually neutral
Advancement Range:	By character class

Description

The halflings of the Scarred Lands are in many ways a beleaguered people. Though they claim their own origins, faith, culture and society, they are often dismissed, abused or overlooked by other "civilized" races, probably because of halflings' diminutive stature and largely non-confrontational demeanor. Perhaps the most widely accepted origin for halflings (accepted by other races anyway) is that the little people were birthed by the deities to quell animosity between the gods' chosen humans and dwarves. Halflings bear qualities of both, after all — they're similar in size to dwarves, and have agrarian inclinations like humans. These "proxies" also tend to live on the outskirts of other races' communities, particularly those of humans and dwarves. Is it any wonder, then, that their more aggressive and self-involved neighbors take halflings for granted? Intruding on their lands, trampling their crops and sometimes waging war on halflings' very villages and homesteads.

Only King Virduk of Calastia has shown anything akin to kindness to the halfling race, though humans and halflings alike generally see this for what it is: a tactic to pit the halflings against the king's dwarven enemies.

Given their abuse, halflings of the Scarred Lands have developed a wariness of other races, especially humans and dwarves. Some entire communities have a transient existence, staying in places only as long as they can support the travelers. Adventurers often emerge from halfling culture to better their lot in life and may come to trust individuals of other races, as long as that confidence is earned.

Although the halflings of the Scarred Lands would like nothing better to live in peace and comfort, they are rarely able to, eking out a meager existence and sometimes being quite thin as a result.

Halflings speak their own language and Common. Most also speak Dwarven.

Combat

Halflings aren't born for the battlefield; they're typically too small and passive to defeat armies. When roused, however, they resort to guerrilla tactics, striking and retreating, staging ambushes and raining missiles down upon a foe.

Throwing: Halflings receive a +2 bonus to attack rolls with thrown weapons. This bonus is included in their Attack statistic above.

Fearless (Ex): Due to their ancestral and cultural abuse, halflings have developed a fearlessness and receive a total +2 morale bonus on saving throws against fear.

Hamadryad

Medium-size Plant

Hit Dice:	6d8+30 (57 hp)
Initiative:	+2 (Dex)
Speed:	50 ft., climb 30 ft.
AC:	20 (+2 Dex, +8 natural)
Attacks:	Strike +10 melee
Damage:	Strike 2d8+4
Face/Reach:	5 ft. by 5 ft./5 ft.
Special Attacks:	Sneak attack
Special Qualities:	Camouflage, plant, sylvan allies
Saves:	Fort +10, Ref +4, Will +7
Abilities:	Str 19, Dex 14, Con 20, Int 13, Wis 15, Cha 17
Skills:	Animal Empathy +1, Bluff + 4, Diplomacy +4, Escape Artist +4, Heal +2, Hide +8, Intuit Direction +8, Listen +4, Move Silently +7, Search +3, Spot +4, Wilderness Lore +10
Feats:	Alertness, Endurance, Improved Trip, Run, Track
Climate/Terrain:	Subarctic, temperate or subtropical forests
Organization:	Solitary, glade (2-7)
Challenge Rating:	5
Treasure:	Standard
Alignment:	Usually neutral
Advancement Range:	4-9 HD (Medium-size); 10-14 HD (Large)

Description

The hamadryads of the Scarred Lands are deceptively dangerous guardians of the deep forest. Although they resemble slight-bodied young girls, usually dressed in the skins of forest creatures, they are in fact wood nymphs (living plants) with all the strength of their tree cousins.

The most obvious thing that sets a hamadryad apart from a human girl is her hair. Hamadryads do not actually have hair per se, but rather a mass of long, slim, flexible branches like those of a willow. Their toes are long and able to lengthen into roots when the hamadryad is hungry or thirsty. Touching a hamadryad is the surest way to determine her true nature. Although a hamadryad seems to have normal human skin, it is actually a thin, birchlike bark over a layer of wood. It's impossible to confuse with living flesh and blood.

Hamadryads are not always hostile to those who enter their forests, but they mark anyone carrying axes or fire as potential enemies. Each hamadryad forest is home to a secret glade where the wood nymphs gather. They keep their communal treasure, which is usually anything

pretty enough to catch their eye, in these glades. If a hamadryad forest is endangered by monsters or mortals, the nymphs are not above using their treasure to bribe other humans to help them defend their lands.

Hamadryads sometimes cooperate with druids, unicorns (even the new breed) or any of Denev's servitors. They speak a faltering Common, and they communicate among themselves with a whispering language like the wind through trees.

Combat

Hamadryads do not enjoy combat, but they fight to defend their woods if they judge intruders to be too great a threat. Many have learned to draw away male stragglers by pretending to be ordinary girls, then murdering the interlopers apart from the group. They prefer using their superior mobility and camouflage to attack those on the fringe of the party, lashing out with powerful blows and then disappearing back into the forest until another attack of opportunity presents itself.

Camouflage (Ex): Hamadryads can become nearly invisible when traveling through the forest. They are treated as invisible to anyone more than 30 feet away from them, unless they choose to be seen. This applies even in combat, but only in their native terrain.

Plant: Hamadryads are impervious to critical hits, subdual damage and death from massive damage trauma. They're not affected by many spells of mind-altering nature (for example, enamoring or charming spells not specifically designed for plants), subject to the GM's adjudication.

Sneak Attack: Hamadryads can sneak attack as a rogue of a level equivalent to half their hit dice, as long as they are in the forest.

Sylvan Allies (Ex): A hamadryad forest usually has other guardians that the nymphs have befriended. The hamadryads can communicate with these creatures — be they unicorns, tree warriors or even dire animals — as a matter of course. A hamadryad's scream can be heard for several miles, and it usually brings guardians running.

Swamp Hamadryad

Certain secluded swamps or bayous enjoy the protection of a swamp-dwelling version of the hamadryad. These "swamp maidens," as they're sometimes called, are much like their forest cousins in most ways. However, the hamadryads of the swamps tend to be a little more malicious toward human interlopers, and they can call on slightly darker allies to protect their homes.

Hanid (or, Spirit Woman of the Flower)

Medium-size Fey

Hit Dice:	9d6+9 (40 hp)
Initiative:	+2 (Dex)
Speed:	30 ft. fly 35 ft.
AC:	12 (+2 Dex)
Attacks:	None
Damage:	None
Face/Reach:	5 ft. by 5 ft. / 5 ft.
Special Attacks:	Spells
Special Qualities:	Damage reduction 15/+1 or cold-iron, SR 14, invisibility, plant home
Saves:	Fort +4, Ref +5, Will +9
Abilities:	Str 9, Dex 14, Con 12, Int 11, Wis 16, Cha 22
Skills:	Hide +18, Intuit Direction +20, Listen +5
Feats:	None
Climate/Terrain:	Desert
Organization:	Solitary
Challenge Rating:	3
Treasure:	Standard
Alignment:	Always chaotic good
Advancement Range:	8-12 HD

Description

The name "hanid", which means "hope" in the parlance of the Ubantu peoples, describes both a desert flower and the spirit that occupies it. The hanid flower is a small, fragile, succulent plant that has long, yellow petals. The dusty gold flower grows flat on the sand and is virtually unnoticeable. Aside from the fact that it holds the hanid spirit, the hanid plant is an otherwise normal plant.

However, the plant may be occupied by a hanid spirit. A hanid spirit appears as a beautiful, faintly translucent desert woman that wanders the desert, moving from flower to flower. Should she meet a creature in distress while wandering, she immediately gives succor, using her magical abilities if need be.

Hanid do not speak. They administer care to those who are at death's door and unattended. Once they have assisted someone, hanid wander away as quickly as they appeared. Because they love small, pretty things, hanid sometimes linger briefly after caring for someone if they offer a small flower, gem or other interesting bauble. A wise old mage once claimed that if certain words of magic were whispered to the hanid by a handsome male while it lingered after assisting him, the spirit would become temporarily enamoured of its patient.

Some desert sorcerers have developed techniques of capturing hanid while they lie in their flower homes

and binding them to the flowers, making the hanid's home into its prison. Like a genie in a bottle, the sorcerer then commands the hanid to his pleasures or sells the imprisoned fey to a sheik or wealthy merchant.

As if that weren't enough to contend with, spiteful sandmaskers rip hanid flowers out of the ground whenever they find them, despite the fact that hanid have helped dying sandmaskers in their times of greatest need.

Combat

Hanid will never fight, even to prevent the destruction of their flowers. Instead they will always try to escape to another flower, perhaps one in a hidden locale.

Invisibility (Su): Hanid may become invisible twice a day for one hour.

Spells: As a 9th-level druid, a hanid focuses on spells which heal, provide food and water, and other means of succor.

Plant Home: As a full round action, a hanid may discorporate and house her spirit in any hanid plant within 10 feet or do the reverse to appear anywhere within 10 feet of the plant she was occupying. The hanid spirit must return to a hanid plant within one day after leaving another plant, or the spirit will die immediately.

Harpy

Medium-size Monstrous Humanoid

Hit Dice:	4d8+4 (22 hp)
Initiative:	+2 (Dex)
Speed:	20 ft., climb 20 ft., fly 90 ft.
AC:	16 (+2 Dex, +4 natural)
Attacks:	Scythe +6 melee; or 2 talons +5 melee; or javelin +6 ranged
Damage:	Scythe 1d8+1; talon 1d4+1; javelin 1d6+1
Face/Reach:	5 ft. by 10 ft./5 ft. (10 ft. with scythe)
Special Attacks:	Reaper dive
Special Qualities:	None
Saves:	Fort +2, Ref +6, Will +1
Abilities:	Str 13, Dex 15, Con 13, Int 12, Wis 10, Cha 9
Skills:	Climb +4, Hide +3, Listen +2, Move Silently +8, Read Lips +2, Spot +6
Feats:	Flyby Attack, Weapon Focus (Scythe)
Climate/Terrain:	Temperate and warm mountains, ravines and desert cliffs
Organization:	Wing (2-5), shriek (4-24)
Challenge Rating:	2
Treasure:	Standard
Alignment:	Usually neutral evil
Advancement Range:	5-8 HD (Medium-size); also by character class

Description

Two hundred years ago, the secretive cult called the Sisterhood of the Sickle Moon was the terror of the Scarred Land's cities. A largely female cult dedicated to the fledgling night-goddess Belsameth, the Sisterhood plied its trade as assassins and spies in the interests of increasing the goddess' influence. But when the Titanswar tore the land apart, the order found that their subtle methods did little good against the armies and beasts massed by the celestial lords. In desperation, the cultists offered up their prayers to Belsameth, hoping that the Slayer could somehow make use of their zeal.

Belsameth answered their prayers with the gift of talons and great vulturelike wings — transforming the Sisterhood into a new race, the harpies.

Most harpies encountered in the Scarred Lands appear to be dark-skinned women with long, brazen talons for hands and feet, and with coal-black plumage adorning their backs, hips, tails and wings. Males are flightless and therefore never seen outside their shriek's rookeries.

The voices of harpies are piercing but not shrill, not unlike an eagle's cry. Harpies prefer to hunt silently, though, dropping from the skies without a sound. Most can speak Common; their own tongue is a garbled dialect of Common and Infernal.

Harpies lair in "rookeries," cave networks that burrow deep into cliff faces. Most rookeries go to some trouble to hide their garbage pits; simply heaving their garbage outside tends to attract human enemies. Each rookery contains at least one crude shrine to Belsameth, typically constructed of bones lashed together with scraps of victims' clothing. Harpies are generally clever enough not to call attention to their lairs, and this includes not attacking armed parties that are seemingly more dangerous than they are. The sole exception to this prudence comes on nights of the lunar eclipse, when the harpies hunt far and wide for sacrifices to their goddess.

Scarred Lands Harpy Characters

Most harpies rely on their natural talents to get by, but a gifted few have levels in rogue, fighter, sorcerer or cleric classes. Harpy clerics use scythes as their favored weapon and tend to draw on the do-mains of Death and Trickery. They seem largely incapable of multiclass; if they favor any class, it's likely cleric (of Belsameth).

Combat

Harpies fight from the air, where they control the battle. If grounded, they become much more desperate, sometimes even losing the will to live. They are not particularly swift fliers, but they are more maneuverable than their large wingspans might suggest. A common harpy tactic is to remain airborne and innocuous (or hidden among cliff faces, treetops or the like) until an opportunity for an ambush presents itself. They begin any combat with their lethal reaper dive attack if at all possible, then continue slashing their foes from above with flyby attacks.

Reaper Dive (Ex): After observing the effective hunting technique of scythe falcons, harpies developed a particularly deadly maneuver of executing their prey. This tactic involves dropping from the sky, slicing at their victim's necks with their scythes as they hurtle past, and then regaining altitude before their foes can retaliate. The reaper dive is possible only at the beginning of combat and counts as a flyby attack. As the harpy begins the dive from a great height and a high speed, her movement is increased to 120 feet for this attack only. The reaper dive does damage as per a normal scythe attack, but the critical range is increased to 18-20. What's more, if an opponent is flat-footed when the harpy makes her attack, the dive gains the bonuses of a rogue's sneak attack (+2d6 damage).

Herald of Vangal

	Large Outsider
Hit Dice:	14d8+56 (119 hp)
Initiative:	+1 (Dex)
Speed:	40 ft., fly 120ft.
AC:	23 (–1 size, +1 Dex, +8 armor, +5 natural)
Attacks:	Greatsword +22 melee and 2 tail stings +13 melee; 2 claws +18 melee, bite +16 melee, 2 tail stings +16 melee
Damage:	Greatsword 2d6+8; claw 1d12+5; bite 1d4+2; tail sting 1d10+2
Face/Reach:	5 ft. by 5 ft./10 ft.
Special Attacks:	Poison tails, diseased bite, fear, magical sword
Special Qualities:	Damage reduction 20/+1, SR 19, outsider
Saves:	Fort +13, Ref +10, Will +13
Abilities:	Str 21, Dex 13, Con 18, Int 13, Wis 14, Cha 19

Skills:	Diplomacy +14, Intimidate +17, Knowledge (geography) +10, Knowledge (history) +8, Knowledge (planes) +12, Knowledge (religion) +11, Listen +17, Spot +15
Feats:	Armor Proficiency (Heavy), Cleave, Combat Reflexes, Flyby Attack, Great Cleave, Improved Critical (Greatsword), Iron Will, Mobility, Multiattack, Leadership, Power Attack, Spring Attack, Weapon Focus (Greatsword)
Climate/Terrain:	Any
Organization:	Solitary (unique)
Challenge Rating:	9
Treasure:	Standard
Alignment:	Always chaotic evil
Advancement Range:	None

Description

Vangal's herald was crafted from one of the dark god's own manticora race. The herald's features are very much that of a manticora, except for the addition of wings and twin scorpion tails, both added to better deliver Vangal's messages. The herald's 12-foot frame is adorned with filth-encrusted armor, lending her a likeness similar to Vangal himself. Her face is human, but her teeth are twisted fangs, capable of tearing through leather with ease. Her twisted claws can rake an opponent, and she is known to carry an immense greatsword that she wields with terrible proficiency.

Though presumably crafted to serve as messenger and to precede Vangal's coming, the herald's true pursuit has been more that of a general. Her skills in war served her master well for centuries. When the Divine War raged across the Scarred Lands, the herald led the followers of Vangal to victory after victory over the armies of the titan races. However, during the battle to defeat the titan Mormo, the herald's army was first to engage Mormo's medusae, and was crushed by the snake-witches' eldritch powers. Though the gods won the day, Vangal had no concern for the shattered remnants of his herald.

But such is the cruelty for those who serve the god of apocalypse and the herald expected no less than for the weak to be left to their pain. Spending the last century and a half in the Abyss repairing her shattered spirit, the herald is now perhaps ready to return to the Scarred Lands to resume her service to Vangal. Though possessing but a fraction of her former power, the herald is still a terrible opponent, all the more cruel and reckless for she will surely seek to gain Vangal's notice once more that he might restore her former strength.

Combat

The herald is a beast of war, and hence is feared for her savage combat ability. She prefers to meet her opponents face to face, but is not against using her flight for flyby attacks.

Poison Tails (Ex): The herald's tail drips a virulent posion. If a victim is struck by her tail he must make a Fortitude save (DC 17) or take 1d6 damage each round for the next five rounds. Effects of multiple strikes are cumulative.

Fear (Su): The herald can summon an aura of fear such that any opponent of 14 HD or level or lower within 60 feet of the herald must pass a Will saving throw (DC 17) or flee in terror for 2d6 rounds. This effect is generated as a standard attack action.

Magical Sword: Vangal's herald possesses the Fellblade, a +3 greatsword which delivers wounds that cannot be healed by any cleric but those dedicated to Vangal (and woe to the cleric who heals such wounds without word or sign from his patron).

Diseased Bite (Ex): The herald's bite carries a debilitating disease. Anyone bitten must pass a Fortitude save (DC 19) or suffer a disease that deals one point of temporary Strength and Constitution damage each day until cured magically or until the victim dies from either ability score dropping to zero.

Outsider: As an outsider, the herald is immune to poison, sleep, paralysis, drowning and disease. She is not subject to ability damage, energy drain or any attack that must target a living victim.

Hill Howler

Large (Tall) Beast

Hit Dice:	4d10+16 (38 hp)
Initiative:	+3 (Dex)
Speed:	45 ft., climb 15 ft.
AC:	15 (-1 size, +3 Dex, +3 natural)
Attacks:	Bite +7 melee and 2 claws +2 melee
Damage:	Bite 1d8+4; claw 1d6+2
Face/Reach:	5ft. by 5ft./10 ft.
Special Attacks:	Terrifying howl
Special Qualities:	Darkvision 90ft.
Saves:	Fort +8, Ref +5, Will +1
Abilities:	Str 18, Dex 16, Con 18, Int 4, Wis 10, Cha 5
Skills:	None
Feats:	Alertness, Cleave, Combat Reflexes, Track
Climate/Terrain:	Temperate foothills, grasslands
Organization:	Solitary
Challenge Rating:	2
Treasure:	Standard
Alignment:	Always chaotic evil
Advancement Range:	4-8 HD

Description

The high, lonely foothills and the wooded hollows of the deep mountains are home to the hill howler, a huge, humanoid beast with broad, hulking shoulders, long, powerfully muscled arms and a misshapen head dominated by a gaping, tooth-filled maw. It moves quickly on its broad feet and knuckles with a rolling, ape-like gait, and it is a nimble climber. When standing fully erect, the hill howler is eight feet tall, although exceptional specimens grow to 10 feet in height. The monster is covered with coarse brown fur, and the thick, curved talons on its feet and hands are black. Its eyes are small and yellow-orange, and they reflect firelight like a cat's.

The hill howler is a flesh-eating creature that makes its lair in a hard-to-reach cave, claiming a hunting ground up to 10 square miles around its home. Once settled, it preys on large game until it has killed or driven away everything in the region. It then moves on in search of better pickings. Hill howlers have a fondness for horseflesh, and they stalk even large groups of travelers passing through their territory. The monster prefers to hunt at night, where its keen senses give it a decided advantage over humans or other animals, and it circles its prey for quite some time as it calculates the best moment to strike. It creeps up on its victim and pounces from the shadows at the last moment with a bone-chilling scream. When it lands, it dashes the prey to the ground to kill it with tooth and claw. Then, as quickly as it appears,

the monster vanishes back into the darkness, carrying its prey back to its lair where it can eat in peace.

Occasionally, a howler develops a taste for human prey and its hunger brings it out of the hills to haunt isolated villages and castles until a sufficiently bold group of hunters is able to put an end to the beast.

Combat

The hill howler uses its keen senses and stealthy tread to catch its prey unawares, then attempts to kill it quickly with its paralyzing howl and powerful teeth and claws. Once its victim is dead, it picks up the body and flees. A typical hill howler can carry off a medium-sized horse without being encumbered significantly. If its sudden attack is not effective and the victim puts up a fierce fight, the monster retreats quickly and waits for another opportunity to catch its prey unawares.

Darkvision (Ex): The hill howler's keen vision allows it to see at night up to 120 feet away as though it were daylight.

Terrifying howl (Ex): When the hill howler springs its attack, it unleashes a hideous, ear-splitting howl. Everyone within earshot must make a Willpower save (DC 18) or suffer a -3 morale modifier to initiative and attack rolls for the duration of the fight.

Hollow Knight

Medium-size Construct

Hit Dice:	6d12+24 (63 hp)
Initiative:	-2 (Dex)
Speed:	20 ft.
AC:	23 (-2 Dex, +5 natural, +8 armor, +2 large shield)
Attacks:	Heavy lance +11 melee; longsword +11 melee
Damage:	Heavy lance 1d8+4 (triple with charge from horseback); longsword 1d8+4
Face/Reach:	5 ft. by 5 ft./5 ft.
Special Attacks:	None
Special Qualities:	Construct, damage reduction 10/+1
Saves:	Fort +9, Ref +0, Will +2
Abilities:	Str 18, Dex 7, Con 18, Int 13, Wis 10, Cha 10
Skills:	Diplomacy +2, Intimidate +6, Listen +1, Ride +8, Search +1, Spot +1
Feats:	Armor Proficiency (heavy), Endurance, Leadership, Mounted Combat, Spirited Charge, Weapon Focus (heavy lance), Weapon Focus (longsword)
Climate/Terrain:	Any
Organization:	Solitary, pair, unit (3-10), army (20-100 plus one 7th-level hollow earl as leader and one 5th-level hollow-baron assistant per 20 knights)
Challenge Rating:	5
Treasure:	Triple standard
Alignment:	Always lawful neutral
Advancement Rate:	By fighter class

Description

The hollow knights are the staunch defenders of the Gleaming Valley. Created by Corean, god of artifice and chivalry, to serve as his army in the Divine War, the constructs are actually the eldritch fusion of metal and spirit. After he forged the mail he required, Corean called upon the resting souls of warriors who had venerated him before, or those whom the Titans had spurned in life and who thus sought revenge against their former tormentors. These ghosts manned the god's armor and strode forth to war against the minions of the celestial tyrants.

As reward for the hollow knights' service and loyalty, Corean decreed after the war that the spirits would be allowed to remain in the world that they had helped claim. However, Vangal the Ravager, jealous of Corean's army and victories during the Divine War, defiled the worldly remains of the knights whom Corean had freed. The soldiers were thus denied their former lives and were forced to continue on as spirits given form only by the armor they wore.

Despite their mistreatment and unnatural existence, the hollow knights have prospered since the Divine War, carving out their own kingdom from the wastes near the Hornsaw Forest. Secretly, however, they fear for their future. With no further need of his

Gleaming Legion, Corean has ceased their creation. Although the knights are stunning combatants, one of them falls in battle from time to time, his soul returning to the next world. The knights' days are therefore numbered, and any army large or bold enough to wage a war of attrition against the knights of the Gleaming Valley could destroy the hollow knights forever.

Hollow knights are identical in appearance, cast as they are from the same mold. They all appear to be knights in full plate armor, although their open face masks reveal a disturbing darkness within — and nothing more. The only variance among hollow knights denotes rank. Common knights are burnished bronze, barons are shining silver, and earls are glittering gold.

Despite the fact that they appear to have no mouths, hollow knights speak Common in a haunting, tinny, reverberating voice.

Hollow Chargers

These are the artificial beasts ridden into battle by the hollow knights. They appear to be metallic statues of warhorses. Their color is appropriate to their riders' station.

Hollow Charger: SZ L (construct); HD 8d12+40; hp 92; Init -1; Spd 50; AC: 16 (-1 Dex, -1 size, +8 natural); Atk: 2 hooves +13 (1d6+6); Face 5 ft.x 10 ft.; Reach 5 ft.; SQ: Construct; SV Fort +11, Ref +1, Will +2; Str 22, Dex 8, Con 20, Int 2, Wis 10, Cha 5; AL LN. Skills: Intuit Direction +2, Listen +1, Spot +1. Feats: Endurance, Run.

Hollow Knight Characters

The only class available to hollow knights is fighter. There are apocryphal tales of hollow paladins, but given the constructs' unwavering lawful neutral alignment, this is probably just a legend.

Combat

When mounted, a hollow knight usually charges with its lance. If possible, the knight attacks other mounted soldiers, but lacking such targets it deigns to attack infantry. On foot, the construct attacks with its longsword, again choosing to attack those it feels to be the most worthy opponents, typically an enemy warrior with the best equipment.

Hollow knights are the very spirit of military precision. When working together, they are able to synchronize their movements in ways no other army can match, allowing them to more easily capitalize on enemy weaknesses and mistakes. Although their reputation on the battlefield defines them as fearless, many hollow knights are terrified of dying again and losing their lease on the world.

Construct: Hollow knights and their mounts are impervious to critical hits, subdual damage and death from massive damage trauma. They're immune to poisons, diseases, blinding, deafness, drowning, electricity and spells or attacks that affect respiration and living physiology. They cannot be stunned. They're not affected by attacks or spells of mind-altering nature (enamoring or charming spells, for example), or by spells based on healing/harming. Fire and acid spells and attacks deal half normal damage.

Hookwing

Tiny Animal

Hit Dice:	2d8-4 (5 hp)
Initiative:	+8 (+4 Improved Initiative, +4 Dex)
Speed:	10 ft., fly 120 ft.
AC:	18 (+2 size, +4 Dex, +2 natural)
Attacks:	Bite +2 melee, 2 claws +1 melee; or flyby strike +4 melee
Damage:	Bite 1d6; claw 1d4; flyby strike 1d12
Face/Reach:	2.5 ft. by 2.5 ft./0 ft.
Special Attacks:	Flyby strike
Special Qualities:	None
Saves:	Fort +1, Ref +4, Will +0
Abilities:	Str 3, Dex 19, Con 6, Int 2, Wis 10, Cha 6
Skills:	None
Feats:	Alertness, Improved Initiative, Dodge
Climate/Terrain:	Temperate forests
Organization:	Solitary, or communal nesting group (10-20)
Challenge Rating:	1/4
Treasure:	Standard
Alignment:	Always neutral
Advancement Range:	2-4 HD

Description

The hookwing is a sleek, muscular flying lizard, measuring up to four feet in length from nose to tail and covered in hard, glossy scales that range from a lustrous greenish-black to an iridescent emerald hue. Sharp flanges and hooks grow from the center of each scale, providing the hookwing with a powerful natural defense against predators as well as an effective weapon in killing its prey. The hookwing's four slim legs have four toes configured much like a bird's talon, tipped with long, curved nails used for gripping and tearing apart its meals.

Hookwings are usually solitary hunters that roost in tall trees or the ruined spires of castle keeps. In the late summer, after mating, groups of females come together to make large, communal nests, where the mothers take turns incubating eggs and hunting for the group as a whole. Females guard these nests very aggressively, swarming over large animals — or people — who stray too near.

These reptiles are very cunning and strong for their size, and they can be trained to hunt on command much like a falcon or hawk. Females can also be trained to guard homes or large, mobile possessions such as trunks or chests. Coupled with their bird-like fascination for colorful shiny objects, hookwings are valued by jewelers and other artificers as watch-animals. A small and discreet class of trainers and handlers has existed among the elves of Eldura-tre near Galumganjus where hookwings are more common, and the humans of Tashon are now adopting this sport. Trainers pay up to 50 gold pieces for healthy eggs.

Combat

Whether hunting or defending its nest, a hookwing attacks its victim by flying high into the air, folding its wings tightly against its body and diving at its prey like an arrow, using its sharp-edged scales like a sword blade as it slashes past a target.

Flyby Strike: The hookwing can attack its opponent at the beginning, middle or end of its move, and it does damage equivalent to the flyby strike listed above.

Hornsaw Unicorn

Large (Long) Magical Beast

Hit Dice:	8d10+48 (92 hp)
Initiative:	+3 (Dex)
Speed:	80 ft.
AC:	20 (-1 size, +3 Dex, +8 natural)
Attacks:	Horn +13 melee, bite +11 melee, and 2 hooves +11 melee
Damage:	Horn 2d8+6; bite 1d10+3; hoof 1d8+3
Face/Reach:	5 ft. by 10 ft./5 ft. (10 ft. with horn)
Special Attacks:	Enhanced natural weapons, rage
Special Qualities:	Immunities, SR 16
Saves:	Fort +12, Ref +9, Will +11
Abilities:	Str 23, Dex 17, Con 23, Int 12, Wis 20, Cha 24
Skills:	Animal Empathy +3, Hide +2, Intimidate +5, Jump +8, Listen +8, Spot +8
Feats:	Multiattack, Track
Climate/Terrain:	Subarctic or temperate forest
Organization:	Solitary, mated pair or herd (3-8)
Challenge Rating:	5
Treasure:	Standard
Alignment:	Usually chaotic neutral
Advancement Range:	6-10 HD (large)

Description

Unicorns have always been ferociously territorial beasts that guarded the heart of Scarn's forests. The Hornsaw unicorn is all the more so. It was one of these beasts, sighted not long after the Titanswar, that gave the Hornsaw Forest its new name — for nothing summed up the changes that forest had undergone better than the savage beasts its unicorns had become.

The Hornsaw unicorn resembles nothing more than a shaggy war horse with a serrated horn, wicked cloven hooves and unusually pointed teeth. It's omnivorous, and although it's usually content to graze, it will gladly eat the bodies of intruders in its domain. It rarely hunts for food or sport, but it can be remarkably aggressive when defending its territory. These beasts possess an unusual level of cunning, and most have learned to understand several languages appropriate to their surroundings (although they cannot speak).

Oddly enough, the Hornsaw unicorn is now apparently the "default" breed of unicorn throughout the Scarred Lands. According to sages, this change is probably due to breeding between unicorns that migrated out of the Hornsaw and the more "common" breed. If so, it would stand to reason that what is now commonly called the Hornsaw unicorn is a mere half-breed — implying that there might still be "true"

Hornsaw unicorns in the depths of the Hornsaw that are even larger and more vicious than these brutes.

Combat

The Hornsaw unicorn prefers to begin battle by charging horn-first into its opponents, although it is canny enough not to do so against any group of foes that possess spears or other weapons that might be set to receive its charge. It is perfectly capable of slashing or stabbing with its horn, and biting and striking with its forehooves all in the same round.

Enhanced Natural Weapons (Ex): The horn, hooves and teeth of a Hornsaw unicorn are nearly metallic to the touch, and they are magically hardened. They count as +4 weapons for purposes of overcoming damage reduction.

Immunities (Ex): The unicorns of the Scarred Lands cannot be poisoned, nor are they subject to disease. They can digest anything that they can chew, although only fresh plant matter or flesh nourishes them. They cannot be charmed.

Rage (Ex): Hornsaw unicorns become maddened when their blood is drawn. Once a unicorn has been wounded, its attack and damage rolls gain an additional +2 bonus for the combat's duration.

Huror (Ice Bear)

Huge (Long) Beast

Hit Dice:	20d10+140 (250 hp)
Initiative:	+0
Speed:	80 ft.
AC:	22 (-2 size, +4 Dex, +10 natural)
Attacks:	Bite +25 melee, 2 claws +20
Damage:	Bite 2d10+7; claw 2d6+3
Face/Reach:	10 ft. by 20 ft./10 ft.
Special Attacks:	Crushing jaws, ice storm,
Special Qualities:	Damage reduction 10/+1, frost pelt
Saves:	Fort +19, Ref +6, Will +10
Abilities:	Str 25, Dex 10, Con 25, Int 18, Wis 15, Cha 15
Skills:	Hide +11, Listen +26, Move Silently +12, Spot +26
Feats:	Alertness, Blind Fighting, Cleave, Great Cleave, Ironwill, Power Attack, Track, Trample
Climate/Terrain:	Arctic mountains
Organization:	Solitary
Challenge Rating:	10
Treasure:	None
Alignment:	Always neutral
Advancement Range:	16-24 HD

Description

As the emperor stags guard the forests in the name of Denev, the ice bears, or huror (hoo-roar) guard the frozen mountains of northern Albadia. The huror appear as massive white bears with unnerving, ice-blue eyes. Crystals of blue ice glitter in their thick pelts, and their claws look like blue steel.

The huror is a rare, almost mythical creature rarely seen even by northern rangers. It is a creature that guards the pristine slopes of the mountains from creatures that would warp the land to their bidding. These bears travel in the heart of great blizzards that sometimes blanket the region for many miles, and they have sometimes come to the aid of travelers lost in snowstorms, leading them to a sheltering cave or a nearby settlement. Most times,

however, a bear appears as a force of vengeance, punishing foolhardy hunters or those who trespass knowingly into the goddesses' holy places.

Legends persist that a huror that is close to death will seek out a great hero in the north lands and fight him in a terrible battle. If the hero loses the fight, he is spared death. If he triumphs, he wins the aged bear's hide as a cloak that is impervious to cold, and the beast's teeth that can pierce the toughest armor. When the hero eventually dies, he is then reborn as a huror himself, and he takes his place as a guardian of the mountains.

Combat

Hurors are awesome creatures in battle, attacking opponents in the midst of a magical blizzard that freezes limbs and blinds eyes. Weapons that strike the huror are bound with layers of ice, weighing them down and potentially shattering them. The bear's immense strength and fearsome teeth allow it to bite through the toughest of armor as though it were mere cloth.

Crushing Jaws (Ex): The huror's massive jaws are capable of biting through the toughest armor. When making a bite attack, the ice bear ignores armor modifiers, although magical, size and Dexterity modifiers still apply.

Frost Pelt (Su): The Huror's pelt is rimed constantly with frost, causing ice to cling to any weapon that touches it. Characters who score a successful hit on an ice bear must make a Reflex save (DC 17) or suffer a -1 penalty to hit on subsequent attacks. This modifier is cumulative with each successful attack the character makes. It takes one full round to free a weapon from its accumulated ice.

Ice Storm (Ex): A blizzard rises to surround a huror wherever it travels. The storm can stretch for more than a mile, and anyone trapped within it must make a Fortitude save (DC 14) or suffer -2 to Strength and Dexterity from frostbite. If the victim remains in the blizzard for eight hours after failing the save, the losses become permanent.

Ice Basilisk

Medium-size Magical Beast

Hit Dice:	10d10 (55 hp)
Initiative:	+2 (Dex)
Speed:	40 ft., swim 30 ft.
AC:	18 (+2 Dex, +6 natural)
Attacks:	Headbutt +10 melee; bite +10 melee
Damage:	Headbutt 2d8; bite 1d8
Face/Reach:	5 ft. by 10 ft./5 ft.
Special Attacks:	Chill gaze
Special Qualities:	Immunities
Saves:	Fort +7, Ref +5, Will +3
Abilities:	Str 11, Dex 14, Con 11, Int 3, Wis 10, Cha 5
Skills:	Hide +12, Spot +10
Feats:	Dodge
Climate/Terrain:	Arctic
Organization:	Solitary, pair, brood (3-5)
Challenge Rating:	6
Treasure:	Standard
Alignment:	Always neutral
Advancement Range:	9-13 HD

Description

Ice basilisks are man-sized, arctic serpents, generally believed to be descended from other Scarred Lands basilisks. The ice basilisk, however, retains only vestigial wings, arms and legs, and it moves across the tundra on its belly like other snakes. A sharp-edged cartilaginous fin protrudes from its head and trails down its spine. The ice basilisk uses this fin to attack prey and defend itself from predators, as well as to break through thin ice to hunt fish in the arctic waters.

Of course, like other basilisks, it is the ice basilisk's dread gaze that makes it one of the most feared predators of the arctic. The basilisk lies in wait for prey and then attacks with its head fin, followed by an attempt to lock eyes with the injured victim. The basilisk can then devour the frozen morsel.

Combat

Ice basilisks are fearless hunters, and they attack anything up to the size of a moose.

Chill Gaze (Ex): Anyone who looks into the ice basilisk's eyes must make a Will saving throw (DC 20) or become numbed and paralyzed by supernatural chill. Left unattended, the victim thaws out in 2d4 days, assuming that they are not eaten and they don't die of thirst or exposure. If he's kept warm, the victim can recover in one day. A victim who is frozen for any period of time, but who survives the experience, suffers 2d10 damage.

Immunities (Ex): Ice basilisks are immune to cold attacks.

Ice Ghoul

	Medium-size Humanoid
Hit Dice:	2d8+8 (17 hp)
Initiative:	+2 (Dex)
Speed:	40 ft.
AC:	14 (+2 Dex, +2 leathers)
Attacks:	Hatchet +6 melee; harpoon +4 ranged
Damage:	Hatchet 1d6+4; harpoon 1d6+4
Face/Reach:	5 ft. by 5 ft./5 ft.
Special Attacks:	Rage
Special Qualities:	Resistances
Saves:	Fort +7, Ref +2, Will -1
Abilities:	Str 18, Dex 14, Con 18, Int 7, Wis 8, Cha 14
Skills:	Escape Artist +2, Hide +5, Intuit Direction +2, Listen +4, Move Silently +5, Spot +4, Swim +7, Wilderness Lore +6
Feats:	Alertness, Power Attack
Climate/Terrain:	Cold to arctic plains, tundra and forests
Organization:	Hunting party (2-8), war party (11-20, led by one 3rd-level berserker), clans (31-50, led by one 7th-level warlord, one 5th-level shaman and five 3rd-level berserkers)
Challenge Rating:	1
Treasure:	Half standard
Alignment:	Usually chaotic evil
Advancement Range:	By character class

Description

The precise origin of the ice ghoul race is uncertain. Very likely, they were once a tribe of human barbarians in northern Asherak who turned to cannibalism during an exceptionally lean winter — the Titans certainly toyed with unnatural weather patterns during their reign. But through unknown methods, these people have become something… other than human.

Ice ghouls are able to draw on some mysterious reserves of energy to keep themselves alive where humans would die; perhaps the human flesh they consume grants them some unusual measure of power. They are able to subsist for months without food — they refuse to eat anything but raw flesh, preferably that of people — but their hunger is almost perpetual. They can endure terrible snowstorms and freezing temperatures without adequate protection, although they likely live in perpetual discomfort.

Ice ghouls organize themselves in family clans, usually living on the outskirts of human territory. Clans can and do war with one another, although ice ghouls seem disinterested in the meat of their own kind, eating it only when absolutely necessary. They scavenge equipment from the human homesteads they ravage, but they aren't above attacking with femurs, rocks and sharpened branches if nothing else is at hand.

Ice Ghoul Characters

The canniest ice ghouls can multiclass (barbarian being their preferred class), usually as rogues (who specialize in stealth), sorcerers or evil druids.

Combat

Ice ghouls rely on base animal cunning to stalk their prey and attack from surprise if possible. When they charge into battle, they do so with bloodcurdling howls of rage and hunger. Particularly famished ice ghouls stop fighting as soon as they make their first kill (or incapacitate a foe) in order to start eating.

Rage (Ex): Ice ghouls are likely to go into a berserker rage when confronted with living prey. While enraged, they gain +2 to Strength, +2 to Constitution, +3 to Will saves and −2 to AC. They cannot end this rage voluntarily until the combat is over.

Resistances (Ex): Ice ghouls take only half damage from cold attacks, and they do not suffer ill effects (frostbite and the like) from natural cold. They can live for up to four months without food.

Ice Haunt

Medium-size Undead

Hit Dice:	7d12+14 (57 hp)
Initiative:	+7 (+4 Improved Initiative, +3 Dex)
Speed:	30 ft.
AC:	13 (+3 Dex)
Attacks:	Bite +10 melee, 2 claws +5 melee
Damage:	Bite 1d8+3; claw 2d4+1
Face/Reach:	5 ft. by 5 ft./5 ft.
Special Attacks:	Numbing grip
Special Qualities:	Vulnerability, undead
Saves:	Fort +7, Ref +5, Will -1
Abilities:	Str 16, Dex 17, Con 15, Int 6, Wis 5, Cha 2
Skills:	Climb +4, Hide +3, Listen +5, Move Silently +6, Spot +5, Wilderness Lore +4
Feats:	Alertness, Improved Critical, Improved Initiative, Track
Climate/Terrain:	Arctic mountains
Organization:	Solitary, Pack (2-20 haunts)
Challenge Rating:	4
Treasure:	Standard
Alignment:	Always chaotic evil
Advancement Range:	6-8 HD

Description

Ice haunts are the tormented souls of travelers who starved to death in the blizzards of the north. Legends say that a man who dies in the snow cursing the god of the mountains will rise again on the night of the full moon, hungry for raw flesh to fill his shrunken belly.

Ice haunts are undead creatures with pale white skin and withered flesh. Their fingers are curled into claws, and their teeth are shaped into fangs. They can hunt only by the light of the full moon; while most are solitary figures, sometimes the cursed souls of an entire village, lost in an avalanche, rise again to torment the living.

Combat

Ice haunts fall upon their victims with tooth and claw, numbing their victims with their icy grip as they rend flesh from bone. Ice haunts will sometimes grapple their prey, holding them in a freezing embrace until the victim is chilled he drops his weapons and meanwhile dig with their teeth for warm blood. If outnumbered, ice haunts will endeavor to use their numbing grip on as many foes as possible before moving to the task of finishing off their chilled victim.

Numbing Grip (Ex): Victims successfully grappled by an ice haunt must make a Fortitude save (DC 16) or become so chilled that they lose sensation for 2d6 rounds. Every round a victim is so effected, he must make a Reflex save (DC 15) to hold on to any handheld items (weapon, shield, wand, etc.) or in order to cast spell requiring a somatic component.

Undead: Ice haunts are immune to mind-influencing effects, poison, sleep, paralysis, stunning and disease. They're not subject to critical hits, subdual damage, ability damage, energy drain or death from massive damage.

Vulnerability (Ex): An ice haunt takes double damage from fire-based attacks.

Ice Weasel

Small Animal

Hit Dice:	2d8+6 (15 hp)
Initiative:	+7 (+3 Dex, +4 Improved Initiative)
Speed:	25 ft., swim 20 ft.
AC:	16 (+1 size, +3 Dex, +2 natural)
Attacks:	Bite +1 melee
Damage:	Bite 1d6-2
Face/Reach:	5 ft. by 5 ft./5 ft.
Special Attacks:	Bleeding wounds
Special Qualities:	Immunities
Saves:	Fort +6, Ref +8, Will +1
Abilities:	Str 6, Dex 16, Con 16, Int 2, Wis 12, Cha 6
Skills:	Escape Artist +12, Listen +7, Move Silently +8, Spot +7
Feats:	Alertness, Dodge, Improved Initiative, Lightning Reflexes, Mobility
Climate/Terrain:	Arctic
Organization:	Solitary, pair or pack (3-12)
Challenge Rating:	1/2
Treasure:	Standard
Alignment:	Always neutral
Advancement Range:	2-3 HD (Small)

Description

Ice weasels are extremely lithe and agile creatures that dwell in cold and desolate regions. Living in burrows deep beneath the permafrost, they eat mostly birds and arctic rodents, although they may eat fish if they live near water. Ice weasels are related to both otters and wolverines, so they are excellent swimmers and ferocious fighters.

Ice weasels are inquisitive creatures that are undeterred by the presence of larger creatures when they are hungry and presented with an opportunity to feed. Groups traveling through tundra or muskeg must be very careful with their food, lest they wake in the middle of the night to find their supplies being dragged away by ice weasels. Worse, ice weasels are incredibly defensive of food when they've found it, and they fight for rations they're in the midst of scavenging.

Combat

Ice weasels prefer not to fight opponents larger than they are, but if they are hungry, cornered or commanded to fight by an ice hag (see "Ice, Hag," in this volume), they are intensely vicious fighters. Ice weasels are also extremely protective of their packs. If a creature attacks one ice weasel, he earns himself a fray with the entire pack.

Bleeding Wounds (Ex): The ice weasel's saliva interferes with the normal blood-clotting process of any living victim that the weasel bites. Any wound from an ice weasel bite continues to bleed for 1 extra point of damage each round until it is healed magically or by a successful first-aid application using the Heal skill.

Immunities (Ex): Ice weasels take half normal damage from cold attacks.

Inn-wight

Small Undead

Hit Dice:	4d12-4 (22 hp)
Initiative:	-1 (Dex)
Speed:	30 ft.
AC:	12 (-1 Dex, +1 size,+2 natural)
Attacks:	1-6 or 1 Thrown objects +4 ranged
Damage:	Thrown object 1d4 or 3d4
Face/Reach:	5 ft. by 5 ft./5 ft.
Special Attacks:	Life drain
Special Qualities:	Damage reduction 10/+1, SR 12, undead
Saves:	Fort +0, Ref +0, Will +3
Abilities:	Str 9, Dex 9, Con 8, Int 8, Wis 9, Cha 9
Skills:	Climb +3, Intuit Direction +12, Listen +5, Move Silently +14, Spot +5
Feats:	None
Climate/Terrain:	Urban areas
Organization:	Solitary
Challenge Rating:	2
Treasure:	None
Alignment:	Always neutral
Advancement Range:	4-5 HD

Description

Very old cities have expensive inns. These establishments sometimes add a "salt surcharge" to the cost of a room, enough to obtain a small bag of salt each night to spread in a protective circle around the bed to keep any wandering inn-wights at bay.

Inn-wights are the ghosts of children who do not realize that they're dead, and they wander a city in search of warmth and comfort. Inns are considered welcoming, and these ghosts crawl into bed with someone who resembles a lost parent, or who at least appears to offer some inkling of kindness or security. The ghost's presence plagues a victim with nightmares full of loneliness and despair. The ghost drains the warmth — and life — from a person's body. If an inn-wight remains with a mortal until dawn, the victim awakens with years of her life stolen away.

These ghosts appear as shimmering, insubstantial forms of children, with sad, lonely faces and hollow spaces where their eyes should be. They are not intentionally malicious; they're unaware of the effects of their suffering.

Combat

If an inn-wight is attacked, it is capable of hurling the objects in a room at its attacker in a typically child-like fit of anger. An inn-wight can hurl 1d6 objects weighing up to 5 pounds (1d4 damage) each per round without penalty, or one object that weighs up to 30 pounds (3d4 damage).

Life Drain (Su): Inn-wights draw energy from sleeping mortals over the course of an entire night. To drain a victim successfully, the inn-wight must be in "contact" with his or her sleeping form for a minimum of six hours. During that time, the victim is wracked by terrible nightmares, and he may wake up with a successful Will save (DC 18). If the victim wakes up, the drain attempt fails and the ghost flees the room. If the life drain is successful, there is a steep price: The victim suffers 1d4 levels of energy drain, and he ages five years, appearing older, with drawn skin and graying hair.

Undead: Inn-wights are immune to poison, sleep, paralysis, stunning and disease. They're not subject to critical hits, subdual damage, ability damage, energy drain or death from massive damage.

Inquisitor

Medium-size Outsider

Hit Dice:	20d8 (90 hp)
Initiative:	-1 (Dex)
Speed:	30 ft.
AC:	9 (-1 Dex)
Attacks:	2 fists +19 melee
Damage:	Fist 1d4 or by weapon
Face/Reach:	5 ft. by 5 ft./5 ft.
Special Attacks:	Charming the masses
Special Qualities:	Shape of the flock, question of true seeing, knowing the heart's sentiment
Saves:	Fort +6, Ref +5, Will +18
Abilities:	Str 10, Dex 9, Con 10, Int 18, Wis 18, Cha 17
Skills:	Gather Information +21, Hide +9, Intimidate +20, Knowledge (societal law) +23, Listen +18, Profession (lawyer) +14, Read Lips +18, Scry +10, Sense Motive +22, Speak Language +15, Spot +15
Feats:	Alertness, Iron Will
Climate/Terrain:	Cities, towns, civilized locales
Organization:	Always solitary
Challenge Rating:	14
Treasure:	Standard
Alignment:	Always lawful neutral
Advancement Range:	19-20 HD

Description

Inquisitors are the spirits of the priests of Hedrada who have been rewarded by their deity with a transformation into eternal (but not undead) sentinels of law. Hedrada, god of cities, is believed to have recognized the quickness with which his civilized demesnes were infected with all manner of chaos and anarchy. In an effort to maintain order, hierarchy and the rule of law, and to reward his most earnest mortal servants, Hedrada added the rank and post of inquisitor to the chain of command among his non-mortal servants.

Should a cleric of Hedrada pass away after having attained the rank of patriarch, his or her fellow clergymen consecrate him in a special ceremony, whereby they commend the

cleric's soul to Hedrada. By the decision of Hedrada, the deceased minister may or may not be elevated to the lowest rung of the god's spiritual service. No one but Hedrada and his celestial court knows if the soul has been taken into special service or not — not even the clerics who perform the consecration.

The inquisitor is charged with rooting out all manner of chaotic activity within areas where Hedrada's lawful touch holds sway. The places in which the Inquisitor operates are many and varied: human cities, dwarven kingdoms under mountains, orc and hobgoblin lairs where hierarchy is respected and deference to one's superiors is the rule. This may include such relatively mundane missions as halting the construction of places of worship dedicated to non-lawful deities, or the destruction of unregulated thieves' guilds. The mission

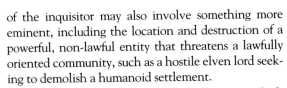

of the inquisitor may also involve something more eminent, including the location and destruction of a powerful, non-lawful entity that threatens a lawfully oriented community, such as a hostile elven lord seeking to demolish a humanoid settlement.

Inquisitors are masters of manipulation, and adventurers may find themselves caught up in the inquisitors' careful plans, even once they have returned home to their communities while not adventuring. On some occasions, high-level heroes are approached by the mysterious inquisitors, who wish to enlist their services. Due to their lawful bent and phenomenal mental capabilities, inquisitors often build elaborate plans and countermeasures, of which their allies may see only a small part.

Combat

Inquisitors usually find they attain best results when they infiltrate a community and work from within to expunge infecting chaotic elements. After all, their mortal clerical brethren are able to fight visible opposition; it is the unseen that inquisitors must combat. Though quite capable in hand-to-hand combat, most inquisitors eschew such unpredictable violence, instead working subtly through manipulation. In order to do this, Hedrada gifts them with some potent capabilities:

Shape of the Flock (Su): The inquisitor is able to take the form of a member of the race with whom it has been appointed to dwell. The inquisitor does not mimic the appearance of another individual, but rather creates its own "mask." It then melds into its social environment, adopting as closely as possible to the life of those around it. This is not a disguise *per se*; rather, the inquisitor has all of the physical characteristics of the race in question, so only supernatural insight can determine the creature's true identity.

Question of True Seeing (Su): The inquisitor is able to ask questions of other members of its apparent race to discern their thoughts and motives. It can immediately tell if a creature is lying, shading the truth, encouraging improper assumptions or the like. Note, however, that this does not tell what the truth *is*, only whether the subject is lying.

Charming the Masses (Su): Some of the most powerful inquisitors are able to work their way up their adopted social ladders and attain prominent positions, where they are able to sway many into doing their bidding. Typically, an inquisitor makes a short speech to any average individual or group in the community (that is, anyone of the race's average Hit Dice, without any additional levels). Those individuals who fail a Will save (DC 20) find themselves swayed to assist the inquisitor in nearly any fashion requested, seeing the inquisitor as a patron figure of society. This power does not function upon chaotic creatures.

Knowing the Heart's Sentiment (Sp): Inquisitors may automatically discern the alignment of creatures they contact. This capacity can be fooled by appropriate concealing spells, though.

Iron Tusker

	Large (long) Beast
Hit Dice:	18d10+126 (225 hp)
Initiative:	+1 (Dex)
Speed:	80 ft.
AC:	27 (-1 size, +1 Dex, +17 natural)
Attacks:	Bite +23 melee; 2 hooves +18 melee
Damage:	Bite 2d8+6; hooves 1d10+3
Face/Reach:	5 ft. by 10 ft./5 ft.
Special Attacks:	Razor tusks
Special Qualities:	Damage reduction 4/—, iron hide
Saves:	Fort +18, Ref +7, Will +5
Abilities:	Str 22, Dex 12, Con 25, Int 16, Wis 9, Cha 9
Skills:	Hide +20, Move Silently +13, Wilderness Lore +15
Feats:	Alertness, Blind Fighting, Combat Reflexes, Sunder, Track, Trample
Climate/Terrain:	Temperate forest
Organization:	Solitary
Challenge Rating:	10
Treasure:	None
Alignment:	Always lawful neutral
Advancement Range:	16-20 HD

Description

The iron tusker is an enormous boar with a black-bristled hide that's covered in hundreds of old scars. Its eyes are wild and bloodshot, and its tusks are more than a foot long, gleaming like polished ivory and sharper than a sword.

Legends claim that the iron tusker is not a living creature at all, but a physical manifestation of a curse imposed by the gods on a foolish and vainglorious noble. The iron tusker simply appears without warning in the forests surrounding a lord's castle and begins to terrorize the local folk, killing hunters and innocent travelers alike, as if daring a hunting party to try and stop it. Hunters that pursue the beast into the forest quickly find the tables turned on them, as the beast is able to move like a shadow through the dense undergrowth and surprise scattered members of the party. Even when cornered, the huge animal is a thing to be feared, with a hide that can shrug off even the strongest blows and tusks that can sever a limb with horrifying ease.

Defeating an iron tusker in combat is considered a mark of immense renown in certain kingdoms; the King's Guard of Darakeene wear the boar head sigil on their shields in honor of an iron tusker they slew in defense of their monarch centuries ago. Stories claim that a man who eats a piece of an iron tusker's heart never feels the touch of fear again.

Combat

The iron tusker is a veritable killing machine. Using an almost supernatural degree of stealth, it surprises its opponents and slashes at them with its fearsome tusks or tramples them under its immense weight. It is swift for its size, and the thickness of its gristly hide allows it to shrug off spears and arrows like raindrops.

Iron Hide (Ex): The hide of an iron tusker is so tough that weapons striking it stand a chance of breaking. If a character rolls a natural 1 to strike the iron tusker, roll 1d6 and add any magical weapon bonus. On a 1-2, the weapon breaks. Any other result has no effect.

Razor Tusks (Ex): If the iron tusker causes a critical hit in combat, there is a chance that it will sever a victim's limb. Roll 1d6: 1-2, no effect; 3-4, arm severed; 5, leg severed; 6, head severed (character killed). If a limb is severed, the victim loses 33% of their current hit points for a lost arm and 50% for a lost leg.

Keffiz

Medium-size Magical Beast

Hit Dice:	8d10+24 (68 hp)
Initiative:	+4 (Dex)
Speed:	60 ft.
AC:	21 (+4 Dex, +7 natural)
Attacks:	Bite +11 melee
Damage:	Bite 2d4+3
Face/Reach:	5 ft. by 5 ft./5 ft.
Special Attacks:	None
Special Qualities:	Animal friendship, SR 10
Saves:	Fort +9, Ref +6, Will +2
Abilities:	Str 16, Dex 18, Con 16, Int 8, Wis 11, Cha 12
Skills:	Animal Empathy +6, Escape Artist +4, Jump +8, Listen +8, Spot +8
Feats:	Dodge, Track
Climate/Terrain:	Any
Organization:	Solitary, brace (2), pack (3-6)
Challenge Rating:	4
Treasure:	None
Alignment:	Always lawful evil
Advancement Range:	6-8 HD (Medium), 9-10 HD (Large)

Description

Keffiz are the hunting hounds of Chardun, who track his enemies and whose steel fangs make his displeasure known. Once normal dogs, these creatures are reshaped by the power of their god. Their fangs and talons are made from glittering steel, and their thick black fur is as tough as wire.

Keffiz are generally encountered under two circumstances. The first is in the company of savant hydrae, another of Chardun's servitor creatures. The savant hydrae use keffiz as hunting hounds and attack dogs, and they seldom travel without a number of these creatures.

However, keffiz can also hunt without the guidance of their hydra handlers. Far more intelligent than a dog of their size, keffiz are often dispatched to remote areas where Chardun or his subordinates suspect that some threat might lurk. These creatures patrol large stretches of territory in an irregular circuit, walking their route on a daily or near-daily basis. As servants of Chardun, keffiz have an innate talent for dominance. A keffiz will typically be accompanied on a patrol of an area by two to four wolves or domestic dogs that it has recruited. These creatures are fanatically loyal to the keffiz, and they will defend it to the death.

Keffiz that are set on patrol are not expected to remedy the situation. However clever and cunning they may be, though, they are still less intelligent than the average human. Keffiz are simply set down to keep an eye on suspicious activities within their run, then report back to their superiors. Their superiors typically dispatch a clutch of savant hydrae, each with a brace of keffiz, to further evaluate the situation.

Occasionally, powerful and devout priests of Chardun will be favored with a brace of keffiz as bodyguards and pets.

Combat

In combat, the keffiz drive any companion canines that they may have recruited into combat first, to soften up their opponents. If they have unreported information, they will use the canines to draw off or slow pursuit so that they can make their report. When under the command of more powerful beings, the keffiz themselves are used in the same role — to soften up powerful opponents and delay or misguide pursuit.

Animal Friendship (Su): Three times per day, a keffiz can invoke a charm effect on a non-magical canine, causing the animal to view the keffiz as an alpha pack member. The canine must succeed at a Will save (DC 16) to resist, or the beguiling lasts for one week.

Lard Worm

Diminutive Vermin

Hit Dice:	1 hp
Initiative:	-1 (Dex)
Speed:	5 ft., climb 5 ft., swim 10 ft.
AC:	13 (+4 size, -1 Dex)
Attacks:	Bite +0 melee
Damage:	1 hit point
Face/Reach:	1 ft. by 1 ft./0 ft.
Special Attacks:	Paralysis
Special Qualities:	Vermin
Saves:	Fort +2, Ref -1, Will +0
Abilities:	Str 3, Dex 8, Con 10, Int 1, Wis 10, Cha 1
Skills:	None
Feats:	None
Climate/Terrain:	Underground or on fatlings
Organization:	Colonies (1-200)
Challenge Rating:	1/4
Treasure:	As per the fatling host
Alignment:	Always neutral
Advancement Range:	None

Description

Just as parasitic fish have a symbiotic relationship with some sharks, so do lard worms have a symbiotic relationship with fatlings (qv.). Around 10 inches long and half-an-inch thick, lard worms live deep in the folds and recesses of fatlings' mounds of flesh, cleaning away the various unwholesome substances (including smothered victims' bodies) that accumulate there. One active fatling can host as many as several hundred worms. Lard worms almost always attack creatures that are enveloped by a fatling, as the paralysis the worms induce makes it more likely that the creature dies there and becomes food for the colony.

Combat

Lard worms strike at anything that gets caught in the folds of a fatling's oily skin. If a fatling is in combat for more than a few rounds, lard worms may become sufficiently agitated that they slither out of the fleshy crevices they inhabit to attack the fatling's enemies.

Paralysis (Ex): Those bitten by a lard worm must succeed at a Fortitude save (DC 10) or be paralyzed for 1d6+5 rounds.

Vermin: Lard worms are immune to mind-altering effects.

Lotus Flower

Tiny Plant

Description

Many varieties of flowering lotus plants exist throughout the tropical regions of the Scarred Lands. While all of the species seem to carry some type of toxin in their pollen, only rare species are toxic enough to affect creatures larger than insects or birds.

These rare species are harvested from the wild and sold at exorbitant prices in black markets to those arcane sorcerers and assassins who are knowledgeable in their uses.

Fresh lotus blossoms carry the full potency of the plant's toxin, but if the flower cannot be used while fresh, it must be properly dried and prepared by an alchemist or herbalist. Anyone preparing a poison from freshly harvested lotus flowers must succeed at an Alchemy or Profession (Herbalist) skill roll (DC 16). Failure wastes the pollen from the plant, and failure on the skill roll by more than five indicates that the alchemist or herbalist has poisoned himself or someone nearby (at GM's discretion).

Some of the lotus varieties whose poisons are potent enough to affect humanoids are described here, but the list is by no means exhaustive.

Black Lotus

The black lotus grows from a thorny creeper vine high in the tree canopy of tropical rain forests, such as the mighty Galumganjus. Its small blossoms range from violet to dark purples that appear nearly black. Anyone searching for this deadly blossom is in for a long and usually fruitless search, as the black lotus is exceedingly rare. Occasionally dead birds and monkeys at the foot of a tree indicate that the deadly blossom hangs somewhere above.

Considered the most powerful poison available, a preparation made from the black lotus is coveted by assassins. If the natural pollen fresh from the plant or a preparation made from dried black lotus flowers is inhaled, the victim must pass a Fortitude saving throw (DC 24) or collapse dead. Even a successful saving throw still has a paralyzing effect on the victim, effectively lowering his Dexterity by 6 (anyone taken to zero or less Dexterity falls to the ground completely paralyzed). Victims who make their save also find their nose, mouth and throat numbed by direct contact from inhaling the poison, making breathing painful and speech nearly impossible.

Victims of black lotus poisoning show a dark purple stain around their nostrils or lips depending on where they inhaled the poison.

One dose of black lotus poison will fetch at least 1000gp the rare time it can even be found on a black market.

Golden Lotus

The golden lotus grows in low light, often creeping through underbrush in a forest floor. The flower is a magnificently large, golden yellow bloom with a long, brilliant red stigma. The flower gives off a potent fruity aroma that can be smelled at some distance, and the flower itself is sweet and succulent to the taste.

Anyone who ingests both the golden pollen and the red stigma of the flower (which anyone eating a whole blossom would certainly do) will wish they had chosen another meal. Once these two parts combine, they form a powerful toxin that will likely kill the person. The unlucky victim's body then becomes the compost from which new golden lotus plants spring.

Anyone ingesting both stigma and pollen suffers 1d4 points of damage each round until he dies from internal hemorrhaging. During this time, the victim is effectively stunned while his muscles go into seizure, and he vomits up blood. However, if the victim passes a Fortitude saving throw (DC 15), he suffers only one point of damage each minute for 2d4 minutes, and he does not suffer any stunning effect.

The golden lotus is prized by assassins (who endeavor to feed their victim both parts of the flower separately). As neither the pollen nor the stigma is poisonous by itself, the two components can sometimes be slipped into a victim's food without detection. The pollen will stay active in an ingester's digestive tract for a day (during which the ingester may feel mild nausea). If the victim eats the stigma during that time, the combined toxic effect will be realized.

One golden lotus blossom will fetch upwards of 400gp on the black market.

Green Lotus

The so-called green lotus is actually a blossom of the blue lotus picked while the flower buds are still green. The buds are dried and then ingested for effect.

The green lotus prevents anyone who ingests it from dreaming properly for 1d4+1 days unless they succeed in a Fortitude saving throw (DC 20). Anyone ingesting the green lotus on purpose to acquire its effect may change any positive level modifier they may have for their Fortitude save to a negative modifier. However, since the ingester's body will try to reject the toxin instinctively, a save must still be made.

Anyone afflicted by the green lotus toxin and thereby prevented from dreaming will lose one point of Wisdom temporarily for each day that they do not dream. Even though they will sleep and rest their body, their mental faculties become impaired without normal dreaming.

Properly timed, subsequent doses of green lotus blossoms will extend the dreamless effect and resultant loss of Wisdom unless the victim makes his saving throw against the new dose(s). Victims brought to 1 Wisdom or lower lose all meaningful willpower and will accept any idea presented to them. Physically self-destructive instructions (such as, "Jump off this cliff.") would still allow the victim a Will saving throw to resist carrying them out (DC 10).

Victims recover any lost Wisdom at a rate of two points per day of normal sleep once they are no longer under the green lotus's effect. However, behaviors or beliefs conditioned into a victim who had fallen to Wisdom 1 or less stand a good chance of enduring even when the green lotus wears off and the victim recovers [GM's discretion or allow a Will saving throw (DC 20)].

Green lotus is commonly used to brainwash or interrogate prisoners. Arcane wizards will sometimes prescribe it as a remedy if someone is being afflicted by a spirit through their dreams or if the wizard himself has raised the ire of a dream spirit and fears being visited. And, like more typical uses for other poisons, it is not unknown for an ambitious prime

minister to slip green lotus into the king's cup and turn the monarch into his puppet. Rich merchants might also contract assassins to slip this drug into the food of the merchant's rival days before an important price negotiation. Finally, the nefarious green lotus brothel in the Seven Sins section of Shelzar is infamous for its use of the drug to convert anyone delivered to the craven establishment's back door into a working slave at the brothel.

Green lotus can sometimes be found at herbalist shops as well as black markets, and it typically costs 50 gp per blossom.

Blue Lotus

The blue lotus pollen can be inhaled or ingested, and it provides a narcotic effect in its user (or victim). Anyone trying to resist its effects may attempt a Fortitude saving throw (DC 13) to shake off its effects.

Anyone afflicted by it will become very drowsy and begin to have hallucinatory effects one minute after inhaling it (or 10 minutes after ingesting it). The effects last 1d4+1 hours.

The effects of blue lotus are almost always euphoric for the user. Many of the Scarred Lands' disaffected wealthy take up the use of blue lotus as a recreational drug, become addicted to its pleasurably effects and spend most of their days in a hallucinatory haze.

The visions offered by the blue lotus seem to have some benefit to oracles and seers however. Anyone under the effects of the lotus may cast divinatory type magic spells as if they were three levels higher. (They do not gain new spells; they just cast their existing spells at greater effect.) Also, anyone using the blue lotus may receive a vision of future or past events relevant to his own life. Such visions are left to the GM for whatever story purposes they might serve.

The side effects of the drug do make it ill suited for adventurers. Anyone under its effects loses two points of Strength and Dexterity temporarily. These points return as soon as the blue lotus runs its course. The victim also sees hallucinatory visions that appear quite real. These hallucinations appear and disappear at the GM's discretion, and each hallucination can be disbelieved like illusion magic. However, those under the drug's effects are at -4 to saving throws against illusionary magic, including disbelieving the blue lotus induced visions.

Additionally, whenever someone under the effects of blue lotus has an adrenaline surge (such as in anger, in combat or during physical exertion), the hallucination effect becomes more pronounced, and the visions become more horrific (e.g., beasts which

attack the victim). Anyone under an adrenaline-related hallucination surge are at -2 to attack rolls and will have 1d4 hallucinatory dangers about.

Blue lotus typically grows in swampy areas. Its thick vines yield lots of blue blossoms. When properly dried and prepared, blue lotus will sell on the black market for 30gp a dose.

Red Lotus

When red lotus pollen is brushed onto its user's skin, its extremely subtle fragrance grants the user +3 Charisma for all social exchanges and skill rolls where the subjects of the skill roll are within range to smell the red lotus (typically 15 feet). The pollen does not change Charisma for any other purpose, so it does not improve a sorcerer's magic bonuses, for example. Its effects last one day or until the user bathes, sweats profusely or something else washes the pollen away.

Applications of Red Lotus pollen cost 25 gp in the rare herbalist shop that carries it, or more on the black market.

White Lotus

Inhalation or ingestion of fresh white lotus pollen or a dried preparation thereof, causes a death-like cataleptic state in its victim (within one minute if inhaled or 10 minutes if ingested), unless the victim passes a Fortitude saving throw (DC 13). The victim gains one additional saving throw each day to awaken from the coma, but the DC goes up by 1 each day.

Additionally, the white lotus is resistant to normal anti-toxin or even magical poison-curing effects. Anti-toxins provide no bonus to the victim's saving throw. Spellcasters seeking to affect the poison through magic must additionally overcome the toxin as if it had a Spell Resistance equal to the current DC of the victim's Fortitude save to recover from the coma before their spell will have any effect.

It is very difficult to discern a white lotus coma from true death, and many a victim has had to go through funeral rites (funeral pyre, burial, mummification, etc.) before actually dying. Superstitious assassins are loath to use white lotus for this reason, believing that any victim killed in such a fashion will rise as undead and seek out the assassin as its first victim.

White lotus grows only in complete shade. If its pollen is exposed to direct sunlight, it turns from white to violet and becomes inert. White lotus coma victims exposed to sunlight may have traces of pollen on their lips or nasal openings turn violet, but this coloration is difficult to differentiate from black lotus stains.

White lotus doses sell for 200 gp in black markets.

Manster

Large (Tall) Magical Beast

Hit Dice:	5d10+15 (42 hp)
Initiative:	+5 (+1 Dex, +4 Improved Initiative)
Speed:	40 ft.
AC:	15 (-1 size, +1 Dex, +5 natural)
Attacks:	Bite +4 melee, 2 claws +9 melee
Damage:	Bite 1d4+5; claw 2d8+5
Face/Reach:	5 ft. by 5 ft./10 ft.
Special Attacks:	None
Special Qualities:	Darkvision 100 ft., invisible in shadow
Saves:	Fort +7, Ref +3, Will +0
Abilities:	Str 21, Dex 13, Con 16, Int 4, Wis 6, Cha 5
Skills:	Hide +10, Jump +4, Listen +6, Move Silently +6, Spot +4
Feats:	Improved Bull Rush, Improved Initiative, Multiattack, Power Attack, Spring Attack, Whirlwind Attack
Climate/Terrain:	Temperate grasslands and forests
Organization:	Solitary or pack (5-8)
Challenge Rating:	3
Treasure:	Standard
Alignment:	Usually neutral evil
Advancement Range:	4-7 HD (Large), 8-10 HD (Huge)

Description

The manster is a pack-oriented primate. They often travel and hunt alone, but frequently return to rejoin an extended family unit. Their rangy bodies are thick and obviously powerful. They have fangs, but these are not nearly so imposing as the dangerous talons on the beasts' front paws. Mansters are much feared for two reasons: their something-more-than-animal intelligence and many special feats that render them very dangerous.

Travelers in particular are wary of mansters because the animals have begun to treat some trade routes, such as the one from Eldura-tre to Tanshon of the continent of Termana, as a sort of humanoid migratory route. In fact, it is not unknown for a pack or two of mansters to take up residence right along such routes and cause so much death and delay that merchants must essentially shut down the route for some time. This has caused food and goods shortages in a number of locations, which leads to profiteering merchants risking the route despite the manster threat. Often these profiteers end up as food for the mansters, which in turn means the mansters have little reason to abandon their position and thus further delay the route's re-opening.

Combat

A manster prefers to ambush its prey. If it can attack a lone victim, so much the better, but otherwise it uses its ability to move unseen in darkness to close within attack distance and leap upon one or more victims (sometimes throwing itself upon all nearby victims with a Whirlwind Attack). Mansters possess enough rudimentary intelligence to know that even camped travelers sometimes wander from the group to relieve themselves, so they often wait for such an opportunity. They also attack and then slip into the shadows beyond a campfire to disappear before attacking again a moment or two later.

Invisible in Shadow (Ex): Whenever a manster stands still or moves slowly (5 feer) in shadow or complete darkness, it becomes invisible to all natural and extraordinary sight, including darkvision and sight-based Keen Senses. Other senses, such as smell, are not affected.

Manticora

Medium-size Monstrous Humanoid

Hit Dice:	2d8+4 (13 hp)
Initiative:	+6 (+2 Dex, +4 Improved Initiative)
Speed:	30 ft. (bipedal), 45 ft. (on all fours)
AC:	16 (+2 Dex, +2 leather armor, +2 natural)
Attacks:	Spiked chain + 4 melee; bite +3 melee, 2 claws -2 melee; harpoon +4 ranged
Damage:	Spiked chain 2d4+1; bite 1d4+1; claw 1d3+1; harpoon 1d8+1
Face/Reach:	5 ft. by 5 ft./5 ft.
Special Attacks:	None
Special Qualities:	Darkvision 60 ft.
Saves:	Fort +2, Ref +5, Will +0
Abilities:	Str 13, Dex 15, Con 14, Int 11, Wis 10, Cha 11
Skills:	Climb +6, Hide +5, Intimidate +4, Jump +5, Listen +4, Move Silently +7, Wilderness Lore +3
Feats:	Improved Initiative, Track, Weapon Finesse (Spiked Chain)
Climate/Terrain:	Any warm, especially savanna or badlands
Organization:	Hunting party (2-5), pride (10-60)
Challenge Rating:	2
Treasure:	Standard
Alignment:	Usually chaotic evil
Advancement Range:	By character class

Description

A vicious, predatory race crafted by Vangal during the Titanswar, the manticora of the Scarred Lands are leonine humanoids with a definite taste for human flesh. Manticora, or "Vangal's cats" as they're sometimes called, are unmistakably inhuman. Their vaguely catlike faces are distended outward, and their teeth are more sharklike than feline. (A manticora, like a shark, sheds and replaces its teeth constantly.) Their bodies are covered with russet-gold fur, and their legs are digitigrade. A manticora also possesses long, retractable black claws on hands and hind paws.

The average member of the race stands somewhere between 5'6" and 6'6", although they tend to lean forward when walking or running on two paws. If its hands are free, a manticora can bound on all fours, increasing its ground speed. They tend to weigh about 150 to 200 pounds, with not a scrap of body fat. Manticora can speak Common, and they can communicate basic concepts ("no," "mine," "kill") to most cat species via body language, growls and snarls.

Manticora embody most of the worst traits of cats and humans. They are affirmed man-eaters; human flesh is a great delicacy among the race. What's more, manticora enjoy hunting for sport, particularly sentient races; they take great pleasure in the fear and pain of their prey. To one of Vangal's cats, there is no greater proof of their hunting superiority than to be able to deliver agonizing, terror-stricken death to the victim of their choice. By tormenting their prey, they believe that they reaffirm their position at the top of the food chain.

Manticora society is based on the pride; these war bands are more inclined to rove from place to place than to stake out a territory of their own. Once they've entered a hunting ground, they take prey with little regard for the long-term health of the ecology. Manticora never mark their territories; that might deprive them of potential prey. A pride is led by a powerful male and his mates (usually three or four of them), all of whom are likely to have a few levels in one or more character classes. Vangal's cats are unlikely to keep domestic animals, although some prides have bred a particularly vicious breed of lion to guard their camps. Only the strongest prides can afford this luxury, for it requires them to bring in all the more meat.

Manticora Characters

Scarred Lands manticora make proficient barbarians, rangers, fighters, rogues and evil druids; their preferred multiclass is barbarian. Manticora clerics typically choose the domains of Destruction and Strength. They have very few wizards, although a few prides are notorious for bloodlines that produce more than their share of sorcerers.

Combat

Vangal's cats can use weapons, but only if they feel that their prey is dangerous. When they're confident in their ability to take a victim down, they resort to tooth and claw for "added intimacy." They're skilled at curing hides, and they typically wear armor sewn together from the hardened skins of their prey, augmented with the occasional scrap of scavenged metal. When using weapons, they prefer short harpoons (like barbed shortspears) designed to sink into flesh and stay there, weighting prey down. When closing for the kill on a dangerous victim, they use spiked chains to entangle their foes or simple chopping or slashing weapons.

Manticora tactics typically involve harrying their prey to tire it out, sneak attacks and even psychological warfare. Although they're sufficiently ferocious to fight in open combat, they prefer keeping a fight on their terms at all times.

Marrow Knight

Large (Long) Undead

Hit Dice:	12d12 (78 hp)
Initiative:	+6 (+2 Dex, +4 Improved Initiative)
Speed:	60 ft.
AC:	19 (-1 size, +8 armor, +2 natural)
Attacks:	Heavy lance +16 melee; or greatsword +15 melee; or longbow +13 ranged
Damage:	Heavy lance 1d8+4; greatsword 2d6+4; arrow 1d8
Face/Reach:	5 ft. by 10 ft./5 ft. (10 ft. with lance)
Special Attacks:	Trample
Special Qualities:	Undead
Saves:	Fort +4, Ref +6, Will +8
Abilities:	Str 18, Dex 14, Con —, Int 10, Wis 10, Cha 14
Skills:	Jump +5, Listen +4, Spot +6
Feats:	Improved Initiative, Weapon Focus (heavy lance)
Climate/Terrain:	Any land
Organization:	Patrol (4-6), column (11-16)
Challenge Rating:	5
Treasure:	None
Alignment:	Always neutral
Advancement Range:	10-15 HD (large)

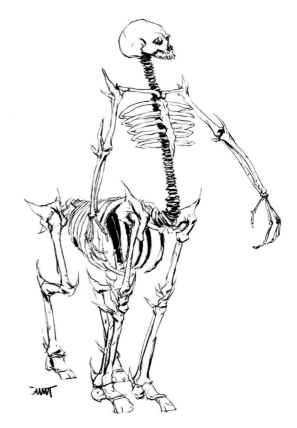

Description

The necromancers of Hollowfaust have devised (or perhaps discovered in some once-forgotten chambers) many undead servitors to guard their labyrinthine home (and to sally forth as an army, should it prove necessary). One of their crowning achievements in this field are the elite cavalry called marrow knights. These knights are crafted from the bones of humans and horses defeated and collected by the necromancers, and resemble skeletal centaurs; they have been armored and barded, and long bone spurs protrude from most major joints.

Marrow knights have a measure of intelligence, even sentience, but they have no independent thought of their own. They are compelled through the rites of creation to obey the necromancers of Hollowfaust; they possess no other ambition. Some serve their masters as steeds. Others patrol the outer corridors of the vast castle, riding down any intruders who might creep in to steal the necromancers' treasures or secrets. Knights without direct orders may come up with some creative or illogical interpretations of their duties, such as slaughtering humans from other lands and bringing back their corpses as raw material.

Combat

Marrow knights are remarkably quick for undead, and often catch their opponents flat-footed with the speed of their assault. They typically begin combat with a massed charge, driving lances into targets, then drawing greatswords to hack at foes. Some, particularly parapet guards, use longbows to whittle down opponents at a range. Marrow knights are not particularly tactically innovative, although those under a necromancer's direction gain the benefit of their master's intelligence and can follow ever more complicated instructions.

Trample (Ex): These undead knights can ride down Small or smaller opponents, crushing them under their hooves. If a Small opponent provokes an attack of opportunity while in melee with a knight, the undead gains an immediate trample attack at +20 on the attack roll. If the knight hits with this attack, the target is knocked down, takes 2d6 damage, and is pinned. The victim must make a successful Reflex save (DC 18) as an action to roll free. If he fails or takes a different action, he suffers an additional 2d6 damage as the skeletal knight continues to trample him. The victim may continue to try to escape in successive actions. A marrow knight may trample only one opponent at a time, but he may fight with his usual weapons while doing so at no penalty.

Spurs (Ex): The bone spurs protruding from marrow knights serve as a measure of defense. Anyone attempting to grapple one in combat (which may include attempts to leap on its back, body slams or bite attacks) must make a successful Reflex saving throw (DC 12) each round of potential contact with a spur or take 1d10 points of damage from striking a spur.

Undead: These beings are immune to poison, sleep, paralysis, stunning and disease. They're not subject to critical hits, subdual damage, ability damage, energy drain or death from massive damage.

Memory-Eater

Medium-size Undead (Ghoul)

Hit Dice:	4d12 (26 hp)
Initiative:	+2 (Dex)
Speed:	30ft.
AC:	15 (+2 Dex, +3 natural)
Attacks:	Bite +5 melee, 2 claws +0 melee
Damage:	Bite 1d8+1; claw 1d4+1
Face/Reach:	5 ft. by 5 ft./5ft.
Special Attacks:	None
Special Qualities:	Undead, memory eating
Saves:	Fort +1, Ref +3, Will +6
Abilities:	Str 13, Dex 15, Con —, Int 16, Wis 14, Cha 16
Skills:	Climb +4, Escape Artist +8, Hide +4, Intuit Direction +5, Jump +4, Listen +4, Move Silently +7, Search +8, Spot +8
Feats:	Multiattack
Climate/Terrain:	Any land
Organization:	Solitary
Challenge Rating:	4
Treasure:	Standard
Alignment:	Usually chaotic evil
Advancement Range:	5-6 HD (Medium-size)

Description

Upon awakening from death, this form of ghoul retains a bit of its former intelligence and memories, often not even recognizing its undead state. Cursed to wander the countryside wracked by the anguish of the dead and the memories of its past life, memory-eaters often seek out clothing, equipment and especially companions that the creature remembers or with which it has some lingering connection.

Sometimes, a memory-eater attempts to reclaim its former role in life through sheer brutality — finding its old home and forcing former loved ones to acknowledge its presence. These attempts soon fail as the ghoul's companions' evident fear enrages the memory-eater by reminding it that it is no longer of the living. When its attempts to reclaim its former life fail, the memory-eater usually flies into a berserk rage, killing anything in its path.

Additionally, a memory-eater gains fractions of memories and experiences from those upon whom it feasts. Sadly, many memory-eaters cannot distinguish these memories from each other, causing them to seek out objects and people that have nothing to do with their former existence and once again try to resume the "normal" life of a person whose memories they have eaten. Typically, a memory-eater wanders by night, looking for a specific lover or friend who can help the ghoul make sense of things. Upon finding that subject, the scene ends in murderous horror with the memory-eater consuming the new victim, and the cycle begins anew.

Combat

Unlike most ghouls, a memory-eater generally does not hide itself from society, but rather attempts to confront former companions that it's able to find. When a memory-eater is reminded of its undead state (usually by the revulsion on the faces of the people it confronts), it attacks those responsible.

Memory Eating (Ex): When devouring a victim, the memory-eater consumes some images and memories of the victim as well. The memory-eater is not able to distinguish these from any others it may have and assumes the memories of the devoured person are his own.

Undead: A memory-eater is immune to poison, sleep, paralysis, stunning and disease. It's not subject to critical hits, subdual damage, ability damage, energy drain or death from massive damage.

Spawn

Like other ghouls, memory-eaters usually devour those they kill. If a body of a victim is left unconsumed and not given sanctified burial rights, it rises from the grave as a memory-eater within a week.

Mere-Lurker

Tiny Animal

Hit Dice:	2d8–4 (5 hp)
Initiative:	+3 (-1 Dex, +4 Improved Initiative)
Speed:	Swim 5 ft.
AC:	11 (+2 size, -1 Dex)
Attacks:	Hooks +1 melee
Damage:	Hooks 1d3
Face/Reach:	2.5 ft. by 2.5 ft./0 ft.
Special Attacks:	Poison hooks, envelop
Special Qualities:	None
Saves:	Fort +1, Ref -1, Will -2
Abilities:	Str 5, Dex 9, Con 6, Int —, Wis 6, Cha 2
Skills:	None
Feats:	None
Climate/Terrain:	Temperate, freshwater pools
Organization:	Colony (5-10)
Challenge Rating:	1/4
Treasure:	Standard
Alignment:	Always neutral
Advancement Range:	1-3 HD

Description

The mere-lurker is a small aquatic animal with a dark greenish-black lower body and muscular tail. The inside of its enveloping hood is a pale green, and resembles an irregular-shaped lily pad or other shallow-water plant. Its eyes — the jewellike lures that give the creature its more romantic name, Lover's Folly — are a deep sapphire blue, and can reflect even the weakest sources of light.

Mere-lurkers are commonly found in shallow ponds or streams where animals and people stop for water. They move about underwater by pumping air through small jets situated around their lower body, and at night they shift to different parts of their territory, moving in among more innocent vegetation for camouflage. Once in position, the mere-luker's powerful tail wraps around a heavy rock or sunken log to anchor itself, and at first light the hood opens and rises to within a few inches of the water's surface, waiting for prey. When an animal drinks nearby — or a curious person attempts to touch the creature's jewellike eyes — its hood closes like the jaws of a trap, and dozens of retractable hooks situated around the hood's rim pump a paralytic poison into the victim. The mere-lurker's tail constricts, pulling the victim below the surface, where either the poison or the water finishes it off. Enzymes secreted from within the hood then liquefy the dead prey for consumption.

The brilliantly hued eyes of the mere-lurker have in recent years come into vogue among lesser nobles of many civilized countries, valued as ornamental inlay or costume jewelry because of their reflective qualities. Though the perils of these creatures are well-known, each year there are stories of hopeful lovers lured to their deaths by the false promise of a glittering clutch of sapphires just beneath the surface of a shallow lake.

Combat

The mere-lurker kills its prey through a combination of suffocation and poisoning. Its hood constricts around its prey with surprising strength, and inward-curving hooks dig deep into the flesh, injecting its poison and making it that much harder for the victim to escape. Finally, the creature uses its powerfully muscled tail to pull itself deeper underwater, hopefully drowning the victim if the poison is not sufficient to the task.

Poison Hooks (Ex): The mere-lurker stings its prey with poison hooks that contain a powerful paralytic toxin (attack bonus included above). Victims must make a Fortitude save (DC 18) or suffer two points of Dexterity ability damage per turn as long as the mere-lurker continues to envelop part of the victim. This loss is temporary.

Envelop (Ex): Victims must make a Reflex save (DC 18) to avoid having their hand or body part enveloped by the creature. Once enveloped, it requires a Strength roll (DC 20) to pry the monster's hood open.

Mill Slug

Gargantuan (Long) Vermin

Hit Dice:	16d8 + 112 (184 hp)
Initiative:	-4 (Dex)
Speed:	20 ft.
AC:	6 (-4 Dex, -4 size, +4 natural)
Attacks:	Bite +18 melee
Damage:	Bite 5d6+6
Face/Reach:	20 ft. by 60 ft./10 ft.
Special Attacks:	Crush
Special Qualities:	Damage reduction 5/—
Saves:	Fort +17, Ref +1, Will +1
Abilities:	Str 22, Dex 3, Con 25, Int —, Wis 3, Cha 10
Skills:	Listen +2, Spot +4
Feats:	None
Climate/Terrain:	Temperate and warm coastal land
Organization:	Solitary
Challenge Rating:	9
Treasure:	None
Alignment:	Always neutral
Advancement Range:	6-10 HD (Large), 11-15 HD (Huge), 17-20 HD (Gargantuan), 21-30 HD (Colossal)

Description

It's almost certain that the mill slug is a by-product of the Divine War — and that it wasn't created intentionally. These monstrous gastropods are dangerous mainly by accident; they lack the sentience or even the instinct to be deliberately menacing. Stretching approximately 70 feet from eyestalk to tail-tip as an adult, a mill slug leaves massive swaths of barren ground behind it, as it must devour everything it can reach just to stay alive.

Mill slugs earn their name for their tendency to destroy windmills. Apparently, the spinning motion of the airfoils attracts the slugs. A mill slug hypnotized by a windmill's motion (or any other repetitive motion of similar size) will attempt to smother the movement under its bulk.

Mill slugs are thankfully rare; although far from ideal prey, they *are* technically edible, and predators otherwise down on their luck may try to take a chunk out of a passing mill slug. Scholars theorize that the mill slug is relatively immune to the ravages of aging, and that they mate largely by accident (when one slug crosses the trail of another).

Combat

Mill slugs aren't predators. When attacked, they crush their enemies under their gigantic bodies if they can and flee if they can't. A mill slug will bite reflexively at any creature fool enough to approach its rasping mouthparts, but it is unlikely to go out of its way to use a bite attack.

Crush (Ex): Although mill slugs have a small range of movement and turn slowly, anyone rash enough to attack them from the front risks ending up underneath the slug. Although their bodies are soft, they are also thick-skinned and unbelievably heavy. Anyone in front of the slug when it moves forward must make a Reflex save (DC 15) or be crushed under the slug's massive body. The slug's weight, combined with the smothering slime that finds its way down throats and into lungs, causes 3d12 points of damage each round. Hungry slugs stop on top of their victims, waiting for the slime to smother them.

Vermin: Immune to mind-altering effects.

Miredweller

Medium-size Monstrous Humanoid

Hit Dice:	4d8-4 (14 hp)
Initiative:	+3 (Dex)
Speed:	40 ft.
AC:	13 (+3 Dex)
Attacks:	Wrap +6 melee; 2 claws +6 melee
Damage:	Wrap1d6+2, claw 1d4+2
Face/Reach:	5 ft. by 5 ft./ 5 ft.
Special Attacks:	Poison, skinfold wrap, smother
Special Qualities:	None
Saves:	Fort +0, Ref +7, Will -1
Abilities:	Str 14, Dex 17, Con 8, Int 7, Wis 7, Cha 4
Skills:	Listen +2, Hide +6
Feats:	Dodge, Spring Attack
Climate/Terrain:	Swamps
Organization:	Solitary (rarely), band (4-10)
Challenge Rating:	2
Treasure:	Standard
Alignment:	Usually chaotic evil
Advancement Range:	4-5 HD (Medium-size) 6-7 HD (Large)

Description

The foul, reptilian race of miredwellers inhabits swamps and marshes, where the beings can ambush passing creatures. They tend to inhabit locales near the lairs of other humanoid races so they have a steady source of creatures to feed upon.

Miredwellers are small for Medium-size creatures. They have scaly, waxy skin and wing-like skinfolds (not unlike a flying squirrel's) that are attached to the sides of their bodies and their arms. A myriad of tiny, sharp, curved hooks protrude from the inside of these large flaps. The miredweller attacks by swooping down on or creeping up behind its victim and wrapping its wings about her.

Miredwellers tend to hunt in bands. A favorite tactic is to have one or two miredwellers bait an opponent, such that victims can be surprised from behind, therefore becoming more susceptible to a skinfold wrap.

Miredwellers worship Luchanig, the demi-god of swamp and mires. Luchanig's main form is that of a large miredweller, and adventurers have spoken of seeing the great miredweller beast roaming the bogs and mires of the Scarred Lands. One tale holds that Luchanig is a master assassin whose expertise in poison is unparalleled and that he creates all manner of lethal substances from the infinite variety of plants, bugs and dark fen.

Yugman the Sage has hypothesized that miredwellers actually draw the living essence out of victims when they wrap them and prick them with their pinhooks. That is to say, not only do the miredweller's pinhooks inject poison but they also absorb small doses of life

energy. This is why, according to Yugman, miredwellers as a race grow slowly larger and more powerful over time.

Combat

In combat, the miredweller may fight normally with its two claws. Of course, it prefers to use its deadly skinfolds to attack.

Skinfold Wrap (Ex): If an opponent is successfully surprised from behind by a miredweller, the miredweller can attempt to wrap its winged skinfolds around its victim. The miredweller need only hit normally to do this, and the victim takes damage from being pricked by thousands of tiny, painful hooks extending from the skinfold. This ability can only be used against Small and Medium-sized creatures. In order to break free, victims must make a Fortitude save (DC 9 for Medium-sized opponents, DC 14 for Small opponents.) Every round of struggling to break free inflicts the normal 1d6+2 damage on the victim as the hooks tear at her.

Smother (Ex): A wrapped opponent can be suffocated while in the miredweller's perilous folds. Every round that a creature fails to break free from the skinfold wrap, it takes 1d3 points of smothering damage.

Poison (Ex): Finally, the tiny needles inject poison into wrapped prey. Opponents must make a Fortitude save (DC 12) or suffer an additional 1d4 points of damage per round from poison. Breaking free of the skinfold wrap stops poison damage, but victims are nauseated for 2d4 rounds and suffer a -1 penalty on all rolls while so nauseated.

Miser Jackal

Small Animal

Hit Dice:	1d8 (4 hp)
Initiative:	+3 (Dex)
Speed:	50 ft.
AC:	14 (+1 size, +3 Dex)
Attacks:	Bite +0 melee
Damage:	Bite 1d4–2
Face/Reach:	5 ft. by 5 ft./5 ft.
Special Attacks:	Narcotic bite
Special Qualities:	Scent
Saves:	Fort +0, Ref +5, Will +1
Abilities:	Str 6, Dex 17, Con 11, Int 3, Wis 13, Cha 13
Skills:	Hide +4, Jump +2, Listen +5, Move Silently +6, Pick Pocket +5, Spot +5
Feats:	Alertness
Climate/Terrain:	Warm plains and savannahs
Organization:	Solitary
Challenge Rating:	1/4
Treasure:	Standard
Alignment:	Always neutral
Advancement Range:	1–2 HD

Description

Miser jackals are a remarkably clever breed of jackal that is relatively common in the plains and savannahs of the Scarred Lands. The animals have a keen sense of smell, and are particularly interested in metal. The miser jackal uses its gift for stealth to steal metallic objects from travelers or local residents, instinctively "caching" them later in secret hiding places. These jackals typically approach targets under the cover of dusk, often while a band is still making camp but before it's settled down and posted sentries. They have an uncanny knack for filching items that a party might need: a miser jackal might steal a group's tent pegs just as it begins to rain, or swipe a warrior's scabbard while he's sharpening his sword. Once the jackal has its latest "toy," it quietly retreats before its victims can discover the loss.

Although this behavior would ordinarily classify the miser jackal as an intolerable nuisance, many fortune-hunters refuse to kill the creatures. The reason is somewhat surprising: Miser jackals often act as guides for large predators or heavily armed bands of humans, leading them to the lairs of local threats — particularly rich ones. The miser jackal's nose for metal and its self-preservation instinct leads it to carefully mark the territories of any creatures in possession of more than a coincidental amount of metal, and that are dangerous as well. If such a creature (or creatures) moves into a miser jackal's hunting range, the jackal generally sniffs out the edges of the newcomer's territory. Once the jackal finds a large predator or band of humans, it tries to lead them toward the lair of the other beast. If all goes well, the predator or humans kill the newcomer, leaving the jackal free to swipe portions of the hoard or feast on the carcass — a most mutual relationship.

Combat

Combat? Never! Miser jackals would much rather flee than fight. They fight only when sick or desperate (such as a mother defending her pups), and even then are limited to biting.

Narcotic Bite (Ex): In order to defend itself a little bit, the miser jackal has taken to chewing the leaves of the julka weed, a potent narcotic to which the jackal possesses a natural immunity. Anyone bitten by a miser jackal must make a Fortitude save (DC14) or take two points of Dexterity and Intelligence ability damage. The ability loss lasts between one to six hours.

Scent (Ex): Miser jackals can smell creatures or sources of metal within 60 feet; if the target is upwind, the range increases to 120 feet, and if downwind, the range decreases to 30 feet.

Mistwalker

Medium-size Undead

Hit Dice:	6d12 (39 hp)
Initiative:	+0
Speed:	120 ft.
AC:	15 (+5 natural)
Attacks:	Chilling touch +6 melee
Damage:	Chilling touch 1d8
Face/Reach:	5 ft. by 5 ft./5 ft.
Special Attacks:	Chilling touch
Special Qualities:	Mist walk, damage reduction 15/+1, vulnerable to fire
Saves:	Fort +2, Ref +2, Will +4
Abilities:	Str 10, Dex 10, Con 10, Int 9, Wis 9, Cha 12
Skills:	Bluff +4, Hide +8, Intuit Direction +4, Knowledge (religion) + 3, Listen +5, Move Silently +9, Spot +5
Feats:	None
Climate/Terrain:	Any
Organization:	Solitary
Challenge Rating:	3
Treasure:	Standard
Alignment:	Usually neutral
Advancement Range:	5-7 HD

Description

Superstitious folk close their doors and shutters on spring and autumn nights, and say prayers against the rising of a fog, for many believe that the swirling cold fingers of mist are in fact the breath of the restless dead. When the fog rises, ghosts walk the earth, looking for mortals out at night who can lay them to rest — or salve their twisted hate.

Mistwalkers emerge only on nights when there is a thick fog; they first appear over the spot where they died, but these spirits are free to roam wherever the fog extends, so they can wander many miles. They appear as wispy, insubstantial forms, sometimes glowing a pale green, like grave mold. Most speak Common; all mistwalkers can apparently understand each of the major languages, but can speak only those they were fluent with in life.

Most of these spirits are tortured souls looking for someone to complete an errand or carry a message to a loved one so they can finally rest. Such actions can usually be completed in a single night, and sometimes these grateful ghosts lead their saviors to hidden caches of treasure as a reward for their compassion.

There are a few such spirits, however, who crave no rest, but seek to vent their bitterness against the living. These cruel ghosts appear in the guise of a forlorn spirit, and try to fool kind souls into errands that lead to hidden traps, misery and death.

Combat

Evil mistwalkers work their mischief through lies and treachery, sending would-be saviors into hazard-ous traps and pitfalls. If confronted, they use their affinity with the mists to their advantage, seeming to strike from every direction at once and leeching the warmth from their victims' bones with their chilling touch.

Mist Walk (Su): Within the bounds of the mist, the spirit can make attacks on a victim at the beginning, middle or end of its movement, as desired.

Chilling Touch (Su): The mistwalker's touch is colder than ice. Victims hit by the mistwalker must make a Fortitude save (DC 19) or take one point of Constitution ability damage, in addition to the damage from the blow. Lost Constitution points return at a rate of one per hour.

Vulnerable to Fire (Ex): Mistwalkers take double damage from fire-based attacks.

Moon Cat

Tiny Magical Beast

Hit Dice:	1d10 (5 hp)
Initiative:	+2 (Dex)
Speed:	40 ft.
AC:	14 (+2 size, +2 Dex)
Attacks:	Bite −1 melee, 2 claws −3 melee
Damage:	Bite 1d4; claws 1d3
Face/Reach:	2.5 ft. by 2.5 ft./0 ft.
Special Attacks:	Mass charm, paralysis
Special Qualities:	Portent, flawless teleport
Saves:	Fort +1, Ref +6, Will +3
Abilities:	Str 3, Dex 15, Con 12, Int 5, Wis 17, Cha 16
Skills:	Hide +8, Listen +12, Move Silently +8, Spot +12
Feats:	Alertness, Dodge, Lightning Reflexes, Multi-Attack, Mobility, Run
Climate/Terrain:	Any land
Organization:	Solitary
Challenge Rating:	1/2
Treasure:	Standard
Alignment:	Always neutral
Advancement Range:	None

Description

The moon cat is a magical creature that appears after moonrise. It is drawn to places or people in impending crisis. Not always as straightforward as someone about to fight for his life, it could be a number of significant events — a treaty signing, the birth of a great villain, the start of a romance and the like.

Sages and scholars argue whether the moon cat is a purely mystic portent or is simply a beast in tune with the moon. Those who have encountered a moon cat are inclined to think the former, as strange luck follows them soon after. Legends agree that encountering a moon cat during a full moon is good luck, while seeing one during the new moon foretells disaster.

It's seldom clear at the time why the moon cat has appeared or whom it may approach. Only in the hours, days or even weeks after it has left is the moon cat's influence felt.

Mages believe that a moon cat offers direct access to powerful magical energy. Not surprisingly, magic-users of all stripes are eager to get their hands on one for study or even to make into a familiar. There is no known instance of a moon cat being successfully captured, though. The rare times one has been caught, it has vanished by sunrise.

A moon cat is the size of a large domesticated cat, with pale silvery fur and intense black eyes. A faint nimbus appears to surround it at times, not unlike the aura that often encompasses the moon.

Combat

A moon cat can use its claws and teeth in combat, but it prefers to rely on its paranormal abilities for defense.

Mass Charm (Ex): The moon cat automatically generates this effect when it appears. It need not speak the targets' language; the moon cat's body language is sufficient to sooth those around it. Treat the creature as a 9th-level sorcerer to determine the number of Hit Dice affected. Subjects must succeed at a Will save (DC 20) to resist.

Paralysis (Ex): Anyone who touches the moon cat must succeed at a Fortitude save (DC 18) or be paralyzed for 1d6+4 minutes.

Portent (Ex): The moon cat rubs against a chosen target, gifting it with a *portent*. The subject may make a Will save (DC 16) to resist. The Game Master rolls 1d8 to determine the effect based on the current moon phase:

Moon Phase	Miracle	Curse
Full Moon	1–7	8
Waning Moon	1–5	6–8
New Moon	1	2–8
Waxing Moon	1–3	4–8

The subject is unaware of which effect he's received until he takes an action that plausibly triggers it. For a miracle, it's important that the Game Master describe circumstances so that the subject has a clear understanding of his situation. The Game Master determines how curse affects the target.

Flawless Teleport (Ex): The moon cat uses this to home in on the site to which it feels drawn. When its task is complete, the creature teleports back to its lair. Many a wizard has spent a lifetime searching for these places, to no avail.

Morgaunt

Medium-size Humanoid

Hit Dice:	3d8+12 (25 hp)
Initiative:	+2 (+2 Dex)
Speed:	60 ft.
AC:	17 (+2 Dex, +4 scale armor, +1 shield)
Attacks:	Bite +5 melee and 2 claws +0 melee; or longsword +5 melee
Damage:	Bite 1d4+2; claw 1d4+1; longsword 1d8+2
Face/Reach:	5 ft. by 5 ft./5 ft.
Special Attacks:	Infect
Special Qualities:	Feats of strength, immunities
Saves:	Fort +7, Ref +2, Will +0
Abilities:	Str 15, Dex 15, Con 18, Int 9, Wis 8, Cha 7
Skills:	Bluff +6, Hide +3, Listen +2, Spot +3
Feats:	Alertness, Armor Proficiency (medium), Blind Fighting
Climate/Terrain:	Any
Organization:	Solitary, colony (2-12)
Challenge Rating:	1
Treasure:	Standard
Alignment:	Always neutral evil
Advancement Range:	By character class

Description

Morgaunts are living beings that have become infected by a parasitic grub that enters the body through a wound or is ingested with infected meat. The grub, initially little larger than a grain of rice, works its way into the host's brain and then begins to multiply. As the colony grows, the host becomes increasingly violent and deranged, and develops an insatiable hunger for meat. Eventually this hunger turns to cannibalism, and the morgaunt feeds upon its neighbors and loved ones, killing them as they sleep. Even if a victim survives an attack, his wounds are almost certainly infected, and before long another morgaunt emerges to spread terror and death among the local folk.

A morgaunt's appearance is variable, depending on how long the host body has been infected. In the early stages, a morgaunt's host looks pale and sickly, but otherwise normal. As the infection spreads, and the grub colony increases, the hosts' skin turns sickly gray, and its eyes become sunken. Soon there are patches of skin sloughing away from the decaying body, and upon first sight the creature appears to be a zombie or other form of undead.

When a town or castle is discovered by the Order of the Morning Sky to be infested with morgaunts, it is quickly surrounded and the inhabitants have three days to wipe out the infestation themselves or else everything is put to the torch to prevent the infection from spreading. This militant order of clerics faithful to Madriel has dedicated itself to rooting out such evil outbreaks of disease and pestilence, and maintains mounted forces in chapter houses across the lands of Ghelspad to race to suspected outbreaks at a moment's notice. In the event that these clerics are unable to answer the call, rulers sometimes turn to mercenaries or adventurers strong enough to do what must be done.

Combat

A morgaunt is capable of using weapons and armor to battle its opponents, but is equally likely to attack using claws and teeth, the better to infect its prey. Most times these creatures are not capable of concocting elaborate schemes or strategies, however, exceptional creatures have been capable of not only acting intelligently on their own, but leading large groups of other morgaunts. The statistics provided are for a typical human morgaunt, but virtually any sentient race can be infected.

Feats of Strength (Ex): Because the morgaunt's body is being driven by a colony of creatures inside its brain, the body can be pushed beyond normal limits of strength and endurance, receiving the following bonuses: Strength +4, Dexterity +4, Constitution +7 (already calculated above).

Immunities (Ex): The morgaunt is immune to the following: sleep, paralysis, stunning and disease.

Infect (Ex): Anyone damaged by the morgaunt's bite must pass a Fortitude save (DC 14) to resist becoming infected by the parasite. Infected victim's will gradual show symptoms of carnivorous hunger and violent mood swings until a number of days equal to their Constitution passes, at which time their transformation into a morgaunt is complete. A spell to magical cure the parasite disease will cleanse the victim if applied before their final transformation.

Murdersprite

Tiny Fey

Hit Dice:	1d6+2 (5 hp)
Initiative:	+6 (+2 Dex, +4 improved initiative)
Speed:	15 ft., 60 ft. flight (good)
AC:	16 (+2 size, +2 Dex, +2 natural)
Attacks:	Pin +5 melee
Damage:	Pin 1
Face/Reach:	2 1/2 ft. by 2 1/2 ft./—
Special Attacks:	Poisoned weapons
Special Qualities:	None
Saves:	Fort +2, Ref +4, Will +0
Abilities:	Str 4, Dex 14, Con 14, Int 6, Wis 10, Cha 6
Skills:	Disable Device +2, Hide +5, Move Silently +4, Pick Lock +2, Search +1, Spot +3, Use Rope +1
Feats:	Dodge, Improved Initiative, Weapon Finesse (pin)
Climate/Terrain:	Any, typically urban or forest
Organization:	Gang (1-4), nest (1-100)
Challenge Rating:	1/2
Treasure:	None (gang); standard (nest)
Alignment:	Always neutral evil
Advancement Range:	2 HD (Tiny)

Description

Cruel and bloodthirsty creatures, murdersprites enjoy undertaking sabotage, deception and observation. Intelligent but by no means swift-witted, these creatures are possessed of a malicious cunning, and they take great pride in inflicting woe. Unlike many of the creatures created by the Titans, murdersprites have prospered in the time since the war. With their fast breeding cycle and malicious intelligence, they have infested many places, displacing rats as vermin or actually herding them for food.

Where they are found, murdersprites are mercilessly hunted and destroyed. They can and will carry out campaigns of terror and sabotage for little more reason than that fear and pain delight them. Where they dwell, small children and the elderly are set upon and blinded or hamstrung, pets are poisoned and tortured, and every grain silo is a bomb waiting to explode.

Murdersprites are certainly clever enough to use tools. Even if they are not intelligent enough to manufacture items, they are certainly able to filch them. These sprites are as brutal to one another as they are to the larger inhabitants of the world around them, and their existence is a squalid caricature of human life, composed of little more than sly manipulation and brutal dominance games.

Combat

Most murdersprites carry pins, sharpened bits of wire or razor-edged fragments of glass they use for self-defense among their own kind or from aggressive animals. Despite their uncanny durability, they prefer to avoid combat with things larger than themselves. Typically, murdersprites attack with poison, pitfall and ambush as a last resort.

Poisoned Weapons (Ex): Anyone stabbed by a murdersprite's weapon must make a Fortitude save (DC 13) or take 1d4 points of Constitution ability damage. Each weapon retains its poison for only one stab, after which the murdersprite must coat it in poison again (as a move action which provokes attacks of opportunity).

Muskhorn

Huge (Long) Animal

Hit Dice:	15d8+150 (217 hp)
Initiative:	-1 (-1 Dex)
Speed:	50 ft.
AC:	27 (-2 size, -1 Dex, +20 natural)
Attacks:	Horns +23 melee
Damage:	Horn 2d10+10
Face/Reach:	10 ft. by 20 ft./10 ft.
Special Attacks:	Corrosive musk
Special Qualities:	None
Saves:	Fort +19, Ref +4, Will +4
Abilities:	Str 30, Dex 8, Con 30, Int —, Wis 9, Cha 9
Skills:	None
Feats:	Trample
Climate/Terrain:	Grasslands
Organization:	Herd (5-10 bulls, 10-20 cows, 1d20 calves)
Challenge Rating:	9
Treasure:	None
Alignment:	Always neutral
Advancement Range:	6-17 HD

Description

Muskhorn herds were once a fixture of the plains of Termana that spread southward from the Iron Steppe, but relentless hunting from tribes of steppe trolls and the recently returned humans have thinned their numbers greatly, leaving the few remaining herds openly hostile to anything that moves on two legs.

Muskhorns are huge, powerful grass-eaters, covered in thick layers of gristle and brown fur. The skulls of muskhorn bulls are made of thick bone, and their four long horns can reach lengths of up to four feet each. Bulls are highly protective of the herd, and immediately rush forward to challenge an interloper who comes too close. During the early spring when muskhorn calves are born, the bulls are exceptionally aggressive and can attack without warning.

Steppe trolls attach considerable mystical significance to the muskhorn, and troll males must successfully stalk and kill a bull as a rite of manhood. The skull and breastbones of the bull are taken back to the tribe and made into armor that the new adult wears with pride.

Combat

Enraged muskhorns emit a deafening bellow and charge opponents, hoping to gore or trample them. At the same time, the angry bull exudes a powerful musk that attacks an opponent's eyes and nose, causing them to burn and itch abominably. The musk has a strong acidic content that corrodes metal on contact, giving rise to the muskhorn's nickname among humans, "swordbreaker."

Corrosive Musk (Ex): Enraged bulls emit an acidic musk that irritates an enemy's eyes and throat, and is corrosive to metals. Creatures within 20 feet of a muskhorn bull must make a Fortitude save (DC 15) or suffer a -2 modifier to initiative and attack rolls for 1d4 rounds. Armor and weapons within this area of effect begin to corrode immediately. Owners of such items should make a Fortitude save (DC 10) per item in each round that it is exposed to the musk. Once an item fails four saves, it is corroded beyond repair. Magical weapons and armor may add their respective bonuses to their saves.

Narleth

	Large (Tall) Aberration
Hit Dice:	8d8+40 (76 hp)
Initiative:	+7 (+4 Improved Initiative, +3 Dex)
Speed:	60 ft., climb 60 ft.
AC:	15 (-1 size, +3 Dex, +3 natural)
Attacks:	Bite +9 melee, 4 claws +4 melee, and web spitter +10 ranged
Damage:	Bite 1d8+2 and posion; claw 1d6+1
Face/Reach:	5 ft. by 5 ft./10 ft.
Special Attacks:	Web spitter, acid venom
Special Qualities:	None
Saves:	Fort +11, Ref +5, Will -1
Abilities:	Str 15, Dex 17, Con 20, Int 6, Wis 5, Cha 3
Skills:	Balance + 10, Hide +10, Jump +8, Listen +4, Move Silently +8, Spot +12
Feats:	Alertness, Combat Reflexes, Improved Initiative
Climate/Terrain:	Temperate forests, foothills
Organization:	Solitary
Challenge Rating:	5
Treasure:	Standard
Alignment:	Always chaotic evil
Advancement Range:	6-9 HD

Description

The narleth, which in Elvish means "silken death," are a horrible blending of human and spider, perhaps created as warriors during the war between the gods and Titans, or perhaps simply mutated during the wild magical storms that occurred shortly afterward. The narleth is larger than a man, with four arms ending in strong, clawed hands, an impossibly broad, bony chest and a large head covered in bristly brown spines and long, fang-tipped mandibles.

In the years following the ancient war, the narleths were a plague against elvenkind, terrorizing their forests and preying upon their children. Finally, the elves came together and hunted these creatures nearly to extinction, and now only a few of the species remain, haunting lonely caverns or nursing their hatred in forgotten ruins. They delight in causing misery to any creature that stumbles into their clutches, immobilizing them in silken cocoons and slowly dissolving them with their venom.

Combat

The narleth prefers to attack from ambush, concealing itself in deep shadows or underneath piles of leaves or rubbish, then springing out and covering a victim with a spray of webbing. Once trapped, the victim feels the narleth's bite, which first paralyzes the body, then begins to dissolve it.

Web Spitter (Ex): The narleth can spit a stream of sticky webbing from an orifice located between its mandibles. The webbing strikes anyone directly in front of the monster up to a distance of 40 feet, unless a target can make a successful Reflex save (DC 17). Anyone hit by the webbing is entangled immediately, requiring no less than three successful Strength rolls (DC 16) to break free. Each attempted Strength roll takes the place of a move action.

Acid Venom (Ex): The venom of the narleth is extremely potent and highly acidic. Any victim (including elves) bitten must make an immediate Fortitude save (DC 18) or be completely paralyzed. If the victim is subjected to multiple bites, the poison builds up in the person's system and begins the horrific process of dissolving flesh and bone. For each subsequent bite after a failed save, a victim loses one point Constitution. This loss is permanent ability drain

Night Singer

	Diminutive Vermin
Hit Dice:	1d8-2 (2 hp)
Initiative:	+1 (+1 Dex)
Speed:	Fly 30 ft.
AC:	15 (+4 size, +1 Dex)
Attacks:	Sting +0 melee
Damage:	Sting 1d4
Face/Reach:	1 ft. by 1 ft./0 ft
Special Attacks:	Poison sting
Special Qualities:	Vermin
Saves:	Fort +0, Ref +1, Will -1
Abilities:	Str 1, Dex 13, Con 6, Int 1, Wis 9, Cha 8
Skills:	None
Feats:	None
Climate/Terrain:	Sub-tropical swamps
Organization:	Solitary
Challenge Rating:	1/4
Treasure:	Half-standard
Alignment:	Always neutral
Advancement Range:	1-3 HD

Description

The beautiful but deadly night singers are large, five-inch-long insects similar to giant dragonflies, with deep green bodies and iridescent wings. The insect's long, whiplike abdomen has an indigo-colored bulb at the tip and a long curved stinger similar to a scorpion's. At night, phosphorescent deposits along the night singer's body causes it to emit a ghostly green glow. The insect's wings create a lilting humming noise that changes pitch as the creature rises and lowers in the air.

Superstitious folk in the swamplands and bayous of southern Ghelspad believe that night singers are the spirits of betrayed lovers, beguiling travelers with their eerie, glowing dance, and their beautiful, complicated "songs." Certainly anyone foolish enough to pursue these dancing, singing motes into the humid night are oftentimes never heard from again.

During the summer months when the night singer is active, it lays eggs along tree trunks close to the water's edge, and the female uses its glow and eerie song to drive away possible predators. If an animal or person is unlucky enough to get too close to the eggs, the insect attacks, stinging the victim and injecting a powerful psychotropic poison. This poison produces immediate and powerful hallucinations, and a rush of terror that is somehow greatly enhanced by the night singer's complex buzzing. Most victims, overcome with nightmarish visions, run screaming deeper into the swamp, where any number of common hazards often seal their doom.

The night singer's poison is greatly valued by both illusionists and assassins, who pay a high price for the insect's venom sacs, or better yet, a cluster of healthy eggs.

Combat

When its eggs are threatened, a night singer attacks immediately, darting in quickly to sting its victim and then flying up and out of reach, where its song can begin work on the hapless individual's senses. It maintains its song until the victim flees the area; the insect does not travel more than 10 yards from its eggs for any reason.

Poison Sting (Ex): The night singer's main defense is a poison sting that causes terrifying hallucinations. Any victim that is successfully stung must make a Fortitude save (DC 22). Illusions, based on the victim's deepest fears, are incredibly vivid and involve all five senses. Each round, the victim may attempt another Fortitude save (DC 18) to throw off the effects. If the victim is still within earshot of the night singer's song, the DC for subsequent saves increases to 22.

Vermin: Immune to mind-altering effects.

Night Terror

Medium-size Animal

Hit Dice:	3d8+6 (19 hp)
Initiative:	+2 (Dex)
Speed:	75 ft., climb 75 ft.
AC:	14 (+2 Dex, +2 natural)
Attacks:	Bite +7 melee and 2 claws +2 melee
Damage:	Bite 1d10+4; claw 1d8+2
Face/Reach:	5 ft. by 5 ft./5 ft.
Special Attacks:	None
Special Qualities:	Nightvision 60ft.
Saves:	Fort +5, Ref +3, Will +0
Abilities:	Str 18, Dex 15, Con 15, Int 9, Wis 8, Cha 7
Skills:	Balance +4, Hide +6, Listen +8, Move Silently +6, Spot +6
Feats:	Alertness, Combat Reflexes, Cleave, Track
Climate/Terrain:	Rain forests, grasslands, plains
Organization:	Pack (6-10)
Challenge Rating:	2
Treasure:	Standard
Alignment:	Always chaotic evil
Advancement Range:	2-6 HD

Description

A night terror is a baboon-like ape slightly smaller than a man, with a long prehensile tail and covered in grayish-black fur. Reddish-orange eyes gleam with startling intelligence from a black-masked face, and yellow tusks bulge from its upper and lower jaws.

Night terrors are legendary predators of the rain forests, feared as much for their frightening degree of intelligence as they are for their terrible savagery. Night terrors have keen senses and are skillful trackers, picking up a likely victim's trail and then stalking it for days, learning its habits and potential weaknesses. Operating in packs, night terrors use barks and long, ululating howls to communicate in the darkness, surrounding their prey and keeping it nervous and off-balance. When the time is right, they ambush a target and overwhelm it with sheer numbers, pulling it down under a writhing mass of fur, talons and teeth.

What is most chilling about these creatures is that, unlike most animals, they have been known to kill simply for the pleasure of it. Night terrors evidently enjoy terrorizing and slaying the animals and people they encounter, and after a kill the trees echo with gibbering shrieks that sound all too cruelly human.

Combat

Night terrors are effective against even large groups of well-armed travelers by virtue of their animal cunning. They're capable of sophisticated tactics such as diversions, ambushes and even stealing a victim's pack or weapons to draw him into a trap. These animals attack with teeth and claws, but have been known to pick up a dropped weapon and flail about with it in the heat of battle.

Nightvision (Ex): A night terror's keen sight allows it to see up to 60 feet at night as though it were in bright sunlight.

Night Tyrant

Large (Long) Vermin

Hit Dice:	8d8+8 (44 hp)
Initiative:	+8 (+4 Improved Initiative, +4 Dex)
Speed:	90 ft., climb 90 ft.
AC:	17 (-1 size, +4 Dex, +4 natural) underbelly is AC 13
Attacks:	Bite +8 melee
Damage:	Bite 1d8+1
Face/Reach:	5 ft. by 10 ft./5 ft.
Special Attacks:	Sedative spray
Special Qualities:	Vermin
Saves:	Fort +7, Ref +6, Will +2
Abilities:	Str 12, Dex 18, Con 12, Int 1, Wis 10, Cha 6
Skills:	Climb +14, Hide +18, Move Silently + 15
Feats:	Dodge, Improved Initiative, Spring Attack, Track
Climate/Terrain:	Rain forests
Organization:	Solitary
Challenge Rating:	4
Treasure:	Standard
Alignment:	Always neutral
Advancement Range:	6-10 HD

Description

The night tyrant is a monstrous hunting spider, its skin colored in mottled shades of black, brown and green, which give it effective natural camouflage high in the forest canopy. The upper side of its body is covered in a thick hide that provides it with a form of natural armor, but its underside is soft and vulnerable.

Deep forests with tall, massive trees provide shelter and conceal- ment for this terrifying breed of spider, a predator that builds no web, but which excretes a fine

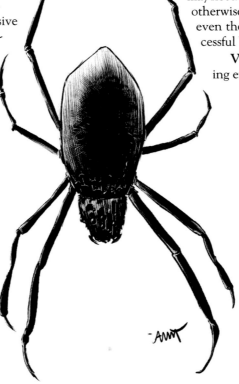

mist from its abdomen that acts as a powerful seda- tive, lulling its victims into a deep, almost catatonic sleep. The night tyrant searches from the forest canopy, seeking likely prey bedded down amid the trees below. Once it locates a likely victim, it slowly, silently descends along a tree trunk until it's within range, and begins pumping its sedative mist into the air. Sensory bristles on the spider's legs monitor the victim's body temperature and breathing, and when it senses that the soporific has taken effect, it comes down and drags the inert form back up into the trees, where it can be killed and eaten at leisure. Night tyrants never claim more than one victim a night, but have been known to stalk traveling parties for days on end, picking away at them a little each night.

Combat

The night tyrant is essentially a coward, and if confronted with fierce resistance it generally flees back into the trees. If cornered, it lashes out with its forelegs and mandibles until it can find an oppor- tunity to escape.

Sedative Spray (Ex): The night tyrant exudes a fine, golden mist from its abdomen. The poison has a strong, honeylike scent and it lulls victims into a deep sleep. Potential victims within 30 feet of the night tyrant must make a Fortitude save (DC 17) or fall asleep. Victims that are already slumbering must save versus a DC of 23. Once affected, victims may not awaken unless shaken violently or otherwise prodded by someone else, and even then the victim must make a suc- cessful Will save (DC 13) to do so.

Vermin: Immune to mind-alter- ing effects.

Orafaun

Large Magical Beast

Hit Dice:	6d10+6 (39 hp)
Initiative:	+0
Speed:	50 ft.
AC:	17 (-1 size, +5 natural, +3 deflection)
Attacks:	Horns +5 melee
Damage:	Horns 2d10
Face/Reach:	5 ft. by 10 ft./5 ft.
Special Attacks:	Cause sleep
Special Qualities:	Immunities, spells, gift of sustenance, turn undead
Saves:	Fort +3, Ref +2, Will +9
Abilities:	Str 10, Dex 10, Con 12, Int 17, Wis 18, Cha 17
Skills:	Diplomacy +9, Listen +6, Sense Motive +4, Speak Dwarven +5, Spot +4
Feats:	Mobility
Climate/Terrain:	Mountains (hills)
Organization:	Herd (21-40, plus a patriarch with 8d10+8 HD)
Challenge Rating:	4
Treasure:	Standard
Alignment:	Always neutral good
Advancement Range:	5-8 HD (Large)

Description

Erias, the renegade son of Belsameth, is the demigod of dreams and none of his creatures represent this dominion better than the orafauna. Erias created the orafauna as his priesthood — he imbued the orafauna with magical powers to allow them to describe and interpret the meaning of dreams for those who come to their temple and make oblation to him. These creatures resemble angora goats, with grand, forked horns and cloven hooves that shine like precious metal.

The temple of the orafauna is located in a region of hills known as the Solemnaic Vale on an island off the western shore of Darakeene. Herein, standing upon the central (and highest) hill of the region, is the fane of Erias. The temple is constructed of white stone and is detailed in pure precious metals. Travelers who wish to have their dreams interpreted make a pilgrimage here.

The orafauna are a good race and, like their deity, they are nonviolent. They gather in herds, which are patriarchical in structure. A male orafaun may have three to six wives, and 12 to 18 kids.

Combat

Orafauna have special powers related to sleep and dreams. The following powers are ones that orafauna may perform for any traveler who meets them anywhere within the sacred vale.

Cause Sleep (Su): Orafauna grant the gift of sleep to all travelers who request such. The sleep lasts for eight hours. Those receiving this slumber drowsily bow to the grass. The sleep heals 1d4 hit points of damage and revitalizes the recipient completely, eradicating all fatigue. Those who have come on a special pilgrimage to the temple and made sacrifices to the god may be granted prophetic dreams, giving them a hint of some future event of particular importance to them. Orafauna may bestow this gift at will. If pressed, an orafaun may use this power against hostile targets who must succeed at a Will save (DC 18) to resist falling asleep.

Gift of Sustenance (Sp): An orafaun can create enough food and water for one person for one day. This gift may be used once per day.

Spells: The patriarch and his chief wife are spellcasters, the equivalent of 9th-level clerics with special access to the domains of Air, Animal, Good, Luck, Magic and Trickery.

Turn Undead (Su): Orafauna may turn undead six times per day as 6th-level clerics.

Immunities (Ex): Orafauna are completely immune to all forms of mind control; they are affected by sleep and paralysis only if they choose to be.

Paragon Crocodile

Huge (Long) Beast

Hit Dice:	8d10+56 (100 hp)
Initiative:	+1 (Dex)
Speed:	30 ft., swim 60 ft.
AC:	19 (-2 size, +1 Dex, +10 natural)
Attacks:	Bite +14 melee, tail slap +8 melee
Damage:	Bite 1d12+7; tail slap 1d10+7
Face/Reach:	5 ft. by 20 ft./10 ft.
Special Attacks:	Improved grab
Special Qualities:	Healing, telepathic communication, underwater prowess, divine protection, SR 15
Saves:	Fort +13, Ref +3, Will +13
Abilities:	Str 24, Dex 13, Con 24, Int 14, Wis 24, Cha 20
Skills:	Hide +8, Intimidate +10, Knowledge (religion) +3, Listen +6, Spot +3
Feats:	Power Attack, Improved Bull Rush
Climate/Terrain:	The city of Hetanu; warm rivers
Organization:	Solitary, mated pair (2), temple clutch (2-8)
Challenge Rating:	5
Treasure:	Standard (jewelry only)
Alignment:	Always neutral good
Advancement Range:	6-7 HD (Large), 9-13 HD (Huge)

Description

As the story goes (and what reason is there to doubt it?), shortly after the Titanswar a horde of barbarians stormed the river city-state of Hetanu, seeking to take advantage of the city's weakened defenses. The citizens were unable to keep the barbarians out, but just as the invaders reached the riverside district, the sacred crocodiles of Madriel's temple surged out of the river. Ignoring their own losses, they tore apart the invaders' strongest foes, and the citizens took this as an omen and rallied. Thanks to the crocodiles, the city survived.

The story records that Madriel was so pleased with the creatures' actions that she gifted the reptiles with sentience and a share of her divine power. Now the paragon crocodiles guard the city of Hetanu with increased vigilance and even religious zeal. Rumor has it that a few pairs have even left the city in order to breed a new generation elsewhere, in order to guard other cities in Madriel's name.

Paragon crocodiles are unusually large, sometimes even exceeding 25 feet in length. Their skin is particularly well maintained, and the priests of their temples adorn them with gold jewelry. They are capable of telepathic communication, but in true reptilian fashion, do not address humans unless they have something truly important to say.

Combat

Like their mortal kin, paragon crocodiles are prone to lie under the surface of the water, waiting for prey to draw near. But when defending a charge, they actively move about with surprising speed. Against multiple opponents, a paragon crocodile maneuvers into position to use both its bite and tail lash against different foes. If allowed to concentrate on a single foe, it generally tries to grapple the opponent and drag him into the water to drown.

Healing (Su): Paragon crocodiles are able to heal wounds by breathing (hissing) upon the wound, restoring 3d8+5 hit points. They may do this 5 times a day.

Improved Grab (Ex): If a crocodile bites a Large or smaller creature, it deals normal damage and attempts to start a grapple as a free action without provoking attacks of opportunity. Each successive attack it makes during successive rounds automatically deals normal damage without provoking attacks of opportunity. The crocodile may move while holding its opponent.

Underwater Prowess (Ex): Paragon crocodiles can hold their breath for three hours with no ill effects and fight underwater with no penalty.

Divine Protection (Ex): Creatures of evil alignment suffer a -3 penalty to any attack rolls made within 30 feet of a paragon crocodile.

Plaguecat

Medium-size Animal

Hit Dice:	4d8-4 (14 hp)
Initiative:	+6 (+2 Dex, +4 Improved Initiative)
Speed:	90 ft., climb 30 ft.
AC:	14 (+2 Dex, +2 natural)
Attacks:	Bite +3 melee, 2 claws -2 melee
Damage:	Bite 1d10-1; Claw 1d6-1
Face/Reach:	5 ft. by 5 ft./10 ft.
Special Attacks:	Infectious claws and bite
Special Qualities:	Darkvision 90 ft.
Saves:	Fort +3, Ref +3, Will +1
Abilities:	Str 8, Dex 15, Con 9, Int —, Wis 10, Cha 6
Skills:	None
Feats:	Improved Initiative, Combat Reflexes, Track
Climate/Terrain:	Temperate grasslands
Organization:	Pack (5-8 adults, 1d4-2 cubs)
Challenge Rating:	3
Treasure:	Standard
Alignment:	Always neutral
Advancement Range:	2-3 HD (Small), 5-7 HD (Medium-size)

Description

The plaguecat is a sleek, long-limbed feline, similar to a jaguar, with a strange greenish-brown pelt. Its coat is often matted and mangy, and its hide sometimes bears weeping sores or strange growths, warning of the diseases the animal invariably carries. Plaguecats are carrion-eaters and for this reason their claws and teeth are capable of causing fast-acting and potentially lethal infections.

The plaguecat is a unique breed of feline predator that relies more on patience than ferocity to find its meals. These cats hunt in small packs and attack virtually anything, using their numbers to surround an intended victim, then rushing in from all sides to bury their claws and teeth in their prey. Once they have inflicted a number of deep wounds, they break off and circle the victim from a distance, waiting for the bacteria to infect their prey. The cats are perfectly willing to shadow a victim for weeks, watching the sickness take its toll until their prey is too weak to fight back. Then the cats close in and finish the job, dragging the body away and either burying it or dragging it up into a tree to "ripen" for a few more days before it's fit to eat.

Plaguecats are justly feared and hated by human settlers in grasslands (such as Virduk's Promise southeast of Tashon) and substantial bounties are offered for their pelts. A traveler who kills one near a village can be assured of a warm welcome and a free bed for the night.

Combat

Plaguecats are very effective pack animals that use coordinated attacks to injure their prey. In practice, the alpha feline of the pack picks out a victim from a herd or traveling party, usually the smallest and apparently weakest of the group. Using growls and roars, the alpha coordinates the pack's effort to surround and strike. Several cats keep potential rescuers at bay while the rest of the pack darts in and hits a victim from all sides, hoping to get at least one or two good strikes in with their claws or teeth. Once the victim is sufficiently injured, the pack retreats to a safe distance and awaits the inevitable.

Infectious Claws and Bite (Ex): The plaguecat's claws and teeth are breeding grounds for hordes of infectious diseases. Victims struck by a cat's claws or bite must make a Fortitude save (DC 18 for claws, DC 20 for bites) for each wound received. Once a victim fails a save, no further rolls are necessary. Within twelve hours, the victim suffers a virulent infection that costs 1d4 temporary Constitution points per day. The infection can be cured magically like any disease or by someone with the Heal skill (DC 22).

Proud, The

Large Monstrous Humanoid

Hit Dice:	3d8+9 (18 hp)
Initiative:	+6 (+2 Dex, +4 Improved Initiative)
Speed:	60 ft.
AC:	17 (-1 size, +2 Dex, +6 natural)
Attacks:	Claws +4 melee; handaxe +4 melee; short sword +4 melee; shortspear +4 melee; javelin +4 ranged; sling +4 ranged; or net +4 ranged
Damage:	Claws 1d6+2; handaxe 1d6+2; short sword 1d6+2; shortspear 1d6+2; javelin 1d6; sling 1d4; net special
Face/Reach:	5 ft. by 10 ft./5 ft.
Special Attacks:	Spells
Special Qualities:	Keen senses
Saves:	Fort +6, Ref +3, Will +2
Abilities:	Str 14, Dex 15, Con 16, Int 10, Wis 13, Cha 10
Skills:	Hide +9, Jump +3, Listen +6, Move Silently +3, Spot +9, Wilderness Lore +3
Feats:	Claw Strike, Cleave, Improved Critical, Improved Initiative, Run, Track
Climate/Terrain:	Temperate and warm plains
Organization:	Solitary, pair, pride (4-8 adults and 1d6+1 offspring), or war pride (10-20 proud warriors and 10-30 lions)
Challenge Rating:	1
Treasure:	Standard
Alignment:	Always chaotic evil
Advancement Range:	By character class

Description

The proud are nomadic cat-centaurs that roam the Plains of Lede and the Bleak Savannah. As with other titan spawn, these creatures bear an intense hatred for the humanoid races. They show no mercy in their attacks on homesteads and caravans and consider the flesh of humanoid children to be a great delicacy.

The proud has the body of a lion with a humanoid torso where the lion's head would normally be. The cat-centaur's own head is a blend of human and feline, with pointed furred ears and large cat eyes. A male has a thick mane that runs from the head down the back of the torso. A proud wears little clothing, generally nothing more than a bandolier and pouches to carry its few belongings and weapons.

The proud speak Leonid and Common.

It is said that the titan Hrinruuk the Hunter created the proud to serve as her warriors. As with many other servitor races, they survived the Divine War in which their titan masters were defeated. In the years that followed, the proud lost what little culture they had and degenerated into savagery and cannibalism.

Combat

The proud hunt in prides during the day as lions do, though the occasional nocturnal attack is not uncommon. When attacking traveling targets, the cat-centaurs pick off stragglers and scouts and harry the main group until the targets' nerves are ragged. This harrying also makes the targets develop a kind of defensive rhythm — which is when the proud attack in full force. The proud prefer surprise attacks against stationary targets, tearing into their midst before the victims know what's happening. They often recruit prides of lions for their raids.

The proud are savage warriors, giving no quarter and expecting none. Still, a pride of proud will retreat if it sees that it is significantly outmatched.

Spells: Once each per day, a proud may cast any spell available to a 7th level druid that deals with charming or speaking to animals. These abilities function as if the spells were cast by a 7th-level druid.

Keen Senses (Ex): The proud see four times as well as humans and have darkvision with a range of 60 feet. They can scent creatures within 30 feet and can discern their direction as a partial action.

Feats: The proud has the following bonus feat:

Claw Strike — The proud can take an additional attack each round with its forelegs at no penalty.

Pyre

Medium-size Elemental (Fire)

Hit Dice:	4d8+12 (30 hp)
Initiative:	+8 (+4 Dex, +4 Improved Initiative)
Speed:	40 ft.
AC:	26 (+4 Dex, +12 natural)
Attacks:	Touch +4 melee
Damage:	Touch 2d6
Face/Reach:	5 ft. by 5 ft./5 ft.
Special Attacks:	Burning residue, engulf
Special Qualities:	Immunities, damage reduction 5/+1, vulnerability
Saves:	Fort +4, Ref +8, Will +1
Abilities:	Str 10, Dex 19, Con 16, Int 14, Wis 10, Cha 4
Skills:	Listen +10, Spot +10
Feats:	None
Climate/Terrain:	Deserts, active volcanoes
Organization:	Raiding Party (3-4), outpost (6-10), settlement (20-30)
Challenge Rating:	5
Treasure:	Standard
Alignment:	Always chaotic neutral
Advancement Range:	3–6 HD (Medium-size)

Description

Pyres are a race of fire elementals that has migrated from the Plane of Fire and now resides exclusively in the hottest regions of the Scarred Lands. They are roughly humanoid-shaped, though fine details like facial features are lost amid the flames. They move quickly, at times seeming to flicker from one spot to the next. Very little of their society has been explored, but it is clear from initial reports that these creatures possess some level of stratification and organization.

Pyres can clearly communicate and coordinate their efforts, but no scholar yet understands how. They rarely travel and can usually be found in the hottest, driest regions, like the Bleak Savannah or the Desert of Onn. Very few encounters with Pyres end peacefully, though in a few cases intruding parties have simply been ignored.

Combat

Pyres flicker about their prey in combat. Even their slightest touch can inflict severe burns. In some cases, pyres have been known to engulf their foes to cause severe burns. In any case, contact with a pyre typically ignites anything flammable.

Engulf (Ex): Instead of a simple touch, a pyre can choose to engulf its foe completely. Doing this exacts a toll on the attacking pyre but has devastating effects on the opponent. An engulf attack is a -2 melee attack and does 4d6+4 fire damage. An attacking pyre takes 1d6 damage to itself if it hits its opponent with this attack, because it exhausts a little of its own life energy in the process. The pyre can only engulf foes that are Medium-size or smaller.

Burning Residue (Ex): Just about anything a pyre touches has a chance of burning. If a target takes damage from a touch, it must succeed at a Reflex save (DC 15) or burn, taking an additional 1d4 damage until it can put the fire out. If a pyre engulfs a foe, the opponent must succeed at a Reflex save (DC 25) or suffer an additional 1d6 damage per round until the fire is extinguished. One character may attempt a Reflex save (DC 15) to extinguish either type of fire. If two characters spend a round putting the fire out, they succeed automatically.

Immunities (Ex): A pyre is immune to all heat and fire attacks.

Vulnerabilities (Ex): A pyre takes double damage from all cold- and water-based spells and attacks. If a pyre is splashed with water, it takes 1d4 damage for a Tiny-sized douse, 1d6 for a Small-sized douse, 2d6 for a Medium-sized douse, 3d8 for a Large-sized douse, 5d8 for a Huge-sized douse, 8d8 for a Gargantuan-sized douse and 10d10 for a Colossal-sized douse. A pyre can make a Reflex save (DC 20) with appropriate size bonuses/penalties to avoid a douse.

Ratman (Slitheren)

Medium-size Monstrous Humanoid

Hit Dice:	1d8+3 (7 hp)
Initiative:	+2 (Dex)
Speed:	30 ft., climb 15 ft.
AC:	16 (+2 Dex, +1 natural, +2 leather armor, +1 small shield)
Attacks:	Bite +1 melee, 2 claws -4 melee; scimitar +1 melee
Damage:	Bite 1d3; claw 1d4; scimitar 1d6
Face/Reach:	5 ft. by 5 ft./5 ft.
Special Attacks:	None
Special Qualities:	Darkvision 60 ft.
Saves:	Fort +5, Ref +2, Will +0
Abilities:	Str 10, Dex 15, Con 16, Int 10, Wis 10, Cha 8
Skills:	Escape Artist +3, Hide +2, Jump +1
Feats:	Dodge
Climate/Terrain:	Any except arctic
Organization:	War band (15-120 ratmen, plus 1 leader of 4th to 7th level per 30 warriors), nest (120-1200 ratmen with leaders as above, plus 1 8th- to 10th-level priest per 100 warriors and 10-24 giant rats)
Challenge Rating:	1/2
Treasure:	Standard
Alignment:	Usually lawful evil
Advancement Range:	By character class

Description

Ratmen are medium-sized, furred humanoids with rodent-like heads and tails. They have long torsos and arms and legs of equal length. They tend to slouch forward when walking upright, giving them an odd, hunchbacked appearance. Their humanoid hands, complete with opposable thumbs, are long and capable of very subtle manipulations. Their fur varies in color depending on their subspecies, but all have red, beady eyes. Ratmen wear clothing and armor that's been stolen or traded for and it's always soiled, dirty and patched together, as the creatures have no concept of cleanliness.

Ratmen speak Slitheren, a language of chittering and sibilant hisses similar to that of rodents, and they can also communicate with giant and normal rats. Most ratmen can speak Common, as well as the secret language of the titans.

Combat

While each subspecies has its own methods of combat, all ratmen share some techniques. They fight only when in a group, preferably with three-to-one odds or better and from ambush. Lone ratmen attempt to flee from any form of conflict, but even they can be driven into a berserk fury if cornered. As with their clothing, their weapons consist of whatever they can scrounge and are typically rusty, pitted and caked with filth. They have been known to bolster their forces by calling upon packs of giant rats and swarms of normal ones to join them in battle.

When led by their priests, ratmen are capable of organized warfare and can use their great numbers to deadly effect.

History

Known as the "scourge of the underealm," the Slitheren lurk in the dark corners of the Scarred Lands, always waiting to prey upon the weak and unwary. It was after the titans fell that the rats came, gnawing and feasting on the Creators' remains. Almost immediately, the dark magical energies that cooled in the titans' flesh began to change the rats' forms and spirits into something more like those of the deities themselves. Deep within the tunnels that they had gnawed through the offal, they bred, and each brood became more humanoid. Now, led by their ruling priest-kings, the various nests, each a pale and twisted reflection of the titan on which it fed, emerge upon an unsuspecting world.

Society

The Slitheren are a superstitious race, filled with a burning fear of starvation and of their own dark titans, a fear that is kept at a fever pitch by the priesthood. Prayers are made twice daily to the priest-king for his intercession with the titans, and the Slitheren year is filled with holy days and rituals. In fact, each tribe has its own calendar of tribute events, and any co-mingling of ratmen from different nests demands observation of the holy days of all participants. Gnawed and carved into ratmen tunnels are shrines and prayer icons. The priesthood — composed strictly of albinos — watches over all these rituals in stern judgement, knowing that it is only by their efforts that the titans are appeased.

This profile details a "traditional" ratman, which could be encountered almost anywhere in the Scarred Lands. The following four nests or sub-species of ratmen — the Brown Gorgers, Diseased, Foamers and Red Witches — are only some of the foul titan offspring and are variations on the common theme.

Ratman, Brown Gorger

Medium-size Monstrous Humanoid

Hit Dice:	1d8+3 (7 hp)
Initiative:	+2 (Dex)
Speed:	30 ft., climb 15 ft.
AC:	17 (+2 Dex, +1 natural, +4 scale mail)
Attacks:	Bite +1 melee, 2 claws -4 melee; scimitar +1 melee; iron dart +3 ranged
Damage:	Bite 1d3; claw 1d4; scimitar 1d6; iron dart 1d4
Face/Reach:	5 ft. by 5 ft./5 ft.
Special Attacks:	None
Special Qualities:	Darkvision 60 ft.
Saves:	Fort +5, Ref +2, Will +0
Abilities:	Str 10, Dex 15, Con 16, Int 10, Wis 10, Cha 8
Skills:	Escape Artist +3, Hide +2, Jump +1, Search +2
Feats:	Dodge
Climate/Terrain:	Any except arctic
Organization:	War band (15-90 ratmen, plus 1 leader of 4th to 7th level per 30 warriors), nest (120-1200 ratmen with leaders as above, plus 1 8th- to 10th-level priest per 100 warriors)
Challenge Rating:	1/2
Treasure:	Standard
Alignment:	Usually lawful evil
Advancement Range:	By character class

Description

As their name implies, these medium-sized, brown-furred ratmen fed from the flesh of Gaurak the Glutton. They were the first of the nests to leave the underealm as they had ravenously devoured the rather large piece of Gaurak that created and sustained them and needed other sources of food.

Their priesthood is composed of grossly obese ratmen who must be carried in order to preside over a regular schedule of holy feast days, yet their priest-king is skeletally thin and eternally hungry, unable to ever eat enough and in constant, gnawing pain.

These ratmen are raiders and pillagers, sending war parties and caravans farther and farther from their settlements in search of food. Entire villages of humanoids have been enslaved and dragged beneath the earth to serve as cattle for the Gorgers. Such is their all-consuming hunger that only metal and such inedible things as gems are worn by these Slitheren — all clothing, wood and leather is inevitably devoured. Unlike the other nests, the Gorgers keep no common or giant rats, seeing them as rivals for food and as food in themselves.

Combat

Brown Gorgers fight as typical ratmen, although their exclusive use of metal armor gives them a higher level of protection. In addition, they generally use large iron darts as missiles. After a battle, the Gorgers feast upon the remains of both their enemies and their own dead. Even more horrific than this battlefield banquet is that which occurs at the Brown Gorgers' warren, to which the remaining, tatterskinned dead are dragged.

Ratman, The Diseased

Medium-size Monstrous Humanoid

Hit Dice:	1d8+3 (7 hp)
Initiative:	+1 (Dex)
Speed:	30 ft., climb 15 ft.
AC:	15 (+1 Dex, +1 natural, +2 leather armor, +1 small shield)
Attacks:	Bite +1 melee, 2 claws –4 melee; scimitar +1 melee; shortbow +2 ranged; sling +2 ranged
Damage:	Bite 1d3; claw 1d4; scimitar 1d6; shortbow 1d6; sling 1d4
Face/Reach:	5 ft. by 5 ft./5 ft.
Special Attacks:	Poisoned weapons
Special Qualities:	Darkvision 60 ft., immunities
Saves:	Fort +5, Ref +1, Will +1
Abilities:	Str 10, Dex 13, Con 16, Int 12, Wis 12, Cha 12
Skills:	Diplomacy +1, Escape Artist +3, Hide +2
Feats:	Dodge
Climate/Terrain:	Any except arctic
Organization:	War band (15-120 ratmen, plus 1 leader of 4th to 7th level per 30 warriors), nest (120-1200 ratmen with leaders as above, plus 1 8th- to 10th-level priest per 60 warriors and 10-24 giant rats)
Challenge Rating:	1/2
Treasure:	Standard
Alignment:	Usually lawful evil
Advancement Range:	By character class

Description

Those rats that partook of the flesh of Chern the Unclean have formed the most civilized of the nests, relatively speaking, with cities hidden beneath those of other races. The Diseased even have several partially aboveground communities in the Mourning Marshes, where legend claims Chern was interred. The Diseased are dull gray in color and wear more clothing, in particular cloaks and cowls, than do other Slitheren. Perhaps this trend is due to these rats' closer association with other humanoids (beyond eating them, that is). This association is also evident in Diseased cities, which, while still dark and labyrinthine to humans, have passages that enable the ratmen to walk erect at all times.

The Diseased priesthood is divided into orders, each of which is responsible for nurturing a clutch of slaves bred as hosts for different plagues and ailments. The Order of the Scarlet Shaking Pox maintains almost 100 humanoids in various stages of the disease, for example, and introduces captives when necessary to insure that the pox is available to be unleashed when needed. While rivalries exist among the orders, there is a limit to how far such conflicts can go; allowing a disease to die out would be considered an offense to the titans. Given their capacity for cooperation, the Diseased are the most likely ratmen to seek joint ventures with other nests, particularly when they require brute strength for conquests. Usually, however, the diseases they inflict for

weeks upon villages and other targets make for easy victories. And while the Diseased prefer to attack from a distance, they have bred a race of depraved humanoids called the dead eaters to serve as their shock troops.

All of these strategies for domination and terror are concocted by the Diseased priest-king, a robed and cowled figure whose concealed body twitches and pulses as he slumps on his throne. His whispered plans for conquest are for the ears of his priesthood alone.

Combat

The Diseased prefer to strike from afar with a variety of missile weapons rather than attack directly. Various archers, crossbowmen and slingers are guarded on the battlefield by dead eaters and by an order of religious zealots called the Shields of Chern; the latter also provide bodyguards for the priesthood. The honor guard protect themselves and their charges with almost full-body rectangular shields and attack with multi-headed spiked flails.

Immunities (Ex): These ratmen are immune to all diseases.

Poisoned Weapons: The Diseased poison their weapons with a variety of deadly toxins brewed from the many plants and oozes available in the marsh. Those hit must make a Fortitude save (DC 13) or suffer an additional 1d6 damage with each blow.

Ratman, Foamer

Medium-size Monstrous Humanoid

Hit Dice:	2d8+6 (15 hp)
Initiative:	+2 (Dex)
Speed:	30 ft., climb 15 ft., swim 40 ft.
AC:	15 (+2 Dex, +1 natural, +2 leather armor)
Attacks:	Bite +4 melee; 2 claws -1 melee; greataxe +4 melee; dagger −1 melee; javelin +4 ranged
Damage:	Bite 1d3+2; claw 1d4+1; greataxe 1d12+2, dagger 1d4+1; javelin 1d6+2
Face/Reach:	5 ft. by 5 ft./5 ft.
Special Attacks:	None
Special Qualities:	Darkvision 60 ft.
Saves:	Fort +6, Ref +5, Will -1
Abilities:	Str 14, Dex 15, Con 16, Int 9, Wis 8, Cha 8
Skills:	Escape Artist +3, Jump +1, Swim +5
Feats:	Power Attack
Climate/Terrain:	Any except arctic
Organization:	War band (15-120 ratmen, plus 1 leader of 4th to 7th level per 30 warriors), nest (120-1200 ratmen with leaders as above, plus 1 8th- to 10th-level priest per 100 warriors and 10-24 giant rats)
Challenge Rating:	1/2
Treasure:	Standard
Alignment:	Usually lawful evil
Advancement Range:	By character class

Description

These are the largest of the Slitheren — seven feet tall at their shoulders, with black oily fur and short, slightly flattened prehensile tails. They are the most barbaric of the ratmen, if that's possible, and are the bane of the seas, having been weaned on the hate-maddened blood of Kadum the Mountainshaker. These ratmen now live only for war and slaughter. Semi-aquatic by nature, they churn out of the water, surrounded by packs of giant rats to rend and tear the life from the unprepared. Instead of dwelling in tunnels, the Foamers reside on bloodstained and half-sunken boats and ships they have captured, sometimes lashing them together as floating bases. Not possessing sailing skills, they rely on captured slaves to propel these makeshift craft, either by sail or oar. In addition to propelling their ships, Foamers' slaves are used to per-

form any task that is not combat-related, as the ratmen consider such chores beneath true warriors.

The Foamer priesthood is comprised of warbands' generals and admirals, with their massive 10-foot-tall priest-king being the most bloodthirsty berserker of them all. His white fur is crusted black by the oceans of blood through which he has waded, and his mad eyes always search for new victims. As might be expected, Foamer priests' rituals are based on blood and slaughter, often pitting captured humanoids against each other in battles to the death.

Combat

Foamers lose all control in combat, disdaining the use of shields and blunt weapons, preferring the freedom of light armor and the satisfaction of slashing and hacking weapons. If missiles are used at all, they're usually javelins, although siege engines are popular for the mayhem they cause. In many cases, a dagger or small axe is held by a Foamer's muscular prehensile tail as a deadly distraction.

Ratman, Red Witch

Medium-size Monstrous Humanoid

Hit Dice:	1d8+3 (7 hp)
Initiative:	+2 (Dex)
Speed:	30 ft., climb 15 ft.
AC:	13 (+2 Dex, +1 natural)
Attacks:	Bite +1 melee, 2 claws -4 melee
Damage:	Bite 1d3; claw 1d4
Face/Reach:	5 ft. by 5 ft./5 ft.
Special Attacks:	Spells
Special Qualities:	Darkvision 60 ft.
Saves:	Fort +3, Ref +2, Will +3
Abilities:	Str 10, Dex 15, Con 16, Int 15, Wis 12, Cha 8
Skills:	Concentration +2, Escape Artist +3, Hide +2, Jump +1, Scry +2, Spellcraft +5
Feats:	Spell Focus (Illusion), Spell Focus (Necromancy)
Climate/Terrain:	Any except arctic
Organization:	Solitary, coven (12-24 witches, plus a 4th- to 7th-level wizard)
Challenge Rating:	1/2
Treasure:	Standard
Alignment:	Usually lawful evil
Advancement Range:	By character class

Description

From the flesh of Mormo comes the most terrifying and mysterious of the ratmen, and also the smallest in number. The Red Witches have been more heavily imprinted by the will and ways of their titan than has any other breed of Slitheren. These vermin are the shortest ratmen, as well, typically standing five feet tall, with reddish fur, and with little interest in armor or weapons. Their power derives from a necromantic or illusionary ability developed by rigorous and deadly training rituals designed to insure that only the wiliest and deadliest spell-casters survive. The Red Witches' priesthood is actually a matri-archy consisting of arch-magi who take groups of lesser male mages, up to two dozen, as covens. These small bands of ratmen seek out areas of magical power and establish underground bases nearby. Their havens are filled with traps, illu-sions and the witches' undead servitors. As they absorb and extract the local magical energy, the witches ingest various potions and powders designed to inspire hallucinatory visions to guide their paths into the future. The resulting prophecies are called the Gifts of Mormo.

The most powerful and telling prophetess is the Witch-Queen, who reclines in a cham-ber that wafts with hallucinatory mists. She is one of the extremely rare shapeshifters among the Red Witches, capable of assuming the form of a giant rat or a member of any of the humanoid races (although she prefers that of a hauntingly beautiful, half-naked human woman). In this form, she amuses herself decadently with her humanoid slaves.

There is one other way that the Witches are unlike the other nests: Some lone ratmen go off on their own to pursue research they don't care to share with the others. These individuals sometimes find their way into civilization, if that's where their visions take them.

Combat

The Witches fight primarily with magic, although they often raise undead troops if a battle is imminent. Unless there is a prophecy that demands they do otherwise, these ratmen typically use their powers of illusion to flee a superior force. Obviously, these are the most intelligent, cunning and subtle of the Slitheren, and their stratagems reflect such deviousness.

Spells: A Red Witch casts spells as a wizard of level equivalent to their hit dice. She specializes in either the Illusion or Necromancy schools.

Ratroo

Tiny Animal

Hit Dice:	1d8-1 (3 hp)
Initiative:	+3 (+2 size, +1 Dex)
Speed:	40 ft.
AC:	16 (+2 size, +1 Dex, +3 natural)
Attacks:	Bite +0 melee
Damage:	Bite 1d4
Face/Reach:	2.5 ft. by 2.5 ft./0 ft.
Special Attacks:	Swarm
Special Qualities:	Immunities, scatter
Saves:	Fort +1, Ref +2, Will -1
Abilities:	Str 4, Dex 15, Con 8, Int —, Wis 8, Cha —
Skills:	Balance +3, Climb +1, Hide +3, Listen +2, Jump +8, Move Silently +4, Spot +4, Wilderness Lore +2
Feats:	Alertness, Track
Climate/Terrain:	Desert
Organization:	Brood (1-12), pack (13-60), swarm (hundreds)
Challenge Rating:	1/4
Treasure:	Standard
Alignment:	Always neutral
Advancement Range:	1-2 HD (Tiny)

Description

Ratroos are a common sight throughout the Desert of Onn. They're the size of large rats, golden-brown in color, with long hind legs that allow them to leap long distances (up to 10 feet in a single bound) and travel very quickly. The creatures also have a pair of needlelike front teeth. Ratroos survive primarily on small lizards and the poisonous water inside spherical desert cacti (to which they are immune), but they also eat spiny toads and bird or lizard eggs — whatever they can scavenge.

Ratroos are pack-oriented and skittish animals, but they are intensely curious. Shiny objects and those with odors distinct from what they're accustomed to encountering in the desert fascinate them. Indeed, although they're cautious as individual animals, ratroos become daring as their accumulated numbers increase. Foreign travelers in the Desert of Onn have reported being followed by increasingly larger gatherings of ratroos, apparently amassed as more and more of the creatures have caught the scent of and investigated the newcomers. Once a swarm gains sufficient momentum — hundreds of the animals — it surges after shiny objects and intruders, each animal hoping to grab (that is, bite) whatever interests it.

Ubantu tribesmen know to dull their weapons and reflective possessions before undertaking hunting expeditions, usually wiping such items with ash or manure. Other desert travelers know that extremely bright lights, explosions or deafeningly loud sounds scatter swarms before they become dangerous. Less informed or incautious travelers are often identified by their remains, found picked clean and left without possessions under the desert sun.

Ratroo warrens are often scattered with the items and remains of swarm victims.

Combat

Individual ratroos avoid attackers at all times, but follow those that interest them from a safe distance. As their numbers swell (over days or sometimes hours), they lose their individual fear and swarm over strangers or attractive items in hopes of grabbing them, even though there's little a rodent could do with an unsheathed sword or a warrior's helmet.

Immunities (Ex): Ratroos are immune to poison.

Scatter (Ex): Extremely bright lights and sounds such as from an explosive spell break up a forming ratroo swarm. Such displays might even avert a swarm attack in the making, as the creatures scatter. A scattered swarm disperses with amazing speed and leaves virtually no tracks, even in the fine sand of Onn.

Swarm (Ex): A ratroo swarm is more a force of nature than a specific attack; opposing it is like parrying a thunderstorm. Unless a target is deaf, he hears the thunder of its approach for two rounds before the animals are upon him. A swarm can't be dodged, but it might be outpaced by a fast runner or mount. Every living thing along a 40-foot front is subjected to attack for one round. Shiny objects are grabbed at and torn from owners. A victim of a swarm may make a Reflex save (DC 12) for each attractive item that the animals might steal, but that means she is struggling with the swarm and will sustain 1d4 damage for every item she preserves. After such an attack, the swarm quickly scatters unless a victim is dead or prone in which case it swarms again. Tracking rolls may be allowed at the Game Master's discretion to attempt to recover especially large or bulky items a member of the swarm snatched.

Reaver, The

	Gargantuan (Tall) Vermin (Spider)
Hit Dice:	20d8 +100 (190 hp)
Initiative:	+8 (+4 Dex, +4 Improved Initiative)
Speed:	30 ft.
AC:	30 (-4 size, +4 Dex, +20 natural)
Attacks:	Bite +24 melee, 8 claws +19 melee; crush +24 melee
Damage:	Bite 2d10+8; claw 1d8+8; crush 5d10+8
Face/Reach:	30 ft. by 30 ft./15ft.
Special Attacks:	Body smash, web
Special Qualities:	Damage reduction 12/+2, SR 20, vermin
Saves:	Fort +17, Ref +10, Will +6
Abilities:	Str 27, Dex 19, Con 20, Int 2, Wis 10, Cha 10
Skills:	Listen +30, Spot +30
Feats:	Improved Initiative
Climate/Terrain:	Any woodland
Organization:	Solitary (Unique)
Challenge Rating:	15
Treasure:	Double Standard
Alignment:	Always chaotic evil
Advancement Range:	None

Description

The Reaver has stalked the wooded areas of the Scarred Lands since before the Titanswar. Any forest will do. Judging from sightings reported in the distant past, the Reaver is thought to be not one creature but a race of enormous, ravenous titanspawn — though no one knows for certain.

The Reaver is appropriately named — its very size guarantees that it destroys whatever woodland it traverses. The only mercy it offers is the warning sound of snapping tree trunks, broken while it travels, which can be heard from miles away. Once encountered, it appears at first glance to be an impossibly large spider. The first time it roars, however, the Reaver is revealed to be one of the primordial servants of the titans — a twisted, deformed creature; a mesh of fur, shell, fang and squirming guts, with no purpose but to devour and destroy.

Fortunately, the beast has not been seen for years. Unfortunately, that means no one is prepared for its potential return.

Combat

The Reaver can't surprise its opponents, but it doesn't need to. Most are destroyed almost incidentally as they are swept up in the Reaver's swath of destruction. If actually attacked, the Reaver responds by instinctively webbing attackers and hacking at the closest opponents with its many legs. Against a single opponent, the Reaver prefers to rear up and slam its body down on the creature.

Body Smash (Ex): Whether it happens as a part of the Reaver's crush attack or as a separate ploy to put opponents off balance, the Reaver can slam its body to the ground and cause shock waves. Anyone within 50 feet must succeed at a Reflex save (DC 16) or fall prone for 1d3 rounds (those within 20 feet who fail drop their weapons, as well). This tactic is also useful for panicking hidden prey or distracting spellcasters.

Any creature within 100 feet of the Reaver when it smashes the earth must succeed at a Will save (DC 16) or suffer a -6 morale penalty to all attacks, saves and skill checks for 1d10 rounds. Spellcasters must make a Concentration check (DC 16) or their spellcasting is disrupted by the shock.

Web (Ex): The Reaver has at least a dozen spinnerets all over its body, allowing it to shoot a sticky thread in nearly any direction, up to 50 feet (make a ranged attack roll at +20 to see if a web hits a particular target). Webs are sturdy enough to support even the mass of the Reaver (there's some speculation that its lair, if it has one, is covered with the stuff). The webbing can also be used to restrain opponents. If the Reaver shoots webbing at an opponent, or an unwary creature walks into a web, the victim must succeed at a Reflex save (DC 16) to avoid becoming ensnared in the sticky strands. Once ensnared, escaping requires a successful Strength roll (DC 25). Slashing melee attacks can also be used to cut webbing; strands are hit automatically and a total of 20 hit points of damage must be done to liberate a Medium-size victim.

Vermin: The Reaver seems more like a force of nature than a sentient creature. It is immune to all magical attacks that affect the target's mental or emotional state, including charms and fear.

Red Colony

Medium-size Plant

Hit Dice:	8d8+16 (52 hp)
Initiative:	-5 (Dex)
Speed:	Swim 10 ft.
AC:	5 (-5 Dex)
Attacks:	Fronds +3 melee
Damage:	Fronds 1d12 (total)
Face/Reach:	5 ft. by 5 ft./0 ft.
Special Attacks:	Acid
Special Qualities:	Plant, keen senses
Saves:	Fort +8, Ref -3, Will +0
Abilities:	Str 1, Dex 1, Con 15, Int 1, Wis 6, Cha 0
Skills:	Hide +11, Intuit Direction +3, Move Silently +11, Spot +5
Feats:	None
Climate/Terrain:	Lake
Organization:	Colony (solitary), clutch (2-3)
Challenge Rating:	3
Treasure:	None
Alignment:	Always neutral
Advancement Range:	6-8 HD (Medium-size)

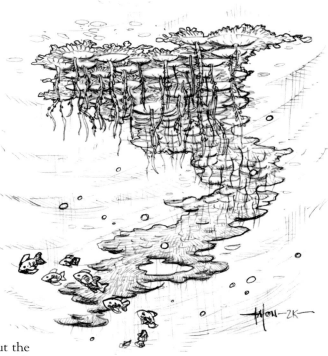

Description

Red colonies are large clumps of algae that inhabit lakes and ponds. They float about the surface where they are able, by lashing gently with fronds, to seek out all kinds of food that they may digest with acid. The non-intelligent red colony usually consumes other floating debris such as branches, leaves or insects, but anything that touches the water's surface is vulnerable to its predation, including wooden docks and boats, which are often the targets of a red colony's hunger.

Red colonies release a powerful acid that rapidly decomposes wood, leather and other non-metallic substances. The red colony floats up to its "prey," surrounds it as much as possible, and releases its digestive secretions. The acid has a slightly reddish tinge and bubbles slowly as it breaks down a potential food source. Lake dwellers have no problem identifying a colony once it releases its acid, but they cannot always distinguish it from harmless plants beforehand.

A red colony has between 20 and 40 fronds that hang down from its body into the water. These fronds are similar to those of jellyfish in that they work to entrap, sting and consume prey. Red-colony fronds are rarely more than two feet long, although specimens with longer ones have been encountered.

Some intelligent creatures extract the acid from a red colony to use it for any number of things, from poisons or metal cleaners. Others (especially aquatic creatures that reside in lakes) cultivate red colonies along shorelines to protect them from ground-dwellers.

Combat

Keen Senses (Ex): Red colonies use a superior nervous system to sense prey. They can detect vibrations in and on the water, and can also recognize changes in light patterns. This sensitivity effectively gives a red colony the Spot skill, as indicated above.

Acid (Ex): Red-colony acid corrodes an inch of wood in about 10 minutes, and destroys a similar volume of leather in about five. Metal is corroded in several hours, but is never destroyed. The acid burns flesh at a rate of 1d4 hit points per round that someone makes contact.

Plant: Red colony is impervious to critical hits, subdual damage and death from massive damage trauma. It's not affected by paralysis, poison, sleep, polymorph, stunning or spells of a mind-altering nature (i.e., enamoring or charming spells that do not specifically affect plants). Water-based attacks or spells have no effect on it.

River Nymph

Medium-size Fey

Hit Dice:	5d6 (17 hp)
Initiative:	+4 (Dex)
Speed:	Swim 90 ft.
AC:	14 (+4 Dex)
Attacks:	Bite +5 melee, 2 claws +0 melee
Damage:	Bite 1d6; claw 1d6
Face/Reach:	5 ft. by 5 ft./5 ft.
Special Attacks:	Siren song
Special Qualities:	None
Saves:	Fort +1, Ref +5, Will +9
Abilities:	Str 10, Dex 19, Con 10, Int 15, Wis 20, Cha 19
Skills:	Listen +10, Move Silently +10, Spot +10
Feats:	Alertness, Dodge
Climate/Terrain:	Rivers
Organization:	Pod (1-15)
Challenge Rating:	3
Treasure:	Standard
Alignment:	Always chaotic neutral
Advancement Range:	3-4 HD (Medium-size), 6-7 HD (Medium-size)

Description

River Nymphs are nocturnal creatures, appearing just after the sun has set and lingering until just before dawn. They appear to be lithe, beautiful beings, vaguely feminine, surrounded by soft, jewel-colored auras of ruby, emerald and sapphire. Their appearance has occasionally earned them the misnomer "river elves," though they are not related to elves in any way.

River nymphs — or river witches, as they are sometimes called — are well known to traders and merchants who ply waterways across the Scarred Lands. These creatures like to frolic and cavort like dolphins in the nighttime waters, tracing glowing paths just beneath the water and circling the hulls of riverboats. They appear fascinated by land-dwellers, lingering around boats and staring at sailors and passengers with wide, luminous eyes. Sometimes a river nymph becomes "infatuated" with a particular person and shows up each night to follow the boat and seek that person out. River nymphs have a reputation for being mischievous, delighting in harmless pranks, but can also warn captains of dangers that lie ahead and sometimes interpose themselves between boats and river predators.

For all their beauty, however, river nymphs have a strange and dark aspect to their nature. Each month, when the new moon falls, the nymphs grow strange and fey. They still circle riverboats, but their eyes are no longer awestruck and childlike. Their gaze calls to sailors with music only they can hear, luring them off the boat and into the water. Those that respond join the nymphs in a dance beneath the waters, and their drowned bodies are found at dawn.

Combat

River nymphs lure land-dwellers to their doom with their powerful glamour, filling target's minds with an aching loneliness that draws them into the water. Victims don't realize they're drowning until it's too late. Those that somehow break the spell frighten the nymphs, who look sadly at their victim and flee into the dark waters.

Siren Song (Su): A river nymph can single out one individual at a time and use its siren song to lure him or her into the water. The victim must succeed at a Will save (DC 22) to avoid being drawn in. Once the victim has succumbed, nothing breaks the charm unless it is dispelled or the river nymph is driven off or defeated. Blocking one's ears is partially effective, lowering the DC to 12.

Rumbler

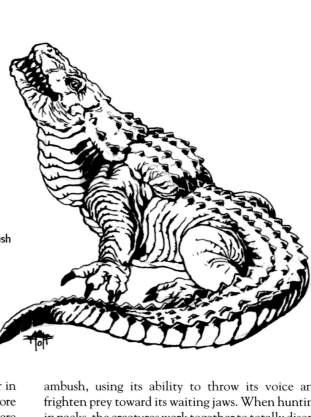

Large (Long) Animal (Reptile)

Hit Dice:	6d8+18 (45 hp)
Initiative:	-1 (Dex)
Speed:	35 ft.
AC:	18 (-1 size, -1 Dex, +10 natural)
Attacks:	Bite +8 melee
Damage:	Bite 2d6+3
Face/Reach:	5 ft. by 5 ft./10 ft.
Special Attacks:	Rumbling bite
Special Qualities:	Deceiving call
Saves:	Fort +8, Ref +1, Will +0
Abilities:	Str 16, Dex 9, Con 17, Int 5, Wis 6, Chr 8
Skills:	Climb +1, Hide +3, Intimidate +8, Intuit Direction +5, Listen +4, Spot +3, Swim +1
Feats:	Combat Reflexes, Improved Bull Rush
Climate/Terrain:	Temparate and warm land and underground
Organization:	Solitary or pack (3-8)
Challenge Rating:	3
Treasure:	None
Alignment:	Always neutral
Advancement Range:	5-6 HD (Large), 7-8 HD (Huge)

Description

The rumbler is a large predatory lizard similar in appearance to an alligator, but much thicker and more powerful around the shoulders and neck. Its jaws are heaviest over folds of thickly scaled throat sacks. It is from these sacks that the beast gets its name, as they are the source of the rumbler's vocal abilities.

Rumblers fill much of the hot hours of the day bellowing, declaring their hunting grounds to rivals and trying to attract mates. These rumblings continue into the evening, but they take on a more dangerous meaning. The rumbler begins to hunt in the late hours of the day and it is best not to believe everything you hear at this time.

Combat

Although these lizards are quite capable of running down much of their prey, they usually do not expend the energy to do so. The rumbler hunts by ambush, using its ability to throw its voice and frighten prey toward its waiting jaws. When hunting in packs, the creatures work together to totally disorient their prey and finally stampede it toward the pack's waiting trap.

Deceiving Call (Ex): The rumbler can convincingly alter the apparent source of its bellows by 140 feet in open ground. This distance increases to 220 feet in hills or canyons. It can likewise alter the volume and tone of its rumblings to deceive the listener into believing that the creature is retreating, while it's actually advancing unseen. A Listen roll (DC 23) is required to recognize a rumbler's deception.

Rumbling Bite (Ex): Rumblers bellow even when their jaws are locked on their prey. When bitten by a rumbler, a victim must make a Fortitude save (DC 14) or be stunned for 1d4-1 rounds and take an additional 1d4 damage per round from the beast's roar.

Runnk

Small Elemental (Ice)

Hit Dice:	1d8+1 (6hp)
Initiative:	+1 (Dex)
Speed:	60 ft., fly 160 ft.
AC:	15 (+1 size, +1 Dex, +3 natural)
Attacks:	2 claws +1 melee, 2 piercing kicks -1 melee
Damage:	Claw 1d2, piercing kick 1d6
Face/Reach:	5 ft. by 5 ft./5 ft.
Special Attacks:	Blizzard band
Special Qualities:	Immunities, ice skills, vulnerability
Saves:	Fort +3, Ref +1, Will +0
Abilities:	Str 8, Dex 13, Con 13, Int 10, Wis 10, Cha 6
Skills:	Hide +1, Intimidation +4, Search +2
Feats:	Multiattack
Climate/Terrain:	Arctic, some tundra
Organization:	Band (10-20), army (80-120)
Challenge Rating:	1/2
Treasure:	Standard
Alignment:	Always chaotic neutral
Advancement Range:	2-6 HD (Small)

Description

Runnks are the living incarnation of the chaotic ice storms and blizzards that blow across the arctic plains of the Scarred Lands. While a single runnk is virtually harmless, a band of runnks is dangerous, and a runnk army can inspire terror. Runnks travel about the arctic lands under the cover of blizzards, and where there are many, they generate their own mobile ice storms. When the storms of winter begin, runnk armies sweep down upon the northern caravans and barbarian settlements of the tundra, wiping away everything in their path.

Taken together, runnks are a chaotic, leaderless force. They delight in razing any semblance of order or structure without concern as to the goodness or wickedness of their actions. Whether wiping out a clan of goblin bandits or causing a merchant road to disappear under snow and ice, such activities are normal for runnks and are engaged in without thought of benevolence or bane.

It is not uncommon for certain peoples and creatures to migrate off of the tundra during the fall in order to avoid the predations of the runnks. Numerous folk legends tell of those foolish souls who were too slow or lazy to remove themselves in time before the runnks came.

No one knows how runnks are made or born, but some of the barbarian shamans hold that runnks are spawned within the heart of the deepest arctic blizzards.

Runnks speak their own tongue.

Combat

Runnks are able to pierce their enemies with their ski-like feet, which are toeless and pointed at the end. They can also attack with two claws. They will usually surround themselves with their Blizzard Band effect and settle over their chosen prey, letting the storm soften up the prey while the ruunks attack and then disappear back into the storm.

Blizzard Band (Su): Ten or more runnks travelling together may form a Blizzard Band, generating a furious ice storm that surrounds the ruunks and follows them as they travel. The ice storm's area of effect has a radius of 20 feet per ruunk inside the storm. So 10 ruunks travel in a 200 ft. radius storm, while 100 ruunks would generate a massive storm almost a mile in diameter.

While travelling within this ice storm, the Ruunk may fly at their flying rate listed above (and may not fly otherwise except in a natural blizzard).

This storm causes 1d6 hit points of damage each minute to all within its radius who are not fully sheltered from the storm's blizzard-like conditions.

Immunities (Ex): Runnks are impervious to cold and air attacks.

Vulnerability (Ex): Runnks have a penalty of −4 to saving throws against fire attacks.

Ice Skills: While under their self-generated blizzards or under the cover of a natural ice storm, runnks are able to Search normally and may Hide at +10. If an army of at least 80 are traveling or attacking under similar conditions, runnks may Intimidate with a +10 bonus.

Sage Camel

Large (Long) Magical Beast

Hit Dice:	11d10+22 (82 hp)
Initiative:	+0
Speed:	30 ft.
AC:	10 (-1 size, +1 natural)
Attacks:	Kick +11 melee
Damage:	Kick 1d8+1
Face/Reach:	5 ft. by 10 ft./5 ft.
Special Attacks:	Spit
Special Qualities:	Immunities, spell-like abilities
Saves:	Fort +9, Ref +2, Will +14
Abilities:	Str 12, Dex 9, Con 14, Int 20, Wis 20, Cha 17
Skills:	Concentration +15, Diplomacy +8, Intuit Direction +17, Knowledge (all) +8, Knowledge (nature) +17, Listen +3, Scry +15, Sense Motive +5, Spellcraft +9
Feats:	Endurance, Iron Will
Climate/Terrain:	Desert
Organization:	1-4
Challenge Rating:	9
Treasure:	Standard
Alignment:	Usually lawful good
Advancement Range:	8-10 HD (Large)

Description

It is written that when the demigod Tamul, "the Old Man of the Desert," was young, he was fascinated by the stars. He always hoped his parents would fly to the heavens and get a star for him. One day, Tamul saw a star fall to the horizon. He ran for many days and nights to reach the horizon. He ran so far and for so long that his legs grew long and spindly. He had no time to shave, and his body was soon covered in hair, all of which became sandy.

He eventually came to the horizon, only to discover that sandmaskers had used their illusions to pose as a star. The sandmaskers chained Tamul to a thorny cactus and left two giant scorpions to guard him for many ages while they held him for ransom.

Tamul studied the stars above him and discovered a way to describe their movements, number and distance from each other, which he called Mathematics. Then, he named the stars and deduced their hidden meanings, which he called Astrology. Tamul looked up at the stars for so long that he stretched his neck. The chains holding his arms were loose enough that he could reach the ground, which he did while writing numbers in the sand. He bent forward writing in the sand for so long that his back grew humped and his arms became long and spindly, like his legs.

Eventually the cactus to which he was tied grew old, sagged and died. With nothing to hold his chains fast, Tamul simply walked away. When the two scorpions who were guarding him tried to sting him, Tamul spat in the face of one and kicked the other with his long arms. Then Tamul, using his new knowledge of the stars to guide him, found his way back home.

Tamul taught his sciences to his siblings, and those who diligently finished their studies became known to the desert tribes as Tamulqawid, meaning "The Wise Ones of Tamul." Those who did not study became beasts of burden for the desert peoples, who named them "Tamuls," or camels.

Sage camels look like large, intelligent camels with wizened, sublime expressions. They wear cloth coverings over their heads and bodies. They are accompanied by different creatures that offer their services in return for the sage camel's knowledge. Sage camels enjoy reclining in huge, plush desert tents and conversing to no end with guests, especially travelers from afar. Sage camels speak many humanoid tongues and are renowned for their ability to speak prophecies and read the stars.

It is rumored that somewhere in the vast Desert of Onn lies the mightiest observatory ever built, wherein The Old Man of the Desert dwells.

Combat

Although sage camels eschew combat, they may kick with their powerful legs.

Immunities (Ex): Sage camels cannot become lost in the desert and are immune to magic that might cause this to happen. They are also immune to sandmasker illusions.

Spell-like Abilities (Sp): Sage camels have spell-like abilities related to their knowledge of astronomy. They are able to cast divinatory spells as a 15th-level sorcerer, and any other spell as a 5th-level sorcerer.

Spit (Ex): Sage camels may spit in their opponent's eyes once every other round, in addition to their normal kick attack. The camel must hit with a ranged touch attack and any opponent struck must succeed at a Fortitude save (DC 12) or be blinded for 1d4+1 rounds.

Sand Burrower

Huge (Long) Beast

Hit Dice:	10d10+43 (98 hp)
Initiative:	-2 (Dex)
Speed:	45 ft., burrow 80 ft.
AC:	10 (-2 size, -2 Dex, +4 natural)
Attacks:	Bite +18 melee, 5 tentacles +13 melee
Damage:	Bite 2d8+10; tentacle 1d6+5
Face/Reach:	10 ft. by 20 ft./5 ft.
Special Attacks:	Poison
Special Qualities:	None
Saves:	Fort +13, Ref +1, Will +8
Abilities:	Str 30, Dex 6, Con 19, Int 9, Wis 18, Cha 13
Skills:	Listen +14, Search +9, Spot +2
Feats:	Great Fortitude, Toughness, Track
Climate/Terrain:	Desert
Organization:	None
Challenge Rating:	6
Treasure:	Standard
Alignment:	Neutral
Advancement Range:	8-9 HD (Large), 10-14 HD (Huge)

Description

Most land-dwelling denizens of the Desert of Onn fear the beasts that the Ubantu tribesman have named sand burrowers. These predators hunt day and night, sliding through the desert sand like serpents through water. They track prey by the vibrations of its passing, and they emerge from the sand to eat their meal on the surface.

The largest sand burrowers hunt the lumbering ancient tortoises, picking them apart as they walk and hollowing out their high-domed shells from within. Sand burrowers of average size terrorize families of bounding ratroos, camel-mounted explorers, wandering Ubantu and grounded desert falcons.

Sand burrowers lair deep beneath the desert, where the sand turns to rock, and it is there that they go to die and give birth at the same time. Newborn sand burrowers are functionally independent, and they devour their parents from the inside. Sand burrowers impregnate themselves and grow larger every year until they deliver. Those who have managed to kill sand burrowers in the Desert of Onn often find the corpses' innards crawling with premature sand burrower larvae.

Combat

Sand burrowers slide-squirm at a depth proportional to their length. When they detect a sizeable vibration above, they surface and attempt to ensnare the victim with the hooked and venomous tentacles that ring the inside of their mouths. Once they have caught their prey, they surface completely to eat. They drop the prey into their 15-deep rows of in-hooking teeth.

Poison (Ex): On a successful hit, a sand burrower's tentacles inject prey with the same poison found in the cacti of the Desert of Onn. It does an extra 1d8 of damage unless a Fortitude save (DC 13) is made.

Sandmasker

Large (Long) Monstrous Humanoids

Hit Dice:	12d8+24 (78 hp)
Initiative:	+2 (+2 Dex)
Speed:	40 ft.
AC:	16 (-1 Size, +2 Dex, +5 natural)
Attacks:	2 claws +9 melee; stinger +9 melee, and weapon type +14 melee; or weapon type +13 ranged
Damage:	Claw 1d10+1, stinger 1d4+1, weapon type +3
Face/Reach:	5 ft. by 10 ft./5 ft.
Special Attacks:	Poison
Special Qualities:	Illusions, leave no sign
Saves:	Fort +10, Ref +6, Will +2
Abilities:	Str 16, Dex 14, Con 14, Int 11, Wis 7, Cha 7
Skills:	Intimidate +3, Search +2
Feats:	None
Climate/Terrain:	Desert
Organization:	Band (1-4, with a leader 13d8+26), troop (10-20, with a leader 14d8+28 and 1d4 giant scorpions), clan (40-60, with a leader 15d10+30 and 3d4 giant scorpions)
Challenge Rating:	7
Treasure:	Double standard
Alignment:	Usually lawful evil
Advancement Range:	10-14 HD

Description

The origin of the sandmaskers is told in the tale of the War of the Broken Vows. The war, which was in its 33rd year, appeared to be all but over. An army of Exemplars was storming the fortress of Tarkun, a renegade from their ranks who had made a terrible bargain with a still-unknown evil power. Finding himself embattled with barely an army left and no avenue of escape, Tarkun sacrificed his last possession — his immortal soul. In a dark ritual, Tarkun cast his blood onto the sand, spat the Incantation of the Unknown and sprinkled dust from the tomb of Urkanet, the first Exemplar to die in the war. From the bloody droplets arose the half-human, half-scorpion sandmaskers. The hideous creatures then formed an army, turned the tide of battle and drove off the Exemplars, who strangely also lost their immorality and physical perfection by virtue of Tarun's terrible magics.

The sandmaskers now roam the deserts of the Scarred Lands, leading bands of giant scorpions on raids and attacks. Fanatical followers of Tarkun, their main goal is to root out Exemplars wherever they find them, but being merciless predators they root out and slay many other innocent creatures.

Sandmaskers appear human from the waist up and giant scorpion from the waist down. They often bear the black crescent moon and scimitar insignia of their lord Tarkun (who is presumed to still live somewhere in the Desert of Onn) branded on their chitin or tattooed on their skin.

Combat

Sandmaskers typically wield desert-style weapons, including spears, cutlasses, scimitars, short bows and crossbows. Although they typically wield one weapon at a time (5% are ambidextrous), they may attack with both claws and stinger.

Poison (Ex): A sandmasker's poison is quite deadly. If the stinger should hit an opponent, the victim must make a Fortitude save (DC 16) or lose 1 temporary point of Constitution each round until they are dead.

Leave No Sign (Ex): Sandmaskers walk through and over sand without leaving tracks (although their giant scorpion pets do leave tracks.)

Create Mirage (Sp): A sandmasker can create the illusion of a mirage or small oasis once per day. A Will save (DC 15) causes the illusion to desist.

Mirage Image (Sp): Sandmaskers can make 1d4 duplicate images of themselves, twice a day. A Will save (DC 13) is required to perceive the original from its images.

Locate Djinn (Ex): Sandmaskers can detect their ancient enemies up to one mile away, automatically. Sandmaskers make all attacks against djinn at +2. The most powerful sandmaskers have been know to carry magical, special-purpose weapons for slaying Exemplars.

Savant Hydra

Medium-size Outsider (Evil)

Hit Dice:	10d8+50 (95 hp)
Initiative:	+5 (Dex)
Speed:	40 ft.
AC:	22 (+5 Dex, +7 natural)
Attacks:	6 bites +13 melee, 2 claws +8 melee
Damage:	Bite 1d4+3 melee; claw 1d6 melee
Face/Reach:	5 ft. by 5 ft./5 ft.
Special Attacks:	Infectious talons, poison, spells
Special Qualities:	SR 18, damage reduction 10/+1, vigilance, outsider
Saves:	Fort +12, Ref +12, Will +10
Abilities:	Str 16, Dex 20, Con 20, Int 18, Wis 16, Cha 12
Skills:	Bluff +8, Concentration +5, Diplomacy +4, Forgery +6, Gather Information +10, Hide +7, Innuendo +5, Intimidate +10, Knowledge (Arcana) +6, Listen +10, Move Silently +6, Read Lips +7, Scry +6, Spellcraft +6, Spot +14
Feats:	Combat Reflexes, Silent Spell, Spell Penetration
Climate/Terrain:	Any
Organization:	Solitary, clutch (2-7)
Challenge Rating:	7
Treasure:	Standard
Alignment:	Usually lawful evil
Advancement Range:	9-12 HD (Medium-size)

Description

Once known as the Ministers of Chardun, savant hydrae were created during the Divine War to hunt down and destroy the servants of Chardun's rival Mormo. Their snake-like shape is both a mockery of Mormo's own servants and a tribute to Chardun. They combine the many heads of vigilance, the reptilian coldness of loyalty to one's duty and the serpentine venom reserved for traitors to the state.

Savant hydrae are less common then they once were, and only a few of the standing hunting parties that once roamed the land, searching for gorgons, hags and Mormo's other servants, remain. Most of the ones that people see now are solitary servants of Chardun who run the god's errands in the world. Some small groups still remain, however, living a shadow existence, hunting those spawn of Mormo that remain hidden.

Roughly half of all savant hydrae one could encounter possess a brace of keffiz (q.v.) as personal bodyguards. As creatures made of the very stuff of hell, the hydrae are brutal, unfeeling creatures — they exist solely to serve Chardun and to destroy his enemies. They have little concern for their own safety and survival, and even less concern for that of others. If it requires the death of dupes or innocent bystanders to destroy their target or accomplish their task, then that's the way it has to be.

Combat

In combat, savant hydrae typically attempt to kill or cripple their opponents from a distance or from surprise with combat magic, then set their keffiz on the enemy. Only if the keffiz are overmatched or losing, or if there are no keffiz with a given clutch, will the hydrae engage in personal combat, where they rend foes with their talons and strike repeatedly with their serpentine heads.

Infectious Talons (Ex): Wounds inflicted by a hydra's talons cannot be healed by magic, only by natural healing.

Poison (Ex): Those bitten by one of the hydra's serpentine heads must make a Fortitude save (DC 15) or take an additional 1d12 points of poison damage.

Spells: A savant hydra has the spellcasting ability and spells of a 7th-level sorcerer.

Vigilance (Ex): Savant hydrae never sleep, and they can see in all directions at once thanks to their many heads. They cannot be flanked or caught flat-footed.

Outsider: Immune to poison, sleep, paralysis, drowning and disease. Not subject to ability damage, energy drain, or any attack that must target a living victim.

Scythe Falcon

Tiny Animal

Hit Dice:	2d8 (9 hp)
Initiative:	+7 (+3 Dex, +4 Improved Initiative)
Speed:	20 ft., fly 240 ft.
AC:	17 (+2 size, +3 Dex, +2 natural)
Attacks:	Claw +3 melee; wing +3 melee
Damage:	Claw 1d3–1; wing 1d6–1
Face/Reach:	2.5 ft. by 2.5 ft./0 ft.
Special Attacks:	Dismemberment
Special Qualities:	Darkvision 120 ft.
Saves:	Fort +0, Ref +8, Will +2
Abilities:	Str 8, Dex 17, Con 10, Int 5, Wis 14, Cha 6
Skills:	Move Silently +5, Spot +8
Feats:	Flyby Attack, Improved Initiative, Lightning Reflexes, Mobility
Climate/Terrain:	Any
Organization:	Solitary, pair or family (1–2 and 2–5 offspring)
Challenge Rating:	2
Treasure:	Standard
Alignment:	Always neutral
Advancement Range:	1 HD (Tiny), 3 HD (Small)

Description

Of all the small animals of the Scarred Lands, none is quite so feared as the scythe falcon. Unlike other small animals that could pose a danger to intelligent races, the scythe falcon energetically seeks prey of virtually any size. Because it is armed with extraordinary natural means of attack, an encounter with the bird is inevitably a dangerous one.

Like most falcons, the scythe falcon is a very fast flyer. In fact, it is one of the fastest animals in the world. Its sleek feathers are normally brown, although the most notable (and most dangerous) feature of the scythe falcon is a razor-sharp ridge of bone that is forward-facing along the length of its wings. This bone is featherless and cuts through flesh as easily as it does the wind.

Scythe falcons mate for life and are frequently encountered in pairs. Unless the pair has young that must be guarded at a nest, they always hunt together. Typically, an attack involves the pair swooping in at great speed from a tremendous height. First, one falcon swoops by. If its dismembering attack is successful, the second bird does not attack but instead grabs hold of the dismembered limb and carries it away. The birds then speed toward their nest, while on the ground their victims are still trying to react or determine what happened.

If the first falcon's attack is unsuccessful, the second bird also attacks. They generally continue thusly until they are able to make away with a meal. When they attack smaller prey such as mice, they shun their wing attack and simply scoop their prey from the ground with their claws.

Beyond the danger they pose, scythe falcons often inadvertently cause other trouble. It is not unknown for

attacked merchants or adventurers to write off the loss of an arm but be unable to stomach the loss of a valuable or magical ring that might have adorned said limb. Therefore, the nests of scythe falcons are often sought by those in the hire of such merchants, or by those simply hoping to find an usual item perhaps lost by another. Game Masters should feel free to add a handful of interesting items to a nest, including items from other beasts of the Scarred Lands, such as a pegasus hoof or a charduni hand still clutching a warscepter.

Combat

Scythe falcons are fearless. Because of their awesome attack potential, they know that virtually any creature, no matter its size, can offer them a meal. They are generally uninterested in fighting longer than is required to gain a meal. However, they are fiercely loyal to their mates, so if one bird of pair is killed, the other almost always fights to the death.

Dismemberment (Ex): When a scythe falcon attacks with its razor-sharp wing bone, the threat range for a critical hit is 18-20. If a critical hit is scored, roll a d6 for the results of dismemberment instead of using a critical multiplier: 1 = head, victim dies instantly; 2 = right arm, victim loses 33% of current hp; 3 = left arm, victim loses 33% of current hp; 4 = right leg, victim loses 50% of current hp; 5 = left leg, victim loses 50% of current hp; 6 = victim badly slashed in chest and loses 50% of normal total hp.

Flyby Attack: A scythe falcon can attack at any point before, during or after its move if it is flying.

Searing Wind

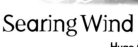

Huge (Tall) Construct

Hit Dice:	12d12+120 (198 hp)
Initiative:	+7 (+3 Dex, +4 Improved Initiative)
Speed:	Fly 50 ft. (good)
AC:	30 (-2 size, +3 Dex, +19 natural)
Attacks:	See below
Damage:	See below
Face/Reach:	10 ft. by 10 ft./30 ft.
Special Attacks:	Barbed whirl
Special Qualities:	Construct, damage reduction 8/+1
Saves:	Fort +18, Ref +7, Will +4
Abilities:	Str 22, Dex 16, Con 30, Int 3, Wis 10, Cha 0
Skills:	Listen +12, Spot +12
Feats:	Improved Initiative
Climate/Terrain:	Any
Organization:	Solitary
Challenge Rating:	10
Treasure:	Standard
Alignment:	Always neutral
Advancement Range:	8-18 HD (Huge), 19-25 HD (Gargantuan), 26-30 HD (Colossal)

Description

Spellcasters can summon entities from other planes to do their bidding in the material world. In the Scarred Lands, the most powerful summoners can trap these entities in weapons. Although almost any kind of small item or weapon can be caught up by one of these creatures, throwing stars or small daggers are the most "popular" (if that term can even be applied to such an unusual entity). Searing winds serve their masters as guardians or — as they did in

the Divine War — as warriors. The wizard Gest Ganest called upon his searing wind, composed of stars, when the titan Gaurak sought to eat the man and was served a mouthful of wounds, instead.

Combat

The searing wind is simple but dangerous. It appears at first to be just a pile of metal weapons, traditionally shuriken. But no adventurer wants this horde — when an intruder enters an area designated by the construct's creator, this pile rises up into a whirling storm of cutting mayhem. The ensuing attack has been described as a gale wind, if that wind carried blades and spikes.

Barbed Whirl (Su): Each round the searing wind is in combat, roll 1d12. That is the number of attacks the construct can make. Roll each attack separately; due to the dispersed nature of the wind, divide the attacks more or less evenly among all the characters within the creature's reach and strike at a full attack value of +16 for each. Each successful attack causes 1d8 damage.

Construct: The searing wind is impervious to critical hits, subdual damage and death from massive damage trauma. It's immune to poisons, diseases, blinding, deafness, drowning, electricity and spells or attacks that affect respiration or living physiology. It cannot be stunned. It's not affected by attacks or spells of mind-altering nature (enamoring or charming spells, for example), or by spells based on healing/harming. Fire and acid spells or attacks deal half normal damage.

Seaspark

Diminutive Elemental (Fire)

Hit Dice:	1d8 (4 hp)
Initiative:	+5 (Dex)
Speed:	Swim 60 ft.
AC:	19 (+4 size, +5 Dex)
Attacks:	None
Damage:	None
Face/Reach:	1 ft. by 1 ft. /10 ft.
Special Attacks:	Flare
Special Qualities:	Immunities, damage reduction 4/+1
Saves:	Fort +0, Ref +7, Will +0
Abilities:	Str 3, Dex 20, Con 10, Int 6, Wis 10, Cha -
Skills:	Swim +20
Feats:	None
Climate/Terrain:	Any marine
Organization:	Clusters (5-9) or swarms (10-120)
Challenge Rating:	1
Treasure:	Standard
Alignment:	Always neutral
Advancement Range:	1-7 HD (Diminutive)

Description

Seasparks are a strange form of fire elemental that thrives in water. Among the more beautiful creatures from the material planes, seasparks look like small multicolored fires about the size of a human fist floating on — or sometimes drifting beneath — the surface of any large body of water. Seasparks beneath the surface can be noted by the trails of steam rising through the water above them. Sages and sailors deliberate the origins of these paradoxical creatures. The former tend to believe that the elementals seek refuge in water, because if they were exposed to air alone they would burn so hot that they would exhaust themselves. Meanwhile, sailors claim that the lights are the souls of drowned sailors, come to claim more victims to light up the seas (more than one ship has been lured to a craggy shore and been wrecked by the deceptive lights).

While they are usually content to drift on the surface, seasparks are capable of very fast movement through water. Depending on your perspective, a swarm of seasparks speeding across the water can be either spectacularly beautiful (if you're on land) or terrifying (if they're headed for your ship).

Wizards have been known to gather seasparks (carefully) and place swarms of the beautiful elementals around their islands for both decorative and security purposes.

Seasparks are generally peaceful creatures, content to dance across the surface of the water. The only danger presented by seasparks is to wooden ships that get too near. Many ships have been set ablaze by aggravated seasparks.

Hitting, prodding or sailing over seasparks are all excellent means of irritating these beautiful creatures, and attempting to remove one from its cluster or swarm is a surefire way to get burned. If the cluster (or swarm) is carefully kept together in water, however, seasparks generally do not take exception to being transported.

Combat

Seasparks prefer to avoid conflict, but they attack as a cluster (or a swarm) if antagonized.

Flare (Ex): When irritated, a seaspark can lash out with a white-hot lash of flame that inflicts 2d10 damage. The spark can choose to direct this at an opponent up to 20 feet distant, or to simply flare up in a five-foot radius. Either way the strike hits automatically, though the victim may make a Reflex save (DC 11) to take half damage.

Immunities (Ex): Seasparks are immune to all fire and water attacks.

Sentry Crow

Tiny Animal (Bird)

Hit Dice:	1d8+1 (5 hp)
Initiative:	+4 (Dex)
Speed:	10 ft., fly 90 ft.
AC:	18 (+2 size, +4 Dex, +2 natural)
Attacks:	Peck +0 melee; 2 talons +0 melee
Damage:	Peck 1d3; talons 1d3
Face/Reach:	2.5 ft. by 2.5 ft./0 ft.
Special Attacks:	None
Special Qualities:	Speak
Saves:	Fort +3, Ref +4, Will +3
Abilities:	Str 5, Dex 18, Con 12, Int 8, Wis 16, Cha 6
Skills:	Hide +3, Listen +8, Read Lips +5, Spot +10, Wilderness Lore +6
Feats:	Mobility, Track
Climate/Terrain:	Mountains (often near dwarven strongholds)
Organization:	Solitary or murder (3-5 and 1d4 offspring)
Challenge Rating:	1/4
Treasure:	None
Alignment:	Always neutral good
Advancement Range:	1-2 HD (Tiny)

Description

"Murder of Crows," a song well-known by minstrels and bards, is given little thought by most people of the Scarred Lands, being played primarily for the entertainment of courtiers and fairgoers. But to the dwarven peoples of the world, the song is a death dirge. It tells of the fall of Iron Tooth Pass to the armies and trickery of the human-land Calastia, led by its boy-king, Virduk. Among the heroes immortalized in the song are the crows raised and trained by the pass' defenders, which acted as sentries for their masters. Indeed, it was the crows that detected Virduk's army before it fell upon the pass, giving the dwarves time to take to their caverns and overlooks and keep the attackers at bay.

The song continues to explain how only the sentry crows escaped the stronghold when it finally fell, commanded by their keepers to take wing and spread the tale of the treachery used against the dwarves. The story told to scattered dwarven kings was captured in song as a warning against future assault, and the phrase "murder of crows" came into use in memory of the horrible story the birds told of Iron Tooth.

To this day, sentry crows are the intelligent, dutiful and beloved pets of the dwarven people who remain in the world. Indeed, they're the revered councilors, spies and scouts of kings, lords and priests, and are sometimes the familiars of the very rare dwarven wizards.

Combat

Sentry crows avoid direct combat whenever possible, but have been known to peck and claw at lone intruders on dwarven lands and at those who attack the birds' masters. They are relied on mostly for their intelligence, guidance and insight.

Speak (Ex): Sentry crows can be trained to speak, usually the dwarven tongue, although they might be taught Common or other languages. Only the most exceptional ones know more than one language each.

Serpent Root

	Large Plant; Tiny Tendril
Hit Dice:	4d8+20 (38 hp) plant;
	1d8+5 (9 hp) tendril
Initiative:	-2 (Dex)
Speed:	Immobile
AC:	11 plant (-1 size, -2 Dex, +4 natural);
	14 tendril (+2 size, -2 Dex, +4 natural)
Attacks:	Tendril lash +4 melee;
	tendril constrict +4 melee;
	plant constrict +3 melee
Damage:	Tendril lash 1d8+1;
	tendril constrict 2d4 +1;
	plant constrict 2d8+1
Face/Reach:	5 ft. by 10 ft./10 ft.
Special Attacks:	Vitality drain
Special Qualities:	Plant, damage reduction 5/+1
Saves:	Fort +9 plant, +7 tendril;
	Ref -1 plant, -2 tendril; Will +0
Abilities:	Str 12, Dex 6, Con 20,
	Int —, Wis —, Cha —
Skills:	Climb +10, Move Silently (tendril) +8
Feats:	Great Fortitude
Climate/Terrain:	Any
Organization:	Grows in patches about 300 feet apart, through runners. Each plant has 1d4+2 large tendrils, and many small ones near the root that grasp victims passed by a large tendril.
Challenge Rating:	4
Treasure:	None
Alignment:	Always neutral
Advancement Range:	2-12 HD (Huge) plant;
	1-3 HD (Medium-size) tendril

Description

When young King Virduk ascended to the Calastia throne — soon after the mysterious death of his father — the new monarch sought to commemorate the event with a "crowning" achievement. After the kingdom's years of relatively peaceful relations with its neighbors, Virduk and his counselors decided that a brilliant military victory would serve to mark the king in the annals of time. The dwarves of the Iron Tooth Pass to the south made likely targets; they had "placed embargoes on trade" and "forced the good people of Calastia into poverty" for too long. Although the human attack came as a surprise, the handful of dwarves manning the Iron Tooth stronghold went to ground and held fast against the invaders, repelling attack after attack.

Finally, the wizard Anteas, chief advisor of Virduk's council, promised a victory where every warlord had failed. He knew the secret — the correct time of year and technique — to harvesting serpent root, a destructive vine that thrived in the Hornsaw Forest. Legend held that the tenacious bramble was born from and fed upon the spilled blood of the titan Mormo or that her serpent children grew roots and became as hard as bark upon her death. The vine was now known to draw the life energy from anything that grew around it, leaving tracts of land in devastation. Transplanting some of the root, Virduk defeated the dwarves within a fortnight, his living weapon literally cracking the earth and sucking the life from its trapped victims.

Combat

Any wise traveler who dares the Hornsaw Forest knows better than to make camp there. If the blight can be transplanted, it is devastating to any town, crop or wood nearby, let alone unwary passersby.

Constriction (Ex): A victim damaged by a tendril attack must make a successful Reflex save (DC 13) or suffer constriction damage in the next round automatically. In addition, the serpent root can pass one opponent from a tendril to its main trunk for intensified constriction. A Strength check (DC 15) is required to break the hold of a tendril or the plant.

Plant: Impervious to critical hits, subdual damage and death from massive damage trauma. Not affected by many spells of mind-altering nature (for example, enamoring or charming spells not specifically designed for plants), subject to Game Master's adjudication.

Regeneration (Ex): The plant regains 1 hp per round, except from attacks made using acid or fire.

Vitality Drain (Ex): The vine drains 1 hp a day from all living things within 10 yards per HD the plant has. Most inanimate objects are eroded or ruined in time as well, drained of any sustenance they might offer.

Siren Vulture

Medium-size Beast

Hit Dice:	1d10+2 (7 hp)
Initiative:	+0
Speed:	30 ft., fly 60 ft.
AC:	10
Attacks:	Bite +5 melee, 2 claws +0 melee
Damage:	Bite 1d4+4; claw 1d4+2
Face/Reach:	5 ft. by 5 ft./5 ft.
Special Attacks:	None
Special Qualities:	Song
Saves:	Fort +4, Ref +0, Will +2
Abilities:	Str 18, Dex 10, Con 15, Int 10, Wis 14, Cha 15
Skills:	Intuit Direction +3, Search +2, Spot+5
Feats:	None
Climate/Terrain:	Desert
Organization:	Flocks (2-12)
Challenge Rating:	1/2
Treasure:	Standard
Alignment:	Usually neutral evil
Advancement Range:	1-3 HD (Medium-size)

Description

Siren vultures are desert falcons' (q.v.) chief rivals for prey, but the way they hunt is entirely different. Where the falcons swoop and strike, siren vultures lure, circle and wait out their prey.

Where siren vultures come from and where they go when they're not hunting is something of a mystery. Ubantu tribesmen tell stories of a crooked tree of desert glass — tall as a mountain — that rings and chimes as the vultures land and take off. Those stories also claim that the siren vultures spear their prey on long shard-branches of the tree for the featherless, newly hatched young to eat. However, since no Ubantu tribesman has returned with proof of these claims in recent history, the stories remain only stories.

What the Ubantu know for certain about siren vultures is how they hunt. These strange beings land near single Ubantu — or other beings — and trill hypnotically. If the performance is forceful enough, it lures the unlucky victim away from his current locale. The siren vulture then leads its thrall out into the desert, ostensibly toward the tree of glass, if legends are reliable. The siren vulture lures the victim away from water and obvious sources of food, landing occasionally to sing and entice the victim further. When the victim inevitably dies of exposure (provided he can be led long enough), the vulture picks him up and flies away with him. The birds are also known to lure prey into dangerous situations or places, such as off a cliff, and carry off their corpses.

Combat

Most siren vultures fly away instantly if attacked, but they can fight. If brought down by an Ubantu slinger or an arrow shot, they draw their wings in close and stand their ground. If one siren vulture in a group dies in battle, the others will pick it up and attempt to escape with it.

Song (Su): The siren vulture's song lulls a victim into a senseless stupor if he fails a Will save (DC 14). The victim follows the siren vulture for 2d6 rounds, at which point the vulture must sing again.

Skin Devil

Medium-size Humanoid

Hit Dice:	5d8+20 (42 hp)
Initiative:	+3 (Dex)
Speed:	60 ft.
AC:	16 (+3 Dex, +3 natural)
Attacks:	Bite +7 melee; 2 claws +2 melee; sword +7 melee
Damage:	Bite 2d4+2; claw 1d6+2; sword 1d8+2
Face/Reach:	5 ft. by 5 ft./5 ft.
Special Attacks:	None
Special Qualities:	Grow new skin
Saves:	Fort +8, Ref +4, Will +0
Abilities:	Str 15, Dex 17, Con 18, Int 12, Wis 9, Cha 14
Skills:	Alertness +4, Bluff +10, Hide +8, Listen +5, Spot +5
Feats:	None
Climate/Terrain:	Any
Organization:	Solitary
Challenge Rating:	4
Treasure:	Standard
Alignment:	Always chaotic neutral
Advancement Range:	By character class

Description

The skin devil is a terrifying creature that in its natural state appears as a human being whose skin has been expertly removed, revealing glistening muscle and pulsing veins from head to toe. Odd patches of skin or hide cling to parts of its body, remnants of former disguises that have fallen into tatters.

The skin devil is a creature in constant agony, knowing peace only when it has clothed its form in another's stolen skin. Intelligent and murderously cunning, these creatures are exceptionally capable mimics and appear to gain a part of a person's skills, mannerisms and personality through a stolen skin. A devil that can take a two-inch square of skin from a victim can place the flesh over its heart and within one night grow skin and hair identical to that of the "donor." This disguise is only temporary, however, starting to rot almost immediately and becoming useless after a single week, at which point the devil has hopefully singled out its next victim. There are stories of skin devils stalking quietly through large towns for months, leaving behind a trail of bodies until they are finally discovered and destroyed.

Skin devils appear to be able to speak and read all the major humanoid languages, though whether this is an innate ability or something absorbed from their victims is unknown. These creatures use weapons and armor like any other person, and in at least one case, a skin devil has been encountered that can cast spells.

Combat

The skin devil prefers to stalk its next victim for some time, working its way into that person's confidence and attacking her unawares with whatever weapons are available. If directly confronted with superior skill or numbers, the creature flees and seek easier prey.

Grow New Skin (Su): If a skin devil succeeds in causing four or more points of damage to an opponent in a single attack, it can successfully remove sufficient skin to grow a disguise identical to its victim. The skin devil needs one full night to grow the skin and, by dawn, has an flawless disguise, similar mannerisms and voice and the ability to call upon the victim's skills and spell abilities at one-half the victim's level. These abilities only last for a week or until the skin itself is destroyed (i.e. the creature suffers more than half its hit points in damage).

Skyquill

Medium-size Fey

Hit Dice:	10d6 (35 hp)
Initiative:	+10 (+6 Dex, +4 Improved Initiative)
Speed:	30 ft., fly 100 ft.
AC:	16 (Dex)
Attacks:	2 Hands +9 melee
Damage:	Hand 1d3
Face/Reach:	5 ft. by 5 ft./5 ft.
Special Attacks:	Quills, spray colors
Special Qualities:	Adhesive glands, cause fog, create cloud, create rain, darkvision 80 ft., voice of the butterfly
Saves:	Fort +3, Ref +15, Will +8
Abilities:	Str 8, Dex 22, Con 10, Int 11, Wis 12, Cha 22
Skills:	Animal Empathy +13, Escape Artist +12, Move Silently +10
Feats:	Improved Initiative, Lightning Reflexes
Climate/Terrain:	Any
Organization:	Solitary, pair, nest (6-8), flock (9-20)
Challenge Rating:	6
Treasure:	Standard
Alignment:	Usually neutral good
Advancement Range:	9-11 HD

Description

Skyquills are the children of Syhana, demigoddess of the clouds, who is herself a daughter of Madriel, goddess of sky. It is Syhana to whom Madriel has entrusted the care and cultivation of the clouds.

Skyquills fly among the clouds and shape them. In fact, the common folk of the Scarred Lands know that skyquills are at work when they look up and see clouds changing shape, even on a day with no breeze. Skyquills are also able to create and walk the rainbow paths, and it is believed that only they of all creatures know what lies at the end of those colorful bands.

Skyquills keep a carefully guarded secret: They know that quillflies can be used to cause clouds to produce rain. Quillflies look like common butterflies, but they produce a magical nectar that skyquills use to prepare the clouds if they wish to reward mortals for a past kindness. Therefore, skyquills are often found near the ground, caring for quillflies and harvesting this magical nectar. Not surprisingly, skyquills are extremely protective of quillflies, and they tend to shoot first and ask questions later if they feel that their charges are endangered.

One old tale holds that a manorial lady planted a number of butterfly bushes about her demesne, which quillflies soon found and fed upon. Seeing this kindness, the skyquills made certain that the lady's fields never wanted for refreshing rain. Therefore, some Scarred Lands farmers consider it taboo to kill any butterfly, lest their own crops go parched.

Combat

If they must, skyquills can hit an opponent with their gluey hands for slight damage, but they typically use the following effects to end a fight:

Adhesive Glands (Ex): The palms of skyquills' hands and the bottoms of their feet are grayish-black, where glands exude an adhesive that lets them cling to surfaces and hang upside-down.

Cause Fog (Sp): A skyquill can create a magical fog once per day that covers a 40-foot radius. This fog obscures all forms of vision and lasts for 2d4 minutes (20-80 rounds).

Create Cloud (Sp): Skyquills are able to create small bits (10 cubic feet) of cloud per round.

Create Rain (Su): These fey are able to use the nectar of quillflies along with their cloud-shaping abilities to make it rain gently. The showers they create last for 1d6 hours and rejuvenate weary folks who've otherwise been hard at work outside.

Quills (Su): By flapping their wings and releasing the quills on the edges of their wings, skyquills can shower opponents with rainbow-colored needles. The needles cover a 15-foot cone, and anyone in the area of effect must make a Reflex save (DC 16) or be struck by 1d3 needles of random color and effect. Consult the following table:

Roll 1d6	Color	Effect
1	Red	Will save (DC 15) or the victim is overcome with amorous love for the closest creature of the appropriate sex and at least somewhat similar racial make-up. The victim stops all activity to proclaim his love to his newfound soulmate. If no compatible creature is nearby, the victim lapses into a narcissistic love and immediately searches for a reflection of himself with which to better admire his beauty. The effect lasts 2d4 minutes before the intensity of the feelings diminishes gradually. The victim defends himself or his new love from attack, but he otherwise remains quite love-struck and docile.
2	Orange	Fortitude save (DC 15) or the victim is overcome with ravenous hunger. He immediately seeks out food from the closest available source. The effect lasts 2d4 minutes.
3	Yellow	As orange, above, except the victim is overcome with thirst.
4	Green	Will save (DC 15) or the victim is overcome with curiosity about some random element of his surroundings (GM's choice). The victim stops all activity to examine the object. It may be another creature, a butterfly, a tree, or just an insatiable curiosity to discover what's on the other side of that distant hill. This effect lasts 3d6 minutes or until the victim is attacked.
5	Blue	Will save (DC 15) or the victim is overcome with a tremendous sense of peace and calm. She does not seek to attack or do anything strenuous. If attacked, she retreats to safety. This effect lasts 2-8 rounds.
6	Violet	Will save (DC 15) or the victim falls into a deep sleep. It lasts 2d4 hours or until the person is forcibly awakened.

Spray Colors (Sp): Skyquills shoot forth rainbow-like color from their hands in a 20-foot cone. Anyone struck by the spray is blinded by the dazzling colors for 1d8 rounds unless they make a Fortitude save (DC 15).

Voice of the Butterfly (Ex): Skyquills are able to speak with and understand butterflies.

Slarecian

Many of the scholars and seers who contemplate, examine and uncover the history of the Scarred Lands share a favorite story of an alternate manner in which the future might have unfolded. If the gods and titans had not sundered the world in their great battle, then perhaps a secretive and almost unknown race known as the slarecians would now rule the world. So, these scholars like to point out to any who will listen and to those who read their works, that the present state of affairs is, perhaps, not a bad thing. To be ruled (probably enslaved) by the slarecians would be a nightmare when compared to living even on a land ravaged by celestial war and among races obliterated by heavenly forces.

Of course, these same scholars can provide little actual facts about the slarecians. They know that this humanoid race lived almost exclusively below ground. The scholars know the slarecians investigated the blackest of arts, but whether such practice was common necromancy or for a more enlightened purpose such as medicine or surgery cannot be determined. Scholars also know that the little slarecian literature written in Common (as the slarecian language has proven resistant even to magical translation) that has been recovered from some buried cities (or even found moldering in the corners of the libraries in such cities as Vashon and Eldrua-tre) deals with death and infernal beings, but it is not clear whether such works are biographical or fictional. In the end, though some scholars claim a repository of artifacts they do not share with others, the majority of them, and so the majority of intelligent races of the Scarred Lands, must make do with judging the slarecians by the remnants of their civilization.

And since that which the slarecians left behind includes the likes of gargoyles and ghouls, most intelligent races fear what might have been if the slarecians had mastered their own destiny. Instead, the stories of the time before the Divine War say that in a final act prior to setting upon each other, the gods and titans annihilated the slarecians, who evidently paid homage to neither group. Whatever the outcome of their war with each other, neither the gods nor the titans desired the slarecians to find a way to emerge the true victors.

The appearance of the slarecians themselves has only been confirmed by illustrations in some ancient tomes and by the aspect of the rarely encountered slarecian ghouls. Only time will tell if anything more can be learned of this mysterious and evidently powerful race. And only time will tell if this knowledge need be put to use.

Slarecian Gargoyle

Large Construct

Hit Dice:	6d12+18 (57 hp)
Initiative:	+5 (+1 Dex, +4 Improved Initiative)
Speed:	30 ft., fly 60 ft.
AC:	22 (-1 size, +1 Dex, +12 natural)
Attacks:	Bite +9 melee, 2 claws +6 melee; horn +9 melee
Damage:	Bite 2d4+4; claw 2d6+4; horn 2d8+4
Face/Reach:	5 ft. by 5 ft./10 ft.
Special Attacks:	Horn special attacks
Special Qualities:	Camouflage, damage reduction 20/+1, SR 13, construct
Saves:	Fort +8, Ref +3, Will +4
Abilities:	Str 18, Dex 13, Con 16, Int 9, Wis 9, Cha 2
Skills:	Hide +2, Listen +12, Move Silently +8, Spot +12
Feats:	Cleave (horn attack only), Improved Initiative, Multiattack
Climate/Terrain:	Any ruins
Organization:	Solitary, pack (1-3)
Challenge Rating:	5
Treasure:	None
Alignment:	Always neutral
Advancement Range:	None

Description

Not a race unto themselves like some others kinds of gargoyles, slarecian gargoyles are believed to be magical constructs that once guarded the tunnels and caverns of a presumed slarecian civilization. The majority of these defenders were likely destroyed when the slarecians were assaulted by the minions of the gods and titans, but some obviously escaped that fate, for they are sometimes encountered, although primarily in very outlying locations. Such is not always the case, though, and there are a couple of reports of a slarecian gargoyle essentially clawing its way out of the ground within or near a town or village and rampaging against the inhabitants. It is assumed that the gargoyles were trapped in tunnels or caves beneath the ground, finally regained their freedom and then turned upon those nearby as though they were intruders. Some people worry about a time when a gargoyle might dig its way up to the streets of a city like Mithril and lay waste to dozens or even hundreds of citizens before it can be stopped (perhaps by the golem there?).

Slarecian gargoyles do not communicate, even with each other, and they cannot be reasoned with or dissuaded from their ends.

Whenever multiple gargoyles are encountered, they always have different colored horns (i.e., a group of three represents each color).

Combat

If possible, a slarecian gargoyle attacks with surprise, often posing as a statue and then springing upon a foe. Although they do not communicate, they do have what must be instinctual or innate tactics, especially when fighting as a trio. A blue-horned one tries to freeze foes while a red-horned one wades into melee, trying to position itself close to as many foes at once (and hopefully nearby a frozen foe, a tactic that draws comrades in to save their friends). Meanwhile, the yellow-horned variety targets spellcasters with its lightning-bolt attack.

Camouflage (Ex): As slarecian gargoyles are made out of stone, they are almost impossible to distinguish from such surroundings. They receive +10 to their Hide skill when hiding against stone backdrops.

Horn Special Attack (Su): Slarecian gargoyles are known to come in three different varieties that are distinguished solely by the color of their gem-like horns. These three colors are red, blue and yellow, each with its own unique power.

The red-horned gargoyle is able to radiate tremendous heat as a free action. Those within five feet of the gargoyle suffer 2d4 damage per melee round, and any metal weapons or armor within that range also heats as per the druid spell effect, so long as such metal is within range of the gargoyle. Those up to 10 feet away simply suffer 1d4 damage per melee round.

The blue-horned gargoyle may attempt to magically hold a victim in place with a powerful freezing effect. It may target one victim per round, who must attempt a Fortitude saving throw (DC 15). Victims who succeed at the saving throw are still slowed to half speed as per the spell effect. Victims who fail their saving throw are frozen immobile. The gargoyle may use this power three times per day.

The yellow-horned slarecian gargoyle can fire a lightning bolt from its horn three times per day. The bolt is treated as a ray effect spell requiring a ranged touch attack from gargoyle to hit (attack +6). The target of the bolt suffers 6d6 damage (Reflex save DC 18 applicable for half damage). The bolt has a range of 60 feet and is used in lieu of a horn attack.

Construct: Gargoyles are impervious to critical hits, subdual damage and death from massive damage trauma. They're immune to poisons, diseases, blinding, deafness, drowning, electricity and to spells or attacks that affect respiration or living physiology. They cannot be stunned. They're not affected by attacks or spells of mind-altering nature (enamoring or charming spells, for example), or by spells based on healing/harming. Fire and acid spells or attacks deal half normal damage.

Slarecian Ghoul

Medium-size Undead

Hit Dice:	6d12 (39 hp)
Initiative:	+2 (Dex)
Speed:	30 ft.
AC:	20 (+2 Dex, +8 natural)
Attacks:	Bite +7 melee, 2 claws +4 melee
Damage:	Bite 1d12+1 and special; claw 1d6+1 and special
Face/Reach:	5 ft. by 5 ft./5 ft.
Special Attacks:	Fetid touch
Special Qualities:	Damage reduction 10/+1, undead, unturnable
Saves:	Fort +2, Ref +4, Will +7
Abilities:	Str 13, Dex 15, Con —, Int 15, Wis 15, Cha 16
Skills:	Climb +6, Escape Artist +9, Hide +9, Intuit Direction +3, Jump +6, Listen +8, Move Silently +7, Search +6, Spot +9
Feats:	Multiattack
Climate/Terrain:	Any land or underground
Organization:	Solitary, pair or pack (1-4)
Challenge Rating:	4
Treasure:	Double Standard
Alignment:	Always chaotic evil
Advancement Range:	5-8 HD (Medium-size)

Description

It's said that when they were set upon at once by the gods and titans, the only way the slarecians could survive was to kill themselves. Wherever they came from, there is little disputing that these ghouls were once slarecians. Whether they became ghouls to escape complete destruction or upon their death because of a predilection for cannibalism is hardly of concern to the unfortunates who face them. Like ordinary ghouls, those of the slarecian variety are emaciated, with rotten and decaying flesh on their tall and now grossly slender frames. They eat only carrion, so fresh kills are left to decay before they are devoured.

The slarecian ghoul has lost none of its desire to dominate "lesser" races. Entire villages or towns may be seized by these terrible beasts, and all the inhabitants are afflicted by the ghouls' fetid touch. The diseased inhabitants are allowed to exist only to later serve as food for the ghouls.

Slarecian ghouls speak Common and a tongue that no one can comprehend (Slarecian, which has proven unintelligible even through magic).

Combat

Slarecian ghouls are deadly foes. However, a great deal of the danger they pose is not faced until after the ghoul itself is destroyed. That's when victims may learn the terrible truth about the ghoul's fetid touch.

Fetid Touch (Su): Living creatures hit by the attack of a slarecian ghoul must succeed at a Fortitude save (DC 12) or suffer a horrific rotting of their flesh. Those who fail their saving throw are stunned for the next 2d4 rounds, during which time the victim's life force is whisked out of and she is essentially turned into undead and gains a zombie-like appearance (ashen gray skin) thereafter.

While victims of the attack gain all the immunities typical of the undead, they are also caught in a terrible limbo between life and death. Until the effects of the fetid touch can be removed, a victim's wounds no longer heal naturally, and even magical healing spells and potions do not aid in healing. Victims in this state can be hurt further, however, so it's an extremely perilous condition.

Other than natural recovery, there is no known cure for the fetid touch, because the affliction is so rarely encountered, but there are certainly some wizards who would pay dearly to examine a victim (willing or not). A victim receives a new saving throw every day to attempt to recover naturally, but the DC increases by one per day. So, the day after the affliction is gained, the Fortitude save is DC 13, and the next day it's DC 14.

Undead: Slarecian ghouls are immune to poison, sleep, paralysis, stunning and disease. They're not subject to critical hits, subdual damage, ability damage, energy drain or death from massive damage.

Unturnable: Unlike other undead, slarecian undead cannot be turned by clerics. The reason for this is unknown, buried with the other secrets of the slarecians themselves.

Slarecian Language Virus
Fine Magical Beast Hazard

Description

Some wizards who have attempted to decipher ancient slarecian texts through the use of high magic have only succeeded in afflicting themselves with a bizarre enchantment or disease. Once afflicted, the victim is unable to speak or write in any language. When she attempts to speak, her voice only enunciates a sing-song of garbled gibberish, and when she attempts to write, her hand moves of its own accord, almost as if ghost-writing, and etches only scrawling knots of lines that resemble no known language. The victim is also unable to read any language. Though victims can still think coherently in any language with which they were fluent before, they lose all ability to communicate externally with such languages.

Were this mental affliction to end there, it would seem to be the result of some curse or mystic rune embedded in the slarecian language. However, the affliction, like a disease, is contagious, and anyone to whom the afflicted speaks or anyone who takes more than a glance of anything the afflicted writes also becomes subject to the disease. It is as if the disease is passed on through the gibberish the afflicted uses in lieu of language. Therefore, where the disease has broken out, it has spread very quickly until a sage has been consulted and the afflicted quarantined and cured.

Any two people afflicted with the disease may communicate with one another, but with no one who is not affected. Additionally, victims of the language virus cannot cast spells with verbal components, speak proper command words to activate magical items, read scrolls or spell books or even pray properly to regain divine spells.

System: Anyone using magical means to decipher the slarecian language or even trying non-magical means of intense study to crack this enigmatic language may be subject to this disease if the text studied happens to carry it. Such linguistic researchers of "diseased" texts must attempt a Will saving throw (DC 22) to resist infection.

All who hear the afflicted speak or read their afflicted writing must pass a Fortitude saving throw (DC 18) to resist picking up the disease themselves.

The language virus can be cured with magic like any other disease, may be removed as though it were a curse or even dispelled as a magical effect (treat as caster level 15).

Slarecian Muse

Tiny Construct

Hit Dice:	3d10+15 (31 hp)
Initiative:	+0
Speed:	0 ft.
AC:	35 (+25 natural)
Attacks:	None
Damage:	None
Face/Reach:	2.5 ft. by 2.5 ft./0 ft.
Special Attacks:	Spell-like abilities, mission
Special Qualities:	Answer, damage reduction 20/+3, SR 15, construct
Saves:	Fort +8, Ref —, Will +6
Abilities:	Str —, Dex —, Con 20, Int 24, Wis 17, Cha 18
Skills:	Alchemy +15, Appraise +15, Decipher Script +15, Diplomacy +10, Innuendo +10, Intuit Direction +15, Knowledges (All) +5, Listen +20, Read Lips +10, Sense Motive +10, Speak Languages (All), Spot +12
Feats:	Silent Spell, Still Spell
Climate/Terrain:	Any
Organization:	Solitary
Challenge Rating:	5
Treasure:	None
Alignment:	Always neutral
Advancement Range:	None

Description

Perhaps at once the most fascinating and most frustrating creature in the Scarred Lands, the slarecian muse appears to be nothing more than a sculpture of a head. The nature of the head can be that of any race from human to dwarf to goblin, but as far as is known only one slarecian muse of each type exists. It's not known whether a muse exists for each intelligent race or not, or whether there are muses for humanoid races only (so none for dragons, etc.). The material from which a muse is sculpted appears to be the same gem-like material found comprising the horns of slarecian gargoyles.

Evidently unable to move even by magical means, these muses are at the disposal of those who claim to own them. Originally given as gifts by ambassadors claiming to represent the slarecians to the rulers of the various races almost 200 years ago, the muses have largely remained in the hands of the original recipients or their descendants. Some have been lost or misplaced through mischief over the course of the last two centuries; in particular, a number of the muses given to the "less civilized" races have been lost. It is known, for instance, that the muses of both human and asaathi likenesses have been lost. Those who claim to "own" muses are highly protective of them and typically restrict access to them.

Each muse is highly intelligent but speaks to only those of the race it depicts. All others seem to be regarded as enemies, though these "enemies" are not attacked unless they in turn attack or attempt to move the muse. With their allies, a muse is quite willing to share its vast knowledge. Though they converse at length, the muses divine the answer to only one direct question per day, and that is the first question put to them after each sunrise. In the event it is unable to answer the question, a muse says as much but still declines to answer further questions that day.

Many — perhaps most — people still distrust muses, feeling they must be part of a ruse or plot of the slarecians. But time dulls paranoia as well as memory, and as muses have ably served without seeming duplicity for so long, most fears have evaporated. Notable in their continued distrust are the dwarves. King Gontric (who then ruled from Burok Torn) locked his muse away when he received it, and his great-grandson who rules today has kept it so (though it's unknown whether it remains in Burok Torn or whether the new dwarven king even cares or knows). Even so, who knows into whose hands some of the missing muses have fallen?

Of course, muses should be mistrusted, for though they hold no specific grudge against those with whom they consort, they do have a mission to complete, the details of which remain unknown. However, those who take advantage of the muses' powers seem to return the favor of the answers by procuring a number of strange, exotic and expensive items. Unknown to any but those rulers who deliver said items after

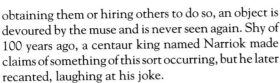

obtaining them or hiring others to do so, an object is devoured by the muse and is never seen again. Shy of 100 years ago, a centaur king named Narriok made claims of something of this sort occurring, but he later recanted, laughing at his joke.

Over the past 200 years, some fortunate handfuls of adventurers and mercenaries have grown rich and powerful by completing errands for various rulers. Retrieve a gemstone from some forgotten cave. Or the scale of a dragon. Or a sacred idol that is later bathed in the waters of the great Vaarooshan Falls. All manner of peculiar items are sought by slarecian muses.

Combat

Slarecian muses do not engage in combat unless forced to do so by aggressive adversaries. Muses in the "possession" of racial leaders are generally protected from such threats, but some of the lost ones may not be so fortunate. However, muses are extremely difficult to injure, and it's most likely that those encountered fall prey to its mind-affecting powers and they attempt to protect it thereafter. The muse then seeks to maintain control long enough to coerce its slave/friend into returning it to the hands of the leaders to whom it "belongs" (i.e., the human head, if ever encountered, might desire to travel to Vashon, home of King Virduk).

Answer (Su): This divination ability can be used by a slarecian muse once per day. Basically, the entity can divine the answer to any "yes or no" question 70 percent of the time. If an answer cannot be obtained, the muse says as much, and that question may never be asked of the same muse again (even by a different individual).

Mission (Sp): This ability can be used to coerce an individual to undertake a specific quest. It may be used once per week on any subject who has ever received an answer from the muse (see "Answer" above). Even if one answer is all an individual ever requests he is still susceptible to multiple missions. In addition, the power operates telepathically and reaches its target anywhere on the same plane as the muse. The victim of the mission gains one Will saving throw (DC30) to ignore each use of this power. Success means the victim has an odd dream that's quickly forgotten. Failure means the victim diligently pursues the completion of the muse's mission, either personally or by delegating the task to others.

If an affected individual attempts to tell another of his coercion or does not attempt to complete the mission, he must make a Will save (DC 30) or fall under the complete mind-control of the muse. Muses, however, do not wish to call attention to this mental domination, so the affected individual maintains a life much as before, yet gains a penchant for undertaking missions on behalf of the muse.

Spell-like Abilities: Slarecian muses may, at will, cast any mind-affecting wizard spell of 1st through 3rd level at the rate of one per round.

Construct: A muse is mpervious to critical hits, subdual damage and death from massive damage trauma. It's immune to poisons, diseases, blinding, deafness, drowning, electricity and spells or attacks that affect respiration or living physiology. It cannot be stunned. It's not affected by attacks or spells of mind-altering nature (enamoring or charming spells, for example) or spells based on healing/harming. Fire and acid spells or attacks deal half normal damage.

Slarecian Shadowman

Medium-size Undead

Hit Dice:	4d12+4 (30 hp)
Initiative:	+10 (Dex)
Speed:	30 ft. or special (see below)
AC:	Always 20
Attacks:	2 Claws +5 melee
Damage:	Claw 1d8+1
Face/Reach:	5 ft. by 5 ft./5 ft. or special (see below)
Special Attacks:	Absorb memory, destroy memory, graft, strength drain
Special Qualities:	Blindsight, immunities, undead, unturnable
Saves:	Fort +2, Ref +14, Will +3
Abilities:	Str 13, Dex 30, Con 12, Int 16, Wis 14, Cha 15
Skills:	Hide +20, Listen +10, Move Silently +15, Spot +6
Feats:	None
Climate/Terrain:	Any
Organization:	Solitary
Challenge Rating:	3
Treasure:	None
Alignment:	Always neutral
Advancement Range:	2–8 HD (Medium-size)

Description

The existence of slarecian shadowmen is a known fact, but their nature and purpose is in question. They are believed to be undead creatures, although clerics seem incapable of turning them. They are also thought to have been spies and/or assassins for the slarecians centuries ago, but that cannot explain the fact that they are still sometimes encountered and evidently still spy on others. Whether this is because they are ageless and continue to carry out orders given long ago or because some slarecians still survive is also unknown.

What is understood is the virtual impossibility of detecting the creatures. Shadowmen typically dwell or hide in darkened areas where they are indistinguishable from the surrounding shadows. Even after they have successfully replaced a victim's natural shadow with their own bodies, they remain difficult to detect, because like the shadows themselves shadowmen are evidently able to twist and stretch their bodies to perfectly duplicate what a natural shadow would do.

A handful of shadowmen continue to wander the Scarred Lands on missions no one can hope to understand. It is rumored that one or even more of these creatures have struck a bargain with the necromancers of Glivid Autel (those renegades originally from Hollowfaust) wherein the death magicians have allowed shadowmen to graft themselves to the sorcerers' bodies. In return for necromantic secrets, the shadowmen are ready to protect their complicit hosts.

Otherwise, they seem to be encountered only in the most well defended locales, including the throne room of Eldura-tre, where one of the vile creatures was found grafted to High Warden Jarwen-awen. After detection, it managed to escape and was subsequently discovered attempting to regain access to the High Warden, who is now reportedly confined to the city, where he is allegedly inaccessible to the shadowman.

Combat

A slarecian shadowman can be either frustratingly invulnerable or fortunately quickly dispatched in combat depending on the foes it faces. Since it is immune to attacks not involving light or fire, a shadowman initially targets enemies with the ability to harm it. This means it first attacks spellcasters who might have light or fire spells at their disposal. The shadowman attempts to graft to the spellcaster and destroy the memory of any spell that might harm it.

Also, because it is made of the stuff of shadows, when it is not interested in remaining camouflaged, a shadowman is capable of stretching as much as 30 feet away from its graft victim to attack another foe. Its shadowstuff composition also explains the creature's AC of 20 regardless of any possible modifiers such as size or facing.

Absorb Memory (Su): A victim to whom a shadowman has grafted (see below) automatically shares his memories and thoughts with the shadowman. Every day that a shadowman remains grafted, the victim receives a Will save (DC 18) that should be rolled by the Game Master. If the victim succeeds, the GM should report to the player that his character has had a restless night of nightmares. If the roll fails, the shadowman becomes privy to 1d100 percent of the victim's memories and thoughts. The shadowman always keeps the highest roll made thus far, so if on Day 1 it absorbs knowledge of 56 percent of the victim's memories and on Day 2 rolls 24 percent, then the shadowman still knows 56 percent of the victim's memories. A shadowman may use this ability once per day per graft victim.

Blindsight (Ex): A slarecian shadowman can see in complete darkness.

Destroy Memory (Su): Seven times per day, but no more than once per round, a shadowman may attempt to destroy a memory of someone to whom it is grafted. The shadowman must have previously absorbed knowledge of the targeted memory. Roll 1d100 and compare to the shadowman's absorb memory rating with this victim to see if this specific memory is known to the shadowman. If the shadowman's roll is successful, then he may target the memory (a password, a memorized spell, the victim's mother's name, etc.). The victim receives a Will save (DC 20) to resist this memory destruction. If the save is failed, then the memory is lost permanently (though it is retained by the shadowman) and the victim does not notice the loss. A memorized spell can be regained normally later. This power may be used during combat in addition to the shadowman's two claw attacks.

Graft (Su): A slarecian shadowman may attempt to graft to no more than three different targets per day, although it may attempt a single target as many times as it wishes and may not be grafted to more than one target at a time. Each attempt to graft takes a full round action, and the target receives a Will save (DC 15). If the saving throw fails, the shadowman has effectively replaced the victim's natural shadow with its own "body," which reshapes itself into an almost perfect match to the victim's own. If the saving throw succeeds, the target knows he has resisted some variety of psychic attack. If the GM makes a successfully Hide roll for the shadowman prior to the attempt, its graft is not noticed.

A victim of graft may automatically be subjected the shadowman's Strength drain once per hour. This attack does not require the shadowman to reveal itself and it affects a victim so gradu-

ally that she generally does not notice the loss until several points have been drained or she needs to call upon her strength for combat, lifting, etc.

A shadowman may attempt to graft humanoids as large as 15 feet tall. Also, a graft cannot be broken by any kind of movement (including teleportation or the like), and a shadowman gains the size and speed of the victim of the graft.

Characters with very high Intelligence (16+) might notice something odd about a grafted victim's shadow. They receive a Spot skill check (DC 20) to note that something is amiss. If they make any obvious sign of this recognition, they are likely to be grafted immediately. The shadowman then attempts to destroy that memory.

Immunities (Ex): Slarecian shadowmen cannot be harmed by any attack that is not light-based. Light or fire does normal damage, but all other attacks are completely ineffective. Light spells that do not typically have damage associated with them do 1d4 hit points of damage per level of the caster.

Strength Drain (Ex): Every time a shadowman hits an opponent with its claws, it does its normal damage, plus it drains 1d6 Strength points from the victim. A victim who is reduced to zero Strength is killed. Drained Strength points return at the rate of one point per hour. All drained points return with a full night's uninterrupted sleep.

Undead: A shadowman is immune to poison, sleep, paralysis, stunning and disease. It's not subject to critical hits, subdual damage, ability damage, energy drain or death from massive damage.

Unturnable: Unlike other undead, slarecian undead cannot be turned by clerics. The reason for this is unknown, buried with the other secrets of the slarecian race.

Sleet Devil

Large (Long) Elemental

Hit Dice:	8d8+24 (60 hp)
Initiative:	+4 (Dex)
Speed:	30 ft., swim 30 ft.
AC:	19 (-1 size, +4 Dex, +6 natural)
Attacks:	Bite +10 melee, 2 claws +8 melee
Damage:	Bite 2d6+3; claw 1d6+1
Face/Reach:	5 ft. by 20 ft./10 ft.
Special Attacks:	Chilling constriction
Special Qualities:	Sense heat sources within 120 feet, sleet cloud, cold defenses, immunities
Saves:	Fort +9, Ref +10, Will +3
Abilities:	Str 16, Dex 19, Con 16, Int 7, Wis 13, Cha 14
Skills:	Climb +3, Escape Artist +5, Hide +8, Intimidate +5, Listen +4, Move Silently +6, Spot +6, Swim +8
Feats:	Multiattack
Climate/Terrain:	Any cold (during winter only) to arctic land
Organization:	Solitary, frolic (2-7)
Challenge Rating:	4
Treasure:	None
Alignment:	Usually neutral evil
Advancement Range:	6-12 HD (Large)

Description

During the severe winters of the northlands, the locals huddle indoors around their fires and tell tales of icy demons stalking the night, waiting to catch and slay anyone they find. At least one of these tales is true — that of the sleet devil. This malicious creature hunts the freezing night air, searching for warm things to kill out of spite.

The sleet devil is hard to perceive at first, due to the constant flurry of ice and snow that surrounds it. Most people outside the cloud see a long, shadowy from with luminescent ice-blue eyes. Those who have penetrated the cloud and survived their encounter describe the sleet devil as a 60-foot-long serpentine creature with two long, clawed forelegs, made entirely out of crackling ice. Its long jaws are filled with hard icicle-teeth.

Wise men aren't quite sure where the sleet devil originally came from, but tales paint it as the embodiment of frozen travelers' anger or a manifestation of the cruelty of long northern winters. Rumor has it that one of the mighty Titans must be buried, in part or entirely, beneath the ice at the top of the world,

Combat

Sleet devils often lie buried under snowbanks to ambush opponents, although they also seem fond of openly and slowly approaching lone travelers, to heighten their prey's feelings of dread. If they feel they can toy with their opponents, they strike casually with teeth and claws, playing a cat-and-mouse game until they tire of the sport and go for the kill. Prey that fights back is a different affair. In such cases, a sleet devil usually tries to constrict a suitable foe (preferably one without a large bladed weapon in hand) while biting and tearing at a second. The devils are not foolhardy, and retreat if combat goes against them.

Chilling Constriction (Ex): Deals 1d8+6 damage on a successful grapple check and each round therafter; constricted victims must make a Fortitude save (DC 16) each round on their action or be chilled to their core by cold so intense that their muscles are frozen to the point of immobility. Whether the save is made or not, the victim sustains an additional 1d6 points of cold damage each round. The sleet devil can constrict one foe while attacking another with claws and bite. Those affected by the chilling constriction who survive may only move at 1/4 speed until they are able to thaw out before a fire or other heat source for at least one hour.

Sleet Cloud (Su): The constant cloud of sleet surrounding a devil impairs its opponents' vision, as well as their scent. Creatures that rely on sight or scent to target opponents suffer a -2 penalty to strike a sleet devil in melee or missile combat.

Cold Defenses (Ex): Being creatures comfortable with the frozen lands, sleet devils are immune to cold, ice and water attacks. They suffer double damage from fire-based attacks on a failed saving throw.

Immunities (Ex): Sleet devils are not affected by critical hits, death from massive injury, poison, paralysis, sleep, disease or any attack that must target a living subject.

Solar Scarab

Diminutive Magical Beast

Hit Dice:	1d10-1 (4 hp)
Initiative:	+4 (Dex)
Speed:	30 ft., climb 30 ft., fly 60 ft.
AC:	18 (+4 size, +4 Dex)
Attacks:	Bite +3 melee
Damage:	Bite 1d6-2
Face/Reach:	1 ft. by 1 ft./1 ft.
Special Attacks:	Solar beam
Special Qualities:	Sunlight storage, heat resistance
Saves:	Fort +0, Ref +4, Will +1
Abilities:	Str 6, Dex 18, Con 8, Int 3, Wis 12, Cha 12
Skills:	Climb +8, Listen +4, Spot +8
Feats:	Alertness
Climate/Terrain:	Desert, warm plains
Organization:	Cluster (11-20), swarm (10-100)
Challenge Rating:	1/2
Treasure:	None
Alignment:	Always neutral
Advancement Range:	1–2HD

Description

The peculiar magical beetles called solar scarabs are a relatively new wrinkle in the Scarred Lands. These golden insects are particularly noteworthy due to their magical ability to store, focus and redirect sunlight. Some branches of the Madrielite church claim that their powers are clearly a gift from the goddess, but this assertion has yet to be proven.

The grapefruit-sized solar scarabs subsist on a diet of anything organic that's available, but they also apparently draw some nourishment from sunlight. At high noon in some areas of the desert, the spiraling flights of shining scarabs reflect like fireworks. They can exist without sunlight for a time, but if a solar scarab spends more than a week without exposure to solar radiation, it simply wastes away.

A few cults of Madriel have managed to raise and train solar scarabs, largely for the purposes of assisting them on undead-hunting expeditions. As the creatures show a level of intelligence comparable to a smart dog, and live for approximately 20 years, they make most interesting — if not overly affectionate — companions.

Combat

Solar scarabs are not particularly aggressive toward most creatures; they are content to eat insects, carrion, deadwood and other scavenged materials. They tend to attack either in self-defense or, peculiarly enough, when in the presence of undead. The beetles swarm overhead any undead that cross their territory in broad daylight, devastating the creatures with a barrage of solar beams. They are less hesitant to use up their stores of light at night, but still strobe sunlight overhead, as if hoping to either injure the undead (who might be vulnerable to sunlight) or to attract other entities to deal with the monsters.

Sunlight Storage (Su): Excited solar scarabs can release stored sunlight, lighting the area around them in a 60-foot radius with genuine solar radiation. This light counts as pure sunlight for purposes of affecting creatures that are vulnerable to sunlight. A solar scarab can maintain this luminescence for up to two hours before needing to recharge its stores. To completely refill its stores, the scarab must be exposed to direct sunlight for four hours.

Solar Beam (Su): While in direct sunlight, solar scarabs can focus the sun's rays into an intense beam of radiation. The scarab must be in flight above a target, although it need not be directly between the sun and its target — the scarab can direct the beam with some precision. Targets must make a Reflex save, DC 13, or take 3d4 points of damage. A scarab may focus this solar beam during cloudy weather or indirect daylight, but it inflicts only 1d4 damage. If hard-pressed, the scarab can even release all its stored solar energy (see above) to produce one full-power beam which deals 4d4 damage, aimed wherever it likes (to a distance of 120 yards).

Heat Resistance (Ex): Solar scarabs take half damage from any heat-based attack and are immune to the adverse effects of high temperatures.

Sour Grub

Tiny Vermin

Hit Dice:	1d8-1 (3 hp)
Initiative:	-1 (Dex)
Speed:	5 ft.
AC:	14 (+2 size, -1 Dex, +3 natural)
Attacks:	Bite -1 melee
Damage:	1d3
Face/Reach:	2.5 ft. by 2.5 ft./0 ft.
Special Attacks:	Paralysis
Special Qualities:	Vermin
Saves:	Fort +1, Ref -1, Will -2
Abilities:	Str 3, Dex 8, Con 8, Int —, Wis 6, Cha —
Skills:	Climb +4, Hide +10, Move Silently +3
Feats:	None
Climate/Terrain:	Any
Organization:	Writhes (2-12)
Challenge Rating:	1/4
Treasure:	Standard
Alignment:	Always neutral
Advancement Range:	1-2 HD (Tiny)

Description

Sour grubs are becoming increasingly dangerous as cities of the Scarred Lands slowly rebuild, spread and grow crowded. The vermin originally lived in the wilds, spawning in cesspits and stagnant pools or beneath the rotting carcasses of animals. Now, however, cities such as Rahoch attract sour grubs in alarming quantities. Sewage drains, refuse piles and even privies are infested.

Although they are disgusting and tenacious creatures, sour grubs do serve a purpose in many modern cities. Citizens tolerate them to a degree because the creatures eliminate disease-carrying rats and other vermin with a singular zeal. They become a problem when their population spreads to inhabit almost all locales that can support them, even the vaults of royalty.

People who intrude upon sour grub nesting areas — which can be anywhere from gutters to back alleys to stables — are bitten and injected with a paralyzing poison. Falling victim to this bite can make a person or animal a meal as other nearby grubs close to feed.

Horrifically, destitute citizens with little other recourse have taken to eating sour grub larvae. In-deed, some erstwhile rat-catchers have become urban filth-farming maggot dealers. These people are typically arrested when caught selling their wares in infested cities, but watches rarely patrol the poorest of markets.

Combat

Sour grubs have no combat style; they typically bite from hiding when disturbed in their filth-domains. Any and all nearby vermin feed upon a poisoned victim.

Paralysis (Ex): The sour grub bite injects a paralysis-inducing poison. A Fortitude save (DC 14) is required to resist it with each bite. Failure causes a victim to collapse for 1d6 rounds. Once paralysis has set in, no further Fortitude rolls need be made for subsequent bites when the grub are merely feeding, but when the victim rouses from paralysis, the feeding grub will inject its poison again. Grubs that feed on an incapacitated victim inflict 1d4 damage automatically for each round that they're allowed to feed.

Vermin: Immune to mind-altering effects.

Spider-eye Goblin

Small Humanoid (Goblinoid)

Hit Dice:	2d8 (9 hp)
Initiative:	+2 (Dex)
Speed:	30 ft., climb 20 ft.
AC:	15 (+1 size, +2 Dex, +2 natural)
Attacks:	Bite +2 melee; 4 claws +2 melee; javelin +4 ranged; dart +4 ranged
Damage:	Bite 1d6; claw 1d4; javelin 1d6; dart 1d4
Face/Reach:	5 ft. by 5 ft./5 ft.
Special Attacks:	Poison
Special Qualities:	Darkvision 60 ft., improved peripheral vision
Saves:	Fort +2, Ref +2, Will +0
Abilities:	Str 11, Dex 14, Con 10, Int 9, Wis 10, Cha 3
Skills:	Balance +2, Hide +7, Jump +5, Listen +4, Move Silently +4, Spot +6
Feats:	None
Climate/Terrain:	Underground caves, deep jungle
Organization:	Gang (1-6), Raiding Band (3-18, plus 2-8 with spider mounts, plus 1 4th-level leader), nest (5-50, plus 2-20 with spider mounts, plus 2 4th-level leaders, plus 1 8th-level cleric matriarch)
Challenge Rating:	1/2
Treasure:	Standard
Alignment:	Usually neutral evil
Advancement Range:	By character class

Description

Spider-eye goblins are among the many races of goblinoids created by the titans during the formation of the world. As one of their first attempts at creating a humanoid race, the goblinoid races fell far short of the titans' demands for servitors, and the titans quickly turned a blind eye to their malformed, imperfect children. Still, in a primordial state and left to fend for themselves, goblins were drawn to and became imbued with various aspects of the world during their genesis, leading to the many varieties of goblinoid races seen across the Scarred Lands today.

Infused with some arachnid spirit during their birth, spider-eye goblins became one of the most hideous of their already ugly kind. They sprouted six long slender limbs, two used for legs and four as arms on the rare occasions that spider-eye goblins go bipedal. Their bodies sprout short thick hairs, and their telltale array of eight eyes rests over a fanged maw.

Like all goblins, the spider-eyed variety breeds quickly. However, since the male is usually killed and eaten by the female during mating and the female herself is consumed by her young when they hatch, spider-eye goblin populations don't grow quite as quickly as those of the other goblin races.

Spider-eyes make their lairs in the canopy of deep jungles or in caverns close to the surface of the earth. Most tribes are relatively small, and all are governed by a matriarchy, with one female priestess ruling the tribe. Since the fall of the titans, most tribes have taken to worshiping the demigoddess Sethris, demon-witch of the web.

A spider-eye goblin tribe of any significant size also has giant wolf spiders as trained mounts (see Wolf Spider, Giant in this volume). The large tribe in the vicinity of the Swamps of Kan Thet are especially renowned for their use of these spider-mounts.

Combat

As with most goblins, spider-eye tactics rely heavily on ambush, particularly by making use of their natural climbing ability to hide in the tree canopy or on cavern ceilings, and raining javelins and darts down on their prey. Though not very bright, the spider-eyes can be cunning bastards when it comes to setting traps. However, in open combat (i.e., a fair fight), the usual goblin cowardice can quickly take hold of a leaderless band.

Poison (Ex): A spider-eye goblin's bite carries a weak poison. Victims who take damage from a successful bite attack must also make a Fortitude save (DC 13) or suffer an additional 1d6 damage from the poison.

Improved Peripheral Vision (Ex): Due to their multiple eyes, spider-eye goblins cannot be flanked. So, for example, attacking rogues cannot gain sneak attacks due to flanking, and multiple opponents fighting on both sides of a spider-eye goblin receive no attack bonuses.

Mounted spider-eye goblins also possess the Ride skill at +7 and the Mounted Combat and Mounted Archery feats.

Spire Wyvern

Medium-size Beast

Hit Dice:	8d10 (44 hp)
Initiative:	+3 (Dex)
Speed:	20 ft.; fly 120 ft.
AC:	18 (+3 Dex, +5 natural)
Attacks:	2 Talons +8 melee, bite +3 melee; tail +8 melee
Damage:	Talon 2d6, bite 1d8, tail 1d10
Face/Reach:	5 ft. by 5 ft./5 ft.
Special Attacks:	Poison
Special Qualities:	Keen senses, screech of the spires
Saves:	Fort +2, Ref +9, Will +0
Abilities:	Str 11, Dex 17, Con 11, Int 5, Wis 6, Cha 6
Skills:	Move Silently +8, Search +11, Spot +11
Feats:	None
Climate/Terrain:	Any (high elevations)
Organization:	Solitary, pair
Challenge Rating:	4
Treasure:	Standard
Alignment:	Always neutral
Advancement Range:	6-9 HD

Description

Spire wyverns are flying reptiles that instinctively occupy the highest points within their domains, which explains the roosts atop the great towers of the Scarred Lands' cities. Young spire wyverns in search of their own territory often find a roost within a city and go unnoticed until they grow large enough to prey upon stray animals or children.

In the wild, spire wyverns inhabit the treetops or build nests into cliff faces. Any treasure possessed by a wyvern is mixed into its nest among the remains of its prey.

Some spire wyverns have been trained as lookouts. Their most common usage is to help patrol frontier lands, coming back to roost in a keep or tower. Some ranger patrols use spire wyverns to accompany them on patrol to act as aerial warning.

Training spire wyverns is no easy task. Only a few of them are patient and intelligent enough to serve adequately, and training must begin as soon as a spire wyvern hatchling has learned to fly. Mother spire wyverns guard their broods tenaciously.

Combat

Spire wyverns may attack with two talons and a bite, or may lance prey with their stinging tail. They typically do not fight except to secure food or protect their nest. When hunting, they attempt to sting prey and fly away until their paralyzing venom sets in. The wyvern then scoops the prey up and carries it back to its nest to devour the helpless victim at the wyvern's leisure.

Keen Senses (Ex): Spire wyverns can see at distances up to a mile with a great degree of accuracy.

Poison (Ex): The spire wyvern's tail delivers a paralyzing venom. Anyone injured by the tail must also pass a Fortitude save (DC 13) or become paralyzed for 1d6 hours. Once injected into prey, the venom takes 1d4 rounds before paralysis sets in (assuming that a player failed his saving throw).

Screech of the Spires (Ex): Spire wyverns are able to let out a great, piercing screech. This sound may be heard up to a mile away, and it is distinctive enough that guards and/or others who are familiar with a spire wyvern can recognize its particular call. The screech also temporarily deafens opponents within 60 feet for 2d4 rounds unless the victim makes a Fortitude save (DC 9).

Spirit of the Plague

Medium-size Undead

Hit Dice:	6d12 (39 hp)
Initiative:	+1 (Dex)
Speed:	15 ft.
AC:	11 (+1 Dex)
Attacks:	Touch +6 melee
Damage:	None
Face/Reach:	5 ft. by 5 ft./5 ft.
Special Attacks:	Plague
Special Qualities:	Damage reduction 10/+1, incorporeal, undead
Saves:	Fort +2, Ref +2, Will +5
Abilities:	Str 10, Dex 13, Con —, Int 10, Wis 9, Cha 9
Skills:	Listen +6, Move Silently +10, Spot +6
Feats:	None
Climate/Terrain:	Any
Organization:	Solitary, wards (10-20), plagues (25-100)
Challenge Rating:	4
Treasure:	None
Alignment:	Usually neutral evil
Advancement Range:	4-9 HD

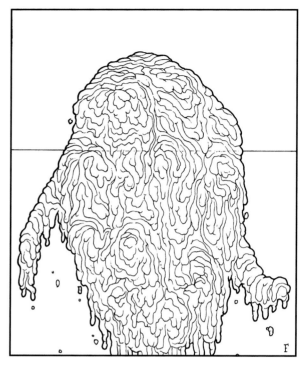

Description

At the height of the Titanswar, the titan Chern of the Last Great Sickness and Suffering unleashed a tide of diseases to destroy all life in Scarn. His plagues were certainly deadly, but the death already caused by the war prevented the diseases from spreading as far as they could in a functioning society. What use was infecting a town if a raid destroyed it the next day? Why infect young boys if they were just sent off to die at war? Travel was all but impossible in those times, and Chern wasn't satisfied by the results of his dwindling illnesses.

His solution was to use the spirits of those claimed by his plagues to spread the sickness to others. After death, the spirits of those who had agonized under the plague the longest, those whose wills were broken and spent at death, returned to the mortal world bound by Chern's will. They traveled through their towns, or along merchant routes, even on the fields of battle to spread their disease.

Now the gods have locked Chern away, but his divine mandate still lingers. A very few souls who die from a communicable illness arise as spirits of the plague a few months later to ignite epidemics. Chern's plague spirits may not have been an effective curse, but they have certainly proved an enduring one.

Combat

Spirits of the plague exist solely to harass the living and spread their horrible diseases. They spend their nights passing through towns, caressing the faces of sleeping people in order to infect them.

Incorporeal (Ex): This creature has no substance in its regular state. It can be seen as only a cloudy apparition. Because it has no form, it can pass through non-magical obstacles such as walls or ceilings. While incorporeal, the plague spirit is immune to all attacks except for purification and exorcism attempts, but it is likewise unable to harm any physical creature. The spirit of the plague can turn corporeal at will, though, at the expense of one attack action.

Plague (Su): Any creature touched by a corporeal spirit of the plague must succeed at a Fortitude save (DC 16) or contract an advanced form of whatever disease killed the spirit originally. GMs can tailor this disease to the epidemiological history of their campaigns, but assume as a default that the disease has an onset period of 1d10 days and that it causes 1d6 hit points of damage per day afterward until it is cured.

Undead: Immune to poison, sleep, paralysis, stunning and disease. Not subject to critical hits, subdual damage, ability damage, energy drain or death from massive damage.

Steel Beetle

Large Construct (Golem)

Hit Dice:	8d12+40 (92 hp)
Initiative:	+2 (Dex)
Speed:	45 ft.
AC:	31 (-1 size, +2 Dex, +20 natural)
Attacks:	2 Claws +14 melee
Damage:	Claw 1d10+7
Face/Reach:	5 ft. by 5 ft./10 ft.
Special Attacks:	None
Special Qualities:	Construct, damage reduction 10/+2
Saves:	Fort +11, Ref +4, Will —
Abilities:	Str 25, Dex 14, Con 20, Int —, Wis —, Cha —
Skills:	Spot +6
Feats:	Cleave, Power Attack
Climate/Terrain:	Any
Organization:	Solitary
Challenge Rating:	8
Treasure:	None
Alignment:	Always neutral
Advancement Range:	None

Description

The steel beetles were built approximately 80 to 120 years ago by the magician Gest Ganest and his apprentices in their (now abandoned) workshop deep in the Kelder Mountains. Some were used as security for the workshop, but most were sold for hefty commissions to private individuals as bodyguards and war machines. Over the years, most of these constructs have been destroyed or worn out, but some still stand at their posts faithfully, and others have long shut down and await only maintenance and refueling before they can be made operational again.

And fuel is the problem with the constructs. They are energized by blood sacrifice — one HD of sacrificed creature is sufficient to power them for a month. While their potential for storing power seems quite limitless, it is only by the sacrifice of living beings that these devices can be charged. Steel beetles that have "wound down" can be revived by anyone who has the Craft Wondrous Item feat and sacrifices an intelligent creature of at least one HD.

Steel beetles respond only to the commands of the person who activated them, or to a single individual designated at the time of awakening. While they are not capable of making plans and judgments on their own, they understand complex and extensive orders given by their owner. Their main failing is that they become inert if ever removed more than one mile from their owner. Once the owner moves back within that range, the construct reactivates.

Combat

In combat, steel beetles fight as directed by their owner. Typically, this means they try to place themselves between attackers and their owner, and lash out with their great steel claws. However, they can be given more complex orders.

Construct: A steel beetle is impervious to critical hits, subdual damage and death from massive damage trauma. It's immune to poisons, diseases, blinding, deafness, drowning, electricity and spells or attacks that affect respiration or living physiology. It cannot be stunned. It's not affected by attacks or spells of mind-altering nature (enamoring or charming spells, for example), or by spells based on healing/harming. Fire and acid spells or attacks deal half normal damage.

Steel Giant

Gargantuan (Tall) Giant

Hit Dice:	14d8+59 (122 hp)
Initiative:	+0
Speed:	45 ft.
AC:	26 (–4 size, +20 natural)
Attacks:	Mallet +19 melee, 2 fists +15 melee; boulder +10 ranged
Damage:	Mallet 2d12+8; fist 1d20+8; boulder 2d10+8
Face/Reach:	20 ft. by 20 ft./20 ft.
Special Attacks:	None
Special Qualities:	Immunities, metal healing
Saves:	Fort +13, Ref +4 Will +4
Abilities:	Str 26, Dex 11, Con 19, Int 13, Wis 11, Cha 9
Skills:	Appraise +10, Craft (metalworking) +22, Spot +19
Feats:	Armor Proficiency (All), Improved Critical (Mallet), Multiattack, Power Attack, Toughness, Weapon Focus (Mallet)
Climate/Terrain:	Volcanoes, volcanic ranges, underground
Organization:	Solitary or group (2-12)
Challenge Rating:	9
Treasure:	Triple Standard
Alignment:	Always lawful neutral
Advancement Range:	14-18 HD (Gargantuan)

Description

The race of steel giants is said to be a gift from Hedrada the Citybuilder to Corean the Avenger after Corean helped Hedrada defeat the titan Hrinruuk the Hunter. In an epic battle, Hrinruuk vanquished Hedrada, took the god up by his bloody mantle and made to cast Hedrada into a great void. But Corean intervened and crippled the titan with a single mighty blow. Hedrada's priests claim that it is the still-living skull of Hrinruuk that now adorns one mallet head of Hedrada's judgment hammer.

In gratitude to Corean, and in appreciation for Corean's affinity for craftwork, Hedrada slaughtered Hrinruuk's servitors and reincarnated them as steel giants, forgers of volcanic metal and rock. To this day, the steel giants work for Corean, providing the god with raw materials for his forge. They delve deeply into the earth below the volcanic ranges to pump out fresh magma from which they smelt mithril to forge armor. Unfortunately, it is not unknown for the steel giants' activities to cause volcanic eruptions on the surface world.

Many smiths, particularly dwarves, seek the metallurgical knowledge that these giants possess. Others dream of finding these metallic giants' lairs, for it is told that they have treasure, brought from the bowels of the earth, that makes a dragon's troves seem a pittance.

Steel giants speak Dwarven and the Common tongue.

Combat

When steel giants fight, they wield their terrible metal mallets with their upper pair of arms, and punch with the lower pair of arms. Steel giants cannot raise their second pair of arms over their head, so throw rocks with their upper arms. Steel giants can throw rocks more than 300 feet.

Immunities (Ex): Steel giants are immune to fire, heat and cold. However, electrical attacks do double damage to them.

Metal Healing (Ex): Steel giants are able to heal their wounds simply by patching themselves up with molten metal straight from the forge. They simply touch the metal to a wound and it heals 2d8 points of damage per round.

Steppe Troll

Large (Tall) Giant

Hit Dice:	8d8+38 (74 hp)
Initiative:	-1 (Dex)
Speed:	40 ft.
AC:	21 (-1 size, -1 Dex, +9 natural, +4 scale armor)
Attacks:	Bite +9 melee, 2 claws +4 melee; or heavy lance +9 melee; or saber +9 melee
Damage:	Bite 1d10+2; claw 1d6+1; heavy lance 1d8+2; saber 1d6+2
Face/Reach:	5 ft. by 5 ft./10 ft.
Special Attacks:	None
Special Qualities:	Regeneration
Saves:	Fort +10, Ref +1, Will +1
Abilities:	Str 15, Dex 8, Con 18, Int 9, Wis 9, Cha 8
Skills:	Animal Empathy +15, Craft +8, Listen +10, Ride +15, Spot +15, Wilderness Lore +10
Feats:	Armor Proficiency (all), Ride-by Attack, Spirited Charge, Toughness (x2), Track
Climate/Terrain:	Steppe, grasslands
Organization:	Hunting/raiding party (1-10), war party (one 4th-level war leader, 5-25 riders), Tribe (1 8th-level chieftain, 2 4th-level war leaders, 5-50 riders, 5-15 children)
Challenge Rating:	5
Treasure:	Standard
Alignment:	Always neutral
Advancement Range:	By character class

Description

Unlike their subterranean cousins, steppe trolls are huge, powerfully muscled creatures, with broad, toothy faces and rough, greenish-brown skin. Their warriors prefer leather leggings and shirts of scale or mail armor, with large iron-banded shields. Members of the steppe tribes also tattoo their bodies with ritual marks, signifying great deeds and events they have witnesses in their lives. Steppe trolls take the heads of mighty warriors they have defeated in battle, incorporating them into their armor or making them into drinking goblets or saddle ornaments.

Steppe trolls are a distant offshoot of the more common troll species, and somehow managed to thrive on the harsh, windswept steppes of eastern Termana.

There are thought to be as many as two dozen nomadic tribes that make their way on annual treks across the grasslands, driving herds of horses and oxen and living fairly peaceful lives, interspersed with occasional livestock raids and war parties. Sometimes young warriors of both sexes leave their tribes on quests mandated by a tribal shaman, and are unable to return until they have fulfilled a great deed required by their gods.

These tribes are suspicious of any outsider, but are honorable in their dealings and willingly trade with travelers passing through their territory. However, their patience with the humans passing through the steppes is beginning to diminish. Troll-horses are a prized breed, famous for their size and strength, and a worthy specimen can fetch a king's ransom in the markets of civilized lands. Steppe trolls speak Giant, and some can also speak Elvish and/or Common.

Combat

Steppe trolls prefer to fight their enemies from the saddle, riding down foes and striking them with long heavy lances or curved sabers. Hunters also favor powerful composite bows with broad iron arrowheads, although their culture frowns on using such weapons in combat, preferring to fight enemies face to face.

Regeneration (Ex): A steppe troll regain 3 hp per round from any damage, except acid, fire or fire-based attacks.

Stick Giant

Colossal Giant

Hit Dice:	20d10+140 (250 hp)
Initiative:	-2 (Dex)
Speed:	50 ft.
AC:	25 (-8 size, -2 Dex, +25 natural)
Attacks:	Fist +22 melee
Damage:	Fist 2d10+10
Face/Reach:	15 ft. by 15 ft./40 ft.
Special Attacks:	Needle spray, spells, splintering
Special Qualities:	Vulnerability (fire)
Saves:	Fort +18, Ref +5, Will +11
Abilities:	Str 30, Dex 7, Con 25, Int 14, Wis 19, Cha 13
Skills:	Animal Empathy +7, Concentration +5, Hide +9, Knowledge (nature) +11, Listen +15, Spot +11, Wilderness Lore +16
Feats:	Cleave, Great Cleave, Power Attack, Track
Climate/Terrain:	Old forests
Organization:	Solitary, pair or family (1-3)
Challenge Rating:	10
Treasure:	Standard
Alignment:	Usually neutral
Advancement Range:	18-24 HD

Description

No one has yet been able to ascertain whether the so-called stick giants are enormous animated ambulatory trees, or whether they are a race of giants with a marked similarity to the forests in which they dwell. Stick giants as tall as 80 feet are not uncommon, and these make for quite an unusual sight considering their near rail-thinness. "Rail" is a good word to describe them in any event, for they appear to be composed of rough-hewn and splintering wood.

They are primarily encountered only in the oldest of forests where the trees can perhaps be as tall as they themselves. They are difficult to spot amidst such camouflage, but they are much sought after for a host of reasons, including their wisdom, magic, treasure, but perhaps most of all for their bodies, portions of which can serve as ingredients for a myriad of enchantments.

Whatever their alignment, stick giants are largely reclusive. However, the good ones go out of the way to make themselves available to like-minded woodland creatures, while evil ones seek to harm any who pass near their homes.

Combat

If a stick giant has the opportunity to prepare for a fight, it uses its spells to the fullest strategic advantage possible. Otherwise, it is perfectly capable of melee combat. Unless foes are weak enough not to require strategic consideration, a stick giant typically attempts to splinter everyone facing it. This is effective against spellcasters who may have trouble concentrating through the pain the splinters can cause them. Finally, a stick giant generally use its needle-spray attack in only two circumstances: if it is close to being defeated, or if it feels certain that use of the effect will almost completely eliminate its opponents.

Needle Spray (Ex): Once per day, a stick giant can cause vast quantities of tiny wood splinters to spray in every direction from its body. Only opponents with a shield are allowed a Reflex save (DC 22) to halve the damage. Otherwise, everyone (friend and foe, though other stick giants are unaffected) within 40 feet sustains 8d10 damage minus AC (without Dex adjustment).

Spells: Stick giants know and cast spells as an 11th-level druid, with restrictions appropriate to the alignment of the giant.

Splintering (Ex): When a stick giant hits a foe with its fists, slivers of its wooden body break off and become wedged in the victim's body. For every round that victim remains active (i.e., doing anything other than sitting still), he sustains 1d6 damage. Splinters can be removed with an action and a successful Strength roll (DC equal to the damage of the blow that dealt the splinter — 12 to 30). Splinters are cumulative, so a single victim could have a dozen or more splinters, each inflicting 1d6 damage every round.

Vulnerability (fire): Stick giants sustain double damage from fire attacks if they fail their saving throws, or against fire damage that warrants no saving throw.

Storm Kin

Medium-size Elemental

Hit Dice:	10d8+40 (85 hp)
Initiative:	+1 (+1 Dex)
Speed:	60 ft., fly 60 ft., swim 60 ft.
AC:	14 (+1 Dex, +3 natural)
Attacks:	Fists +15 melee
Damage:	Fists 2d6+5
Face/Reach:	5 ft. by 5 ft./5 ft.
Special Attacks:	Elemental eruption
Special Qualities:	Damage reduction 8/+2, immunities, locate element
Saves:	Fort +11, Ref +4, Will +9
Abilities:	Str 20, Dex 12, Con 19, Int 13, Wis 19, Cha 14
Skills:	Hide +8, Knowledge (nature) +15
Feats:	Iron Will
Climate/Terrain:	Cataclysms, natural disasters and any large assembly of zealous elementals
Organization:	Solitary, packs (2–8, depending on size of disaster)
Challenge Rating:	7
Treasure:	Standard
Alignment:	Always chaotic neutral
Advancement Range:	11–15 (Large), 20–25 HD (Huge)

Description

Storm kin are the spirits of nature commonly associated with natural disasters such as hurricanes, volcanic eruptions, tsunamis and earthquakes. Before her defeat, the titan Lethene unleashed the elemental forces of chaos on the upstart gods in the form of the storm kin. The Untamed One thought of living storms and storm kin as her elemental shock troops, and more than one god fell before the combined onslaught of volcanic infernos, shrieking tornadoes and enormous maelstroms. Though the largest of these spirits were, in large part, snuffed out in the Titanswar, storm kin are still found inciting volcanoes to erupt and rivers to flood, dwelling in the pellucid eyes of storms or in the smoke-choked hearts of infernos. Legend says that any who face and defeat one of the storm kin at the heart of the cataclysm it inhabits can dispel the elemental phenomenon itself. Many have tried, and many are the charred and battered bodies of those heroes who believed they could best a volcano, a tornado or a tidal wave.

Storm kin will sometimes coalesce into packs to bring about truly magnificent displays of elemental fury; a group of four or more storm kin can easily consume a large forest with fire or raze a coastal city with a combination of tsunamis and hurricane winds. Finding and defeating a storm kin when they work in concert is a daunting if not impossible task, but if brave adventurers will not or cannot stop them, entire civilizations might be snuffed out by these zealous forces of nature.

Combat

If its foes have not been burned or blasted to death by whatever cataclysm the elemental resides in, a storm kin will focus all the elemental might it can summon against them. If the disaster is large enough, the storm kin may stay hidden and direct the storm or conflagration from afar, letting it consume the hapless victims without making the elemental itself vulnerable.

Elemental Eruption (Su): Storm kin command wild eruptions of elemental force that they can use as weapons if provoked. Outside of their particular cataclysm, storm kin can turn small manifestations of elemental phenomena into enormous ones. Light rain becomes a monsoon or a terrible hail storm, and cook fires flare into infernos. Targets of these attacks take 2d6 points of damage per round of exposure.

While inhabiting its particular disaster, on the other hand, the storm kin can inflict devastating amounts of damage — winds lift its victims off the ground and blow them into cliffs, storm surges smack victims flat and suck them down into the depths in an overwhelming undertow, and lava wells up from the ground itself to burn victims alive. Targets of these catastrophic attacks take 10d6 damage per round as they are engulfed by nature's most destructive energies. A successful Reflex save (DC 17) halves this damage. Should the storm kin leave the area of its eruption, the effects subside in 2d4 rounds.

Immunities (Ex): Storm kin are immune to all elemental effects, including lightning, fire and cold. They are also immune to poison, polymorph, drowning and paralysis.

Locate Element (Ex): A Storm kin is able to sense any manifestation of elemental energy, like high winds, a river or a campfire within 500 feet of itself.

Strife Elemental

Medium-size Elemental

Hit Dice:	4d8+4 (22 hp)
Initiative:	+1 (Dex)
Speed:	30 ft., fly 30 ft
AC:	18 (+1 Dex, +3 studded leather, +1 small shield, +3 natural)
Attacks:	Longsword +4 melee
Damage:	Longsword 1d8
Face/Reach:	5 ft. by 5 ft./5 ft.
Special Attacks:	Cause strife
Special Qualities:	Damage reduction 10/+1, impersonate
Saves:	Fort +5, Ref +2, Will +1
Abilities:	Str 11, Dex 13, Con 13, Int 10, Wis 10, Cha 10
Skills:	None
Feats:	None
Climate/Terrain:	Cities or villages
Organization:	Solitary
Challenge Rating:	2
Treasure:	Standard
Alignment:	Usually chaotic neutral
Advancement Range:	By character class

Description

Strife elementals can be found wherever man faces challenges, be it the heat of battle or the ongoing struggles of daily survival in the Scarred Lands. Using its power to take the guise of a soldier, peasant or adventurer, an elemental generally tries to be as close to the actual strife itself as possible without dealing with it directly. In a town or village, a strife elemental may be found working among the peasants as a simple farmer, laboring daily under oppressive heat and struggling to grow crops in a nearly infertile land. In times of war, the elemental may take the guise of an archer or lieutenant, so that it may admire the event from afar without succumbing to the hazards of war. It might also seek to join a group of adventurers during a quest.

Wherever a strife elemental goes, life becomes harsher, more contentious and violent for the people around it. In fact, should the strife elemental find an area too comfortable and harmonious, it attempts to incite arguments and even conflict. The peasants might revolt, the soldiers might ignore a retreat in order to keep fighting, or the adventurers find cause to argue over treasure. For this reason, the elemental has gained a reputation as a prankster at the least, and a murderous beast at the worst.

These elementals seem to be created spontaneously in areas of massive strife, and some Scarred Lands scholars believe that they were all formed during the cataclysmic conflicts of the Divine War. Strife elementals travel the land now, drawn to conflict like moths to a flame. They adopt guises that allow them to fit into a new situation, but each time they adopt a new persona, they lose most of their memories gained in former guises.

Combat

If attacked, a strife elemental fights as per its normal class (usually fighter or bard, at a level equal to its hit dice), relying on the same skills as any commoner to defeat the challenge before it.

Cause Strife (Ex): Generally, a strife elemental's mere presence is enough to cause problems. Anyone within 30 feet of the elemental must pass a Will save (DC 12) to resist being compelled along a contentious, argumentative or violent course of action, whenever a situation unfolds that might conceivably warrant such a response. This effect is considered a type of mind-altering magic.

This power should be handled very subtly, and the GM may wish to make Will saves on players' behalf and inform them of unexpected changes in characters' emotional state. Examples of situations adventurers might face that would call upon the cause strife effect include parleying with potential opponents instead of fighting, haggling with a merchant over a price, sneaking past enemies instead of fighting, arguing as a result of pre-existing divisions between party members, or splitting up treasure.

Impersonate (Su): Upon taking a new form, a strife elemental may choose its hit dice in skills at hit dice level, and half its hit dice in applicable feats. For example, a 4 hit dice strife elemental impersonating a homeless street performer may take the skills Bluff, Hide, Perform and Tumble (each at +4) and the feats Dodge and Alertness. Each impersonation transformation takes about five minutes, and it persists until the elemental decides to move on to another guise.

Swamp Gobbler

	Small Monstrous Humanoid
Hit Dice:	6d8 (27 hp)
Initiative:	+1 (Dex)
Speed:	30 ft.
AC:	14 (+1 size, +1 Dex, +2 natural)
Attacks:	Bite +8 melee, 2 claws +3 melee; tail bludgeon +8 melee
Damage:	Bite 2d4+1; claw 1d6+1; tail bludgeon 3d8+1
Special Attacks:	None
Special Qualities:	Camouflage, darkvision 40 ft., breathe underwater
Saves:	Fort +2, Ref +6, Will -1
Abilities:	Str 12, Dex 13, Con 11, Int 7, Wis 5, Cha 4
Skills:	Climb +7, Hide +4, Listen +8, Search +9, Spot +4, Wilderness Lore +3
Feats:	Alertness, Tracking
Climate/Terrain:	Swamps
Organization:	Group (2-6), band (10-16)
Challenge Rating:	3
Treasure:	Standard
Alignment:	Usually chaotic neutral
Advancement Range:	4-7 HD

Description

Swamp gobblers come from a clan of poor halflings that was tricked in a game with the god Enkili, or so goes the story among those who scorn and abuse halflings in the Scarred Lands (i.e., everyone). Many moons ago, a clan of halflings traveled across the face of Scarn, looking for lush green meadows to make their shire. Unfortunately, they became lost in a vast swamp and they wandered there for many months. Eventually, they ran out of food and began to starve.

Enkili the Trickster came to the swamp and became intrigued with the laughable little people. He made them an offer. If they would give up their dreams of finding a shire and agree to live in the swamp as his playmates, Enkili would see that they were fed. Although they were famished, the halflings refused, for they could never live and be happy in a swamp! So Enkili made the halflings another offer. He produced a knucklebone die with 500 sides. The clan's sheriff would roll the die, and if it produced any number other than 392, Enkili would lead the halflings to a place where they could be safe and build a shire. But if the sheriff rolled 392, the halflings would become Enkili's playmates in the swamp forever.

The halflings were skeptical, believing the die was loaded, but Enkili convinced them that it was not. And it wasn't. What he didn't tell them was that the die was magically attuned to the number of moles on Enkili's backside, and that whenever he rolled his die, it always rolled that number of moles, a feature he could polymorph at will. When the die was cast,

Enkili made it show the appropriate number, and the halflings lost the game. To this day, the transformed halflings run pell-mell through the swamps, constantly ravenous.

Swamp gobblers are about four feet tall, and they are covered in thin, black fur (and usually mud). Their pale yellow faces and yellow, glowing eyes are the only parts of the gobbler that can be seen clearly at night. Their sharp claws allow them to climb trees quickly or dig swiftly through mud. They have large, thick but flat tails, not unlike a beaver's, which they can use to deliver a tremendous blow or which they pound of the earth to communicate with one another over a distance.

Combat

Swamp gobblers are constantly hungry, and they aggressively attack anything that they believe may fill their bellies. Adventurers traveling through swamps inhabited by swamp gobblers are always attacked. Swamp gobblers initially go for a party's rations. Should they steal or win such through combat, they disappear back into the swamps only long enough to consume the rations. Then they return for mounts or familiars, followed by leather goods that they the adventurers might be carrying. Eventually, the swamp gobblers try to consume party members themselves.

Swamp gobblers may drop from tree branches to deliver a powerful initial tail-blow to their prey. They literally fall from trees and vines (where they are camouflaged). Attacking from above is the only situation in which this tail attack may used.

Breathe Underwater (Ex): Swamp gobblers can breathe in the murky waters of swamps.

Camouflage (Ex): The fur of these creatures and their filthy, dark coats allow them to blend in perfectly with the surrounding environment. Gobblers receive a +4 bonus to their Hide skill (already included above).

Tanil's Fox

Tiny Animal

Hit Dice:	1d8 (4 hp)
Initiative:	+12 (+8 Dex, +4 Improved Initiative)
Speed:	40 ft., run 200 ft.
AC:	31 (+2 size, +8 Dex, +11 natural)
Attacks:	Bite +1 melee
Damage:	Bite 1d6-2
Face/Reach:	2.5 ft. by 2.5 ft./0 ft.
Special Attacks:	None
Special Qualities:	Skill mastery
Saves:	Fort +0, Ref +12, Will +2
Abilities:	Str 6, Dex 27, Con 10, Int 2, Wis 15, Cha 8
Skills:	Climb +2, Escape Artist +4, Hide +12, Jump +4, Listen +3, Move Silently +5, Spot +3, Swim +1
Feats:	Endurance, Improved Initiative, Lightning Reflexes, Mobility, Run
Climate/Terrain:	Temperate and warm woodlands
Organization:	Solitary
Challenge Rating:	5
Treasure:	Standard
Alignment:	Always neutral
Advancement Range:	None

Description

Legend holds that Tanil, the goddess of the hunt, blessed a family of foxes with supernatural speed and guile. She then amused herself by hunting the descendants of this breed. Tanil's foxes are quick, clever and divinely lucky, some believe. Although every hunter in the Scarred Lands has a tale of how he came "this close" to catching Tanil's fox, the rare person who actually catches one does so only if he is among the finest hunters to have ever lived. At most, a hunter with an arrow or sling gets one shot at one of these foxes. One shot, to make his name legend.

Combat

War is not the divine function of Tanil's fox. Though one might put up a struggle if cornered (a near-impossibility), such foxes are more likely to flee at any sign of danger.

Skill Mastery (Ex): Tanil's foxes are considered masters at the Hide skill. As a result, such a fox may take 10 when hiding, even in stress situations, just like a high-level rogue.

Thunder Orb

Medium-size Construct

Hit Dice:	5d12 (32 hp)
Initiative:	+0
Speed:	25 ft. flying
AC:	20 (+10 natural)
Attacks:	Lightning +3 ranged; grand lightning +8 ranged
Damage:	See below
Face/Reach:	5ft. by 5ft./5ft.
Special Attacks:	Grand lightning, lightning
Special Qualities:	Blindsight, construct, damage reduction 10/+1
Saves:	Fort +4, Ref +1, Will +1
Abilities:	Str 10, Dex 10, Con 10, Int 10, Wis 10, Cha 10
Skills:	None
Feats:	None
Climate/Terrain:	Any
Organization:	Solitary, pair, sentinel group (3-5)
Challenge Rating:	3
Treasure:	None
Alignment:	Usually lawful neutral
Advancement Range:	None

Description

Thunder orbs are magical constructs that guard vaults, tombs or other such places. Created by an arcane spellcaster who summons an elemental spirit and imprisons it inside an enchanted basalt construct, thunder orbs are a unique construct powered by the intelligent mind of the elemental spirit housed within.

The orb's body is a sphere about four feet in diameter, sculpted from dark stone. The surface is deeply carved with arcane signs and restraining circles, some of which can be seen to glow, lit from within by the elemental imprisoned in the hollow core. The orbs are suspended magically in the air, floating two feet off the ground and moving about by a form of levitation. They spark with electricity whenever they sense anyone near, and they attack if the intruder is not one of the few whom the orb's creators have instructed to be allowed safe passage.

Combat

Thunder orbs are bold and fearless in combat. They take their task of guardianship very seriously, and they drive away any who come too close. (They kill if the trespasser fights back.) If confronted with a powerful foe capable of destroying them, the orb does not back down but attacks with abandon, instead. If the orb is destroyed, the elemental spirit within is freed of its prison to return to its plane of origin.

Blindsight (Su): The orb has no sensory organs, but it locates objects and creatures within 90 feet with a complex form of magical sensitivity. This sensitivity makes the orb extremely difficult to fool, but it also means that a spellcaster who dispels the power successfully renders the orb blind for 2d4 rounds.

Construct: Impervious to critical hits, subdual damage and death from massive damage trauma. Immune to poisons, diseases, blinding, deafness, drowning, electricity and spells and attacks that affect respiration or living physiology. Cannot be stunned. Not affected by attacks or spells of mind-altering nature (enamoring or charming spells, for example), or by spells based on healing/harming. Fire and acid spells or attacks deal half normal damage.

Grand Lightning (Su): Once every 1d4 rounds, the orb can unleash a bolt of lightning 45 feet long and five feet wide, in lieu of its normal lightning attack. Those caught within it take 8d6 points of damage. A successful Reflex save (DC 19) halves the damage.

Lightning (Su): Once each round, the orb can generate a small stroke of lightning that inflicts 2d6 points of damage on one opponent within 30 feet. A successful Reflex save (DC 15) halves the damage.

Tokal

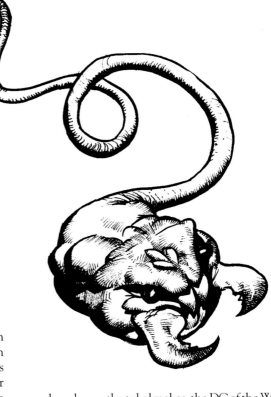

Fine Aberration

Hit Dice:	1 hp
Initiative:	—
Speed:	—
AC:	18 (+8 size)
Attacks:	—
Damage:	—
Face/Reach:	—
Special Attacks:	Infest, control
Special Qualities:	Symbiotic link
Saves:	Fort +1, Ref +1, Will +10
Abilities:	Str 1, Dex 11, Con 11, Int 14, Wis 14, Cha 8
Skills:	None
Feats:	None
Climate/Terrain:	Jungle
Organization:	Solitary
Challenge Rating:	1
Treasure:	None
Alignment:	Always neutral
Advancement Range:	None

Description

Tokal are tiny parasitic creatures that thrive in moist jungle regions. They infest a new host when an established host bites a victim, implanting the tokal's eggs in the process. While tokal always die with their host, tokal parasites often live long enough to infest a new host with eggs before dying. Once infested, a tokal host typically wastes away within a few months as the tokal consumes it from within to make new eggs.

Being sentient, the tokal wages a constant battle with its host's mind for control of the body. Strong-willed hosts have been known to control the tokal, while lesser beasts do the bidding of this creature. Tokal typically exist for one reason only: to reach gestation within their host and infest a new host with their eggs.

Some tribal societies, deep in the jungles, have developed an immunity to the destructive effects of the tokal's infestation and live in a state of relative equilibrium with their parasites. How this works remains a mystery.

Combat

While the tokal do not fight per se, a battle with a tokal infestation does indeed occur. A mature tokal wages a constant struggle with the mind of the host to advance its breeding instinct. Often, the tokal strikes in the heat of combat, while the host is slave to his more savage impulses.

A host can survive an infestation for a number of months equal to her Constitution before dying from the infestation. The parasite is treated as a disease for the purposes of determining which spells can affect and remove it. The tokal gets a Will save (DC 25) to resist any attempts to "cure" it from the host's system. For each such save the tokal makes, the DC of the Will save is reduced by one as the tokal becomes immune.

Infest (Ex): The tokal has a chance of infesting a new host with its eggs if that host is bitten by the tokal's current host. If bitten, the prospective host must make a Fortitude save (DC 20). Failure means a successful infestation. Tokal eggs require 2d20 days to gestate before they can use their other abilities.

Control (Ex): A mature tokal can vie for control of its host at any time if the tokal's Intelligence is greater than its host's. If the host's Intelligence is greater than the tokal's, the tokal must wait for a period of combat or other strenuous activity (physical exertion, arguments, intercourse) before attempting to take control. When the tokal attempts to assert itself, the host must make a Will save (DC 15) to keep control. If successful, the tokal cannot try again for the next four rounds. If the agitated state is controlled within that time (e.g., combat ends), the tokal cannot try again until the next strenuous activity. If the host fails the save, the tokal takes over and attempts to infest a new host (through a bite). The current host can make a Will save (DC 18) every round to regain control of his actions.

Symbiotic Link (Ex): A tokal develops a symbiotic connection with the host, and at times, the host is richer for it. A host with a mature tokal gains the following adjustments to his abilities: Str +1, Dex +2, Int –1, Wis –1, Cha –2, all saves +1, initiative +1. A host under a tokal's control is immune to mind-influencing attacks and magic.

Tokal Tribesman

Medium-size Humanoid

Hit Dice:	2d8+4 (13 hp)
Initiative:	+4 (+3 Dex, +1 tokal parasite)
Speed:	30 ft.
AC:	16 (+3 armor, +3 Dex)
Attacks:	Bite +5 melee; club +5 melee
Damage:	Bite 1d6+3; club 1d6+3
Face/Reach:	5 ft. by 5 ft./5 ft.
Special Attacks:	Infest
Special Qualities:	None
Saves:	Fort +5, Ref +6, Will -1
Abilities:	Str 16, Dex 17, Con 14, Int 9, Wis 9, Cha 7
Skills:	Listen +2, Spot +2
Feats:	Alertness
Climate/Terrain:	Jungle/woodlands
Organization:	Hunting Party (3-6), Village (15-45)
Challenge Rating:	1/2
Treasure:	Standard
Alignment:	Usually neutral
Advancement Range:	By character class

Description

Dwelling deep in the jungles and dense woods of the Scarred Lands, these tribesmen are living, breathing breeding grounds for the parasites known as tokal. They have developed an immunity to the parasites that infest them, and they are not consumed from within by the growth of the tokal.

Their motives seem simple enough: hunt for food, shelter themselves, protect themselves from predators and find new hosts for the tokal whenever possible.

It is the presence of the tokal parasite that makes these otherwise primitive humanoids truly dangerous. The tribesmen and the tokal parasites often think as one, and the tribesmen gather into raiding parties three or four times a year to seek out neighboring tribes and infest them with the parasites. Fortunately for civilization as a whole, the newly infested tribes do not share the tokal tribesmen's natural symbiosis with the parasites and are thus consumed by the tokal within a few months. Meanwhile, the tokal tribesmen continue to breed, slowly increasing their numbers.

Tokal Tribesmen Characters

Tokal tribesmen are usually fighters or barbarians. The tribe's holy man is typically a druid. Their few rogues act as scouts. The tribe's rare arcane spellcasters are invariably sorcerers.

Combat

Tokal tribesmen are savage fighters who wield simple weapons — clubs, spears and anything they may have acquired during a war party. They learn and adapt quickly, perhaps a side benefit of sharing their bodies with an intelligent parasite. When the tokal tribesmen outnumber their foes, they surround them as a pack of dogs would and wear them down through attrition. When the tribesmen themselves are outnumbered, they seek to bring as many foes down with them as possible and infest them.

Infest (Ex): These tribesmen are all hosts for the tokal parasites. As such, one bite stands a good chance of passing the tokal parasite on to a victim. If bitten, the prospective host must make a Fortitude save (DC 20); failure indicates a successful infestation. Tokal eggs require 2d20 days to gestate before they can use their other abilities.

Trogodon

Large (Long) Monstrous Humanoid

Hit Dice:	5d8+15 (37 hp)
Initiative:	+1 (Dex)
Speed:	40 ft, swim 40 ft
AC:	14 (−1 size, +1 Dex, +4 natural)
Attacks:	Bite +6 melee, 2 claws +1 melee; tail slap +6 melee; and trident +1 melee
Damage:	Bite 1d8+2; claws 1d6+1; tail slap 1d8+2; trident 1d8+1
Face/Reach:	5 ft. by 10 ft./5 ft.
Special Attacks:	Tail strike
Special Qualities:	Darkvision, regeneration
Saves:	Fort +7, Ref +2, Will +0
Abilities:	Str 15, Dex 13, Con 16, Int 4, Wis 9, Cha 3
Skills:	Listen +6, Spot +9, Swim +18
Feats:	Cleave, Improved Bull Rush, Spirited Charge
Climate/Terrain:	Temperate and warm swamps
Organization:	Solitary, pair or swarm (3-7)
Challenge Rating:	3
Treasure:	Standard
Alignment:	Always chaotic evil
Advancement Range:	4-8 HD (Large); 9-12 HD (Huge)

Description

The trogodon is a bizarre combination of reptile and man that infests the Swamps of Kan Thet. Stupid and savage, this creature does little more than swim in the dank waters, hunt for food and attack anything that disturbs it. The ancient race of asaatthi are known to use trogodons to guard the marshes around their few remaining cities.

A trogodon has the lower body of a crocodile and the torso of a man. Its head is reptilian, with razor-sharp teeth and wide-spaced eyes. The trogodon's hide is rough and patterned in green and black. A row of bony plates extends from the trogodon's head to its tail, which itself ends in a vicious bladed point.

An intelligent trogodon emerges infrequently. Such a creature makes a formidable foe, able to add reasoning and cunning to its physical power and durability. These greater trogodons have been known to lead their lesser cousins in raids against nearby civilization, even recruiting normal crocodiles in attacks. Asaatthi lend their martial expertise to develop simple tactics for trogodons on these raids. The asaatthi seldom take part themselves, however, since trogodons don't take direction well in the thick of battle.

Combat

Powerful and brutish, a trogodon knows little of things like tactics. It has a degree of cunning, though, hiding in the water to leap on unsuspecting prey. Beyond that, it comes down to a simple matter of striking hard and fast. If a trogodon suffers a significant amount of damage early on in a fight, it flees to safety. Otherwise, blood lust overwhelms it, and the trogodon battles to the death.

Regeneration (Ex): Part of what makes a trogodon so tough is its ability to heal damage. The monster regains 2 hp each round, but it cannot regenerate electrical damage.

Tail Strike (Ex): The trogodon can make an additional attack each round with its tail at no penalty.

Ubantu Tribesman

Small Humanoid

Hit Dice:	1d8 (4 hp)
Initiative:	+1 (Dex)
Speed:	30 ft.
AC:	15 (+1 size, +1 Dex, +3 hide armor)
Attacks:	Hammer +2 melee; knife +2 melee; sling +3 ranged; javelin +3 ranged
Damage:	Hammer 1d4; knife 1d4; sling 1d4; javelin 1d6
Face/Reach:	5 ft. by 5 ft./5 ft.
Special Attacks:	Poison
Special Qualities:	None
Saves:	Fort +0, Ref +3, Will +0
Abilities:	Str 10, Dex 13, Con 11, Int 10, Wis 11, Cha 8
Skills:	Craft +2, Handle Animal +2, Intuit Direction +3, Listen +2, Ride +2, Search +3, Spot +3, Wilderness (Desert) Lore +2
Feats:	Endurance, Mounted Combat, Point Blank Shot, Precise Shot, Ride-By Attack, Run, Track
Climate/Terrain:	Desert
Organization:	Hunting party (1-3), band (4-20, with one 3rd-level pathfinder), community (21-100, with one 7th-level leader, two 5th-level priests and five 3rd-level pathfinders)
Challenge Rating:	1/4
Treasure:	Standard
Alignment:	Usually lawful neutral
Advancement Range:	By character class

Description

By their reckoning, the Ubantu are the only truly intelligent creatures that reside in the Desert of Onn. They believe that Hedrada set them aside to keep them safe from the ravages of the mad Dame of Storms, the Titan Lethene. They claim that the desert's colossal, ancient tortoises arose from Hedrada's footsteps when the god scratched out the desert for the Ubantu. The desert's other predators reputedly exist to protect these people from outsiders and to punish the weak and sinful among them.

Their beliefs aside, the Ubantu are devoted to maintaining a civilization even in the trackless waste in which they live. They construct sprawling tent-cities of bone and ratroo skin beneath the empty and sun-flaked shells of dead tortoises.

Given the desert's harsh conditions, their lives are otherwise devoted to survival. They herd ratroos for food (although remotely from their homesteads). They distill water to drink and poisons to coat hunting weapons, both from the desert's many cacti. They are even willing to lead visitors into the heart of the Desert of Onn or to one of the few treacherous mountain passes that allows travelers egress to the Blood Sea (although the Ubantu themselves have no desire to pass into the "unclean" lands beyond). The people are polite if abrupt with guests who choose to

stay with them, as long as those outlanders don't upset Ubantu society overmuch. Disruptive guests are escorted deep into the deserts and left to fend for themselves. If they survive, it's because Hedrada wills it, and the Ubantu must tolerate the person.

Like any intelligent, civilized people, however, the Ubantu war among themselves over living space, resources and feuds. Indeed, many resent those of their race who forsook Hedrada for Madriel to construct the city-state Hetanu on the Ba Delta. Ubantu defend their homes against any overt threat with vicious, unbridled cruelty.

All Ubantu speak their own language. Some who have conducted trade with outsiders know a broken Common.

Ubantu Characters

The Ubantu people are natural warriors (particularly of the barbarian class), although they make effective rogues given their size and agility. Sorcerers and wizards are rare among them, but priests are venerated as the eyes, ears, hands and mouths of Hedrada (whom their culture depicts as a giant bird). Priests focus on the Sun, Law and Earth domains.

Combat

Ubantu commonly use knives made from the teeth of sand burrowers, bone *adl adls* with poison-tipped spears, ratroo-hide slings and hand-crafted hammers. They hunt in parties and fight in bands. When they attack in war or defense, they swarm their enemies in as great a number as possible.

Poison (Ex): The poison the Ubantu use to coat weapons inflicts an extra 1d6 damage to those who are hit, unless the victim passes a Fort saving throw (DC 13). The Ubantu themselves are immune to this substance, having developed an immunity over generations.

Undead Ooze

Huge Ooze

Hit Dice:	6d12 (39 hp)
Initiative:	-2 (Dex)
Speed:	25 ft., climb 25 ft.
AC:	6 (-2 size, -2 Dex)
Attacks:	Crush +4 melee
Damage:	Crush 2d8
Face/Reach:	10ft. by 10ft/10ft.
Special Attacks:	Cold, engulf, skeletons
Special Qualities:	Blindsight, creeping, ooze, undead
Saves:	Fort +8, Ref -2, Will +6
Abilities:	Str 10, Dex 7, Con —, Int 8, Wis 14, Chr 1
Skills:	None
Feats:	None
Climate/Terrain:	Any land or underground
Organization:	Solitary
Challenge Rating:	4
Treasure:	None
Alignment:	Always chaotic evil
Advancement Range:	6-9 HD (huge)

Description

The undead ooze is created when an ooze of any other sort violates the grave of a restless and evil soul. The malevolent spirit, still tied to the rotting flesh consumed by the ooze, enters the ooze as well. This is the last meal the ooze takes as a living creature; it is changed into a thing of undeath and filled with a hatred of the living, and a cunning intelligence.

Once the transformation is complete, the ooze's former breed is undeterminable. It becomes a huge, viscous, black mass from which the bones of its victims' corpses occasionally protrude. Hereafter it stalks the living, preferring intelligent prey who are the most terrified of it.

Combat

The undead ooze always tries to approach its victim from behind. If the target is unarmed and likely to be easy prey, the ooze takes a moment to reveal its presence and revel in the victim's terror before making the kill. Otherwise, it tries to strike from surprise.

Engulf (Ex): Any opponent who has been hit by a successful crush attack may be engulfed in the next round. The victim can make an attack of opportunity against the ooze as it seeks to engulf. If the victim does not attack, it may instead make a Reflex save (DC 18) to avoid being engulfed.

Engulfed victims are subject to cold damage each round and are considered to be grappled and trapped within the body of the ooze. The ooze is free to make other crush attacks in subsequent rounds, but can only engulf one medium-size victim per three HD of

the undead ooze (one small per two HD, and one large per four HD).

Cold (Ex): Any victim engulfed by the ooze suffers 1d8 cold damage per round.

Skeletons (Su): If confronted with multiple enemies, the ooze expels 1d6 skeletons from its mass. These skeletons conform to the stats of standard, medium-size skeletons and attack any living thing in the area. If no living things remain in the vicinity of the ooze, the skeletons collapse into piles of bones and await the ooze to pour over them and re-absorb them.

Blindsight (Ex): The ooze is blind, but it can sense objects by degrees of heat and cold, and can sense and track any living being within 60 feet.

Creeping (Ex): The ooze can climb any vertical surface and can hang from the underside of any horizontal surface as long as a third of its mass touches a vertical surface. It can pass through openings as small as a human head.

Undead: As an undead, this creature is immune to poison, sleep, paralysis, stunning and disease. It is not subject to critical hits, subdual damage, ability damage, energy drain or death from massive damage.

Ooze: The ooze is not affected by attacks or spells that involve poison, sleep, paralysis, polymorph or stunning, or that influence the mind. It has no physiological weak points and is therefore immune to critical hits.

Unhallowed, The

Sometimes, perhaps once in a hundred years, a child is born bearing signs that he or she is beloved of the gods. She may be stronger, smarter, swifter or more beautiful than any other child. Above all, she is gifted with abundant blessings and is clearly destined for greatness in the fullness of time. These souls go on to become mighty warriors, legendary paramours, silver-tongued thieves or righteous holy men, meant to share their talents with those in need. It is a fundamental truth of the universe that the gods expect much of those to whom they give the greatest gifts.

Sometimes that trust is betrayed. With a single act, these blessed individuals turn their backs on their sacred pacts with the gods and heed the call of self-interest and evil.

People are fallible, and power can corrupt. Not everyone is up to the challenges of a disciplined and compassionate life, and they give in to their base natures. Usually, once these heroes lose their way and use their mighty skills to indulge their dark sides, there is no turning back. Such a violation of sacred trust earns them the eternal enmity of the gods. When these fallen souls reach the end of their lives, nothing but an eternity of torment awaits them.

Along with all the gods' wonderful gifts can comes an equally powerful ego, and many corrupted heroes do not go so easily into the afterlife. They linger in the world of the living by sheer black will. The more their bodies rot, the more they cling to their physical existence, knowing that everything they feel is just a pale shadow of the punishments that await them.

These tormented spirits, called the Unhallowed because of their abandonment by the gods, are very powerful undead creatures whose influence can bring ruin not just to individuals, but to entire kingdoms. These creatures often worm their way into the ruling families of a land, spreading their corruption like a cancer until the entire kingdom is plunged into years of horror and despair.

The Unhallowed cannot be destroyed by sword or spell alone; their crimes must be exposed before the gods and their unholy will broken before their protection can be stripped away and justice served. The first step in laying one of these creatures to rest is to learn its true name and the terrible act committed that set its feet on the path of evil. This discovery alone can be the object of a major quest, as these spirits frequently roam from place to place, far from the lands of their birth, and many are centuries or millennia old, their exploits now only fragments of forgotten lore. If and when this knowledge is uncovered, the creature must be confronted in a holy place, its name and crime spoken aloud to call the attention of the gods. Once this is done, the being may be fought and destroyed, but even then the battle is certain to be bloody and grim.

Stories and accusations abound regarding the Unhallowed among the ranks of the living in the Scarred Lands. Perhaps the most persuasive case is made for Tankaras the Tortured, the present leader of the pirates of Bloodport. An often-told rumor relates that King Virduk himself is an Unhallowed, or in the very least his young wife Queen Geleeda is one. And there are always accusations among the clerics of Vesh that one or the other of them has stolen from the true path of Corean.

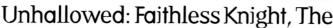

Unhallowed: Faithless Knight, The

Medium-size Undead (Unhallowed)

Hit Dice:	10d12+40 (105 hp)
Initiative:	+10 (+4 Dex, +4 Improved Initiative, +2 natural)
Speed:	60 ft.
AC:	31 (+4 Dex, +13 magical full plate armor, +4 natural)
Attacks:	Bastard sword +15 melee
Damage:	Bastard sword 1d10+6
Face/Reach:	5 ft. by 5 ft./5 ft.
Special Attacks:	Cursed sword
Special Qualities:	Invulnerable, frightful presence, undead
Saves:	Fort +11, Ref +7, Will +5
Abilities:	Str 18, Dex 18, Con 18, Int 19, Wis 12, Cha 18
Skills:	Diplomacy +25, Innuendo +20, Intimidate +24, Listen +24, Ride +30, Spot +24
Feats:	Alertness, Ambidexterity, Armor Proficiency (heavy), Blind Fighting, Cleave, Combat Reflexes, Great Cleave, Improved Critical, Improved Initiative, Iron Will, Power Attack, Ride-by Attack, Spirited Charge, Trample, Weapon Focus (bastard sword), Weapon Specialization (bastard sword)
Climate/Terrain:	Any
Organization:	Solitary
Challenge Rating:	8
Treasure:	Standard
Alignment:	Always lawful evil
Advancement Range:	10-16 HD (Medium-size)

Description

The faithless knight was once a bold and noble warrior who, in a moment of rashness or passion, committed an act of terrible cowardice or dishonor so great that it violated everything for which his patron deity stood. Now the craven fiend travels the world spreading terror and pain, drowning innocent kingdoms in blood and leading many young knights to their doom.

The faithless knight appears as a hideous, near-skeletal corpse, its skin gleaming an unholy greenish-white. It wears enchanted plate armor and clothes that were once of the finest quality, now rotted and scarred by years of pitiless campaigning. Most times, the knight also rides a terrible black warhorse, caparisoned in matching armor, or, in much rarer cases, has a bloodmare as its steed. Occasionally, a particularly mighty knight may also have a pack of hellhounds or even blight wolves circling his heels.

These dark warriors plague the living in many ways, some leading huge war bands of evil creatures on crusades of conquest, while others operate alone, bringing whole kingdoms to ruin by corrupting their knights or slaughtering the rest on the battlefield.

Combat

With its fearsome powers and terrible weapons, the faithless knight is a veritable engine of destruction, scything through ranks of warriors like so much ripe wheat. Most importantly, these warriors are utterly ruthless and dishonorable, thinking nothing of murdering an unarmed or helpless foe or using a hostage as a shield.

Invulnerable (Ex): Until confronted by its crimes on holy ground, a faithless knight cannot be slain. If the knight is reduced to 0 hit points in battle, it and any companions (horses or hounds) simply vanish before attackers' eyes, only to return to the mortal plane the following night.

Frightful Presence (Su): The faithless knight exudes an aura of terror so intense that any individuals (with 10 or fewer HD) within 60 feet must make a Will save (DC 20). Targets with 6 or fewer hit dice that fail their saves are panicked for 1d4 turns, suffering a -2 modifier on saves and fleeing the knight. Targets with 7 to 10 hit dice are shaken for 1d4 turns, suffering a -1 modifier on saves.

Cursed Sword (Ex): The faithless night wields an enchanted bastard sword woven with unholy spells. If the sword hits an opponent, the victim must immediately make a Fortitude save (DC 17). If she fails the roll, she takes damage from the sword and suffers one of the following effects, determined by rolling 1d6: 1-3, take 1 point of Strength, Dexterity or Constitution (respectively on the 1-3 die result) ability drain; 4-6, energy drain (victim gains 1d3 negative levels).

Undead: The faithless knight is immune to poison, sleep, paralysis, stunning and disease. It's not subject to critical hits, subdual damage, ability damage, energy drain or death from massive damage.

Unhallowed: False Lover, The

Medium-size Undead (Unhallowed)

Hit Dice:	10d12+40 (105 hp)
Initiative:	+2 (Dex)
Speed:	60 ft.
AC:	18 (+2 Dex, +6 natural)
Attacks:	None
Damage:	None
Face/Reach:	5 ft. by 5 ft./5 ft.
Special Attacks:	None
Special Qualities:	Invulnerable, pleasing illusion, unearthly glamour, undead
Saves:	Fort +7, Ref +5, Will +13
Abilities:	Str 15, Dex 15, Con 18, Int 18, Wis 18, Cha 21
Skills:	Bluff +13, Diplomacy +13, Gather Information +11, Innuendo +12, Listen +9, Sense Motive +13, Spot +9
Feats:	Iron Will, Leadership
Climate/Terrain:	Any
Organization:	Solitary
Challenge Rating:	7
Treasure:	Double standard
Alignment:	Always lawful evil
Advancement Range:	10-12 HD (Medium-size)

Description

The false lover was once the paragon of charm and beauty, who effortlessly won the hearts and souls of any who looked upon him. He inspired heroes and heroines to great deeds, gave birth to new forms of art and literature and transformed the cultures of entire kingdoms with his wit and grace. Ultimately, however, he betrayed those dreams, crushing the spirits of those who loved him, sometimes simply because he could. He left a trail of broken lives in his wake, exulting in raw sensuality and power. As the years passed and his looks began to wane, he lapsed into bitterness, spitefully using his powers to manipulate those around him and leech every last drop of happiness from their lives.

The false lover hides his true nature behind powerful illusions that maintain the semblance of the radiant person he once was. He can still seduce the strongest of hearts, filling them with love one moment and jealousy the next. These creatures delight in destroying relationships and turning powerful figures against one another, oftentimes setting entire families at one another's throats and embroiling the land in bitter feuds and civil wars.

The false lover presents a face of unearthly beauty and grace, charming even the most callous hearts with his glamour. He surrounds himself with rich and exotic clothes and gifts, the better to accentuate his image.

Combat

The false lover does not fight; he has innocent victims ready to hurl themselves in the path of any attacker, willing to fight to the death to uphold the reputation of their paramour. At any given time, this creature has 2-10 paramours and escorts accompanying him wherever he goes, who gladly sacrifice their lives to buy time for the creature to escape.

Invulnerable (Ex): Until confronted by their crimes on holy ground, the Unhallowed cannot be slain. If they are reduced to 0 hit points during a battle, they simply vanish before attackers' eyes, only to return to the mortal plane the following night.

Pleasing Illusion (Su): The false lover is capable of concealing his undead features with clever illusions, allowing him to change appearance at will. For this reason, these creatures have an effective Charisma of 21 when determining reaction rolls, followers, etc. Victims may see through the illusion only with a successful Will save (DC 19) and *only* if they know to look for it specifically.

Unearthly Glamour (Su): Such is the power of the false lover's glamour that even the hardest hearts can be seduced into his service. The false lover can pick a single target in a combat round and subject the victim to the full force of his charms. The target must immediately make a Will save (DC 20) or fall under the false lover's sway. The victim is under the creature's direct control so long as they remain within sight of each another. Once the two are separated the control ebbs, but the victim is never quite the same again, and if the creature uses its glamour on the person again the victim's DC is increased to 28.

Undead: The false lover is immune to poison, sleep, paralysis, stunning and disease. It's not subject to critical hits, subdual damage, ability damage, energy drain or death from massive damage.

Unhallowed: Forsaken Priest, The

Medium-size Undead (Unhallowed)

Hit Dice:	10d12+40 (105 hp)
Initiative:	+7 (+3 Dex, +4 Improved Initiative)
Speed:	60 ft.
AC:	21 (+3 Dex, +8 magical leather armor)
Attacks:	Mace +12
Damage:	Mace 1d8+2
Face/Reach:	5 ft. by 5 ft./5 ft.
Special Attacks:	None
Special Qualities:	Invulnerable, unholy arts, sweet-sounding lies, pleasing illusion, undead
Saves:	Fort +7, Ref +6, Will +14
Abilities:	Str 14, Dex 16, Con 18, Int 19, Wis 20, Cha 20
Skills:	Alchemy +10, Concentration +13, Diplomacy +13, Gather Information +13, Innuendo +12, Intimidate +13, Listen +10, Spellcraft +12, Spot +10, Use Magic Device +12
Feats:	Alertness, Combat Casting, Empower Spell, Enlarge Spell, Extend Spell, Improved Initiative, Iron Will, Leadership, Maximize Spell, Quicken Spell
Climate/Terrain:	Any
Organization:	Solitary
Challenge Rating:	8
Treasure:	Standard
Alignment:	Always lawful evil
Advancement Range:	10-16 HD (Medium-size)

Description

There is no greater crime in the eyes of the gods than when one of their holy men forsakes his vows of obedience and uses his influence to lead innocent members of the faith down paths of corruption and iniquity. The forsaken priest is a creature who betrayed the highest offices of his patron deity and, since that time, has been a force of malevolence and temptation to any soul caught in his clutches.

Like many of the Unhallowed, the forsaken priest can cloak his true nature behind pleasant-seeming illusions, worming his way into the trust of rulers and true holy men, then slowly subverting them to the cause of evil. He drives those in power to abuse their followers and to perform acts of brutality and greed, sowing the seeds of war, rapine and famine everywhere he goes.

These creatures appear to the uninitiated as grand, dignified men and women whose wisdom is vast and beyond reproach. They are always eager to lend an ear and offer advice, filling their victims' minds with honeyed words that turn to poison in the fullness of time.

Combat

The faithless priest surrounds himself with fanatical acolytes and supporters who defend his person with their lives. If an opponent is willing to cut her way through a barricade of innocent people, she must still contend with the cleric's fearsome array of spells and frightful powers of summoning.

Invulnerable (Ex): Until confronted by their crimes on holy ground, the Unhallowed cannot be slain. If they are reduced to 0 hit points during a battle, they simply vanish before attackers' eyes, only to return to the mortal plane the following night.

Unholy Arts (Sp): The forsaken priest can cast spells of the Evil domain as a 10th-level cleric.

Sweet-sounding Lies (Su): The forsaken priest spreads his corruption by seducing noble souls with blasphemous advice that nevertheless sounds sweet on the priest's tongue. The priest may whisper a suggestion, no matter how vile, into a person's ear, and the victim follows it unless he makes a successful Will save (DC 24).

Pleasing Illusion (Su): The forsaken priest is capable of concealing his undead features with clever illusions, allowing him to change appearance at will. For this reason, these creatures have an effective Charisma of 20 when determining reaction rolls, followers, etc. Victims may see through the illusion only with a successful Will save (DC 19) and *only* if they know to look for it specifically.

Undead: The forsaken priest is immune to mind-influencing effects, poison, sleep, paralysis, stunning and disease. It's not subject to critical hits, subdual damage, ability damage, energy drain or death from massive damage.

Unhallowed: Treacherous Thief, The

Medium-size Undead (Unhallowed)

Hit Dice:	10d12+40 (105 hp)
Initiative:	+10 (+6 Dex, +4 Improved Initiative)
Speed:	60 ft., climb 60 ft.
AC:	22 (+6 Dex, +6 magical padded armor)
Attacks:	Short sword +10, dagger +10
Damage:	Short sword 1d6+2, dagger 1d4+2
Face/Reach:	5 ft. by 5 ft./5 ft.
Special Attacks:	None
Special Qualities:	Invulnerable, pleasing illusion, silent as the wind, undead
Saves:	Fort +11, Ref +10, Will +3
Abilities:	Str 15, Dex 25, Con 18, Int 18, Wis 12, Cha 19
Skills:	Appraise +15, Balance +15, Bluff +18, Climb +15, Escape Artist +20, Forgery +15, Innuendo +15, Listen +20, Open Lock +24, Pick Pocket +30, Spot +20
Feats:	Alertness, Ambidexterity, Improved Initiative, Iron Will, Two-Weapon Fighting
Climate/Terrain:	Any
Organization:	Solitary
Challenge Rating:	7
Treasure:	Triple standard
Alignment:	Always chaotic evil
Advancement Range:	10-14 HD (Medium-size)

Description

The treacherous thief was cursed by the gods for betraying those who trusted him, all for the sake of nothing more than petty greed. He used his skills to steal from those who had almost nothing to call their own, simply for the joy of taking what did not belong to him. He murdered people for nothing more than a handful of coins. And now, in death, there is no treasure in the world great enough to buy his way out of damnation.

The treacherous thief can disguise his hideous features with spells of illusion that allow him to take different faces at will. His powers of stealth and sleight of hand permit him to slip inside the best-guarded vaults or the most secure sanctums, allowing him to make away with whatever strikes his fancy.

Unfortunately, to one who is centuries dead, wealth is nothing but a cruel joke. The thief now takes what pleasure it can by depriving others of precious or holy artifacts or turns brother against brother by stealing from one and placing the blame on the other. Or worst of all, he earns the confidence of powerful nobles and corrupts them into a life of callous thievery as well.

The treacherous thief wears a pleasing face and rich attire, always dressing in the finest clothes to beguile his unwitting victims.

Combat

The treacherous thief is no fighter; if confronted, he flees or, better yet, uses gullible dupes to do the fighting for him. Then, when his foes are distracted, he fades into the background and delivers a devastating sneak attack in the confusion.

Invulnerable (Ex): Until confronted by his crimes on holy ground, a treacherous thief cannot be slain. If he is reduced to 0 hit points during a battle, he simply vanishes before the attackers' eyes, only to return to the mortal plane the following night.

Silent as the Wind (Su): The treacherous thief can blend into shadow and move so silently that none can detect his approach. The being is automatically successful when Hide or Move Silently rolls are required.

Pleasing Illusion (Su): The treacherous thief is capable of concealing his undead features with clever illusions, allowing him to change appearances at will. These creatures therefore have an effective charisma of 19 when determining reaction rolls, followers, etc. Victims may see through the illusion only with a successful Will save (DC 25) and *only* if they know to look for it specifically.

Undead: The treacherous thief is immune to poison, sleep, paralysis, stunning and disease. It's not subject to critical hits, subdual damage, ability damage, energy drain or death from massive damage.

Unholy Child

Tiny Undead

Hit Dice:	4d12 (26 hp)
Initiative:	+0
Speed:	Crawl 10 ft., fly 20 ft.
AC:	14 (+2 size, +2 natural)
Attacks:	Bite +2 melee, claw +0 melee
Damage:	Bite 1d3; claw 1d2
Face/Reach:	2.5 ft. by 2.5 ft./0 ft.
Special Attacks:	Dread presence, frost touch, frost breath
Special Qualities:	Non-corporeal, smile of innocence, undead
Saves:	Fort +4, Ref +1, Will +3
Abilities:	Str 3, Dex 9, Con —, Int 9, Wis 14, Cha 8
Skills:	Listen +2, Move Silently +1
Feats:	None
Climate/Terrain:	Any populated
Organization:	Solitary
Challenge Rating:	3
Treasure:	None
Alignment:	Usually neutral evil
Advancement Range:	3-15 HD

Description

These deceptive creatures are the spirits of infants murdered or left to die by their parents. None know what happens after death to instill such rage in such a young heart, but there is no doubting the sincerity of an unholy child's consuming hatred.

Some unholy children merely seek revenge against their killers and move on, while others may haunt a family or house for generations. The spirit may be exorcised and bound, but many clerics believe that what the spirit truly needs is to be given a proper name (many such infants die unnamed) and funeral rites. This folklore is a popular one, and often scoffed at by those who regularly deal with spirits.

The unholy child appears as an emaciated infant still scarred by its means of death, and arrayed in a rotting swaddling blanket or whatever it was wearing when it died. Normally the spirit floats at head height across the ground, its eyes piercing any observers with an unnatural hatred so out of place in the image of an infant. The child's cooing and crying only add to the juxtaposed horror and innocence.

Combat

The unholy child prefers to use its beguiling ways to get close to its intended victims and then strike.

Dread Presence (Ex): The unholy child's very presence can inspire dread and depression, though if the child remains unseen, most victims do not understand the reason for their mood change. When materialized, the sight of a ghostly child with murder in its eyes is enough to stop the bravest heart. Those within 30 feet or eyesight of the creature must succeed at a Will save (DC 16) or have their resolve shaken and perform all actions at -1 to the roll for 4d6 rounds.

Non-corporeal (Su): The unholy child can materialize or dematerialize (turn ethereal) as an attack action. While ethereal, it cannot harm creatures in the physical plane.

Frost Touch (Ex): When materialized, the unholy child may lay its hand on an opponent as a touch attack, and the person suffers the effects of frostbite, taking 2d6 damage. The frost touch also takes effect if the child claws an opponent.

Frost Breath (Su): In addition to its physical attacks, the unholy child may breath out a 10-foot cone of supernaturally chilled air. Anyone caught in the breath must pass a Fortitude saving throw (DC 14) or temporarily lose 1d4 points of Constitution. Those reduced to zero Constitution are killed. Lost Constitution is recovered at a rate of one point per 10 minutes of rest.

Smile of Innocence (Su): This is the most insidious weapon the unholy child has in its arsenal, because it plays upon its target's compassion and pity. As a move action, the unholy child can stifle its dread presence and cloak itself in an illusion to appear as a normal baby. It cries like a normal baby, gurgles when picked up, and if its skin feels a little cold, the natural instinct is to hold it close to warm it. This is usually when the creature sinks its teeth into its would-be caretakers' neck, or reaches up tiny hands to rip out his eyes. The unholy child reverts to its "normal" appearance once it attacks or uses any of its special attacks.

Undead: The unholy child is immune to poison, sleep, paralysis, stunning and disease. Its not subject to critical hits, subdual damage, ability damage, energy drain or death from massive damage.

Valraven

Huge (Tall) Animal

Hit Dice:	8d8+16 (52 hp)
Initiative:	+2 (+2 Dex)
Speed:	10 ft., fly 100 ft.
AC:	19 (−2 size, +2 Dex, +9 natural)
Attacks:	Beak +11 melee, 2 talons +6 melee
Damage:	Beak 2d4+5, talon 1d8+5
Face/Reach:	15 ft. by 15 ft./10 ft.
Special Attacks:	None
Special Qualities:	Keen senses
Saves:	Fort +4, Ref +5, Will +6
Abilities:	Str 20, Dex 15, Con 14, Int 10, Wis 10, Cha 12
Skills:	Listen +8, Speak Language (Common), Spot +8
Feats:	Alertness
Climate/Terrain:	Temperate and warm hills and mountains
Organization:	Solitary, family (2-5)
Challenge Rating:	4
Treasure:	Standard
Alignment:	Usually neutral good
Advancement Range:	7-15 HD (Huge)

Description

In the final days of the Divine War, the gods granted their greatest heroes the use of valravens — gigantic, reliable mounts from the realm of the gods themselves. Tales of the greatest battles of the Divine War inevitably invoke the majestic image of thousands of the gods' heroes flying on the backs of their valravens to overwhelm the forces of the titans.

The gods grant such prizes rarely today, but nests of young valravens still inhabit the Scarred Lands. Although the greatest birds of legend have returned home, their scattered offspring nest in mountains and hills. Divinely charged to honor glory, triumph and holy power, modern heroes can sometimes tame members of this new generation to serve as their mounts.

Combat

When ridden into combat, valravens prove to be adaptable fighters. They can maneuver to allow their riders good firing vantages while avoiding similar opportunities for enemies. They can attack other aerial creatures with beak and talons. Valravens can even swoop down on their enemies, grapple them, carry them aloft then let gravity take care of the rest.

Keen Senses (Ex): Valravens can see eight times as far as a normal human, and they have effective Darkvision up to 400 feet.

Vengaurak

Large Vermin

Hit Dice:	7d8+7 (38 hp)
Initiative:	-1 (Dex)
Speed:	30 ft., burrowing 5 ft.
AC:	20 (-1 size, -1 Dex, +12 natural)
Attacks:	Bite +12 melee, 4 claws +7 melee
Damage:	Bite 2d6+6; claw 1d8 +2
Face/Reach:	5ft. by 5ft./10ft.
Special Attacks:	Frenzied charge, seize
Special Qualities:	Blindsight, immunities
Saves:	Fort +6, Ref +1, Will +1
Abilities:	Str 22, Dex 8, Con 13, Int 4, Wis 8, Chr 3
Skills:	Climb +10, Escape Artist +6, Listen +6, Spot +12, Wilderness Lore +3
Feats:	Track
Climate/Terrain:	Any land and underground
Organization:	Solitary
Challenge Rating:	4
Treasure:	None
Alignment:	Always chaotic evil
Advancemant Range:	5-8 HD (Large); 9-11 HD (Huge)

Description

Vengaurak are horribly transformed creatures who have come under the influence of the titan Gaurak. These creatures, usually burrowing insects that are mutated by the titan's buried essence, tunnel up from the depths in search of anything edible. Rapidly growing to monstrous proportions and totally fearless, the vengaurak hunt anything in sight, but have a special hunger for those favored by the gods who cast Gaurak down (i.e., races such as elves, dwarves and humans). They relentlessly attack any being that tries to bar their way; Gaurak's hatred of being restrained forms much of the vengaurak's warped instincts.

Combat

Though not particularly intelligent, vengaurak often have opportunity to ambush prey at the beginning of a rampage. When moving into a new area, they burrow tunnels, then sit and listen. Waiting under the earth until its hunger spurs it on, the vermin have been known to errupt into city streets, unerringly discovering and devouring any who choose to hide rather than flee.

Vengaurak are single-minded in combat — they do not see enemies, only things to be eaten. Their clawing attacks are intended to drag food to their teeth, but still cause horrendous wounds. Once set on a target, vengauraks never cease pursuit unless another tasty bit tries to bar their path.

Frenzied Charge (Ex): A vengaurak can make a special charge attack. Charging 60 feet in a straight line, it can make a bite attack against any foes within five feet of the charge's path. A successful Reflex save (DC 20) halves the damage from the snapping bites delivered during this charge. Additionally, anyone directly in the vengaurak's path during the charge is also subject to a bull rush attack which, if successful, knocks the opponent away five feet laterally so the vengaurak may continue its charge. The vengaurak does not attack with its claws during this charge attack.

Seize (Ex): If the vengaurak hits its opponent with three or more of its claw attacks in the same round, the opponent is treated as a helpless defender for the vengaurak's bite attack.

Blindsight (Ex): Vengauraks, being tunneling creatures, have developed the skills to hunt by hearing and vibration. Likewise, their sense of taste is so accute they may also use it to track prey, keeping them aware of creatures within 180 feet.

Immunities (Ex): Poisons of any sort have no effect on the vengaurak. It is also immune to sleep, paralysis and visual illusions, as well as any illusion that does not include a taste component.

Skills: Vengaurak gain a +5 bonus when tracking prey due to their keen sense of taste.

Vrail

Tiny Animal

Hit Dice:	2d8 (9 hp)
Initiative:	+4 (Dex)
Speed:	fly 60 ft., aerial dive 150 ft.
AC:	22 (+2 size, +4 Dex, +6 natural)
Attacks:	Talon +8 melee
Damage:	Talon 1d10-3 (diving) or 1d6-3 (grounded)
Face/Reach:	2.5 ft. by 2.5 ft./0 ft.
Special Attacks:	None
Special Qualities:	None
Saves:	Fort +0, Ref +7, Will +0
Abilities:	Str 4, Dex 18, Con 10, Int 2, Wis 10, Cha 10
Skills:	Listen +3, Spot +12
Feats:	Dodge, Weapon Finesse (Talons), Flyby Attack
Climate/Terrain:	Alpine and alpine highlands
Organization:	Flock (5-8), bloodletting (21-32)
Challenge Rating:	1
Treasure:	None
Alignment:	Always neutral
Advancement Range:	1-4 HD (Tiny)

Description

Vrail are communal raptors, and a serious threat in many alpine wilderness areas. Unlike most raptors, which dive onto smaller prey and carry them off in their talons, Vrail hunt as groups. They swoop down in quick succession from different directions, each slashing the target with its razor sharp talons as it flashes past. After the target has bled to death, the vrail descend on the body as a flock and feed. Vrail are still dangerous on the ground; they attack targets with their knifelike talons to protect their kills. Vrail make their rookeries in high, rocky cliff faces, which are typically quite inaccessible. The harpies of the Scarred Lands have been known to keep individual vrail as pets upon occasion.

Combat

In the air, Vrail are incredibly difficult to hit. They may be attacked in melee combat by their target only on the round that they swoop in. They may be attacked with missile fire in that round or the next, but afterward are generally too far away to be shot at. All vrail in a flock attack on the same round and then circle to survey the results. Vrail can make airborne attacks a maximum of once every three rounds. Vrail do not typically attack groups of more than three individuals, but circle, waiting for one to stray too far from the group.

Flyby Attack: A Vrail can attack at any point before, during or after its move if it is flying.

Well Spirit

Medium-size Undead

Hit Dice:	5d12 (32 hp)
Initiative:	+8 (+4 Dex, +4 Improved Initiative)
Speed:	40ft. swimming
AC:	20 (+4 Dex, +6 natural)
Attacks:	None
Damage:	None
Face/Reach:	5 ft. by 5ft./5 ft.
Special Attacks:	Drown
Special Qualities:	Damage reduction, undead
Saves:	Fort +1, Ref +5, Will +3
Abilities:	Str 16, Dex 19, Con —, Int 9, Wis 9, Cha 0
Skills:	Listen +5, spot +5
Feats:	Improved Initiative
Climate/Terrain:	Any, always in wells
Organization:	Solitary
Challenge Rating:	3
Treasure:	Triple Standard
Alignment:	Always neutral evil
Advancement Range:	3-10 HD (Medium-size), 11-20 HD (Large)

Description

Unless a town lies on a river or lake, it probably gets its water from a well. How inconvenient then, when the ghost of a being that drowned in that well comes back to share the experience with others. Even the poorest of towns finds the wherewithal to hire a magically inclined mercenary or two to cleanse its water supply of such an unholy presence. If one looks past the skeletons, the accumulation of loot at the bottom of some such wells can be incentive enough to take on the challenge.

Combat

Well spirits seek to drown others, or else they hated the settlement enough in life to haunt its water supply in death. The spirit waits in the well until someone comes by to draw water. Then the spirit manifests itself, rising up in a flood, as a knot of watery tentacles or as a vaguely human shape suggested by the form of the water. Regardless, the spirit envelops the victim and drags him down into the well. The spirit bangs its victim around, knocking the air out of him and making him easier to drown.

Damage Reduction (Ex): Well spirits have no material bodies. They animate the water they inhabit. As such, well spirits can be harmed only by magical weapons and attacks.

Drown (Su): Once the well spirit has made a successful grappling attack on the victim, it drags him down into the well and holds him submerged until he drowns. Each round, the victim must succeed at a Fortitude save (DC 20) or lose 1d12 hit points as the spirit slams him into the walls of the well and keeps him submerged. A character killed in this fashion has drowned. When the well spirit drowns someone, it is restored to full hit points as it claims its victim's life force for its own.

Undead: Immune to poison, sleep, paralysis, stunning and disease. Not subject to critical hits, subdual damage, ability damage, energy drain or death from massive damage.

Were-Vulture

Medium-size Magical Beast (Lycanthrope)

Hit Dice:	4d10+4 (30 hp)
Initiative:	+6 (+4 Dex, +2 natural)
Speed:	30 ft., fly 30 ft
AC:	17 (+4 Dex, +3 natural)
Attacks:	Beak +8 melee, 2 claws +3 melee
Damage:	Beak 1d12+3; claw 1d8
Face/Reach:	5 ft. by 5 ft./10 ft.
Special Attacks:	None
Special Qualities:	Lycanthrope, damage reduction 12/+1 or silver
Saves:	Fort +5, Ref +5, Will -1
Abilities:	Str 16, Dex 18, Con 12, Int 7, Wis 7, Cha 2
Skills:	Listen +4, Spot +7
Feats:	Weapon Focus (Beak), Flyby Attack
Climate/Terrain:	Subtropical or tropical plains and deserts
Organization:	Solitary, gaggle (2-8)
Challenge Rating:	2
Treasure:	Standard
Alignment:	Usually chaotic evil
Advancement Range:	2-9 HD (Large); also by character class

Description

When Belsameth set out to give birth to the greatest of her children, she determined that they would carry the visage of the vulture, the grace of an angel and the grim wrath of her most poisonous dagger. As the first were-vulture lay in its black egg, she cast the vilest enchantments on her sleeping child to ensure he would be the strongest and most terrifying creature to stalk the night. When the egg was ready to hatch, she gathered all her children together to witness, and it was during this time that Enkili took notice and cast some spells of his own.

No one knows who told Enkili of the coming birth, but amongst the children of Belsameth news of the "blessed child" spread quickly, and even before its hatching, the creatures of the night were consumed with jealousy. When the egg finally hatched and Belsameth looked on greedily, the creature was her greatest embarrassment.

The were-vulture is an ugly, balding thing, generally afflicted with some type of skin disease and rarely possessing a mind greater than that of a spoiled child. It is rumored that Enkili sometimes puts them to use, and thus spared them from utter extinction. When not in service, were-vultures wander the desert, feeding on the carcasses of the dead as the carrion birds to which they were likened. Sometimes, a were-vulture may adopt the guise of man and attempt to live in a small village or town, but these creatures are of such limited intelligence that such attempts generally prove futile. It is only a matter of time before the creature is discovered for what it is and is driven back to the desert.

Combat

Belsameth did ensure one thing — these creatures are terrifying opponents when provoked. If forced into combat, a were-vulture attempts to win by any means necessary, eating the victim afterward.

Lycanthrope (Ex): Like other lycanthropes, were-vultures receive damage reduction against any blow unless it comes from a silver or magical weapon. Additionally, those who survive a were-vulture attack but are injured by the lycanthrope must make a Fortitude saving throw (DC 13) or be themselves afflicted with were-vulture lycanthropy.

Flyby Attack: A were-vulture can attack at any point during, before, or after its move when it is flying.

Willow Tree Warrior

Large (Tall) Plant

Hit Dice:	8d8+40 (76 hp)
Initiative:	+1 (Dex)
Speed:	20 ft.
AC:	16 (-1 size, +1 Dex, +6 natural)
Attacks:	2 branches +13 melee
Damage:	Branch 1d10+6
Face/Reach:	5 ft. by 5 ft./10 ft.
Special Attacks:	Entangle, constriction
Special Qualities:	Plant
Saves:	Fort +8, Ref +3, Will +3
Abilities:	Str 22, Dex 14, Con 20, Int 12, Wis 14, Cha 15
Skills:	Hide +2, Listen +4, Spot +2, Wilderness Lore +10
Feats:	Track
Climate/Terrain:	Any tropic or temperate forest, especially swamp
Organization:	Solitary, pack (1d4+1), forest (3-18)
Challenge Rating:	6
Treasure:	None
Alignment:	Usually neutral
Advancement Range:	None

Description

One of the species of the treantlike Arborian races, the willow tree warriors were created by Denev the Earth Mother to be her soldiers in the Divine War. Since the ascendancy of the gods over the titans and the end of the Divine War, Denev has not had as much use for her warriors and so the Earth Mother creates relatively few new willow tree warriors. The warriors can still be found, though, usually defending groves, springs, mountains and other places sacred to Denev, and occasionally in packs or even forest-size troops on the offensive to right a wrong done to Denev, her holdings or her followers.

Willow tree warriors stand 10 to 14 feet tall, and are generally humanoid in shape. They are lean and supple, with smooth bark and long hair strands like willow branches. Their two branch-arms end in hands that are masses of thick corded willow branches. In combat, these "hands" are used to flail at an opponent, and writhe around the opponent to entangle and constrict her.

Combat

Willow tree warriors carry on fighting until they perish, unless the situation calls for a strategic retreat. Depending on the odds, willow tree warriors generally use one branch-arm for entanglement and the other for strikes against entangled opponents or other nearby foes.

Entangle (Ex): The willow tree warrior may attempt to entangle opponents using the vinelike branches grown from its hands. The warrior may either make a touch attack if it chooses to only entangle, or may attempt to entangle an opponent it hit with its normal branch attack (in addition to the damage from the attack). If the willow tree warrior succeeds with its touch or normal attack, the opponent is entangled just as if she had been hit with a net, except the opponent receives one Escape Artist skill check to avoid entanglement (DC16). Once a willow tree warrior has used one of its two branches to entangle an opponent, it may not use that branch-arm to attack. Like a net with a control rope, the willow tree warrior may restrict an entangled victim's movement.

Constriction (Ex): Any opponent entangled by a willow tree warrior takes damage automatically. Damage is 1d6+6 per round.

Plant: Willow tree warriors are impervious to critical hits, subdual damage and death from massive damage trauma. They are not affected by many spells of mind-altering nature (for example, enamoring or charming spells not specifically designed for plants), subject to Game Master adjudication.

Wolf Spider, Giant

Large Beast

Hit Dice:	5d10 (27 hp)
Initiative:	+3 (Dex)
Speed:	40 ft., climb 30 ft.
AC:	13 (-1 size, +1 natural, +3 Dex)
Attacks:	Bite +6 melee
Damage:	Bite 1d10+2
Face/Reach:	5 ft. by 10 ft./5 ft.
Special Attacks:	Leaping attack, poison
Special Qualities:	None
Saves:	Fort +4, Ref +4, Will +1
Abilities:	Str 14, Dex 16, Con 10, Int 3, Wis 11, Cha 4
Skills:	Hide +8, Listen +5, Spot +1
Feats:	None
Climate/Terrain:	Any tropical or temperate
Organization:	Solitary, or with spider-eye goblin nest (2-20)
Challenge Rating:	3
Treasure:	None
Alignment:	Always neutral
Advancement Range:	4-7 HD

Description

Giant wolf spiders commonly make their homes in shallow pits that they instinctively cover with debris. This type of nest lends the spiders the nickname "trapdoor spider" since they usually ambush prey by leaping from a covered pit. When hungry, the spider attacks most anything of its size or smaller.

The giant wolf spider is the size of a small horse. Its body is covered with fine gray or brown hair, and its most remarkable feature is its array of eight eyes.

Giant wolf spiders are also found among spider-eye goblins, who use the wolf spiders as trained mounts.

Combat

The wolf spider ambushes prey by leaping from its covered pit, and then typically maintain its attack on its chosen victim until the prey is dead. However, injured spiders can be driven off, and despite their size and fearsome appearance giant wolf spiders are prone to fleeing unless they are extremely hungry.

Leaping Attack (Ex): The giant wolf spider can leap up to 35 feet, either while running or standing still. This can be used as a charging attack and the spider receives a +4 modifier to its attack roll when it leaps onto prey. However, the spider does not suffer any penalties to its defense as with normal charging attacks. When not used as a charging attack, this leap is a standard move action.

Poison (Ex): A wolf spider's bite carries a weak poison. Victims who take damage from a successful bite attack must also make a Fortitude save (DC 13) or suffer an additional 1d8 damage from the poison.

Woods Haunt

Tiny Elemental

Hit Dice:	5d8 (22 hp)
Initiative:	+0
Speed:	Fly 240 ft.
AC:	18 (+2 size, +6 natural)
Attacks:	None
Damage:	None
Face/Reach:	2.5 ft. by 2.5 ft./0 ft.
Special Attacks:	Wilderness mastery
Special Qualities:	Partial invisibility, SR 17, damage reduction 6/+2, immunities
Saves:	Fort +4, Ref +4, Will +1
Abilities:	Str 10, Dex 10, Con 10, Int 16, Wis 5, Cha 6
Skills:	Animal Empathy +18, Hide +10, Listen +11, Spot +11, Wilderness Lore +20
Feats:	None
Climate/Terrain:	Primeval forests
Organization:	Solitary
Challenge Rating:	3
Treasure:	Standard
Alignment:	Always neutral evil
Advancement Range:	4-7 HD

Description

Most spirits of the forest are benign creatures, content to observe and sometimes assist travelers in times of need. But there are certain deep forests across the land that are ancient and twisted, and have no love for any man or elf. Such a forest is often the home of a woods haunt, a twisted and spiteful spirit that delights in leading traveling parties to their doom.

The woods haunt is rarely seen, preferring to observe its victims from a distance and use its magic to alter their perceptions. Ranger lore describes these spirits by the effect they have on their surroundings; sometimes the knot of a tree twists into a cruel, leering face, or a swirl of leaves takes on the shape of a gaunt, hateful man. These strange effects are the only means to detect the spirit's presence without magic, and thus many wanderers are unaware of the peril they're in until it's too late.

Combat

The woods haunt uses its powers of illusion to lure forest travelers into many dangerous situations: tricking them into walking in circles for days on end, deceiving them as to the strength and depth of a river, or leading them straight to the lair of a fearsome predator, to name just a few. Followers of Denev may sometimes be able to draw out the spirit and convince it to cease its interference, but something is always demanded in return, such as a special act of devotion or a hazardous errand on behalf of the forest.

Wilderness Mastery (Su): The woods haunt's affinity with the forest is so strong that it can create powerful and subtle illusions to confuse and deceive travelers. A haunt can affect up to 10 targets at once, and victims must each make a successful Will save (DC 17) or be tricked into seeing what the haunt wants him to see.

Partial Invisibility (Su): The woods haunt can only be seen by mortal eyes through the manner in which it affects the forest around it. Attempts to spot a woods haunt always involve a -5 modifier to the roll.

Immunities (Ex): Woods haunts are not affected by critical hits, death from massive injury, poison, paralysis, sleep, disease or any attack that must target a living subject.

Wyrmspawn

	Wyrmspawn, Young Tiny Magical Beast	Wyrmspawn, Adult Small Magical Beast
Hit Dice:	1d10-1 (4 hp)	3d10+3 (19 hp)
Initiative:	+1 (+1 Dex)	+5 (+1 Dex, +4 Improved Initiative)
Speed:	20 ft., climb 20 ft.	20 ft., climb 20 ft., fly 80 ft.
AC:	16 (+2 size, +1 Dex, +3 natural)	15 (+1 size, +1 Dex, +3 natural)
Attacks:	Bite +0 melee, 2 claws +0 melee	Bite +4 melee, 2 claws +4 melee
Damage:	Bite 2d4-3; claws 2d4-3	Bite 2d4; claws 2d4
Face/Reach:	2.5 ft. by 2.5 ft./0 ft.	5 ft. by 5 ft./5 ft.
Special Attacks:	Poison	Larval cloud, poison
Saves:	Fort +1, Ref +3, Will -2	Fort +3, Ref +4, Will +1
Abilities:	Str 5, Dex 13, Con 9, Int 2, Wis 6, Cha 4	Str 10, Dex 13, Con 12, Int 3, Wis 10, Cha 6
Skills:	Hide +4, Listen +2, Spot +4	Hide +9, Listen +5, Move Silently +3, Spot +9
Feats:		Flyby Attack, Improved Initiative
Climate/Terrain:	Temperate and warm forests, hills and mountains	Temperate and warm forests, hills and mountains
Organization:	Solitary, pair or flock (3-7)	Solitary, pair or flock (3-7)
Challenge Rating:	1/4	2
Treasure:	Standard	Standard
Alignment:	Always chaotic evil	Always chaotic evil
Advancement Range:	2 HD	3-9 HD (Medium-size)

Description

Also known as "gut wyrms," wyrmspawn are wyvernlike beasts found everywhere from the Hornsaw Forest to the Kelder Mountains. Dangerous though the creatures are, it is their mysterious method of reproduction that incites the most fear in humanoids.

Scholars of the Scarred Lands do not yet understand how wyrmspawn disseminate their young. Some legends suggest that gut wyrms lay eggs in fruit, while others claim that the monsters take form within someone who performs an evil deed. However they get there, these horrid creatures gestate inside a living host to burst forth as snakelike beasts.

The beasts look much like snakes when young, being only a foot long with vestigial limbs. A wyrmspawn reaches maturity within three months. The adult is roughly the size of a dog, with a long serpentine body and four narrow limbs. A wing membrane stretches from its forelegs to the rear, not unlike a bat. It nests in trees and ventures out at night to feast upon rodents and other small animals.

Combat

Young wyrmspawn have an overwhelming desire to feed, but flee if attacked. Adult wyrmspawn are similarly cowardly, preferring to attack weak and exposed targets from the air. A flock of wyrmspawn can take down a large victim so that all may benefit from the feast.

Poison (Ex): When a wyrmspawn strikes with a successful bite attack, the victim must succeed at a Fortitude save (DC 13) or suffer paralysis for 1d6+2 minutes.

Larval Cloud (Ex): An adult wyrmspawn can expel a foul cloud at an opponent once each day. The cloud covers a 10-foot diameter; those caught within it must succeed at a Fortitude save (DC 13) or be blinded and unable to breathe for 1d6+2 rounds. The victim must make a second Fortitude save (DC 13) to avoid ingesting gut wyrm larvae.

Flyby Attack: The wyrmspawn can attack at any point during, before, or after its move when it is flying.

Spawning

The asexual wyrmspawn spreads its young by flying low over a living creature and expelling a larval cloud from its abdomen. At such an early stage of gestation, the wyrm larvae survive only a few seconds of exposure. The target usually breathes in at least a few. The wyrmspawn typically sows its seed at night, so the unfortunate victim often knows nothing is amiss other than waking with a brief cough from the strangely noxious air. A wyrmspawn does not discriminate; sentient beings and livestock alike may be subject to larval infestation.

The larvae attach themselves to the inside of the host's lungs and hatch 1d4+2 days later. They chew their way out from the inside and begin feeding on the host. Victims suffer 2d6+2 points of damage when the spawn emerge; a successful Fortitude save (DC 15) reduces the amount by half. Horrifically, creatures that survive the gut wyrms' initial emergence still must contend with the hungry larvae that wish to consume the rest of their host.

Gut wyrm larvae can be removed through use of disease- or poison-curing magic. Larvae-infested victims who are subjected to poisonous gases might also find that the gas kills the dormant larvae, assuming the victim himself survives the gas.

Appendix One

The Gods

Worship in the Scarred Lands has real and immediate consequences. It was only a century-and-a-half ago that the gods' avatars walked the land, contesting the titans for supremacy, while mortal races sided with the gods or titans and fought at their feet.

With such colossal events in recent history, religious practice is never a matter of rote ritual or prayers mumbled to an unresponsive heaven. Certainly the most audacious displays of divine might occur when the gods allow their divine power to flow through chosen saints and champions, granting these mortals the strength to perform miracles. The gods respond regularly to any of their worshipers, however, whether favorably or not. The smith who fails to have his forge blessed to Corean finds that his ironwork shatters under the hammer. The doctor who fails to draw wards on her medicines, displaying the proper fear and respect for Vangal, invites plague upon herself and her patients. Madriel's voice resounds like a deafening wind through a temple of farmers who fail to pray for a good harvest. The gods and goddesses of the Scarred Lands make their presence known daily across the world.

The intelligent races of the Scarred Lands openly worship the eight major deities, and the sole remaining titan Denev, the Earth Mother. Though these deities have begotten many lesser demigods and goddesses who are also worshipped, these nine are venerated (or appeased) above all others.

Corean

(CORE-ay-ahn), the Avenger, the Champion (LG; Chivalry, Craftwork, Strength, Protection, Wisdom)

The very picture of the paladin's ideal, Corean is an unflinching crusader among the gods. He has the strength of mountains, and his smoky armor reflects his ties to the earth and the metals that run through it. He bears a longsword that he forged himself from scraps gleaned from a titan's forge — that of Golthagga, who was the first to taste the blade's edge. Corean is generally unwilling to compromise, although he generally errs on the side of compassion rather than on the side of law. Many people praise him as the ideal of virtue, although more people pay lip service to him than are willing to live up to his standards.

Domains: Fire, Good, Law, Protection, War

Holy Symbol: Four longswords forming a compass rose

Madriel

(MA-dree-el), the Redeemer, the First Angel of Mercy (NG; Sun, Light, Sky, Redemption, Healing, Agriculture)

Madriel flies on wings of peacock feathers, an armored angel with a spear formed from the purest, whitest sunlight. Although relentless in her struggle against suffering (and particularly against her rival Belsameth), she is the most merciful and compassionate of the gods. Her temples are popular across the Scarred Lands, particularly in areas where people pray for fertility to return to their fields.

Domains: Air, Good, Healing, Plants, Sun

Holy Symbol: Spear with a tassel of peacock feathers

Tanil

(TAH-nil), the Huntress (CG; Travel, Hunting, Forestry, Music, Archery, Freedom, Good Fortune)

Of all the gods, Tanil is most likely to spend some of her time quietly walking the face of the Scarred Lands. However, this doesn't make her sociable — she prefers back roads and untrod wilderness to highways and villages. The ultimate champion of the underdog, she is the queen of archery and stealth, generally favored by rogues, bards and wayfarers. She appears as a lithe archer wearing flexible bronze armor. Her arrows are silver-tipped, as she dislikes the poor treatment of animals and considers the world's werebeasts an insult. Many elves venerate her; her other servants include dryads and unicorns.

Domains: Animals, Chaos, Luck, Plants, Travel, Trickery

Holy Symbol: Three bronze arrows lying parallel

Hedrada

(heh-DRAH-dah), the Lawgiver, the Judge (LN; Law, Justice, Wealth, Order, Cities, Knowledge)

The Lawgiver is keeper of all the things that civilized beings have learned, and is the patron of society itself. He is the ultimate impartial judge, striving to make certain that each person receives what he or she has earned (for good or ill). He's commonly shown as a stern man in somber robes, crowned with gold and wielding a massive two-handed hammer. He is particularly popular among dwarves, mages, prosperous merchants and regional governments, and is the patron of many cities (foremost of which, of course, is Hedrad).

Domains: Knowledge, Law, Protection

Holy Symbol: Two-handed hammer

Denev

(den-EV), the Earth Mother (N; Earth, Nature, Death — natural, the Seasons)

The only surviving titan, Denev sided with the gods — in particular, her children — against her brothers and sisters who ravaged Scarn. However, the long battle left even more wounds on the world's surface, driving her to retreat to its heart in frustration and fatigue. She still answers prayers from those who venerate her, and is honored by the other gods. She is not a generous or merciful mother, though; she respects nature at its bloodiest as well as at its most beautiful. She is rarely depicted in humanlike form — tales paint her as a mountain range or forest come to life — although she is said to wield a stone sickle when roused to make war. She is venerated by cults of druids who stubbornly refuse to pray to any of the newcomer gods, and by many elementals and other spirits of the land.

Domains: Air, Animals, Earth, Fire, Plants, Water

Holy Symbol: Stone sickle with a flowering wooden hilt

Enkili

(en-KEE-lee), the Trickster, the Shapeshifter, the Unlucky (CN; Storms, Trickery, Chaos, Misfortune)

The real wild card of the gods, Enkili can't really be said to be on anyone's side — not even his own. His tempestuous and stormy personality is mirrored in each freak storm or sudden calm. He commonly shapeshifts from form to form, even changing gender so regularly that no two temples portray the same image of him (or her). As the trickster figure of the pantheon, he also gets into trouble far more often than any divine being should. When he uses a weapon, he commonly wields a thunderbolt-hurling flail that lashes so wildly that others doubt it's under his control.

Domains: Air, Chaos, Luck, Travel, Trickery

Holy Symbol: Mask decorated with lightning shooting from the eye slits

Chardun

(char-DOON), the Slayer, the Overlord, the Great General (LE; War, Domination, Conquest, Avarice, Pain)

Tyrant among gods, Chardun exemplifies the worst traits of the most despotic generals, emperors and masters. His weapon is a golden macelike scepter that's stained deeply with blood. He wears the white regalia of a conquering hero, but his robes and sandaled feet are splattered with blood and dusted with powdered bone. He is particularly venerated by militaristic people with powerful ambitions, but anyone who craves domination is a worthy follower. A general who seeks a throne and a man who covets absolute obedience from his woman are both near to Chardun's black heart.

Domains: Evil, Law, Strength, War

Holy Symbol: Blood-soaked golden scepter, crowned with a thorny laurel wreath

Belsameth

(BEL-sa-meth), the Slayer, the Assassin (NE; Darkness, Death, Nightmares, Deception, Witchcraft, Madness)

The vulture-winged goddess Belsameth is the incarnation of everything people fear about the night. Her basalt throne sits on the dark side of the moon; her power over the moon grants her power over lunacy and makes her the patron goddess of Scarn's werebeasts. Her preferred weapon is a jet-black dagger, and she is favored by evil sorcerers and witches, Scarn's harpies, wily and murderous goblins, and of course by werewolves and their like.

Domains: Death, Evil, Magic, Trickery

Holy Symbol: Thin silver circle on a black field (signifying the lunar eclipse)

Vangal

(VAN-gahl), the Reaver, the Ravager (CE; Destruction, Pestilence, Famine, Bloodshed, Thunder, Disaster)

The volcano-god Vangal is the very embodiment of war. He is commonly depicted as a huge charioteer in filth-covered armor, beard and dreadlocks matted with blood. He wields two massive axes still encrusted with the blood of the titans he overcame. He has few human followers, as it's said that when he gains sufficient power, he'll bring about the destruction of Scarn itself. The few cults dedicated to him, called the Horsemen, are much-dreaded doomsayers and warriors.

Domains: Chaos, Destruction, Evil, Strength, War

Holy Symbol: Cloven shield dripping blood

The Titans

Many of the various races created by the titans survived the Divine War and still populate the Scarred Lands. Whether they are pockets of brigands, remote remnants of shattered civilizations or sovereign nations still contesting the people of the gods for supremacy, the titans' races have not walked meekly into oblivion. Many carve out power in the new world, drawing on what latent vitality they can from their fallen masters. Other titan races seek to resurrect their fallen lords and rule the world at their side.

A few of the titans are listed here.

Mormo, Mother of Serpents, Queen of Witches

This gruesome crone was the patron of all witches and hags and was responsible for the creation of serpentine races such as the medusae. Her spilled blood has turned the Hornsaw Forest into the homeland of mutated terrors that it is today. Some say her followers seek to recover the pieces of the Serpent Mother that were strewn across the Scarred Lands. They hope to bring these grisly trophies together so that Mormo may be reborn.

Gaurak, the Glutton

A hideously obese and always ravenous titan, Gaurak is said to have devoured all the life from the once verdant moon. After his defeat, the gods pulled out every last one of Gaurak's hundred teeth before burying him deep in the earth. His fallen teeth are said to have taken the form of mountains, colossal obelisks and even trees, always tainting the land near them.

Kadum, the Mountainshaker, the Bleeding One

This great beast would uproot entire mountains when enraged, but his strength alone could not save him. Belsameth cut his heart from him and Chardun chained him to a rock, which Vangal in turn sank to the bottom of the deepest ocean chasm. To this day, the deepest waters of the Scarred Lands run red with the Bleeding One's ichor. It is said that whole new races of horrific merfolk, krakens and other fell sea monsters have arisen from exposure to Kadum's blood.

Appendix Two

The following are the most current draft versions of the Open Game and D20 Logo licenses. For more information and updated versions of these licenses, go to www.opengamingfoundation.org and read more about the open gaming movement. Future printings of Creature Collection will include the final versions of these licenses.

OPEN GAME LICENSE
Version 1.0

The following text is the property of Wizards of the Coast, Inc. and is Copyright 2000 Wizards of the Coast, Inc ("Wizards"). All Rights Reserved. No permission is granted to reprint or redistribute this text in any media without the prior written consent of the Copyright Holder.

1. Definitions: (a)"Contributors" means the copyright and/or trademark owners who have contributed Open Game Content; (b)"Derivative Material" means copyrighted material including derivative works and translations (including into other computer languages), potation, modification, correction, addition, extension, upgrade, improvement, compilation, abridgment or other form in which an existing work may be recast, transformed or adapted; (c) "Distribute" means to reproduce, license, rent, lease, sell, broadcast, publicly display, transmit or otherwise distribute; (d)"Open Game Content" means the game mechanic and includes the methods, procedures, processes and routines to the extent such content does not embody the Product Identity and is an enhancement over the prior art; any additional content clearly identified as Open Game Content by the Contributor and means any work covered by this License, including translations and derivative works under copyright law, but specifically excludes Product Identity. (e) "Product Identity" means product and product line names, logos and identifying marks including trade dress; artifacts; creatures characters; stories, storylines, plots, thematic elements, dialogue, incidents, language, artwork, symbols, designs, depictions, likenesses, formats, poses, concepts, themes and graphic, photographic and other visual or audio representations; names and descriptions of characters, spells, enchantments, personalities, teams, personas, likenesses and special abilities; places, locations, environments, creatures, equipment, magical or supernatural abilities or effects, logos, symbols, or graphic designs; and any other trademark or registered trademark clearly identified as Product Identity by the owner of the Product Identity; (f) "Use", "Used" or "Using" means to use, Distribute, copy, edit, format, modify, translate and otherwise create Derivative Material of Open Game Content. (g) "You" or "Your" means the licensee in terms of this agreement.

2. The License: This License applies to any Open Game Content that contains a notice indicating that the Open Game Content may only be Used under and in terms of this License. You must affix such a notice to any Open Game Content that you Use. No terms may be added to or subtracted from this License except as described by the License itself. No other terms or conditions may be applied to any Open Game Content distributed using this License.

3. Offer and Acceptance: By Using the Open Game Content You indicate Your acceptance of the terms of this License.

4. Grant and Consideration: In consideration for agreeing to use this License, the Contributors grant You a perpetual, worldwide, royalty-free, non-exclusive license with the exact terms of this License to Use, the Open Game Content.

5. Representation of Authority to Contribute: If You are contributing original material as Open Game Content, You represent that Your Contributions are Your original creation and/or You have sufficient rights to grant the rights conveyed by this License.

6. Notice of License Copyright: You must update the COPYRIGHT NOTICE portion of this License to include the exact text of the COPYRIGHT NOTICE of any Open Game Content You are copying, modifying or distributing, and You must add the title, the copyright date, and the copyright holder's name to the COPYRIGHT NOTICE of any original Open Game Content you Distribute.

7. Use of Product Identity: You agree not to Use any Product Identity, including as an indication as to compatibility, except as expressly licensed in another, independent Agreement with the owner of each element of that Product Identity. You agree not to indicate compatibility or co-adaptability with any Trademark in conjunction with a work containing Open Game Content except as expressly licensed in another, independent Agreement with the owner of such Trademark. The use of any Product Identity in Open Game Content does not constitute a challenge to the ownership of that Product Identity. The owner of any Product Identity used in Open Game Content shall retain all rights, title and interest in and to that Product Identity.

8. Identification: If you distribute Open Game Content You must clearly indicate which portions of the work that you are distributing are Open Game Content.

9. Updating the License: Wizards or its designated Agents may publish updated versions of this License. You may use any authorized version of this License to copy, modify and distribute any Open Game Content originally distributed under any version of this License.

10. Copy of this License: You MUST include a copy of this License with every copy of the Open Game Content You Distribute.

11. Use of Contributor Credits: You may not market or advertise the Open Game Content using the name of any Contributor unless You have written permission from the Contributor to do so.

12. Inability to Comply: If it is impossible for You to comply with any of the terms of this License with respect to some or all of the Open Game Content due to statute, judicial order, or governmental regulation then You may not Use any Open Game Material so affected

13. Termination: This License will terminate automatically if You fail to comply with all terms herein and fail to cure such breach within 30 days of becoming aware of the breach. All sublicenses shall survive the termination of this License.

14. Reformation: If any provision of this License is held to be unenforceable, such provision shall be reformed only to the extent necessary to make it enforceable.

15. COPYRIGHT NOTICE

D20 System Reference Document ©2000 Wizards of the Coast, Inc.

D20 SYSTEM

TRADEMARK LICENSE

Version 0.4

1. Definitions.

1.1. "License" means this document.

1.2. "Publication" means any distribution of material under the terms of this License.

1.3. "D20 System Trademarks" means the words "D20 System", and the D20 System logo.

1.4. "D20 System Reference Document" means the copyrighted work owned by Wizards of the Coast identified by that name.

1.5. Each licensee is addressed as "You".

2. The License.

2.1 Offer and Acceptance:

Wizards of the Coast offers You the right to Accept the terms of this License.

You are permitted to use the D20 System Trademarks only in compliance with this License. Use of the Trademarks under any other

COMING NEXT FROM
SWORD & SORCERY STUDIO...

RELICS & RITUALS

OVER 100 NEW ARTIFACTS, RELICS, AND MAGIC ITEMS
OVER 200 NEW ARCANE AND DIVINE SPELLS
RULES FOR RITUAL MAGIC ALLOW CASTERS TO WORK
TOGETHER FOR GREATER SPELL EFFECTS

ALL 100% 3RD EDITION COMPATIBLE

SWORD &
SORCERY
STUDIOS

⋆ The d20 logo is a trademark
of Wizards of the Coast.

A NEW WORLD
OF ADVENTURE
COMING SOON

SWORD &
SORCERY
STUDIOS

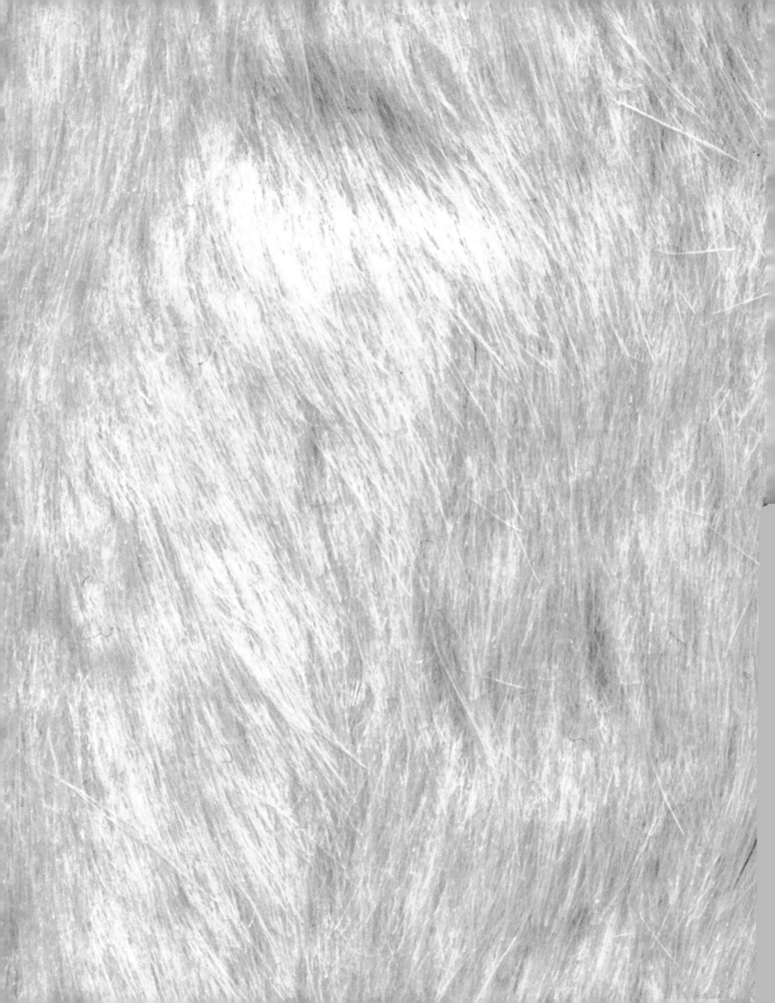